CJ Grabham emigrated from the UK to Canada when he was six and has had a foot in both countries ever since, having been educated and taught in both. A major turning point came when, in his early twenties, he stumbled into Durham University one drizzly, autumn afternoon and asked if they would let him in. They did, and his life changed forever. Changed for the better, it might be said. But then, this was not unusual, for that place has a similar effect on all who go there.

To my dear, dear friends.

CJ Grabham

PALACE GREEN

Yes, I am still here, and
I am still yours

AUSTIN MACAULEY PUBLISHERS™
LONDON ∗ CAMBRIDGE ∗ NEW YORK ∗ SHARJAH

A CIP catalogue record for this title is available from the British Library.

ISBN 9781398431614 (Paperback)
ISBN 9781398431621 (ePub e-book)

www.austinmacauley.com

First Published 2022
Austin Macauley Publishers Ltd®
1 Canada Square
Canary Wharf
London
E14 5AA

Chapter 1
Palace Green

Palace Green is a medieval jewel, a fairy tale town square balanced precariously atop ancient Durham City. The Green occupies the space contained between the Norman Cathedral at one end and the castle at the other. The adjacent sides of the Green are lined with other beautiful, ancient university buildings – the library and lecture rooms. At the centre spreads a large rectangular lawn around which motorcars circulate and park, some properly, some improperly according to the spaces available. No one ever parks on the lawn though. This would be unthinkable. Pedestrians, however, use the lawn as a short cut across the square to and from the lecture rooms and library.

The magnificent cathedral dominates not only Palace Green and the town roundabout it but the entire countryside for miles. In the evening, its illuminated towers can be seen rising out of the gentle, surrounding hills by returning travellers as far away as the A1 M. There is nothing else in the world quite like it. Its majesty, its calm reassurance, whispering, "Yes, I am still here, and I am still yours."

We in Cuth's (St Cuthbert's Society) never cared much for the castle itself. You see, it housed students from University College, stuck up and pampered prigs from well-to-do English aristocracy. Who else would be given the chance to live in a castle whilst at a university? Privileged, well to do sn\obs, that's who, or so we liked to think. I suppose there had to be some genuine people at Castle, as they called University College, but we didn't come across many.

Errol Renwick, son of the Earl of Stanfordham, was one such Castle undergraduate. A handsome fellow, moustachioed with long, flowing locks, a product of the Home Counties – proper accent, money up to his arsehole, he drove around in a clapped-out old Daimler that did the rounds of college parties trawling for women. I must say, he looked, acted and spoke the part of a would-be Home Counties dilettante youth. As a result, he was in a position to pull the best totty in the university. What self-respecting young lady wouldn't fall for his flowing, shoulder-length locks, tapered moustaches, skin-tight flares and Daimler bought for him by his parents to ease the trials of academia in the cold, cold North. Not only was he mobile and well to do, his ostentatious wealth placed him at the very top of the university totty pecking order. And peck he did.

An idle sod, he had an engaging smile and condescending manner that had the women swooning and queuing up for a ride in his jalopy. He rarely attended lectures or worked at anything. He disdained sports and any type of common, lower-class activity. Renwick fed off the adoration that privilege and his Daimler brought him, and he played it to the hilt.

One such young beauty taken in by his condescension was Carol Drysedale, an undergraduate attending St Mary's, an all-girls' college, located just over Prebend's Bridge across the river from Cuth's. A product of the Mary Quant Sixties, Carol was undoubtedly stunningly beautiful. A tall, elegant, blue-eyed red head, which, on the face of it, was enough to turn any young man's fancy. But that wasn't all. Oh, no, not in the least. She was a delight to talk to, an unintentional beauty and not at all suitable for Errol's kind of shallow, up-market romancing. When you got to know her, she brimmed over with genuine, happy, innocent laughter, was considerate, highly intellectual and not at all right for Errol.

I fell deeply in love with Carol the first time I set eyes on her, before I knew what she was really like or who she really was. I was willing to overlook the Mary Quant fashion-statement for a chance to get to know her. And she looked so bloody-well unattainable that I thought she was well worth a go. Know what I mean? She looked so incredibly beautiful, I thought, what the hell. Nothing ventured, nothing gained or nothing lost for that matter, so I dared to have a go. I knew I probably wouldn't get anywhere with her anyway. The attempt would be enough. I just had to talk to this elegant, elusive-looking, unattainable angel.

And when I got to know her much later, I fell deeper and deeper. I was easy with her. She was very relaxed with me, and despite our different backgrounds, we hit it off. Looking back though, our backgrounds weren't that dissimilar. Her dad ran a hardware store. They lived modestly in a nice house near Coventry. She didn't come from aristocracy or mock privilege. She was really an ordinary girl with a knockout shape, sensational eyes and a very charming manner. Sweet, innocent, thoughtful and caring. She laughed at my idiosyncrasies but somehow always made me feel so comfortable.

I knew from the start that it was going to be difficult to wrest her from Errol's evil grip. It would take time and patience. I was willing to wait because she was so worth it. As time went on, we got to know each other really well. We chatted, laughed and developed an easy, uncomplicated, undemanding love affair.

The first time I saw Carol was in the university library on Palace Green.

She didn't need to be there at that particular time. I didn't need to be there either. But there we were. We happened to be in the library at the same time sitting across from each other, ignoring each other, pouring over books, guarded, rarely looking up. She apparently doing her Russian and me, English.

Interesting, I thought at first from a distance before I sat down opposite her, seeing the virginal, white hair band and sweeping shoulder-length hair. I don't know whether I was initially reluctant to think any more of the coincidence because she looked so fabulous and out of my league. Or was it because I thought she was just another phoney? Anyway, I looked up once or twice during our first meeting but initially never gave her much thought. I knew I didn't stand a chance at that point, anyway.

As time went on, though, during that first hour, I grew tired of Pope's *Essay on Criticism* and so, becoming inquisitive about her, raised my head to take a peek. From what I could see head on – because her face remained buried in her books – she looked respectable, maybe even nice – from what I could see. Had I made a mistake in my initial impression of her? Maybe, maybe not. And so I contented myself that she might not be all that bad, in the library, pouring over her books, looking like that.

Then she sighed.

That's all.

She sighed so sweetly.

Her voice was springtime.

Not what I'd first thought it might be. I first thought that she must be some sort of brainless dolly bird done up to mimic the Carnaby Street set. All fashion and no brains. But I was so so wrong.

Her sigh was sweetness and innocence. It suddenly dawned on me that she might be unintentionally beautiful and couldn't help it, no matter what I thought. Her looks were not her fault. It was wrong of me to have ever thought they were.

Still, I repressed the burning desire to say something in order to begin some kind of introduction. Something in me said, "No. Do nothing, dammit. Don't spoil the moment."

How could I dare break the spell?

So I did nothing. Instead, I went back to Pope leaving her to her Tolstoy.

And there we were directly opposite each other in the library on Palace Green ignoring each other. Frozen in isolation, yet together. It was kinda nice. Comfy. Safe.

Yet together.

Peaceful.

It was as if we had done it for years and couldn't be bothered with each other anymore, didn't feel the need to engage, to explore, to pose. Leave it at that. Enjoy it for what it was.

I felt able to get to work and so forced the pace. I was pleased that I could go on reading without the distraction of her being there across the table from me. For the best part of an hour, we ignored each other, worked apart, yet…

Then she was gone.

Suddenly, she was gone.

With another sweet sigh, she had closed her books, put her pens and pencils into her cute little, plastic pencil case, her pencil case and her books into her bag, stood up and was gone.

But what a standing up!

Hard to describe, but what I do remember is that she looked stunning, so stunningly sweet, like a fawn trying to rise in the woods, print miniskirt, tall, well-shaped legs. Her hair flowing out behind her as she hustled away from me towards the door. Clearly, she was the most astonishing creature I had ever seen, and I cursed myself that I hadn't made more of the chance. At the same time, though, I was content that I had not sullied the water by being pushy in my lovemaking, for lovemaking it was. Oh, I didn't know it at the time – I had merely seen a glorious girl in a library – nothing special in that. Not around these parts. But later I would come to realise that it had all started that day, in that library with her gentle sigh. Intended or not. She was elegant, innocent, unapproachable and exquisite.

Days passed. I would divide my time between two libraries – the modern Elvet Riverside Library, with its big windows and a view of the traffic on the river, and the gorgeous, ancient, dusty old library on Palace Green where breathless time stood still. I had spotted my muse that once and almost immediately forgot her. There were too many other knockout women around the place, all of whom tested my fancy and daily presented new possibilities, new distractions to my studies of the great poets. Carol went to the back of the queue for some weeks.

Until.

Struggling one day in Palace Green library with other literary giants, Milton perhaps or Wordsworth, I happened to look up across my mountain of books, and there she was again, calmly sitting down opposite me. Had she made a mistake? It was certainly not intentional, couldn't be. She had just wandered in and sat down at a table, some random table with no significance in it whatsoever. Thing was, the library was practically empty.

Why opposite me?

My lovely, blue-eyed, innocent goddess.

I felt honoured and at the same time sullied – played with. She hadn't remembered me from weeks ago – couldn't have. Probably recognised me now as a safe bet, someone who wouldn't disturb her studies. So, she sat neatly down directly across the table, struggled to take out her books and pencil case from her bag, her pens and pencils from her pencil case with many an 'Oomph' and hefty sigh. She finally arranged her pens, pencils and notebook neatly on the table in front of her, didn't look at me once during this, pulled her chair around her and dived into her work.

This was a true academic I decided, not to be disturbed. A businesswoman on her way to a good degree, probably a First. Brains as well as beauty. Approach with care!

I thought I knew now that this was why she had chosen to sit down opposite me. She sensed I would not disturb her, not like the half dozen or so bozos in there who probably would have a go at her, try to chat her up, get in the way of her work. In this was a kind of honour, a pact. And so I honoured our unspoken contract, poured through my work without looking up, absorbing the closeness of this amazing woman on the other side of the table for all the right reasons, subduing multiple urges to do more, to find out, until something wonderful happened.

Suddenly, there was an unexpected nudge under the table. In twisting sideways to get her long legs more comfortable, her foot bumped mine.

Without thinking, I looked defensively up. Was it my fault?

She too looked up in shock.

"Sorry," she said with a blushing smile.

That sweet voice again but this time articulating the English language with angelic tones. The bells that chimed in her voice were from the Home Counties. Didn't matter. I was smitten.

I guess I gawped some inaudible, goofy apology for being in her way. I can't remember what I said, but I do know she calmly raised her eyebrows to herself and smiled again at me. Electric joy flooded the whole room. Then she turned her attention safely back to her Tolstoy.

I was mesmerised, gobsmacked, out of breath. She looked back up at me again for reassurance, disabled me with another smile then disconnected totally. Our work filled the rest of the hour until it was time for her next lecture. She left but not without saying 'Bye' amid a flurry of sweeping up her texts, notebooks and other paraphernalia round about.

'Bye'. Is that all I get? You break my foot and stop my heart, raise my blood pressure to near bursting, and all I get is some throwaway 'Bye'.

I said nothing but managed a nod, a condescending, stupid, grovelling, little, twerpy, sideways nod that must have made me look like some kind of outlandish, southern fop.

It was then that I suddenly realised she hadn't been keeping score at all. But I had. She was as natural as could be, pure, honest, delightful, and I was the one who was keeping score, playing a game. Amazing. What a jerk. I couldn't believe I hadn't at least said something before she left. My second chance and I muffed it again. Why? Because I had been subconsciously keeping score.

Jerk!

This was all getting very stressful, so with two near misses and no hope for a third, I confidently entered the library the next day knowing there was no chance at all of her being there as well. Not so soon after yesterday. Not two days in a row. I could get some work done on my classics essay in peace knowing I wouldn't be disturbed by another out of body experience with my angel this soon after yesterday.

Bugger it. She was there when I walked in. Sitting right there in her favourite place opposite my empty seat with nobody else for miles around. So I sat down making as much noise as I could to let her know I was there and also to disturb her cone of silence, shake her up a bit, get on her nerves, in her face a bit.

Don't ask me why. I guess I was still peeved at the way she stormed out yesterday with nothing more than a 'Bye' leaving me rotating and bobbing dizzily in her wake.

"Do you always make such a clatter?" she smile-whispered without raising her head, still without looking up at me.

"Of course. Always," I hiss-whispered back. "I clattahhhh wherever I go," I said, only I said it, not in my native Canadian but mimicking her Home Counties accent, softening the 'er' of 'clatter' to 'ahhhh' and making a right pig's ear of it.

Squeezing her shoulders together, she squealed with delight under her breath at my hambone attempt at her dialect but still didn't raise her head. I was being punished. For being late? For making such a noise? For being there at all? For being North American? You tell me.

She was too busy to respond and dug deeper into her books.

Two could play at that, I thought, so I followed suit trying my best to ignore her, clattering my books out of my haversack onto the table, crashing my pens all over the place and scraping my chair into position a number of times, flipping the pages of *A History of Greece* back and forth before deciding on the page I wanted to read.

"Sssssshhhhh," she shushed, still without looking up.

"You must be quiet," she whispered into her book. Then as if to emphasise the point, a little scrap of paper inched its way across to me at the end of her index finger.

A note.

"Quiet Please!!! (:" it said with lots of exclamation marks and a smiley face. That's all.

And at that moment, my life changed forever. At that moment, Carol formally entered my life with all her fun, her laughter, her joy and playfulness.

"Sorry," my returning note said. "I am a lummox."

"Yes, you are!!! (: (:" came the next instalment with two smiley faces.

"Be Quiet!

Or you'll get us both put out."

She still wasn't going to look up, though and idly pushed the reply back to me with her left index finger whilst scribbling away at her notebook with her right hand, still not recognising my existence at all, or so it seemed. She was far too busy for that.

So, I got stuck into my work. There was total silence for about half an hour, and believe me, the feeling at that table was one of a shared contentment, a felicity that felt warm and cosy, as if aged for years in the deep-delved earth, as if we had been married for years and didn't need to spell anything out anymore. Two old students ruminating quietly with no need to prove anything anymore. No need to posture, no need to win or score points because the winning had already been done. An agreement had been struck.

She sighed.

I looked up.

She looked up.

She smiled at me and went back to work, struggling over *Crime and Punishment*. I thought to help her out with it but thought again. It was her problem, and I knew nothing about the novel anyway, so all I could accomplish would be me revealing my ignorance in the face of her vast knowledge.

Something had to be done though. About us, I mean. We couldn't just go on like this, letting things stagnate without finding time to talk. So, I became very brave just before the end of the hour when I knew she would have her next lecture.

"Coffee?" the note said – from me this time.

"Can't," she sent back with a little drawn grimace.

"Lecture in five mins.

"Some other time? (:" she added with a smiley face and then looked across at me directly into my soul and mouthed, "Sorry."

And got up and left me there, once again bobbing dizzily in her wake.

And then she did something I would get used to. She stopped at the end of the aisle, bent her knees crookedly, comically inward, turned on her heel and scuttered back to her seat.

"How about some time next week? We could leave time," she actually said out loud to the dismay of several grumpy old students further along who looked up and grumbled at the disturbance in the ether.

I grimaced first at the thought of speaking in this sanctorum, then nodded happily.

She returned my happy nod, turned on her heels and hauled ass out of the room to get to her lecture on time.

Some ass.

Chapter 2
Weetabix

"Will you marry me? Answer in ten words or less on the back of a postage stamp and within the next minute or so."

I slipped my note across to her and waited for an eruption of some sort. She merely scrunched her shoulders up in a giggle, scribbled a reply and slid it over.

"Takes more than a minute or so to consider marriage."

More notes ensued.

"Two minutes then. Come on. I'm waiting."

"Don't get cross, but you'll have to ask my father first. That's the way it's done over here."

"Don't want to marry your father. And what do you mean, 'over here'?"

She feigned study, but I could tell she was waiting eagerly for each message. She was enjoying herself within the parameters of her work.

"He won't be best pleased about that. And I meant that you aren't from around here, are you? I can tell by your handwriting." came her tactful reply.

"Did you ever notice how your writing and mine slope at 90 degrees to each other? There must be some significance in it."

Carol slid the note across to me and went back to her Tolstoy. Her long red hair flowed over her headband and down across her face.

"Probably because I have Wheetabix for breakfast and you don't," I noted back.

"Weetabix not Wheetabix. There's no h in it, silly. And your handwriting is getting progressively worse. You are becoming illegible.

"Reform!!!!

"And by the way, I too have Weetabix for breakfast."

"Oh? How do you have it? I scrunch mine up in a pile in the middle of the bowl and make a milky moat around the outside of it."

"I have them like little boats floating in the milk and nibble away at the soggy edges."

"There. You see? We are totally compatible. This amounts to an acceptance of my proposal. We'll have to set a date. I'll have a word with your dad."

"While you're at it, please ask him to send money, as I am soon to be out of funds."

"He has a solution," I noted.

"Good. What is it?"

"Stop spending so much."

"Can't. Anyway, that's no solution. Not when you have to pay such high costs of living."

"Like what?"

"Battels. Makeup. Clothes. Heating and lighting. Food. Books. Pens. Pencils. Makeup."

"You listed makeup twice."

"Need it twice as much as anybody else."

"Don't need it at all, not with a face like yours."

"Yes I do. Look at this…"

And as I read the last note, she looked up at me pulling the worst face I have ever seen.

"Ugh! You're right. More makeup, please. Layers of the stuff. Get that face covered up. Don't know why I ever thought you the most beautiful creature on earth. Must have been the makeup all the time."

At which she silently (because we were in a library) blazed up at me and stuck out her tongue, shook her head and didn't send any more notes for the rest of the hour.

Just before our time was up, sensing disaster, I sent across, "Didn't mean it."

She stuck out her tongue again and coyly looked up at me, and I sent across:

"We've just had our first fight, haven't we?"

Nothing came back. I was scared to death but looking over at her saw a little self-satisfied smile crinkle her nose.

"That's better. Thought you were mad at me."

Apparently, that couldn't have been farther from the truth.

Chapter 3
Lucien Fenwood-Gross

Lucien grimaced. "You see, young Flynn, being in Durham and staying in this wondrous university are two completely different propositions."

Lucien and I were having an afternoon pint in the bar of The Three Tuns Hotel. Basic accommodation. Bare wooden tables and benches. He was about to put on his serious face; the one where he puffs out heavily into eternity, squints back into the past and considers with scalded eyes his future. He pushed his pint gently to one side and leaned on his elbows across the table, leering at me for some seconds, for some seconds exhaling, his large hippopotamus nostrils expanding with the depth and gravity of the coming pronouncement.

Finally, Lucien came to terms with the turmoil inside his head, opened his mouth to speak then closed it again with an audible hippo-like 'clop', considering his circumstances, changing his mind at the last second. Then impetuosity took him by the scruff of the neck and he declared in a rush:

"Father is going to pull the plug."

Eyes bulging at the thought of his father's decision, he swallowed deeply at finally having published his dilemma, pulled it closely around his shoulders and drummed the fingertips of his left hand upon quivering lips.

"Can you imagine?

"My dear old dad cutting me off. Me!"

"What about your grant?" I said after an appropriately sympathetic pause to weigh the enormity of his revelation.

"Dear boy!" he said dismally, dismissing the suggestion for what it was – next to useless. Lucien could never hope to exist on just an LEA grant. His bar tabs alone throughout the town totally exhausted that incidental income and then some.

"Work harder?" I ventured with little conviction.

"Haven't worked a day since coming up. Couldn't now if I wanted. Wouldn't know how. I'm afraid, dear friend, Daddy's stipend is essential to life as I know it."

I had never seen Lucien this glum.

"Sell your body," I offered with rising enthusiasm.

"What? This offensive tub of blubber?" he said looking desperately around about his worthless hulk.

"Who on earth …?"

"You never know," I said, trying desperately to cheer him up. "There's a market for almost anything these days. Bit of body filler. Dab of paint here and there…

"Jeremy's Pam, for example," I offered.

"Jeremy's Pam is a looker, I'm afraid. Couldn't compete with the likes of that Page Three totty."

"You don't have to compete with anybody. Horses for courses an' all that. Those paintings of big people by whatisname – Renoir or somebody…He liked big people. Most of 'em did. All I'm saying is …"

"All you are saying, dear boy, is, it's hopeless. If that's the best anybody can offer. Well…Hopeless. Couldn't even sell this," he said, looking dismally round about at himself again "this foetid, old carcase.

"As a last resort…It is a last resort, isn't it? I mean, there's nothing else after my worthless carcase, is there? That's it. Last resort is gone, and I'm … buggered."

"Could be," I said.

Lucien's drinking head start had left the poor soul bereft of any sober hope at all. He'd got to The Three Tuns an hour before me and drunk himself into maudlin self-deprecation well before my arrival.

"Might just as well go out …" he said, rummaging around in his coat pocket for his little jar of Valium. Finding the jar, he opened it and hurried one of those life-giving pills down his throat chased by a swig of beer.

"Might as well …" he repeated, searching for his train of thought, lost it completely and so returned to his beer for support.

"Where was I, dear friend?"

"Looking for a means of staying up without Daddy's help. Selling your bottom to the highest bidders."

"That's it in a nutshell," he concurred. He considered my advice for a moment, breathing out harder now.

"You have a way of putting things, so that even I can understand."

"Alternatively to applying yourself to your studies or selling your bottom, you could get a little job to offset your poverty. Something part-time. You could do it standing on your head. Go on. Frampton's Chip Shop always has a little notice in the window. They are always looking for someone to help sell their fish and chips."

"Work?

"Again?" he said desperately.

"You see … You see, I'm not cut out for work of any kind." He fretted, fingers to his lips.

"Could you see me behind that greasy glass counter, tiny apron, paper tiara, dispensing fish and chips?

"Horrid thought.

"No. Couldn't do it.

"Besides, dear boy, when would I ever get my studies done?" he lamented, lifting his glass to his lips, eyes bulging out of his head in self-righteous, accusatory alarm.

"There is a tide in the affairs of men…" he added miserably. "Mine has gone out, I'm afraid, and left me high and dry," he said, setting his empty glass down and peering into the very bottom of his bottomless doom.

Lucien pissed me off. He had a gift for the overly dramatic. His father had very probably said nothing of the sort to him, had most likely asked him very politely to pull up his socks in order to get at least a third out of his years at Durham, so that he wouldn't have to support his profligate son for the rest of his life.

His father was a treasure. I met him at Christmas when he drove all the way up from Weymouth in his clapped-out old Morris Minor Shooting Brake delivering a hamper full of 'essentials', as he put it, and he seemed the salt of the earth then. Wonderful man. Of course, the dad had spoiled the woebegone son all his life and was now paying the price for it, poor old soul.

But Henry couldn't be budged. He was adamant his dad was the Attila the Hun of all fathers. He let me buy several more rounds before suddenly lurching to his feet and staggering outside to the bog in the backyard. I fell into line. He was in no state to be left now, and so I pissed next to him, barely able to keep my head up, repelled by the nauseating smell of everybody else's effluent trickling merrily along that gruesome trench past my toes.

"Do you think I could, old man?"

"Could what?" I asked.

"Sell my bottom."

"Should bring a pretty penny," I lied looking back along past that very bottom.

"You could make your fortune," I said, in a hurry now to get out of The Three Tuns and off up the street to Sweaty Betty's chip shop at the bottom of Church Street. The mention of Frampton's had made me hungry.

"Fancy a fish?" I asked as we struggled out into the drizzling, cold, soggy November night.

"Excellent thought, old boy. Excellent. Dining at Betty's. What could be better? My treat. Cod or Haddock?

"Oh, no. I insist. I think I'll have extra batter. And a dollop of mushy peas."

Chapter 4
The Supreme Fornicator

Carlos Del Fuego was Argentinian. He had just successfully dropped out of his posh college at home to follow his family to London. His English was impeccable.

Tall and skinny, athletic-looking, helter-skelter talker, he finished every statement off with his patented, glorious grin that stretched from ear to ear. His father was a diplomat who, for the time being, was lodged in formidable apartments in London – Belgravia to be exact – while his son finished university in Durham. I'm not so sure they were over here solely for that though. I got the impression that they were on an extended tour in Europe and that Carlos was being given another chance at academia. Anyway, they were temporarily inhabiting posh apartments in the heart of the best part of London.

It seemed that Carlos' second attempt at getting a degree was falling short as well. Probably because of his well-to-do parents, he hadn't felt the need to push anything. Mediocrity was good enough. He pleased the parents by taking up a place in Durham, but he seemed to have no inclination to finish the job properly. In time, he would inhabit a park bench in New York until, eventually pulling himself up by his boot straps, he would head up a moderately successful company on the internet selling horticultural supplies. He housed the soul of a hippie in the tall, gangly body of a lost little boy. Given to emotions that ran from gushing enthusiasm to hellish self-doubt, he ran either blisteringly hot or morbidly cold.

Carlos was reading business studies. This was puzzling because he gave the impression that inside his well-heeled Harris Tweed sports jacket beat the heart of a nomad – an Argentinian nomad wearing tatty running shoes with jeans held up by a length of rope. Given half a chance, Carlos would have gladly gone around in a Bedouin robe and headdress. I guess the business studies was for his dad, whom I never met, although I felt his plutocratic pressure all about his son who spent a lifetime rebelling against him and yet in small ways here and there honouring his wishes.

Carlos fell in love with everything English and everything happening at St Cuthbert's Society. We all did. How could anyone not? It was the making and at the same time the undoing of us all. A more structured place would have us attendant and on time for everything scholarly. We didn't feel that was necessarily why we were there. There were actually some people at Cuth's who were given to studious endeavours. I never met any of 'em, but I was told they really did exist.

The only real structure any of us ever adhered to were the piss-ups at The Angel every Thursday night.

The Angel was Cuth's pub. Nothing special. Just a pub. The clientele was special, though, given to overindulging the beer and singsongs around the piano with our mates. The food was average; the beer was good, but the singing… Well, ranging from *Cushy Butterfield* to *Wandering Star* to *Harry* (Cuth's own ridiculous, nonsensical drinking anthem), some dirty, some raunchy, some even clean and sentimental. Pork pies, a few pints – nobody ever counted – everybody bought rounds, everybody sang their hearts out, everybody ended up in a drunken heap one way or another at the end of the evening and staggered off to their digs thoroughly paralytic.

It was after one such evening that, following behind two shadowy figures in the distance along the riverside path towards the glorious stone arches of Prebend's Bridge, Leo Tucker and I finally brought our blurred vision into focus long enough to make out the tall and short forms of Carlos and Herbert (Specky) Neville.

They were both in a bad way. Barely able to stay on the path, they disappeared at one point, just below the big weir that spanned the river between Durham School boathouse and the old mill. The weir held back a wall of water ten feet deep, which in bygone days fed the mill (now occupied by the university archaeology department).

High on the opposite side of the river from us, the illuminated towers of the cathedral rose majestically into the night sky, portentous yet reassuring like a benevolent parent lording over its mischievous children. The river was particularly high this night due to excessive rains over the last few weeks. A dangerous, howling waterfall poured over the weir, crashing across its top edge and forming a raging set of rapids that swirled away below it.

Cuth's infamous pinball wizard, Leo Tucker, and I staggered as best we could along the winding path, tripping over the odd tree root, gashing the odd ankle, gaining slowly on the two wrangling figures ahead until just as they reached Durham School boathouse they disappeared from view. Nothing unusual in that; the towpath meandered back and forth and up and down the bankside. It wasn't until we ascended the path and got to Prebend's Bridge that we decided something was amiss. Specky and Carlos were nowhere to be seen in any direction: up or down river or across the bridge.

The night was quiet. The river above the weir was still and silent. Nothing stirred. The enormous, illuminated towers of the cathedral seemed to move against the brilliant moon.

Dead silence.

Then the shouting started.

"Oh fuck. Look at that.

"You prick. You pissing bastard."

It was Specky Neville in a rage in a bush somewhere behind us down near the weir.

"You bloody fool, Del Fuego. Aww, you pissed all over my foot. You pissed all over my bloody foot. Aw, gawd," he shrieked, "you pissed all over my bleedin' foot and all up and down me leg."

Silence again. Then Carlos appeared from the bushes down by the water's edge.

"Blessed your leg, Herbert," Del Fuego replied calmly, drunkenly zipping up as he forced his way back up the riverbank.

"You have been blessed. By me," he said with a final tug on his zipper to complete the job.

Specky followed, lamely whingeing all the way up the bankside.

"Yeah, right! Honoured. What would you say if I happened to crap all up and down your leg?" he said, kicking his foot out, kick, kick, kicking as if kicking would rid him of the insult.

"What would you say, eh?" Specky nagged.

"I would say, what's that awful stink, and where did it come from? Ah! It's only Specky stinking out the world again. Too bad somebody couldn't do something about it, coz it's around him wherever he goes," Carlos answered, nipping his nose between thumb and forefinger and leading himself by his nipped nose away from Specky and back up the bank.

"People have noticed."

"Is that why you pissed on my foot? Because people think I smell? Is that supposed to make me smell better?"

"Wreak," Carlos corrected.

"OK. Wreak then. Is that going to make things any better?"

"I had the chance. So I did it. Who wouldn't?"

"Who's noticed then?" the outraged Specky stormed. "Who? Are you saying I smell like shit?"

"You smell…" Del Fuego replied after a second or two, "You smell like a baby's diaper that's been left in the sink for days."

"Nappy," Specky corrected.

"Nappy then. Diaper, nappy. Specky, you stink, whether you like it or not.

"But not so much now, though. Not now that you've been anointed by my waters. It has cut through the stink. You should be grateful. You wouldn't notice the difference, but many of your friends will.

"And I'll tell them it was me who did them the favour – did the whole world the favour."

Specky struggled back onto the path following his friend, grumbling to himself, out of breath, considering Del Fuego's advice. He stood with his hands on his knees for a minute or two coming to terms with things, breathing and things.

"Bastard," he said at last.

"You're always doing that to me," he wheezed, still out of breath.

"Doing what to you, Specky?"

"Turning things around like that. Making me feel like the guilty one, when it's you all the time. Giving me a hard time."

"Face it. You deserve it. Anyone who smells like that deserves to be given a hard time until he learns."

"Learns! Learns what?"

"Learns to have a bath every now and then."

"Aw, fuck off."

"No, you fuck off, Herbert. It's time you knew who your friends are."

And with that, and seeing us on the bridge in the distance, Del Fuego raised a hand and started along the path towards us.

Specky decided to split with his friend and stumbled off in our direction ahead of Del Fuego.

"Did you see that?" Specky asked, out of breath, almost walking backwards as he approached us, pointing at something he'd seen back there off the trail in the dark.

"Did you see it? Did you?

"They're doing it. Right there beside the tow path," he said, incredulous and lighting a spliff. The spliff flared up illuminating his face and NHS spectacles.

"What, Specky? Doing what?" Leo asked.

"Fucking," he said lowering his voice lest the cathedral across the river heard him and took offence.

"Back there. Behind that log. Going at it like a couple of rabbits. Franklin, I think it was."

"That would be Beau," Leo confirmed and then continued, "back in the Angel he told me he was going to bonk Jill for me before the night was out.

"Bastard. Couldn't wait 'til he got her back to his digs, could he? Does it right out in the open like that just to prove a point."

"And his point being?" Specky had to ask.

"He can do her, and I can't. That's his point. He knows I've been after Jill for months. He caught sight of her in the Angel tonight. Never said boo to her all the time she's been here and – Bastard – gets her in his cross hairs…"

"Some blokes have that kind of savoir faire," Specky said, lamenting the fate of the rest of us.

"Aye, and a bloody big nob."

"Yes, right, Leo. You might be right there, but they don't know it, do they til…til he's on 'em and in 'em. Do they? I mean…" Specky offered.

"You'd be surprised, Specky, me old son. Word gets around one way or another, or haven't you seen the queue. It's like a bloody chip shop on Friday night outside his room. They are queued up from teatime on, just to get at it."

"It's horrible," Leo said with true terror in his voice.

Leo continued his lament. "And he's at it all night long. I can't get a minute's peace, can't get a good night's kip. And he sleeps all day just to get enough rest for the next night. And so on, and so on.

"Bastard!

"He knew I'd be walking back this way," Leo said, nodding his head and leering back in the direction of the supreme fornicator.

"How come you didn't notice them back there then?" Specky asked, swaying under the weight of too many pints.

"Oh, I noticed. I noticed all right. Heard them a mile off, didn't I. Didn't want to give him the satisfaction, that's all. And wouldn't have if you hadn't blabbed it all to the whole town."

"Sorry, Leo. Didn't know you had such a thing about it, about him and women, I mean. Want me to go back there and tell him to pack it in? I could go back there right now and tell him you don't like the way he's always ambushing you at night from the bushes with a girl – your girl – he'd just picked up minutes earlier just to show off what a big nob he's got. I'll tell him that it bothers you how he's always fucking your lass before you've even had a chance to bonk her yourself. I'm sure he'll understand, Leo. Being such a good bloke an' all. He'll probably stop it all tomorrow – if I tell him."

"Fuck off, Specky," Leo spat walking off across the bridge, sticking two fingers in the air.

"Do you want me to fuck off and tell him then, or just fuck off and not say another word to him?"

"Just fuck off, Specky," Leo shouted back over his shoulder, lifting two fingers into the night.

"Oh. Do you want me to fuck off and tell him, or fuck off and not tell him?" Specky shouted at the figure on the other end of the bridge. Specky was out of sorts now, and he could be an irritating little rat when he was out of sorts.

Chapter 5
Cuth's

North and South Bailey is a cobblestone lane that stretches from the middle of the town, up past shops, colleges and the cathedral and ends up going down over the river across Prebend's Bridge. St Cuthbert's Society (otherwise known as just plain old Cuth's) is situated on the left-hand side of South Bailey just before you get down to the river at Prebend's. It was a college of allsorts that catered specifically to the brilliant or unusual in society. Generally academic wonders, none of your usual students here. Unusual people were only ever accepted into Cuth's. Everyone in it was brilliantly unique. Requirements for entry were similarly unique. Dodge past Henry Havelock, the principal's second in command on the first floor and end up having a chat with Prof Osborne, principal, in his office at the top of the stairs, and you were in. Cuth's considered and admitted only those who disdained the rest of Durham's other, ordinary colleges.

The forefathers of this wonderful university, in their infinite wisdom, must have said, "Now that we've catered for all of the ordinary, boring young men and women in the country who might want to come to this place in order to learn, we must find a place somewhere for the unusual students, the academic wonders, the students with a difference, students who will make a difference, the gremlins of society who won't be afraid to give the world two fingers when it was needed."

It was one such deflated gremlin who earlier in the evening had thrown two fingers in the air over his shoulder and now trudged downheartedly across Prebend's Bridge and nipped into Cuth's bar for a quick pint of Best Scotch.

Scholars claim that Cuth's bar was erected on that ancient site by the monks of Lindisfarne years before the cathedral or castle were ever thought of. Legend has it that in times gone-by Cuth's bar was originally a Meade House that the monks built as a refreshment stopover when making their way from their Abbey

27

on Holy Island to York Cathedral – two weeks' travel by donkey cart to the south. When St Cuthbert finally popped his clogs, it was under Cuth's Meade House that his remains were first laid to rest before the lads set-to and built him a more suitable resting place just across South Bailey where that glorious cathedral now stands.

But enough history. This is getting too academic for me. Back to a legendary Cuthsman.

Leo Tucker staggered up to Cuth's JCR, ducked in a side door and suddenly, miraculously, like the gremlin he was, and still is – I might add – reappeared in front of the pinball machine next to the bar, his natural habitat. (Cue: The Who – *Pinball Wizard*) His pint jiggled precariously on the glass top of the pinball machine as he struggled with the mechanical intricacies of that blazing, whirling cabinet. Wonderful to behold, an otherwise eccentrically co-ordinated athlete, Leo was a pinball genius. The flashing lights soon proclaimed his wizardry when once again he bettered the best scores of the day by many hundreds of points. Finally spent, he slumped over the table, totally knackered yet grateful that he still had the touch.

Ladies and gentlemen of the Junior Common Room who had gathered around to watch the performance applauded politely and raised their glasses to him. He was a minor sensation. But also a humble man, Leo waved away their praise, disdaining any form of acclaim for himself that was not on the inside a pint glass. Moments later, he lifted one of the many pints he had been offered and staggered across to the chalkboard to write his name and total score at the very top of the list of recent scores. Chuffed to death, he just happened to notice that next under his name was that of Beau Franklin, fornicator extraordinaire, who earlier in the afternoon had posted a result that nobody thought could be touched anytime this side of the next millennium.

Savouring the moment, Leo swigged back the first half of his drink and wiped his gob clean with the well-worn sleeve of his jacket.

"You might be a better fucker than me, Franklin…" he issued before finishing off the first of many pints he would drink that night. He didn't complete the warning, didn't need to. Everybody in the JCR quietly understood.

Later that evening, that same fornicator extraordinaire wandered by, chest puffed out in triumph and bowlegged after an exceptionally long dalliance in the long grass behind a log down the hill from Prebend's Bridge.

"Tucker, you bastard," he exclaimed. Beau came from somewhere near York, I seem to remember, and I'll try to represent his northern accent without totally wrecking it, but, dear reader, bear with me in this.

"Surely, that's not yewer score up there. Imposseeble!" he said, amazed, and somewhat deflated whilst ordering a pint from the bar.

"Mine's a pint, Beau, me old mate," Leo said, savouring this very special moment, raising his glass to his own humble triumph. "It seems I've set a new worldwide best score or something.

"Just put it down there, there's a good chap, at the end of the queue," Leo said, meaning the pint Beau was getting him in fealty to his achievement. "I'll get to it in due course.

"Did you enjoy your walk with my Jill?" he asked, head lolling back and forth.

"Down by the river, I mean."

"Now lewk, Leo. Nobody said she was yewers." (To be read in a Yorkshire accent, remember.).

"Oh, then you haven't been lodging here for the past three months. You don't have the room next to mine and you haven't seen me come and go with her umpteen times, at least, over the course of this term? Haven't heard us next door to you sharing a game or two of monopoly and a bottle of green chartreuse well into the wee, small hours?"

"Aye. But also, by the sounds of things next door, Leo, you din't really get very far with her. Even by your own admission on many nights in the JCR, your success has been limited." (Sorry about that pathetic attempt at dialect. I'll let you put the appropriate turn on it from now on.)

"I was working up to it, Beau. Working up to it, mate. And there you go in one fell swoop, scooping up the woman I lust in the space of, oh, forty-five minutes," Leo said, grimacing at his watch.

"True," Beau had to admit. "Can't help it if I'm afflicted, though, can I, pal?" He giggled defensively and shrugged his shoulders in mitigation. "I can't help it if they throw themselves at me from every corner of the room."

"Not what I'm talking about."

"What are you talking about, then, Leo?"

"The Cuth's code of honour."

"Never heard of it."

"Oh? Then let me elucidate for you. The Cuth's code of honour states that you do not shag another bloke's dolly bird before he's had his leg over first."

"Still never heard of it."

"It's on the Cuth's crest."

"What bloody crest, you maniac?"

"That one there. See? That one there above the bar," Leo said turning around and pointing at an ancient looking seal right above where they were sitting that had a picture of Holy Island and an inscription below in Latin that neither of them could understand.

"See, me old mate. It says, 'Keep your filthy hands and other rude body parts to yourself until you are invited to.'"

"Fair enough. Fair enough. But she's the one who dragged me out of the Angel. I had nothing to do with it, mate. She invited me – forced me."

"Bollocks."

"She bloody well did.

"Ask her. She dragged us out to the riverbank to have her wicked way with us. Nothing to do wi' me. I told her I wanted to stay for the singsong. She wouldn't hear of it, wouldn't be told. You must have bloody well seen her dragging me screaming and kicking out of the Angel before we'd even sung *Harry*."

Leo mulled this over but couldn't remember what time he'd left the pub, never mind Franklin and his catch for the evening.

"It's true. I was in the snug wi' you lot, suppin' up like good uns, and over she walks, bold as brass, tells us she wants to say sommat to us outside. Next thing I know…Well…We're down the bankside and she's climbing all over me wi' a tongue down me throat."

As testament to the veracity of his evidence, he raised his pint to his lips. His big, liquid, bloodshot, delphinium-blue eyes bulged out over the top of the glass.

"Couldn't get her off us. Didn't want her in the first place. Don't know what she wanted in me. Don't know what any of 'em see in us, anyroads," he explained to his inquisitor who by now had passed completely out with his head lying sideways on the table and drool from his mouth forming a perfect circle on the tabletop.

"Leo!

"Leo, mate!"

"Here, Colin, give us a hand to get him back to his room. I think he's had too much for one night. Poowa lad. This whole thing has come as quite a shock to him."

Colin and Leo shared a room in Number 8.

With Colin's help, Beau managed to get Leo back to his room before sidling along to his own, which had a gaggle of hopeful admirers queued up for him outside his door.

"Now then," he said on his way over to the squirming mob, rubbing his hands together in anticipation, "where were we? Form a queue, ladies. Form a queue, and let's see…er…who's first…?"

And so ended the night for Beau, in the arms of his beloveds.

Leo sat slumped over in his chair, oblivious of Beau's merry-making next door. Better too that he was unconscious while this was going on. The row coming from Beau's room wouldn't have been good for his beleaguered mojo, coming hard on the heels of events down by the river.

Leo's roommate, Colin, dodged in later with his young lady, Vicky, in tow.

"Maybe we should undress him and get him into bed," Vicky whispered with a look of grim disgust on her face, not relishing the thought of what lay under Leo's camouflage combat jacket and jeans. Colin didn't think undressing Leo was such a good idea but compromised by tugging him up out of his chair and tilting him backward onto his bed.

"Throw that blanket over it, Colin, pet. Don't want him to get cold and wake up while we're at it."

Leo sighed, stuck a thumb into his mouth and turned over into the foetal position, dead to the world.

"Just like a wee babbie," Vicky whispered.

"Just like a babbie," Colin agreed ripping off her top and jeans and throwing her onto his bed not more than a dozen feet from the sleeping babbie. He reached over and turned off the light.

A shuffling sound.

A sigh.

Another sigh, more shuffling.

"Ouch. That hurts."

"Sorry, thought you liked it."

"Do…But not that hard."

"How hard then? That?"

"No. You can do it harder."

"That then?"

"Harder than that, pillock."

"Harder than that?"

"Uuuunmmm."

"That's harder than the first one."

"Uuuuuum. You're learning. Harder now."

"Like that?"

"Yeeeeeeessssss," she shrieked. "That's it. Now. Now. Now!

"Oh, now, Colin. Do it nowwwwwww!"

"Gracious," Colin uttered in disbelief. "You're a right randy masochist, you are."

"Ummmmm," she murmured. Turning over to offer him the other one, she demanded. "Now…

"Do the other one just like that, but not too hard at first. Licking's good too at first, then gobble me all up."

An early-next-morning-sun struggled through the misty bedroom windows. Wood pigeons cooed in the trees outside. Colin opened an eye to the disturbance, then shut it again, straight away. The room was spinning. The pain in his head remained. He knew that opening his mouth to speak would upset some sort of delicate balance he felt in his guts, so he clenched his teeth and called out to Vicky.

"You awake?"

Vicky was still dead to the world and snoring.

"Vicky…Vicky!"

Colin threw back the covers and sat up on the side of the bed.

Not a good idea. His head spun around and around accompanied by an urgent need in his gut to spew.

His gut wrenched up into his oesophagus, and before he could get to his feet, a spume of vomit described an arc through the air and deposited itself in a perfect circle on the mat next to his bed. Fascinated by this, Colin was about to mention the phenomenon to his bedmate when another urge to spew grabbed his intestines. He wretched and wretched, but nothing more than a dribble emerged to fall in little drops onto the pancake of sick, spoiling its symmetry. He shivered back the agony of expectation but nothing more emerged. Breathing became easier as a cool breeze from the gardens at the back of Number 8 drifted into the room and across his fevered brow.

"Bugger."

"Colin, pet, close the window. There's an awful smell coming in from the river." Feeling not too well herself, Vicky lay inert, smelling Colin's effluent, wanting to get up to close the window but held petrified by her own aching bones.

"Colin. Can't you do something about that repulsive smell? Close the window or something."

On the verge of adding to his delivery on the floor and knowing full well that any movement on his part would lead to another upchuck, Colin held his position and his silence and concentrated on breathing slowly in and breathing out slowly. He sensed that speaking or moving might set him off again. And so, like a dummy he sat fast, immobilised by the last little drip of puke that had landed in the middle of the pancake at his feet.

"Bugga me. What's that smell?"

It was the Pinball Wizard coming back to life.

"Colin. Colin, did you shit the bed last night?

"I do believe … oh, hello, Victoria," Leo said, rolling over and squinting across at their guest in the next bed.

"You're looking unbelievably lovely this morning, my dear. Did…er…did Colin shit the bed last night, or something? There's an awful smell in here," he said sniffing round at his own body parts in case it was him.

Not content with the silence that was coming from both of them, Leo persisted.

"Colin…"

"No, Leo," Colin hissed. "I didn't."

"Ah, well," Leo continued on irreverently, still in a daze.

"I didn't. So it must have been…" meaning Vicky, then thinking better of going on with this line of investigation, rolled back over and pulled the covers around his head to continue his sleep.

"Might be Old Timmy Bickerstaff out in the garden," he mumbled under the covers.

"Lets his innards get the best of him when he's raking around in the bushes. Loses track of time. Gets carried away, caught short," he chuntered on to no one in particular.

33

"Him and his dog, but I've never ever smelled dog shit quite like this. This is some kind of human waste," he deduced, going silent for a bit, conjuring up a solution.

"Pisses on his flowerbeds out there in the gardens, does Timmy. Says it's good for them.

"Fertiliser.

"But he grows the nicest flowers around, so he must know a thing or two about horticulture. It's going to be a pain in the arse though if every time he wants to improve his flowers he has to roll down his trousers.

"Can't see Mrs Manners approving, never mind Prof Osborne."

A nose appeared from under the covers then disappeared again.

A note or two here about Cuth's gardener and Mrs Manners, the bursar. Tim Bickerstaff was in his eighties at least, maybe nineties. A lot of people thought that he might have been around when the college was founded by the monks from Lindisfarne, but that is just silly. He wasn't really that old but still…True to his trade, he wore huge black wellies, a cloth cap, leathern breeches held up with braces, a stripy shirt that looked like pyjama tops and a stripy waistcoat that was never done up. None of his apparel matched, and that was good, for Old Tim didn't match anything himself. He came from good old Northumbrian stock and talked in a beautiful, guttural Northumbrian brogue that would have been well understood by Geoffrey Chaucer and his mates. These days pure Northumbrian, although a gentle, lilting language, is understood by few outside that county.

Tim rummaged all day long in the gardens behind St Cuthbert's amid an assortment of trees, and rhododendron bushes and gravel paths that wandered eventually down to the river. In the spring and summer, these gardens were glorious, full of colours and aromas. In the autumn, wild garlic replaced the gentler summer fragrances.

Behind Number 8 South Bailey, a croquet lawn hosted many bloody battles. On the other side of Cuth's croquet lawn, other, more normal, less warlike lawns spread along behind adjacent colleges lending tranquillity and peace and quiet to buildings that were normally brimming cauldrons of student dramas.

Tim didn't pay much attention to the students. They came and went, year in and year out in their turn, but he remained steadfast as the only permanent Cuth's resident. He rummaged, dug, planted, pruned, pissed, shat and cursed at will with his faithful dog always nearby and just outside of easy reach of its master's wellington boot. The dog, a wily old collie-lab cross was called 'Yabooga', or

34

so the students thought, for every command levelled at the poor beast was accompanied by that particular epithet.

"Come eeya, ya booga," Tim growled as he plunged and swung at his pet, back and forth through the rhododendrons, wisteria, myrtle and stinging nettles.

Yabooga growled and snapped back at his adoring master, barking his head off at him but never venturing closer than the length of Tim's swingeing welly.

"Gerroff, Yabooga," Tim snarled. And Yabooga scuttered well out of welly-shot howling indignantly. It was a love-hate relationship that punctuated the air along Cuth's riverbank from dawn 'til dusk. Tim had a racing boat – an eight – named after him by admiring Cuth's rowers, but Timmy didn't give a shit about them or their fucking boats.

Mrs Manners was the matronly college bursar. Befitting her station, she wore a tidy, dispassionate, Harris Tweed suit, and along with Joyce and Elizabeth, her two crony secretaries-in-crime, she inhabited the little office at the foot of Prof Osborne's stairs, seeing to the needs of the students, organising their billets and battels, ducking responsibilities as best she could all day long until three o'clock when, in relief of the day's toil, the office sherry bottle was brought out.

It didn't take long before a happily reckless atmosphere spread throughout that ancient office.

"He's here, ladies," Mrs Manners said, in a rush, one afternoon, stuffing letters into the pigeon holes outside the office, craning her neck around to get a better look at the object of her affection, her eyes bulging out at the figure who had just entered the building.

"Ee mind, but ee's got lovely blue eyes," Joyce remarked from behind her second generous glass of sherry, looking up over her spectacles.

"Wavy blond hair," Elizabeth said from her desk in the corner. "Beautiful hair. Beautiful."

Mrs Manners leaned back in through the office door so as not to be heard outside and whispered confidentially out of the corner of her mouth. "Never mind that you two. Just look at the bum on it," she said pointing at the student who was just disappearing up the stairs to Prof Osborne's little office at the top.

"Glorious," Joyce agreed.

"Aye, ah know," said Elizabeth, drooling at the spectacle.

Mrs Manners rotated on a heel to follow the spectacular bottom all the way to the top of the stairs. "They shouldn't be allowed."

"The jeans or the bum?" Elizabeth giggled, holding her breath, blushing red and salivating.

"Glorious," Joyce whispered again, mesmerised by the thought of that bum inside those tight, flared jeans.

"Buttoned up flies an' all. They make me ache, Lizzy. Oooh, they make me ache in places, ah, can't tell you about, do those bulging buttons. I'd just like to bite each one of them off one at a time until the whole thing dropped out," she added with a gleeful shriek, scrunching her shoulders up.

"Delicious."

"What drops out, Joyce?"

Dead silence.

Then.

"His aspidistra?" Lizzie ventured just before the office exploded and collapsed in dirty, raucous lady laughter.

"You two have had too much sherry," Mrs Manners said entering the office and taking her official place at the side of Elizabeth's desk. She shifted her chair.

"Why are you doing that, Mrs Manners?"

"What, pet?"

"Scrunching around like that."

"To keep an eye on you two and that sherry. Somebody has to."

"It wouldn't be," Joyce asked, raising her eyebrows, "to get a better look when it comes downstairs again?"

Mrs Manners was scandalised.

"Stuff and nonsense," she blustered.

"Doesn't bother me. Doesn't bother me one bit. I can take male bottoms or leave 'em. Doesn't matter at all to me," she said, glancing from time to time toward the top of the stairs, which only she could see – sitting where she was.

"No, you two are too enamoured by them. Or is it the sherry? A woman of the world, like myself, is able to control these urges …" she said, suddenly breaking off and staring transfixed at something that was happening outside the office.

"Aye?" Joyce said, following the train of thought that now came back down the stairs.

"You were saying, Olive …" But she too was cut short by the sudden emergence of a pair of tight jeans and bulging, buttoned-up flies slipping around the banister and descending towards the office doorway. A wavy blond head and liquid delphinium-blue eyes peered in.

"Scandalous," Joyce whispered, her widening eyes riveted to the bulging display.

"Good morning, ladies. Prof Osborne says I should see somebody in here about me battels. I think ah've been overcharged for me dinners last month."

'Oh!' was the shocked response of the three women inside, petrified solid by the sudden emergence of this unimaginable gift from heaven.

Mrs Manners was the first to move.

"Let me see it—

"—your battels, I mean." And she couldn't think why 'aspidistra' wanted to fly out of her mouth. Lizzie and Joyce could only sit and admire her shameless display, as she quickly jumped to her feet and moved in ever so close to him. Joyce nervously tipped in another glass of sherry. Elizabeth giddily passed her glass over for replenishment. Mrs Manners fumbled with the battels sheet.

"You seem confused, Mrs Manners," Joyce said nodding to Elizabeth at the other desk.

"Can I help? I'm in charge of aspidistras, er … I mean battels," Joyce said, getting to her feet, taking the offending piece of paper and pushing in between Mrs Manners and the student.

"If there is some kind of error, the fault is all mine. Let me see. Oh, yes. There it is, shameless thing. An error in accounting, that's all. Could have happened to anyone. Could've…" she said arrested by the eyes that glowed not one foot from her reddening cheek.

"Just come around to my desk a minute, pet," she said, grinning at her companion who grinned back, wantonly.

"I'll have to check the accounts book. Mrs Manners, can you get a chair to place under Mr Franklin's lovely bottom while I check his…"

"…Aspidistra," Elizabeth whispered over to Mrs Manners whose tongue, it must be said, was hanging out by the roots.

When the problem had been sorted and the aspidistra sent happily on its way, Elizabeth turned to Joyce.

"You!" she spat.

"What?"

"Why did you have to go and mention aspidistra like that?"

"Couldn't help it, pet. Anyroads, it's just an expression, just a turn of phrase."

"Talk like that might never get him back."

"Our talk, not his. He didn't mind. Probably thought I was just bonkers, which I am when you think on…"

"Well. Next time, mind your manners."

"Aye, but he is lovely, our Lizzie."

Lizzie looked askance over at her cousin who looked off in the distance at something special disappearing across the TV room and out the door leading to the JCR bar.

Chapter 6
Specky

Later that week, the Saloon Bar in the back room of the Student's Union, North Bailey was packed. We managed eventually to find a side table and squash around it with our pints and ham baps smothered in 'blow your socks off' Keynes mustard. Specky came in after a bit, found Leo standing at the bar and although I motioned to him to come join us, he glowered and chose instead to stand at the bar beside Leo, light a cigar and order a drink. I could tell he was in a mood. He stood with his back to us, furtively chatting to Leo and glaring every now and then in our direction – or was it my direction. There was never any knowing with Specky. He was always a bit of a loose cannon. We were never sure when he was going to blow up or fizzle out. And looking back at those times now, I marvel at how many undergraduates on Valium managed to stay out of the gutter.

The university was awash with anti-depressants. God knows what might have happened to the place without their so-called calming effect. I guess it spoke large about the pressure students were under in those days to come good to get a university place – any place and then live up to their parents' massive expectations of them. Social necessity or just getting a job? Getting a job – any job – in order to put food on the table or get their parents off their backs. Most got through university all right, with or without those little pills, despite nagging parents. Some fell by the wayside or flat on their faces. Most managed one way or another. Few seemed to ever get the job they wanted, though. Choice was taken out of their hands by necessity or by fate. Some hard-working sods with vision managed to rise to the top of their year, find their desired job after graduation and command a profession. Most didn't. Teaching, the civil service, the banks or the like were good enough.

The little pills got them through, calming the tensions of life, enabling a kind of fumbled fulfilment, a muzzled second choice.

This evening, however, the effect of those little pills was not going to be calming enough for Specky.

The night had all started off fine, quite pleasant as a matter of fact. Cuth's Boat Club had all agreed to meet in the Students' Union after 'work', have a few drinks, something to eat and see what the night brought. When we arrived, it was obvious it was going to be a struggle to find a seat, but we spied Vicky on the inside of the throng in the back room peering back at us through those thick, thick spectacles. She signalled that a table was about to be vacated in there, so we jumped in juggling our pints and nuclear ham baps. Vicky, Colin, Carl, Carlos, Lucien and I scrunched in around the table waiting for Specky to show.

When he finally appeared and set out to snub us by standing at the bar, we laughed it off. It was just Specky's way. We ordered another round. It was my 'shout', so I plunged through to the bar beside Specky, ordered the drinks and tried to engage him with chitchat while I waited for the barmaid to pull the pints. His back was to me. I thought the extended snub no big deal and was even grateful that I didn't have to participate in his lugubrious conversation. Leo was on the other side of him, and Jill was on the other side of Leo.

Tonight was the night, as far as Leo was concerned. He'd been working hard on Jill for weeks. By the time I got to the bar, he was looking well in, ignoring Specky and focussing totally on his pretty little prey.

"Ta, mate," Leo said after I slid his pint of Best Scotch across the bar to him and a Cherry B for Jill. He looked at me triumphantly then returned to the hunt, sliding a surreptitious arm surreptitiously across her back. I pushed a pint of Guinness across to Specky, but he just ignored it, choosing to focus instead on his cigar – one of several he'd nicked from a box on my mantle shelf two nights prior.

"Yeah, right," he snarled in thanks under his breath, exhaling cigar smoke across at the barmaid with that wiseacre, Humphrey Bogart sneer across his face.

"Don't mention it," I whispered into the general bar hubbub, as I carried the tray of drinks to our table. He ignored the sarcasm, intent on making the perfect smoke ring for the barmaid or for me. I couldn't decide which. The last I heard before getting back to the table was her laughing hysterically and him chortling at an apparently successful puff of rings twirling above their heads.

"Mind your subject-verb agreement there, young Flynn," Lucien said, officiously rearranging the pints I had placed on the table. "I'm on the lager and

Carl here's on the shandy. God knows why anybody would ruin a perfectly good bitter by diluting it with filth like that.

"By the way, what did you say to Specky just now?" Lucien nudged me when I had finally settled back into my seat and quaffed off the top half of my drink.

"If looks could kill," he said, pointing over to Specky who had lost the attention of the barmaid and was now glowering first at me then down into his untouched Guinness.

"Not me," I said, seeing nothing unusual in Specky's morose behaviour.

"Seems to hate the whole world tonight," Lucien said. "But then again, when doesn't he? Seem to hate everybody, I mean. Solemn chap at the best of times, our Specky. Maybe another pint or two will mellow him out, although he hasn't touched a bit of his first, just sits and stares into it like it was some kind of poison he wants no part of – his fount of doom."

"Didn't manage to pull the barmaid with that silly smoke trick," I said. "That's all that's wrong with him. Needs to get his leg over."

"Don't we all?" said Lucien. "Don't we a…dear friends," he said, suddenly raising his pint in the air, "here's to all of us getting our legs over – or under, in the case of Vicky – in the very near future. Sometime this side of Christmas, if poss – if not, very soon thereafter."

"Very good," Colin said with a wry smile. "Some time, anyway."

"Yes. Soon. May it be some time soon," Lucien added.

We raised our pints to his amended toast then broke back into small talk again. I looked over at Specky to see if he concurred, but…nothing. He hovered malevolently over his drink.

Never one to miss out on a toast, though, Leo raised his glass and turned to us with that lurid, dirty grin on his face, nodding deeply as if he were certain of his chances tonight. Then, returning his attentions to Jill, he lorded over her, ordered her an orange juice, attending to her every need, for she, it seemed, was his tonight – poor thing.

Tomorrow he would claim that it was not his inadequate love making that lost him the night with Jill. It was the change over from Cherry B to orange juice.

"I had her," he lamented the following evening whilst pissing in the bog of The Travellers' Rest. "I had her in the palm of me 'and. All it needed was one more alcoholic drink to tip her over the edge …" He paused to consider his calamity.

"Then I went and ordered her that bloody orange."

"Bad luck," Colin said.

"But I thought it was Jill who asked for the orange juice."

"Maybe she didn't like the way things were going," I said.

"…averted a fate worse than death," I added, doing up my flies and wandering out of the bog and back onto Claypath.

"What is it that you said, Lucien? Something about a tide?" I asked.

"Ah, yes, dear friends – a tide in the affairs of men …"

"Yours was ebbing last night, Leo," Colin said, "but you didn't know it."

"Bugger!" the poor sod added to his lament.

"Counting your chickens again," Colin said.

"I'm always bloody well counting me bloody chickens," he said with true exasperation. "Why do I always count me bloody chickens?"

"I'll tell you why, dear chap," Lucien said, looping an arm around Leo's shoulder so that he might steer him up Claypath away from The Travellers' Rest and toward The General Gordon.

"It's because you are the eternal optimist. You have hope for … er … how can I put it …? Improvement. You see hope in situations that really have no hope at all."

"Jill, last night, for instance?"

"Yes. Jill for one thing."

"What other things, then?" Leo squirmed, expecting the worst then holding up his hand to intercede, anticipating Lucien's fell declaration.

"I know what you are going to say, and it wasn't my fault."

"What? What wasn't your fault?"

The rest of us crowded around, held our breaths, awaited Leo's defence of who knew what.

"Specky's tirade last night."

"Oh, you think it was your fault?"

"No. I'm saying it wasn't my fault. I was just there at the bar …"

"Trying to get a leg over your sweet Jill …"

"No, not that, not there. Some other time. Any other time," he said becoming more flustered.

"Well, what then?"

"Yeah," Colin interceded, the way he does – that mischievous grin, egging them both on.

"What then, Leo?"

"Specky throwing his pint of Guinness across the room at Flynn last night in the Union."

"Did he?" Lucien was astonished at this news and turned to me for confirmation. "Did he, Flynn? I must have been in the bog at the time."

I nodded, sheepish that it had happened at all, and that I was the main target.

It was all I could do to duck out of the way in time, as I saw in slow motion this black and frothy-white pint tumbling through the air towards me. I can see it now, slowly tumbling and tumbling in mid-air, miraculously retaining its full contents until suddenly it exploded against the wall, only inches above and behind an otherwise civilised conversation.

Crash!

The glass smashed on the wall behind us missing all of its targets who ducked for a split second, then as if by some unspoken accord – that it didn't really matter, that it had been a harmless prank and that nothing needed to be said, that no blame needed be apportioned – we all sat back up and continued our conversations as if nothing untoward had happened at all, and that it was no big deal. It wasn't assault; no one had been hurt. It was just Specky in a mood trying to kill us – me. Trying to kill me.

And a waste of a bloody good pint. To take notice or offence would have meant that we acknowledged his grievance as a grievance. But I guess he had a right to do what he did, and we all agreed with that right, and we all loved him anyway, despite the fact that he had attempted to kill us – or at least one of us, me, that is.

But it was just Specky. He needed to get it all out, and he did in spades. Then he barged his way out through that packed bar, more pissed off than ever, because nobody had even noticed his passionate outburst. No compassion for his humiliation. Everybody in the bar went on talking, as if nothing had happened at all. The smashed shards of glass tinkled to the floor behind our chairs, and the splashed Guinness dribbled down the wall.

All eminently fixable.

But what about Specky's humiliation? Who would fix that? This was in the back of our minds as we went on talking. Another round was ordered – Leo's shout this time. Carlos squashed his way out to the refectory to get more mustard-laden ham baps for everyone. They gave him a tray full, and he beamed above that wobbling pyramid of buns as he hurried back in to us.

Chapter 7
Reginald Leonard Edward Buxton-Phipps

Reginald Leonard Edward Buxton-Phipps was an enigma. To be a member of Cuth's at all with a name like that was odd. His name and accompanying upper-class idiosyncrasies said that he should belong to Castle or Hatfield or Grey College, all of whose undergraduates, as we well know, are enigmas. But he was truly one of us, and we loved him and all of his screwball, upper-class eccentricities. Reggie was our pet snob. He talked with his nose in the air, so that he had to peek down over it to see his audience. This wasn't intentional, it was probably genetic, idiomatic like most of his other crazy mannerisms. He would make a statement, check with you with a sidelong glance to make sure that you understood, then whether you understood him or not, he would carry on explaining whether you were still listening or not. And by that time, you probably weren't. But that didn't bother him either. Nothing ever seemed to bother Reg. He would slough off any opposition to what he was saying with a little laugh and a warm, knowing smile. There was always an element of unintentional condescension in his tone, though, partly because he wasn't sure of his audience and partly because he wasn't sure whether he was making any sense at all.

We humoured Reggie. He was used to it.

He was a lovable little rascal snob who intended no offense and gave none.

Still, he was full of himself, loved cricket and loved to go off and practise his bowling technique whenever the conversation grew sluggish. I never really ever saw him play cricket, but being a novice rower like me, he agreed to take part in the annual Cuth's Rowing Club v Rugby Club rugby match. It was his first and last attempt at rugby.

Being a tiny soul, it was imagined that he might be effective out on the wing where, once given the ball, he might run like the wind with it over the try line. But he preferred picking daisies out there on the wing beyond the touchline, where, he declared, "The flowers hadn't been torn down yet by hordes of lumpy old rugby boots." While the rest of us were careering back and forth up and down the pitch, crashing into each other, fumbling the ball and making a general balls-up of the game, Reggie was wandering back and forth looking for four-leaf clovers. He didn't seem to care that the game was life and death to the rest of us. He had decided that rugby could be a gentle ramble in the countryside, beyond the clarts and gouts of blood willingly given to the cause by the rest of us.

When half time arrived, he was found back in the pavilion, guzzling tea and lovingly peeling the crusts off his watercress sandwiches. The rugger buggers – big brawny fellows from places like Grimsby, Huddersfield and Wigan who ate nothing but burgers and chips – could only sneer at our tiny winger who, delighted at seeing that he had unintentionally become the centre of their attention, lifted his chin, opened his mouth, closed his brain and began to lecture us all on his beloved cricket. This did not go down well with the rugger buggers who ate namby-pamby cricketers like him for breakfast, nor did it please us rowers who were losing badly to the rugby team. Just about to demonstrate the action of his favourite demon fast bowler, John Snow, Reggie was suddenly laid out by a right cross from one of our disgruntled halfbacks.

Cuddling his bloodied nose in his hanky on our way back into town along the riverbank from Maiden Castle rugby pitch, Reggie couldn't quite grasp the fact that a player on his own team had taken exception to his cricketing demonstration.

"Why on earth did you want to go and do a thing like that, Leo?" Reggie said trying to pick the scabbing blood off his swollen honker.

"Seemed like a good idea at the time," Tucker replied, still pissed off by the ball that Reggie had fumbled right into the hands of their hooker.

"Leo's pissed off that you gave up their first try," Colin said.

"Their second try was the worst" Leo fumed. "When in fact, I was passing the ball to you, Reggie, you bastard. But you weren't bloody well there, were you."

"Oh, where was he then?" Colin said trying to agitate between the warring parties.

"Off having his orange, that's where he was. Off having his fuckin' orange five bleeding minutes before the bloody ref blew for fuckin' halftime."

"Didn't like that ref," Carl chirped in. "Didn't blow for any of their fouls."

"That's because they didn't have any," Colin said. "They knew what they were doing. They knew how to play the game, and we didn't."

Reginald danced around a puddle on the towpath trying to keep up with the rest of us.

"We were on to a loser right from the start. Who agreed to play the rugby team at rugby, anyway? Stupid idea in the first place," Carl whinged.

"Archie set it up."

"The bleedin' Boat Club captain should stay out of decisions like that if he doesn't intend to play."

"We all agreed to take on the rugby club at their own game. Thought we could handle 'em. Don't blame Archie," Beau said.

"Should've agreed to something in between," Carl observed but immediately wished he hadn't.

Reggie's little bloodshot eyes lit up. When he came up with the bright idea of playing them at cricket, he was chased all the way back along the riverbank to the Dun Cow Inn where his littleness got the best of his irate pursuers through the narrow passageway beside the pub and out onto Old Elvet. Fortunately for Reggie, distracted enough by the beery aromas coming from their local watering hole, they allowed him to scramble his way through the narrow passage ways and out of their clutches. On his own now and bowling his way down Old Elvet, he offered up his googlie to them as a means of levelling up the score with the rugger buggers. But as usual, no one was listening.

It was Leo's shout in the Dun Cow. The tiny back room was barely big enough to contain the Boat Club, but it managed. At the bar, Leo carried on a lively one-sided conversation with the barmaid while she poured the pints for him and fitted them all onto one tray.

"Clever girl," Leo announced back at the table, "and I think I've scored there. She's new here, and I think she's in love with me already," he said grinning proudly, handing around the pints and dragging over another stool to sit on.

"How do you know, Leo?" Colin asked in this usual shit-disturbing manner.

"Did you see the way she looked at me with those big doe eyes?"

"She was out on the razz last night. That was her being rat-arsed wi' booze. I don't think she noticed you at all, Leo. She looked as though she couldn't focus if her life depended on it. You thought she was besotted with you, and she was just being dense. Just your type," Beau said in his condescending, encouraging way.

"She held my hand when she handed me back the change."

"Held your hand?" Beau exploded.

"Just for a second. A brief moment in time. Didn't you see it?"

About to open his account on the fair maiden, Beau was immediately stifled by Leo. "And we don't need anything from you about it, Franklin. I saw her first, so just leave it."

"Ah …"

"Leave it …"

"But …"

"… Just get it out of your head, Franklin. I saw her first, and I get first dibs."

Beau gave up any more interest in the lass without a fight. Couldn't even be bothered to turn around and look her over, sat with his back to her for the rest of our meeting. Colin bought the next round and came back from the bar with very little to report except that Leo had a good 'un there.

Leo beamed, raised his glass to himself, but when Franklin shoved his pint across to Carl to announce that he was finished, citing lots to do down at the river and stood up to leave, we all knew something was up. He scraped back his stool and turned to go. We all watched him past the bar – now empty of the barmaid and out the door with nary a glance back at us. Satisfied that he really had rights over this girl, Leo raised his glass to his lips and savoured victory. The door closed and Beau was gone.

Colin was puzzled. Carl couldn't believe what we had just witnessed. He was astonished. We raised our pints to Leo and fifteen minutes later rose as one to dog Beau's tracks back to the boathouse. One by one, we left by the side door, the one that leads out into the little alleyway that runs out the back of the pub and down beside a yard filled with deep grass and surrounded by a shoulder high creosote fence. On our way past that yard, Colin just happened to look over the fence and gasped. One by one, we stopped to gaze in disbelief over the fence, speechless, for there in the deep deep grass was Beau on his back and his new conquest bending over him, helping herself to his most urgent needs.

"Filthy beast," Carl remarked on his way past.

"Dizzy lass," Leo said, suddenly unsmitten.

"Lucky bastard," Colin observed of her obvious ardour for Beau's needs and the blissfully helpless, almost apologetic look on his face, as if it were not his intention or fault at all that this had happened, that he had merely been on his way back to the boathouse, and that she had lain in wait for him in the long grass with her tongue hanging out as well as other indecently delicious parts of her anatomy.

"How does he do it?" Leo was heard to remark as he vaulted the dry stonewall at the end of the pub garden.

"He's a kind of magician," Colin said following Leo over the wall. "He just has to wave that magic wand of his, and women appear from behind creosote fences for him."

"It must be magic. If I did something like that, I'd end up on a charge for indecent exposure."

"Nothing indecent about yours, Leo. Quizzical, maybe. Without equal. Definitely humorous. Minimalist?"

"All right. All right. No need to go on about it. Like I tell all the lasses, find it and it's yours," Leo said, striding off down the lane in a huff.

"That's twice in the same week. I'll do for him, if he tries it on again. I will. I'll bloody do for 'im."

Chapter 8
'Doing for' Beau Franklin

Not to be confused with Palace Green mentioned in chapter one, the medieval town square, or marketplace, in the middle of Durham is compact and to this day largely functional with shops, pubs, banks and businesses surrounding it. A massive statue of the Marquess of Londonderry stands in the centre of the square beckoning to all to come and use the public bogs located below him. The ornate frontispiece of Durham Town Hall holds court along one side of the square. Mainly a venue for local as well as college discos, the Town Hall was simply a big, wood panelled room with a bar and a stage in it. Tonight, it was throbbing with partying students. Beer flowed freely from the bar. Instead of the usual DJ, a little-known band hammered out its tunes on a stage in the middle of the floor surrounded by all manner of students gyrating to the band's blues-based drawl. It was pretty intoxicating. The drummer, as usual, was too loud, almost drowning out the drawling lead singer, but the lead guitar was amazing, flicking off down home riffs and rising above the rest of the group while maintaining a close connection with the drums and the base.

The excitement in that place was indescribable, so I won't try to describe it and just say it was very noisy. You couldn't hear the person next to you unless you were up really close. Strobe lights crashed back and forth across the murky interior. Girls in short, tight miniskirts and guys in tatty old flared jeans, fashionably ripped at the knees, flailed against one another in a pre-coital invitation to submissive hours later on in the night when the beer and the noise and the hormones of youth would eventually mix for some of the lucky punters.

Having already spent some time in the Dun Cow and The Shakespeare, we arrived on the scene late and in the latter stages of lost sobriety. I don't know how he managed to do it, but Leo was always able to worm his way to the bar past terraces of surging, predatory, agitated drinkers. He purchased a round and ferried the beers surreptitiously back to us without anyone putting up an argument. We were all soon supping on Best Scotch back at the edge of the dance floor, eyeing the totty over the tops of our drinks, evaluating the possibilities.

Sensibly, Beau had forgone the beer in favour of getting straight down to business. He was already gyrating away in the centre of the melee in front of a canny-looking local lass who was responding as expected to his advances. He was a sex machine. He knew it; the totty knew it, and he couldn't be held back.

"I give up," Leo shouted across the racket to the rest of us who were only inches away from his shoulder. "He's already at it. Couldn't he at least give the rest of us a fighting chance?"

"What?" Colin chimed in. "Shave his head and put on fifty pounds."

Colin took another sup of his drink and shouted thoughtfully back, "Nothing for it but to get stuck in, Leo. I'll hold your pint while you get over there and have the next dance with that lass at the bar. Go on, man. Get stuck in. The night is young."

Suddenly, the night exploded.

"Hello."

Carol appeared out of nowhere on the edge of the dance floor, reaching her hands out eagerly to me, inviting me to enter the fray with her. She backed up into the dancing crush, appealing to me to follow her into it, and I did, reaching out for her dangling, enticing fingertips. Colin took my pint just before the crowd engulfed us. She was a knockout. Short light blue miniskirt, pretty psychedelic top and black, knee-length boots. She had come to party and wouldn't take no for an answer.

(Cue: Free: *All Right Now*)

I couldn't believe my luck.

The strobe lights flashed around the room. The crowd stomped and crashed in hedonistic abandonment. The band shook the stage above us, the floor below us. Carol beamed at my ham-fisted efforts to follow her raunchy moves then exploded, jumped up and down and clapped with glee when I managed to invent some moves of my own. Her hair flew out in all directions. Nothing was off-limits. Hands, elbows, arms and hips pumped in all directions. Her hips and bum and shoulders rotated seductively, feet stomped and elbows declared themselves off-limits to all but the heartiest of movers. She was in a trance, sliding further and further away from me into the crowd. I lunged after her into the depths of that sexually charged mob.

The floor shook and just as suddenly as it had started, the band stopped in a heap. The skinny little scruffy singer on stage dressed in a denim jacket and torn jeans, looking for all the world like he had just come out of the Ozarks, stepped to the front of the stage, took a deep bow amid raucous applause and cries for more, put his hands in the air and started clapping rhythmically and banging one heel down to begin the next number. But it was over for me. In the interlude, Carol had been pulled reluctantly away to the other side of the room by an unidentified hand or hands. With a weak little wave and a bleak, unwilling look on her face, shaking her head, she disappeared totally from view, engulfed by the mob, the strobes, the ear-shattering band and the night.

Her friends had rescued her from certain capitulation, but who was I to argue. Couldn't have argued if I wanted to. She was gone, but at that point, judging by the look on her face, as she was being unwillingly dragged back out of sight, I knew I would get her back. I didn't know how, and I didn't know who I was up against, but I knew time was on my side, and I knew something else. I saw the look in her eyes as she enticed me out onto the dance floor. That was no lie. That was her telling me secrets she had told no one else.

"Flynn, you jammy bastard. Who was that?" Colin shouted as he handed me back my pint.

"Some girl just fancied a dance," I said.

"Some girl? Fancied a dance? Fancied a fuckin' dance? You jammy bugger. If a girl like that came up to me and dragged me onto the dance floor like that, I'd fall all over me tongue. Who was the bastard, the one dragging her off?"

"Don't know. Just some guy. A friend of hers, I guess."

"Aren't you going to chase off after her?"

"Something tells me she'll be back," Leo said, sidling up behind me and whispering into my ear.

"Now ..." he said sternly, measuring the contents of his glass.

"...to more important things. I seem to be empty. Whose shout is it? Can't hunt totty in this dehydrated state. I think it must be yours," he said, handing me his empty glass and nudging me in the direction of the mob lining the bar, six deep and clamouring for booze, arms and glasses and elbows going in every direction. It was hopeless. I'd never make it through that, so, deciding to edge round to the far end of the bar, I found an opening and squeezed in.

Just before I got to ground zero, a little female voice, a little, cultured female voice at my left elbow drifted up towards me.

"You're the one from the library," the little voice said, but looking across at the bar, I could see nothing. I could see no one.

"Here. Down here. You're the one, aren't you?" she said in a clipped, breathless rush as if she had discovered something sacred. "The one she's always talking about. Won't let her get any work done."

She sounded cross.

When I finally located the source of the voice, I couldn't believe my eyes. The girl beside me at the bar was small but extremely well packaged. Her hair flew around her head in a remarkable brunette swirl. Her face beamed with stunning brown eyes that pinned me to the spot. A savage kind of sullen beauty holding two glasses of wine to her fabulous breasts, daring me to contradict her, stopped me in my tracks.

"You ARE the one from the library, aren't you?" she insisted.

She enunciated her words with a clipped, Home Counties authority. Steely-eyed, she pinned me again, daring me to answer, daring me to deny it.

"I get to the library quite a bit," I managed to stammer, hating myself for succumbing to her intimidating gaze so easily, feeling somehow guilty for intruding into their well-established pattern of life, which I obviously didn't fit.

"Yes, you DO," she said vehemently, swishing that fabulous coiffure across her savagely beautiful, vermillion lips.

"You most certainly do. Tell me, what do you do in there besides sending notes back and forth to Carol all the time, disturbing her concentration. She'll not get through the year, you know, if you keep on," she smirked.

Bloody cheek, I thought. Who does this gorgeous shrimp think she is, apart from being the second most beautiful woman I had seen since coming to town.

"Sorry. Didn't know I was having that kind of effect," I said, easing my way up to the bar when a space appeared and squeezing in beside her.

"Louisa…Lulu," she said as a kind of introduction, putting her drinks down on the bar and vigorously shaking my hand.

"We're in digs together up Western Hill."

"Sorry, err, Lulu. Didn't know I was causing such a disturbance. I'll study somewhere else in future. Wouldn't want her to fail her course."

"NO!" Lulu exploded.

"DON'T DO THAT," she said holding on to my hand.

"Don't do THAT! It's all rather, well, rather nice," she said, softening and urging me at the same time.

"She'd be put out if she thought I was…well…I was interfering, but…" she said looking up at me in earnest, her eyes crossing a little in concentration in that endearing way that makes some women so appealing, so vulnerable. "… you do know about her significant other, don't you? Attached pretty well, they are. Have been for years. Well … ever since last Christmas, anyway," she stumbled, trying to hold it all together.

"Oh," I said, knowing all the while that there had to be at least one other bloke in her life, if not more. But what the hell. Nothing ventured … I was willing to do some queue jumping. The prize was worth it.

"I'm not really surprised," I said. "Bet he drives a Rolls Royce."

But Lulu wasn't smiling now or listening. She was thinking hard.

Finally, she ventured, "I was wondering if you might … if you might be interested …" she said hesitantly.

Then in a rush, she added, "We're having a little soiree next week at our digs. Come along, if you like. Should be fun. Bring wine or something, or nothing at all. Just your lovely self, if you like. One or two friends, that's all. Seven o'clock, Friday night, 50 Western Hill, bottom floor apartment. And you're not allowed to bring anybody else with you, if you know what I mean," she said, looking over at the lads, "Ladies mostly, I mean."

"There, I've done it, and I'm not sorry," she said taking a deep breath and examining the damage.

"I've done it," she repeated to herself, picking up her drinks and pushing back away from the bar.

"Bye. See you next week," she shouted back over her shoulder above the din with a flip of those gorgeous eyes. Her little bottom squiggled out of sight, engulfed in the crowd, and I was left alone at the bar to navigate five pints back to my mates.

I decided right there and then that I liked Lulu too, and who knows, if Carol didn't work out, maybe…Fearless, thoughtful, caring. Who knows…? Definitely mind blowingly gorgeous. What a lass!

"Haway, Flynn. Get 'em in, lad," Leo shouted in a poor imitation of the local Geordie dialect.

"Scored again, I see. You're a regular little Lothario, aren't you? I'm not bringing you out any more if you're going to go around sweeping all the lasses off their feet before any of the rest of us get a look in. And young Beau isn't looking too impressed over there either. Seems he's lost his first lass in many years to that bloke doing the cancan.

"Isn't he the bloke who was up on stage before? The singer?" Leo said, spotting the worn-out jeans and high-heeled boots.

"The singer. Scruffy little git. Needs a shave. Look at the state of that. Looks like he hasn't had a decent meal in months, tatty jeans and worn-out denim jacket and yet he pulls like he's Mick Jagger. Just like I would if I had a mind to."

"And the body," Colin said, halfway down his pint already.

"Or the moves," said Carl.

"I have moves," Leo said feigning offence and putting out his foot in a sorry imitation of the singer. "See there. And there," he added, replacing the first foot with the other, teetering back and forth. "It's called 'The Undertaker'."

"And you're the corpse," Colin said.

"It's a dance step I've been working on for ages," he insisted in a drunken garble.

"Go on then, Leo," Colin said, pushing him nearer the dance floor than he cared to be.

"Get out there and try it on them lasses, the ones dancing in a circle around their handbags."

And by god, he did. Minutes later, Leo was in the circle of girls sticking first one foot out, drawing it back decisively like a matador pulling back his cape, stumbling a bit off balance then stabbing out with his other foot. Pissed out of his mind, he teetered as he transferred his weight from one foot to the other.

"…The undertaker," he was heard explaining to the assembled circle of beauties, patiently waiting for him to bugger off out of it so that they could carry on their own dancing.

"…Easy. All you have to do is first do this." Teeter.

"…Then you do…" Totter.

"That."

But his legs couldn't follow his own instructions, and he fell backwards into the arms of a woman who had been the only one in the circle even remotely interested in his antics, the same woman who had just been gyrating with the lead singer of the band and before that our Beau.

"Like that," he said over his shoulder looking back and up at the young lady who had saved him from falling flat on his arse.

"'Ello, 'ello, 'ello," he boozily said to her.

"And what's your name, my dear? You are very strong," he groaned as she helped him to his feet, turning around to her and holding on to her for support.

"And excellent, strong, child-bearing hips, I see," he said hanging on to her for dear life.

"Did you like 'The Undertaker', my dear? I'll show you again. There. That's it. Now. All you have to do – are you watching? Put your foot out like this," he said, wobbling back and forth as he did his best to demonstrate.

"Have a little drink. That's it. That's good! You're catching on to the drinking bit already…have a little drink, then do this.

"Nice one dahlin'. You're one o' them women on Top of the Pops, aren't you? Must be. Yes, Pan's People. That's it. You must be a Pan's Person," he mumbled, struggling with his words and with standing up and stumbling about all over the place.

"No. Not like that. Like her. Like her. She's got it. That's it, my dear," he said trying to applaud with his empty pint glass.

"And I'm going to give you first prize. Do you know what I'm going to do? Do you? Do you know what I'm going to give you? I'm going to give you the honour of getting me another pint before I whisk you off into the night away from all this noise and interference in our love life," he said handing her his empty glass.

"The winner," he pronounced before falling flat on his arse again in the middle of the dance floor. This time all the girls followed suit, and it wasn't long before everybody on the dance floor was flat on their arses doing 'The Undertaker'.

"You said you'd do for him, Leo. And that's just what you did," Colin said later that night as we wobbled back up Saddler Street towards Cuth's.

"That's right, my old son," Leo said.

"What did I do?"

"Just what he's done to you loads of times."

"Right," Leo agreed. He stumbled on some more then asked, "Which is what, Colin, precisely?"

"Stole his lass."

"Oh, yes. Right!" Leo said, barely able to place one foot in front of the other.

"Stole his lass…Right," he said, proud as punch with himself.

"Who?"

"Angela. The lass you spent most of the night with before you passed out on the Town Hall steps."

"Oh, yes, right. Angela. Nice girl. Did I dance with her, Chris?" he brightened, turning to me.

"You were almost shagging her right out there in the middle of the dance floor."

"Oh, yes. Right. Shagged her right in the middle of the dance floor. Now I relembler." Leo stumbled over 'remember' the way any of us would who had just drunk multiple pints of ale.

"Relembler? We were dancing," he miss-remembered all of a sudden, with exploding glee.

"That's right. That's right. I shagged her right in the middle of the dance floor."

"Almost. Almost, but not quite," Colin said.

"Almost shagged her, then. Almost." He turned the words over to get it all straight.

"Whilst you were doing 'The Undertaker'. You were both sitting on the floor at the time. It seems to be part of the dance."

At this, we all fell about the place laughing, tripping over the cobblestones in the road and the curb.

"Beau was not amused."

"Aw…Wasn't he?" Leo tried to commiserate.

"You 'did for him', Leo. He wanted to beat you to a pulp. But you were out cold by then, so he went off with Agnes, Angela's mate, to have a quick shag behind the Town Hall."

"Did he?"

"Aye, he did."

"And what happened to Angela, then, the one I was shagging on the dance floor?"

"Ah, that's the good bit."

"Is it? Yes. That's the good bit. She says you two should get together tomorrow night when you're feeling better, and you can have a nice, quiet drink together."

"Good! Good! Seems like a nice girl after all, Colin. Not a tart at all. Seems like a really nice girl then, Chris," he said earnestly, looking from one of us to the other, desperately trying to focus his eyes.

"She is Leo," Colin said. "Too nice for you. But never mind that. So we're going to get you back home and put you to bed so you'll be right as rain for tomorrow's drink with her."

"Good plan. But now, if you don't mind, I'm going to puke me ring out into that garden over there," he said, hurrying over to the side of the lane.

And he did just what he said and felt ever so much better for it, but tomorrow was another story.

Chapter 9
Cannibal Croquet

The gentle clack of wooden mallet on wooden ball drifted across the gardens behind St Cuthbert's Society. Despite the seemingly idyllic pastoral, a battle royal stormed back and forth across the croquet lawn.

"Can't do that, Leo," Colin whinged.

"I just did, me old son," Leo replied with saltpetre in his voice.

"You cannot just hoik my ball all the way into the bushes like that. The rules state – and Archie will back me up on this – the rules clearly state that all competition paraphernalia must remain on the pitch and in sight at all times. Rule 27, paragraph 3(ii)."

"Bollocks. You will have to play it from behind the azalea bush or forfeit a go. And the rulebook clearly states that if you forfeit a go, I get to whack you again, mate. And this time I will not be so gentle. Your ball will end up down there in the river. Good thing it floats. You'll be able to fish it out below the weir early tomorrow morning at the cost of one more penalty stroke. 'There is a willow grows aslant a brook' down there behind which all river flotsam rotates around and around and around in a whirlpool. Your ball should be caught in it for some time before it is released to the sea and lost to you forever. Game over."

"You won't get away with quoting *Hamlet* at me in order to justify your bent interpretation of the rules of croquet, mate," Colin said giving his ball an almighty whack and sending it fortuitously into a high loop through the azaleas and then through a rhododendron bush, back onto the croquet lawn and through the next hoop. Colin punched the air.

"Jammy bugger," Leo railed. "Couldn't do that again in a hundred tries. I'll just have to punish you again for being such a bad sport about it," he said, lining his mallet up behind his ball and taking careful aim again at Colin's several yards distant.

"Leo, the rules state…"

"Whack."

"Clop," Leo's ball enunciated, crashing into its target…

"… that you can't …"

"Crunk." Leo put his ball next to Colin's again and gave it another almighty bash.

"… do that …"

"Bollocks," Leo crowed in triumph. "All's fair in love and croquet. Especially croquet, mate."

A bum suddenly appeared backing out through a hole in the privet hedge.

"Mind me ball, Tim," Leo shouted, as the gardener's large, denim covered bottom edged its way toward the final hoop.

Tim, though, wasn't paying attention to the final of Cuth's Annual Cannibal Croquet Tournament. He had something in his hand he'd picked up in the privets.

"What the bleedin' 'ell's this?" Tim said to himself.

"I've bin in and around them bushes dozens of times but never seen this afore." He turned it over and over walking carelessly back to his manure pile at yon end of the lawn.

"Musta fell outa somebody's winda up there," he said, suddenly stopping and looking up.

"Eeyah, young'un," he said turning to Leo, "you live in that winda up there. Did you lose summat?"

"Never seen it before in my life," Leo said in a hurry to get on with the game.

"Yes, you did, you lying bugger," Colin said, lining up his next shot.

"That's your box of rubbers from your secret stash behind your mirror. What's it doing down here in the garden, Leo? Couldn't have been from last night, could it? Not the full, unopened box Angela chucked out here last night after you made that lewd suggestion to her?"

"Er…right…game over…I win. Timing fault," Leo said, deftly snatching the box from Tim and hurrying through the games room door into Number 8.

"Timing fault? What bloody timing fault?"

"Rules state you must take your shot within 45 seconds of the last shot or forfeit the game to your opponent," he said, crashing through the darkened interior of the games room.

"Read the rules," he added over his shoulder, just before catching his knee on the edge of the Ping-Pong table and crashing in a whirling, writhing heap to the floor.

"Ooooh, me bleedin' leg," he squealed clutching his knee whilst circling in agony under the table. "This is all your damn fault, Crabtree. I shall probably never walk again after this."

"Serves you bloody well right for trying to win the game by default, is all I can say. Can you stand up?"

"Here, give us a hand. It's the least you can do for a fallen comrade. And it wasn't lewd. I merely asked her if she wanted a quick shag, placing the appropriate accessories for her security on the table for her to examine. She could have done the decent thing and said, 'No, Leo, not tonight. Let's have a cup of cocoa instead.' But no. She had to go and chuck the damn box out the window into the laurel bushes in the middle of the night with no chance of retrieving them, least ways, not in the dark in the state I was in."

"Inebriated?" Colin asked, leading his opponent friend through the door and onto the stairs that would take them up to their room at the top of Number 8.

"You know, mate. You were with us."

"I was, Leo, but you were in a world of your own. Face it. Even if she had wanted to, you wouldn't have been able to perform for the young lady anyway."

"Course I would," Leo said, hobbling up the stairs, the sound of his voice diminishing as he ascended.

"Course I would. Never been known to fail the call of a damsel in distress."

"She would have had to have been in some distress to accept the likes of you as her knight errant. Err, just wait a minute, Miss, while I drink me usual 12 pints, get totally paralytic, and then we can go back to my place so I can shag you rotten for the rest of the night – after, of course…after I've puked me guts out on the way home."

"I bought her fish and chips at Sweaty Betty's," Leo remonstrated, minutes later, hobbling his way into their room.

"Course you did. What a hero. You go and spew your guts up outside the Union and then drag her off to Betty's for fish and chips claiming you're feeling a mite peckish, make her wait outside the chip shop whilst in your drunken stupor you chat up the waitress in Betty's, then almost get arrested for pissing onto the river off Kingsgate Bridge. Two more feet to the right and it would have been right on top of that copper's head. Just lucky…all I can say is that you were just bloody lucky you missed and that he was looking the other way when you did."

"Almost got 'im though. The wind…And it was a long way down. Otherwise…"

"Otherwise, Bingo, you go to jail, and I'm off out of it, mate. Leggin' it up South Bailey with Angela in tow.

"Off out of it.

"We were off out of it, mate and getting on quite well back here until you finally show up, rat-arse drunk and shouting your conjugal rights with her as soon as you got back. Didn't even see that we were hitting it off really well – me and her. You thought I had brought her back just for you, rescued her out of the night just for you. Butted right in when we were right in the middle of some meaningful conversation. Buying a lass a soddin' cod and chips doesn't necessarily entitle you to barge in and tell her to get her knickers off."

Leo looked hurt, deflated and a little confused.

"Doesn't?

"Don't forget the ham roll in the Union," he urged. "With extra mustard." He was sincerely aggrieved that his account had been misunderstood.

"You had that lass in the palm of your hand. Then you had to go and get stinking drunk. You threw any chance you had with her out the window. She's a nice lass, and you go and treat her like shit."

"Bought her a ham roll," Leo said in sullen mitigation. "Britvic too."

Chapter 10
Party

On my way to Carol and Lulu's party I stopped in at that cute wine store located on the bottom end of Elvet Bridge. Not being a wine person, I had no idea what to get, so I went by cost and bought what I thought would be a suitably expensive bottle. The girl at the checkout concurred enthusiastically. Feeling that at least the wine would be up to the occasion, I set off along the cobbled streets of Durham with my imagination running wild. Western Hill was all the way across the other side of town and quite a climb. Number 50 was right at the top. By the time I got to it, my sense of anticipation was numb with equivocating possibilities. Maybe I should turn around and give my excuses tomorrow. Although I hoped for the best, I had no way of knowing what to expect.

So, with an open mind, I took a deep breath and knocked.

Carol opened the door and for a split second her lovely smile filled the universe until, peering out at me over her shoulder with his hand clutching that shoulder possessively, a bloke with a rakish Terry Thomas moustache and cheery smile said, "So you've been hitting on my woman, have you?"

And with that charming introduction to Errol, Carol's 'other', the bottle was lifted from my possession, and I was ushered inside to mingle with the assembled guests. It was all very civilised and cultured in there. Lulu and her boyfriend, Oliver, with Carol and Errol, held centre stage leaving me to pick up the odd conversation with courteous and friendly members of the party all interested and interesting but none of them Carol – the one I most wanted to see and talk to and absorb in the worst possible way. Throughout the chitchat, my eyes strayed in her direction, but she held her nerve and never once looked my way. Was I being strategically snubbed? Why was I there? Why had Lulu invited me in the first place?

Things were looking pretty grim and cut adrift until Carol managed to pull herself free from her other party duties and sneak over to me with a glass of wine. I could see now that she wanted to make me feel comfortable when the time was right, and although I expected us to be invaded by Errol at any minute, we were left alone to talk, absorb each other and test and find out more about one another, admire, concur and commiserate on loads of topical stuff.

This was better.

She was a delight.

I was once again stunned by her beauty. My heart was in my mouth in case I put my foot in it or was found out to be inappropriate. About what, I didn't know, but I had this pervading Prufrockian feeling of guilt about not really belonging in that place, well founded because, with one or two exceptions, they were generally a pack of toffs. But whatever I felt, I was sure that she sensed my unease, and within minutes, I was generating ideas and leading the conversation with total confidence. She had that kind of effect.

Over her shoulder, I could see the sensational Lulu next to the fireplace chatting with Errol and Oliver but anxiously glancing out of the corner of her eye in our direction now and then. Finally, she made her excuses with them, lightly touching Oliver on the arm before breaking off with him and drifting across the room to Carol and me. She looked as though she had achieved some great victory as she snuggled in between us and seemed to be saying, 'See? I told you so' with those huge brown eyes. She flicked her fabulous hair to one side, looked back and forth from me to Carol and back again and demanded,

"Well?"

Carol giggled, scrunched her shoulders and depressed her eyebrows as if not understanding the question.

"Good idea? Inviting him?" Lulu asked, nodding vigorously. I could see that in Lulu I had a champion whose testimonial might be needed at some point.

Carol smiled broadly.

"He brought a great bottle of wine," she admitted, raising her glass.

"Excellent guest. You couldn't have done better, Lou."

"No. I mean…you know," Lulu said, looking tersely up at both of us, from one to the other, then staring at Carol.

"You know…!" she stamped.

"Don't have any idea what on earth you're talking about," Carol teased then relented.

"Oh. Next weekend. Yes. Well. Err, no." Carol was flustered. "I haven't mentioned it yet.

"Do go away Lulu, you pest. You're interrupting our high-level conference and getting in the way of very intellectual things," she said trying to fuss Louisa away.

But Louisa wouldn't be put off. She flicked her eyes towards me and crossing her arms under her magnificent breasts, idled indignantly between us, demanding a result.

"Later. I'll ask him in a minute. Right now, we're deeply involved in much more important things. Do go away, shorty, won't you. We're right in the middle of *War and Peace*"

"Humph," the petite beauty said with mock indignation. Her lips glistened petulance and her eyes flared annoyance.

"Well, get on with it, won't you, or I'll have to ask him myself."

"All right. All right," Carol teased.

"Get out of the way, little person. Give big, grown-up people some room.

"For such a minimus you do take up such a lot of space and create quite a distraction. I was just coming to it before you barged in.

"Get away. Get away. Shoo, you bug. Shoo," she said shooing little Lulu off to the nearest chair where she sat down like a child in a huff, her wonderful breasts rising and falling with her heavy breathing.

"Now. Where were we?" Carol said taunting her dearest friend with a smile.

"Ah, yes, *War and Peace*. Never read it myself," she whispered confidentially to me. "Too long. Hope to one day when I've oodles of time on my hands and nothing worthwhile to do. Started to, but like most Russian literature found it tedious and boring. "What about you?" she asked me, turning that fabulous smile on.

"Me either," I said, producing an even bigger smile from her.

"You're just saying that because I said I didn't like it, aren't you? Are you currying favour with me, Christopher?"

This took my breath away, just took my breath away.

Apart from my immediate family, no one ever used my full name, and now this woman had assumed a familiarity with me that left me speechless.

I took a drink of wine to buy some time, but it went down the wrong way, and I ended up spluttering it back into the glass. As a good hostess, or mother, should, Carol came to my rescue with her napkin, wiping my shirt dry and ending up tidying up my face with due care and attention. This brought us closer in more ways than one. For an instant, with her face less than half a breath away from mine, she stopped in mid-wipe, a strange, concerned look in her eyes, a look of dread, took a deep breath and as if coming to some sort of conclusion, turned her head sideways towards her dear Lulu.

"Lou wants to know…" she said, with a suitable pause between her words.

"… if … you … err … if you would escort her to Mary's Ball next weekend," she finished finally in a rush, nodding at Louisa who had brightened up and was staring expectantly at us both.

"Ollie's off home that weekend and won't be able to perform said duty for her, and we, well, I…we…were wondering if you'd come to the aid of a maiden in distress," she said turning back to me and whispering ever so quietly in my ear, "and perform said duty, as irksome as it may be, and believe me, it will be irksome with such a little, peevish person," she nodded in Lulu's direction so that she would know we were talking about her.

"Don't do it if you don't want to," Carol whispered.

"She's really an awful dancer, will get on your nerves, cause you all kinds of grief, and believe me, you will regret it."

"What?" Louisa said, hearing the slander and coming back to us.

"What's that you said, Carol?"

"What did she say to you, Christopher Robin, just now?" she demanded, expanding my name to a playful intimacy I never thought possible.

"I'll bet it was something awful about me, wasn't it?" she scolded in a huff, coming right up to both of our chins with her mock outrage.

"I heard that, Carol. You said … well … you said I'm an evil witch or something, didn't you? I heard it," she shouted wagging her finger up at Carol's nose.

"Not quite, Lou. I said you were an evil bitch, and he wouldn't enjoy a minute of your company, that he should take me to Mary's Ball instead, and you could have Errol for the evening.

"There!"

"Where?" Errol asked over Carol's shoulder.

"I've just given you to Lou for Mary's Ball," Carol answered without hesitation.

"Who are you going with?"

"Christopher has agreed to step into the breach."

"Ooh. You poor old sod," Errol said. "Fate worse than death. Believe me. She's not a lot of fun at a dance. A known hazard. You'd do better going with Louisa and leaving the leviathan to me. At least Lulu doesn't trample your toes out on the dance floor."

"I don't trample," Carol said, stamping her foot to emphasise her point. A near miss on Errol's big toe made him jump back in fright.

"You do," Lulu intervened. "Yes, you do. Errol has to bathe his poor feet often after discos. There are bloodied bandages all over the place. Poor Errol. He puts up with a lot, ushering your great lump around the dance floor. And that's why Christopher Robin better take ME to Mary's. I don't want to be the reason he hobbles around the town with a cane for months afterwards.

"Just look at Errol if you don't believe me."

"I don't hobble."

"Yes, you do," Lulu confirmed.

"Yes, you do," Carol chimed in. "But not from me. It's congenerative. Runs in the family," she said dismissively, "along with many other malformations you have that we all have to put up with."

"Congenerative?" Errol said. "What the bloody hell is congenerative?"

"You know, genetically passed on. Oh … congenital. That's what I mean. That's the word, congenital," Carol said, catching up to her meaning in a flap.

"I am not bloody well congenital. Never heard such rubbish. Don't believe her, Chris. See? If you spend any time at all with her, you too will become subject to her lunatic accusations."

"Not lunatic," Carol insisted. "A priori cognitions. Facts. Everybody knows about your congenital defects. Adelia, for example…"

"Ah. Now you intend bringing that sad case into the conversation."

"Adelia is a very clever girl. Gets firsts for all her work. She knows a congenital when she sees one. And she says…"

"Never mind about all that," Errol cut in, suspiciously quickly. "Adelia's opinions on things that really matter are suspect at the best of times," he said turning to me.

"What we really need to establish is which one of these two other sad cases poor old Chris will have to drag through Mary's Ball. Neither is going to be easy. Quite a sacrifice for him. I would advise him to decline both."

"Me," Lulu said waving her hand in the air with all the authority her little body possessed, but thankfully, Carol stepped in and said:

"Me," with just as much vigour.

"Anyway, I saw him first."

"But you said you were going to go with Errol," Lulu said peevishly. "There's no need for you to butt in. I'm escortless and need one, so it should be me. It's a simple matter of maths – takeaways and things."

Deciding that either was beyond anything I had ever dreamt of, I took stock of both. Little Lulu with her succulent figure and wild, gypsy looks or Carol, who had, it must be said, already taken complete possession of my heart and head and every other part of my anatomy for that matter. But I knew somehow it wasn't going to be up to me. To accept one would be to deny the other. And how could I possibly safely do that to either of these two. They would have to work it out, and as it turned out, by the end of the evening, as the wine flowed freely and competition between the two of them grew, it was decided that I would take both of them to Mary's Ball to the total satisfaction of everyone concerned, especially the guys, who were given the chance to 'be bloody well rid of them both' – Errol's words – 'for the weekend'.

I couldn't believe it. To be in the presence of either or both of them for a second was bliss, and I was going to revel in an entire night's entertainment – or so I thought.

Funny, despite being drawn into their little circle, by the end of the night I felt, strangely, still excluded from it. It was clear the two couples were unassailable, and for me to try to break into one or the other would be churlish at this stage. Anyway, breaking up Carol and Errol would be impossible, or so I thought. Over the course of the evening, I had begun to modify my original opinion of him, saw him as less of a prig and more of a human being, almost a friend, although his cavalier attitude toward Carol left me wondering where his brain was.

Nevertheless, there was always a chance with her, a slim one maybe. But after seeing the way she behaved at the party, the way she danced rings around everyone's hearts, her loving abuse of Lulu and Errol and me, but mainly the way on one particular occasion when she lowered her voice and looked at me in that intimate way, a look that was to be repeated by her on more and more occasions, as time went on, I was convinced that she was the one. I wanted this girl more than ever and decided that patience would win the day. After all, there was no rush. Yes, there were rules that I couldn't ignore. In the meantime, acting the escort to both beauties would give me the chance to establish a beachhead.

As I was leaving, both saw me to the door, but it was Lulu who walked with me to the gate, Carol having been called back in by Errol. We exchanged the usual pleasantries, but when I turned down the lane, Lulu shouted after me that I was forbidden to see anymore of Carol in the library. Strange.

"And don't forget your copy of *The Romantic Poets* you promised to get to me. I won't be in until late tomorrow night, say tenish," she said. "These doors will be locked, but you could bring it to my window, first room along on the south wall."

The thought of seeing Lulu in her nightie leaning out of her window into the moonlight like a latter-day Juliette filled my head with all sorts of delicious possibilities.

The next morning after breakfast, I decided to take the long way across Prebend's Bridge from Cuth's to Prof Lynwood's lecture in Elvet Riverside. Don't ask me why. I guess it was the tranquillity of the riverbank that sent me in that direction or fate or idleness, but I started out on the walk thinking about the book delivery I had to make to Lulu.

Seagulls wheeled overhead.

As I got halfway across Prebend's Bridge, I noticed a tall, elegant young woman carefully descending the steep, rugged path toward me from the other side of the river beyond the bridge. From a distance, she looked very stylish, very elegant, like someone out of a Jane Austin novel, dressed in a full-length black coat, black boots with a walk that said delicate sophistication, the epitome of Byron's *She Walks in Beauty Like the Night*. From a distance, this vision in black was unapproachable, outside of my league, someone I would normally admire as she passed and let her walk on. As she got nearer and as she saw me, her face lit up. It was Carol on her way from Mary's to Palace Green Library.

She beamed and waved hello.

I struggled to catch my breath and waved back.

The distance between us closed very quickly. We met in the middle of Prebend's and stopped amidst the dense, hurrying student traffic that passed that way every morning.

"Hello," she said in a breathless way, turning her head and scrunching her shoulders as if to ask me what I was doing there at that time of day.

"Cuth's," I said in a grinning, stupid rush, pointing back the way I had come.

"Ah, yes. Cuth's…I'm at Mary's, but you know that. Sorry. I should've…," she said, also in an embarrassed rush.

"You go to Cuth's," she repeated, looking around her to find some way of relieving herself of the sweet homily.

"You're at Mary's...Mary's," I said, pointing back up in the direction that she had come.

"Yes, but you already know that. I'm..."

"Where are you going?" we said in unison and laughed.

"Lectures: Elvet Riverside," I managed lamely. "English / Prof Lynwood, Wordsworth."

"Ahhh," she nodded, thus informed. "I'm off to Palace Green."

"Why not walk down by the river?" I asked, changing directions in order to allow both of us to walk together along the river.

"We could walk together."

"We could walk together as far as Kingsgate."

"As far as Kingsgate," we both said.

And so, stepping down the path that led below Cuth's side of the river, we accompanied each other along the winding, tree-lined towpath that would take us both halfway to our separate destinations. I couldn't help feeling that I would much rather spend the next hour in the library with her but stuck to my original plans. I needed to come to terms with Wordsworth, and Lynwood was the world authority.

The river was soft flowing, the towpath was overhung with willows, and roses filled the air. Someone above us in Cuth's gardens was playing tennis. A coxed-four rowing downstream passed us, leaving a quiet, widening, watery V to slosh gently against the bankside. The rowers soon disappeared around the bend at Count's House leaving us alone and stranded in thought, fumbling for words, making jagged, angular attempts at conversation.

It was Carol who finally came to the rescue.

"You aren't in the library this morning," she said, quietly concerned.

"Lulu said I was forbidden."

"Oh! ... Lou ...!? Why on earth not?"

"Don't know. Said I couldn't go."

"Funny," she said, dismayed. "I was hoping... We need to talk ...about ... Mary's Ball."

"Yes. Well?"

"Well. Among other things," I plied.

69

"Other things?" she said, surprised and immediately changed the subject, sensing that 'other things' were unmanageable at the moment.

A rowing coach on a bike approached us from behind, forcing us to the inside of the path. Carol stepped delicately around a puddle. As the boat he was coaching came upstream, we stopped to watch it slide past. I said something about its technique and she nodded doubtfully. The boat disappeared around the bend past St John's boathouse with its coach shouting at it, and we were left in peaceful silence again.

"Can't say that I know anything about that sort of thing," she said, elegantly, delicately dodging more puddles to keep her boots clean.

"Looks jolly hard work," she said as the last echoes of the clunking oars faded upstream in the morning mist.

"I could show you."

"You could what?"

"Put you in a boat. Show you how it's done."

She shook her head vehemently, her eyes widening in mock fright.

"Yes," I decided. "I'll put you in one of our women's novice crews, or a sculling boat by yourself, if you like. You'll love it. Don't knock it until you've tried it. Sunday morning. Cuth's boathouse. There, that's decided. Bring Lulu, if you like."

But at the mention of Lulu's name, Carol pulled a face.

"No. I'll come myself for my first time. Anyway, she's busy Sunday. Let's keep her out of it for the time being," she said in a rush.

"What will I need to bring? Not a lifejacket, I hope. Don't want to fall in."

"You won't need a lifejacket, leastways not in a four. A single scull's a different thing altogether though. Everybody falls in, in a sculling boat on their first go."

"Oh?"

"Very tipsy. Tricky to balance."

"Oh!" Carol said, taking this as some sort of challenge, making up her mind that she would not be one of those weak, falling-in people, not if she had anything to do with it.

"Good," she decided, just like that

"I'm for it – this sculling lark."

I nodded, interested with the adventurous, sporty side of her I was seeing.

"Sunday at nine."

"Oh, in the morning? Not so sure about nine o'clock in the morning. That's sleeping-in time."

"Nine in the morning. No sleeping-in."

"After Mary's Ball the night before?" she said, quickly making allowances, coming to terms with things.

"Pretty much."

"Can we do it?"

"Course."

"Not so sure about that," she said, putting on her doubtful face.

"Hmmmm," she said, assessing the possibilities.

"How will you get in from your digs that early? Won't be any busses in on Sunday that early from Langley Moore, surely?" she asked, seriously puzzled.

Then she suddenly brightened. "You'll have to stay over after Mary's Ball," she said, making her mind up.

"Then we could come down together in the morning after breakfast.

"Good," she decided unilaterally. That's what we'll do…

"That's settled," she said firmly. "Early breakfast then…

"Who knows?"

"Who knows?" I agreed but not to the rowing. This was a sporty, risk-taking side to her I thought I would never see.

"Do I need to bring a towel?" she asked.

"What for?"

"In case I fall in, silly."

"There must be some hanging around the boathouse. But you won't fall in."

"Promise?"

"Yes. I'll teach you how not to fall in."

"How not to fall in?" She turned this proposition over for a bit.

"If I do, will you jump in and rescue me?"

"Yes," I said with decision.

"But you won't fall in. It's easy. Just don't let go of the blades, and you won't fall in."

"Don't let go of the blades," she said, with innocent dread in her eyes.

"Don't let go of the blades?"

"Right."

"What are blades? Sounds sharp and dangerous. Do I really want to be holding them in the first place? Sounds sharp," she said, turning to go up the steps at Kingsgate Bridge. I followed her up giving her all the assurances I could that the blades weren't sharp, and that she wouldn't fall in, but if she did, I had a towel and that I would jump in after her, which I knew I wouldn't do. You never jumped in after a capsizing. Just wasn't done. Unthinkable. Procedures were in place for such eventualities.

"All right," she agreed, not really sure what she was getting into.

When we reached the top of Kingsgate steps, she turned to go her way towards Palace Green library, doubtful about whether she had made the right decision about sculling. As I made my way in the opposite direction, I turned over in my mind whether she had made the right decision about me staying over, whether I had heard her right in the first place.

"Flynn, you sly bastard." A familiar voice rang out from across the river.

Tucker waited for me at the far end of Kingsgate Bridge.

"Just some girl," I lied.

"Some girl," he said.

"That's more than just some girl. She's the one in the Town Hall that night, isn't she? You fuckin' liar. I think you're well in there, mate."

"Yeah, maybe," I said, not wanting to count my chickens. The cost could be too dear, so I kept my interest low key and simply said, "Just some girl that wants to learn how to row. Nothing special in that. I'm gonna put her out in a single scull when I get the time."

"Oh, aye," he said with that funny, disbelieving look in his eye.

"Novice sculler, eh? You bloody liar."

Guess I was. I was a bloody liar but far too far in love to chance admitting it, letting the world know or to even consider the consequences of what Carol and I were going through at that moment. This was becoming more than an act of patience. As Leo and I made our way to Lynwood's lecture, I could think of nothing else but her. Leo carried the conversation. I nodded and grunted agreement from time to time, but underneath it all was the vision of this girl I totally and utterly adored.

Chapter 11
Lulu

"Well. Did he?" Lulu squared up to her friend, intent on making some sense of the solemn look in her eyes.

"Who? Did who, Lou? Did what?" Carol teased.

"You know who. Christopher Robin. Did he see you in the library this morning? Still hasn't delivered that book I asked him to. Stop being so obtuse. You know what we're talking about.

"That fellow, then," she murmured, utterly frustrated with Carol's lack of sense or communications.

"No," was all Carol would admit to, then blurted out, "oh, Lou, don't let's go on talking about it."

"He's an 'it' then now, is he? Now he's an 'it'."

"No, he's not. He is certainly not. Stop putting words into my mouth."

"You didn't see him then," Lulu said, brightening, pecking gently at her coffee and Carol's patience.

"No," Carol lied again.

"He wasn't there?"

"Didn't show up today. There. Are you happy now?" Carol said with some anguish.

This was not Lulu's Carol. This was not the bright, effusive girl Louisa knew. This was some moribund imitation of a friend who moped and fretted and twisted her fingers inside out and sighed deeply and looked off past Louisa's shoulder, as if Louisa wasn't even there.

"Good," Lou said.

"Good? What do you mean, 'Good'?"

"Good. That's all. Just good."

"There's a subtext here somewhere, Lou," Carol said, fixing her with her squinty eyes and moving in closer.

"What are you up to? What's going on in that foetid little mind of yours? Come on. Out with it."

"Not foetid, just wondering what's set you off like this, that's all. I was hoping he'd pass on his book to you for me. Nothing foetid in that, is there?"

"Not if that's all you've got on your evil brain. Face it, Lou, you were hoping he'd show up with it at your moonlit window, so that you could do the Juliette trick, languishing out of your window with your ample bosoms accidentally unfettered and swaying in the breeze. 'Oh, are they my boobs wafting around in front of your nose, Christopher Robin? So sorry. Should have lashed them down before coming to the window. Do come in and let's have sex before you go back to your digs.'"

"So that's it," Lulu exclaimed with murderous intent.

"What's it?"

"Just like you …"

"Just like me, what?"

"Just like you to make fun of my boobs and my innocent intentions…you…!"

"Not so innocent, Lou. We've all seen through your desperate harlotry and we are not impressed," Carol teased raising her eyebrows to a point.

"Desperate bloody harlotry? Desperate bloody harlotry? Here I am trying my damnedest to help you with your dirty little weekend, and look at what I get for my efforts. You make fun of my physical—"

"… deformities …" Carol interjected.

"Well, bloody hell. Now I'm deformed!"

"Right. Or haven't you taken a close look at yourself lately? Oh, no, sorry you can't. You can't see down past those massive breasts of yours to see the rest of your anatomy."

"Now it's the bloody rest of my anatomy."

"And you can stop swearing, Louisa … most unbecoming.

"You'll acquire a reputation. 'Not only is she an ugly little person with a pair of massive paps, but she's foul mouthed into the bargain. She'll be spitting and smoking cigarettes soon. Probably does already or pot or something. How is her drinking addiction going?'"

"What reputation? What drinking addiction? What have you been saying behind my back? What have you been telling everyone, Christopher Robin, everyone?"

"No need. NO need. Your reputation precedes you," Carol said playfully flicking Louisa's breasts sending her a step backwards.

"Stop it. Stop doing that.

"Anyway," Louisa said, calming down a bit, "you know they're sensational, and you're just jealous of them as well as the rest of my perfect figure. Compact and bijoux, so the saying goes. Compact and bijoux. So there," she said, doing a triumphant, strumpet twirl to show off her shapes.

"Much rather have a shape to get hold of than twigs like you."

"What do you mean, twigs?"

"Nothing – and that's what I mean. There's nothing to you that anybody – any boy, at least – would find in the least bit interesting. Beanpole. Nothing to cuddle up to on a cold winter's night. I'm not surprised one bit that nobody's really interested in you. Nothing to be interested in. Errol's bored, won't take you to Mary's Ball. Christopher Robin has gone off you already—"

"Stoppit, Louisa. You are becoming ridiculous. Everybody knows I'm gorgeous and very desirable where you are merely an oddity of funny bits tethered together on a dwarf-like frame. Your bottom for example—"

"What's wrong with it? What's wrong with my bottom, eh? Eh? Eh?" she demanded, bumping Carol back and back and back with her breasts to sit on the edge of the table.

"Just like these … these … these overgrown, out of control mammaries.

"And your bottom, my dear, burgeons out of the back of you like some kind of, some sort of, of, of grotesque, monster mushroom. Not at all like my petite little bum that men find exceptionally erotic and would love to get to know better, given half the chance." She nodded to confirm her own points.

"That's you in a nutshell, I'm afraid, Carol. In a nutshell."

"Oh?"

"You never give anybody half a chance – and I don't blame you there – nothing to look at there. But you don't even give them a look-in. No wonder they all see you as a frigid old frump not worth bothering with, coz if they did bother, there would be nothing out of the ordinary to admire – visually or, or, or … physically.

"Frump! While I am the beauty round here with these," Lulu said erotically encircling, lifting and bouncing her breasts with her hands, "and this" – turning round and showing a pert bottom – "and most of all this," she said indicating her astonishingly beautiful face.

"This most of all. And you know it's true, Carol. Don't deny it. You'd be lying if you did.

"I am a tasty package worthy of any man's attentions.

"And you, I am afraid, just aren't.

"Well, you are pretty enough but not in my league of beauty …

"Ah," Lulu said putting a finger to Carol's lips. "You would just be making a fool of yourself if you did. Just be happy that from time to time I am willing to throw you one of my cast-offs.

"Errol for example …"

"I saw him first," Carol objected.

"Yes, you did, but he didn't become totally aroused until he saw this" – pointing to her bottom – "and these" – her breasts – "and finally this masterpiece."

"What? Shockingly shoddy make-up?"

"Beautiful face, that's what. My gorgeous face. You know it. They know it. Errol knew it as soon as he saw it. As soon as he saw it, he was in love with it. Couldn't keep him away. Thing was, I had Ollie at the time, so I passed Errol back to you.

"And now Christopher Robin. I did my best for you. Set you up at the Town Hall then our party and Mary's Ball, saw to it that you were on his mind. And you can't even follow that up properly. He should be cloying to you by now, but he's not. Is he?

"Is he, Carol?"

Carol remained noncommittal.

"Is he?" Lulu pressed a little harder, seeing that Carol remained unusually, strategically quiet.

"What have you going on in that tiny mind of yours?"

"Something's up, isn't it? You have seen him, you bugger. Haven't you? Haven't you, eh?" Lulu said, prodding her friend up and down as they both began to giggle.

"You've been holding out on me all this time, haven't you?" Prod. Prod.

"Help! Stop it, Lou, you'll hurt them. They weren't meant for that sort of digging."

"Then tell me what you two are up to, or I will twist them off."

But Carol was so helpless with laughter she wouldn't have been able to stop Louisa if she had wanted to. Finally, they both collapsed in a rollicking heap into the same chair; Lulu on top of Carol; Lulu pummelling Carol to tell her; Carol too full of laughter to speak.

Minutes later after they had both calmed down, arms around each other and Louisa's head on Carol's shoulder, Lou tried again:

"Tell me. I won't beat you anymore, but tell me. I have to know."

"Why? It's nothing."

"I have to look after you, that's why. Even over nothings."

"Look after me? Why do you have to look after me for goodness' sake?"

"Because, dear heart ... you ... are ... incapable ..."

". . . of looking after myself?" Carol answered for herself.

"Yes. I don't want you to get hurt. After all, I am the sensible, practical one, and you, well, you ... you are not," Louisa said as sweetly as she could, not wanting to start another war.

"Rot."

"You might end up – well – having a baby or something without knowing you're even doing it. 'Oops, is that a baby? How on earth did that get there? I'll have to ask Louisa. She'll know.'"

"Bollocks. A baby or something? Or something? What do you mean by 'something' – a chimpanzee, a hippopotamus? And I can assure you, dear girl, I am well aware of how and where babies come from," she added, disentangling herself from the pile and getting up.

"And do you really think I am that naïve? That I am taken in by these bullyboy tactics of yours? Louisa, I am surprised at you. You're nothing but a gossipy old goose, not really interested in anything but gossip."

"Not," Louisa said.

"Too," said Carol.

"We'll see," Carol added.

"See what?" Louisa asked.

"Just whether you are an old gossip or not; whether you are really interested in my welfare or not."

Chapter 12
Anyone for Tennis

"Block 'im! Block 'im," Specky screamed at Del Fuego.

"Do for 'im, good and propa," Specky shrieked, pissing himself with the thought of my total croquet annihilation.

Carlos had his boot on top of his ball, about to smash mine off the lawn.

He tapped me off to the side.

"Awwwww. That's lame, Del Fuego. That's bloody lame. You had a chance to send him into the middle of tomorrow, and look what you've gone and done."

"Strategy, Herbert, strategy. Watch and learn," Carlos said, his head on an angle, lining up his next strike. Tapped it. His ball rolled gently through the hoop.

"See?" he said rolling his next shot up to mine again, clicking it gently.

"Two for the price of one ..."

"Bastard."

"Capitulate, Flynn, before you end up in the river," Specky spurted with demonic intent.

"Not quite so fast, young master Specky," Tucker said, measuring up an impossible recovery shot from the other side of the lawn. His mallet swung. His ball was sent whizzing off the lawn, hit a tree stump somewhere and rebounded back onto the lawn again to hit Del Fuego's ball full in the face.

"Good," Leo said. "Just right. Now let's see who will capitulate," he said, stopping for a second, raising an ear to a sudden urgency, a sudden foreign sound going on somewhere nearby.

"What's that?"

"It's something going on over there in the bushes," Specky said referring to the giggling, moaning that had started off in there minutes ago but was now rising to an undeniable crescendo. We all tried to ignore it at first, but now...well, things were getting out of hand somewhere deep in the bushes, halfway down the bankside.

Croquet players were being put off their aim.

"Lucky bastard," Leo said in reference to the moaning. Placing his ball beside Carlos', he prepared for the inevitable thwack. Not having been successful lately in the art of love, Tucker had a heartfelt grievance against the morning activity that was taking place not many yards from the croquet lawn.

The moaning continued, and it was obvious that the woman was oblivious to the match that was taking place not far from her ecstasy.

"Perhaps somebody should go over there and tell her to tone it down a bit," the disgruntled Tucker emitted from between gritted teeth.

"I cannot get me aim," he fretted.

"Now, now, Leo." Ian appeared from Number 8 to hand around pints and referee the rest of the match.

"Just because you haven't managed to get your leg over…" he said.

"Yes…well. Shit!" Leo spat missing his shot and setting Specky up for the grand finale shot of a lifetime.

"Seems to me, Beau could turn it off for a couple of hours to allow us to finish our World Championship in peace."

"That's a bit harsh, Tucker. How'd you know it is Beau?"

"Believe me, it's him. It bears all the hallmarks of an orgasmic Franklin moment. That mellifluous prelude, the subsequent panic and, listen, listen – any time now…Yes, here it comes now. Listen…the sibilant, overwhelming release at the end of a lengthy, uncontrolled pounding. I know all about these things," Tucker said, putting a finger to the side of his nose. "I have made a study of these things. I have—"

"You've been a victim of this many times over. You have spent many jealous hours planning your revenge, but alas, revenge has never been realised," Ian said.

"Not yet," Tucker said. "Not yet. But I will be avenged," he said with a raised eyebrow after the style of a thwarted super villain.

"Still don't know it's him down there," Specky protested lining up his shot. He hit the hoop and bounced back.

"Fuckin' hell."

Specky stood up straight to measure the extent of his error.

"Couldn't be anybody else," Leo said, convinced.

"Who else but Franklin would be on the rand in the middle of the morning like this? Poor bugger just doesn't know when to start – or stop. Probably been at it all night down there in the bushes. Just never takes time to check the clock when he's at it," he said, about to make his shot but stopping a minute to shoo away a nosey dog that had wandered onto the lawn to sniff at his croquet ball.

"Get away you beggar …"

"I mean … gerroff me ball," he screamed, as the dog lifted his leg to sprinkle directly over it.

"That bloody dog's got it in for me," he lamented. "I claim a penalty stroke. "Referee, that dog's spoiled me next stroke. Just look at me ball. It's sodden."

"Get on with it, Tucker. It's perfectly usable," Ian said, dousing the offended ball with half a pint of ale. At this, the dog snaffled up Leo's ball and charged off into the bushes with it. Deep into the bushes.

"That does it. Game's a draw," Leo shouted and threw his mallet after the dog. It missed and clattered halfway down the hill, out of site.

"Franklin!" he screamed off in the direction of the river. "You bastard. Can't we even have a quiet game of croquet without your damned interference."

Just then there came a tap at a window and a muffled call from somewhere behind us. We turned around, surprised to see a figure waving and leering out at us from a second-floor bedroom window, holding his morning cup of coffee up to us in greetings. It was Beau, scratching his bum in his PJ's, looking for all the world as if he had just got up.

The window slid open.

"Can't a bloke get a decent lie in around here without you lot wrecking the morning for 'im," he said drowsily, slammed the window shut, lifted two fingers at us and staggered out of sight back to bed.

Del Fuego was always one to measure things carefully before making any kind of pronouncement. He looked deep into Beau's bedroom then across the lawn to the spot behind which he was sure the lovemaking was coming from, looked back at Number 8 and concluded for Leo.

"…Wasn't him, Leo. Wasn't Beau."

Leo too looked dumbfounded and visually traced the same path back and forth several times, then nodded with some degree of understanding as Yabooga, Tim Bickerstaff's faithful old collie, reappeared from the bushes in the vicinity of Tim's gardening tool shed with Leo's ball gripped safely in his mouth. He dropped the ball at Leo's feet and sat down like a 'Good Boy' wagging his tail and awaiting his reward.

"He's a good dog," Specky said. Specky was fond of dogs. Leaning down to pat him, he added, "You're a good old dog, Timmy," he said, fond of dogs but not always accurate with names.

"No, no, no, no, no," Leo reminded him kindly. It's Yabooga, Tim's dog. Timmy's the one that does the gardens. That's his tool shed down there…

"Oh…oh…oh, hello Mrs Manners." Leo smiled kindly and waved to the college bursar who seemed to be having some difficulty making her way back up the bankside through the shrubs.

She smiled grimly back at the assembled company, mentioning each one by name under her breath as she struggled past and into Number 8.

Leo eked out a pained, knowing smile to the rest of us.

"Yes…Well…" he said, recovering from the shock.

"Er … yes … well … anyone for tennis?"

Chapter 13
Lucien's Troubles with
the English Department

In The Three Tuns, Lucien was more sombre than usual, as I slipped along the bench across from him, spilling my pint in the process. His large, round, pink face offered a pained grimace as solicitude. Busily handing me a couple of beer matts to help sop up the mess, he seemed momentarily taken out of his doldrums.

"You missed a bit.

"There," he said.

"Can't leave this place in a worse state than we found it. Terrible mess to begin with," he huffed, hunched over his beer and falling back into his own morass.

I had always found the bare tables and benches of the Three Tuns welcoming, but I could see his point. It was like sitting in a British rail waiting room, bare of the wall trappings you usually find in a pub, bare of anything pubby.

"Can't stay long," he said, munching down into the thick, juicy meat of a pork pie he got at the bar.

"Lunch," he muffled through a mouth full and took a drink to wash it down.

"Prof Lynwood wants to see me at 1:30," he said, inclining his head seriously. Can't think why. I went to one of his lectures once. Took notes even. There …" he said poking a finger at a scruffy little spiral, dog-eared notebook, tea stained and beer stained, covered in crumbs on the table next to his pie plate.

"Evidence," he said with supreme pride.

"Even asked him a question."

"Oh?" I asked, incredulous. One never dared ask questions during a Lynwood lecture. It just wasn't done.

"What did you ask him?"

"I asked him where the nearest bog was, actually," Lucien said with his mouth wide open, halted in mid-air preparatory to another bite of pie.

"Round the corner on your way out," he said to me kindly, as if it had been his fault in the first place that I didn't know where it was. And, by god, there it was. I was ever so grateful. Awful squits that morning. Barely made it in time. Nearly blew my arse off. Terrible goings-on. Certain he and the rest of the lecture room heard it all. Didn't dare go back in after. Couldn't, could I?"

"You could have disguised yourself as somebody else and gone back in."

"Who else?"

"Sir Andrew Aguecheek, for example."

"Sir Andrew," Henry said, mulling the solution over in his head.

"Yes …Yes … Could've been Sir Andrew. Yes …Toby Belch would have been better, though."

I had to agree with him on that one. Sir Toby would have been a better disguise for a mad, surreptitious farter.

"But," he said, facing up to the ordeal to come, "I think I'll be Andrew today when I see him."

"You think he's going to torture your soul?"

"No. Never that. Whatever Prof Lynwood is, he's never a torturer. Kindest man I've ever met. Honestly. He'll ply me with tea and scones first and make me feel I'm the most important fellow on god's earth before he does anything."

"Before he sticks the knife in?"

"If he does, he'll make it feel like the most wonderful experience in the world. Believe me. No … I'm looking forward to it, whatever he wants. I'm sure to leave his office feeling absolutely wonderful. Never does anything without a cup of tea and scones first.

"Cannot think what he wants. Handed in a paper once, so it can't be that."

"Last year. Remember? You read it back to me."

"It was crap," I had to tell him.

"Yes," he said sadly. "Yes, it was. But it was only a week or two late."

"I'll give you credit for that."

"The Prof did too. Couldn't thank me enough for it. When he graded it, he apologised for giving it a 'D'. Silly old fool.

"I had to tell him a 'D' was lovely. Best grade I ever got. It was crap, though," he lamented.

"Yes," I said, lowering my head in sympathy. "'Twas. 'twas. Not really your fault though. You had been ill."

"I had been ill. It was my bad cold that he used in mitigation at the end of the year."

"He gave you an aegrotat for your bad cold."

"My usual aegrotat. Best one I ever got."

"Still. Here I sit supping beer with you and almost another term has passed. I must be doing something right in his eyes. For the life of me, I cannot think what.

"Still…" He raised his glass.

"Cheers. Your very good health, Flynn, old chap."

"To your next aegrotat," I agreed, raising my glass.

"My next aegrotat. And many more of 'em," he said, fishing in his pocket for something. He pulled out a little plastic bottle, opened it and swallowed a little pill.

"Nerves," he said.

"You are a hostage to your nerves," I said.

"Life is fraught. Term papers. Money. Parents. The cost of things, beer and things. I mean, take beer for example. It's a necessity, a staple. Keeps one right. Ought to be on the NHS like these pills.

"Don't you think? I mean, beer on the NHS."

I mumbled something, which I think he took as agreement, and he shoved the little plastic bottle back into his pocket.

"Another necessity of life, I'm afraid," he mumbled surreptitiously, meaning the pills and his need to take them."

"Only because of term papers, etc.," I said trying to reconcile his addiction.

"Life would be so much easier, so much more manageable without them," he said hopefully.

"Think so? Really?"

"Course. Don't you?" he said.

"Maybe. Maybe not," I equivocated. "I often think that they are the irritant, the sand in the shell that finally produces the pearl."

"Oh. Interesting thought. Never thought of it that way. Never thought of me that way. A pearl. Ha!" He thought some more and then pronounced in his drollery, "Cruel way of producing worthless beauty.

"But. One way of rationalising beauty – or insanity – if they are one in the same. I must tell Prof your theory. He'll think it poetic, but then again, he thinks everything's poetic."

"A necessary thing in life – poetry. Not a bad way of looking at everything though. That everything is necessarily poetry and therefore that poetry, as poetry, doesn't really exist at all."

"As a separate thing, you mean."

"Can't be separate if it's everything. It's like saying, well, it's like saying we're here because we're not here. Like—"

"Like the speed of light," Henry helped without thinking.

"Must be some sort of equation or algorithm for all this prattle," Henry mused over his new pint.

"If there isn't one yet, somebody somewhere will invent one.

"Someone who has had too much time on their hands and too much beer in their belly.

"Whatever Prof wants, I'll plead insanity," he said, tapping his pocket where his pills were housed.

"Lynwood wouldn't dare throw out an insane person. Just wouldn't do."

"You think he wants to send you down?"

"Not 'wants'. Needs. Can't blame him really.

"I am an idle sod if the truth be told. No. Wouldn't blame him in the least if he did. Papa won't pay any more, and Prof is fed up. Tried getting a job at the post office sorting mail to offset penury. They wouldn't have me, in the end. Kept putting the post in the wrong holes. Awful mess. Posties were up in arms all over town. Don't blame 'em, really. You'd think that I could at least put the post in the right holes, wouldn't you."

"Not your strength," I said.

"No. Prof's got me pegged. I should just leave and save him the agony. Fall on my sword. Do the decent thing…"

"Find out what he wants first. Might be nothing of the kind. You might be up for some kind of English Department award."

"Yes," he said in his disbelieving way, "piss artist of the year. I'd win that one hands down."

Chapter 14
St. Mary's Ball

Lulu's large brown eyes peered out through the crowds pouring into St Mary's through the big main oak doors.

"You're here!!!" she squeaked.

"At last. Thought you'd never arrive. In here. In here," she said, reaching out between people for my hand.

"Round this corner and down the hall."

"Come on. You're late," she grinned back at me over her surging hips, urging me to hurry, pulling me along. Her bottom wiggled away from me, disappearing from time to time into the throng. For such a little person, she had a mighty tug. I stumbled on dutifully, out of breath.

"Get a move on. We're late. We'll miss the food," I heard her say somewhere up ahead.

"You'll have to try the blancmange.

"I made it," she grinned back at me, squeezing my hand tighter.

"It's rather good. We all had to submit a dish for the feast. Carol made an Italian quiche. It's not very good, really. Tastes like sick. Italian sick but sick nonetheless.

"But don't tell her I said so. She's very proud. Make believe you like it. Make a fuss of her cooking. You'll have to have at least a taste. There's a bin nearby if you want to spit it out or be sick in without her seeing. Really! That girl! She has no idea about cuisine."

Suddenly, we were in the Great Room of the college – tables around the outside full of food, and conversations with full plates grazing in the middle.

"All looks pretty great to me," I said, twisting my head in search of Carol.

"You have to be careful. Most of it should have a warning from the Ministry of Health," Louisa said.

"Should be condemned!

"There's a nice bean salad you should be safe with. Adelia made it. We're bivouacking in her room tonight. She said there was space. Carol's in there putting on her face. Quite a job, that face. Needs a lot of work, unlike mine, which you will have noticed needs nothing at all," she said puckering her lips, imitating a French manikin.

"My job – feed you first. Then the Ball. Carol should have disguised her plain bits to look scandalisingly wonderful by then. Then you are anybody's," she declared.

"Hers and mine, I mean. No need to choose though. We had a powwow and decided to split you up evenly over the night. You will have to be prepared to do double shift on the dance floor and in the bar and canteen, the…er…Great Hall, I mean. Then afterwards…Well, we don't intend to have you make a choice, but I'm vying very hard for the romantic midnight, moonlit walk with you down by Prebend's Bridge. I don't know what she's got in mind…Probably get you drunk, then god knows what. Whatever it is, it won't be as good as my romantic moonlit walk along the river under the cathedral. I think she wants you in Adelia's to ply you with her records and things. Adelia's away. Gone home for a rest from all of this," she said, doing a twirl to emphasise that 'all of this' meant the stresses of university life.

"Poor Adelia. I'm afraid it's all got too much for her. She can do the lectures and exams bit okay but can't seem to come to terms with the social whirl – what whirl there is. I just try to tell her to relax and don't worry. The men will flock to her in due course. You've met Adelia, haven't you?

"No?" she went on without seeming ever to need to take a breath.

"Well, she's very pretty but a bit of a recluse. Works very hard on her studies and says she hasn't got time for anything else – like boys and such. It's just an excuse. Got dropped by a boy in the first month here and hasn't gone back to the well since. Poor Adelia. She's a lovely girl and a good friend, and I do hope she'll find somebody soon. Perhaps you!" She suddenly realised.

My heart sank.

Nodding her head, she said, "Yes. That's it. We'll have to introduce you – if you want to, that is. She's very pretty and ever so clever. Too clever for my liking – and too pretty if the truth be known, but she is going to waste and rot if she doesn't get over Fred – or whatever his name was. Anyway…" she said marching on ahead of me along the corridor of rooms, "Adelia has loaned us her room for the night as a rendezvous place, and here it is," she said doing another one of her delightful twirls in front of Adelia's door.

"Carol!…Should be inside trying to turn her sow's ear into a silk purse. I've told her not to bother; it will be almost impossible, but she never listens. Promise you won't laugh," she said, knocking and pushing straight through the door regardless of what might have been going on in there.

"We're here," she sang out, and barging in pushed the door fully open for my sake.

"Here we are. Are you decent?" she called through.

But whether Carol was decent or not, Lulu didn't care. She pushed straight in leaving me at the doorway. I walked in. Two beauties sat on the bed awaiting my inspection. The brunette was out of breath from talking so much, the other one beamed at her for being such a 'chump' as she liked to say.

I should describe Carol at this point, sitting there on the bed opposite her Lulu, but I won't. She was lovely and also breathless and blushing pink, beaming and happy. She was the one I wanted to see tonight, hear and totally absorb just by being in the same room with her.

"I told him about your Italian quiche," Lou said, still out of breath. "But steered him right away from it," she said with horror in her voice.

"Pizza, silly," Carol said, reaching over and giving Lulu a playful smack on the arm.

"And, no, it doesn't need a government health warning. She probably told you it needed a government health warning, didn't she, Christopher Robin?

"It's supposed to taste like that. Do you like pizza?" Carol asked patting the bed beside her for me to come and sit down.

I sat down.

"I make pizza too," I had to admit. "You'll have to let me cook for you some time, but I know it'll never match up to yours."

"Very diplomatic. I like your kind of diplomacy. You can come back anytime." Carol smiled, inclining her eyes.

"Bought mine at Tesco's," she said biting her lip and scrunching up her shoulders anticipating being smacked by Lulu.

"You fraud, Carol!" Lulu shouted, jumping up.

"You said you made it for him yesterday. I'll never believe another word you say; will we, Christopher Robin?" she stamped, feigning indignity, her eyes blazing with love for her friend.

"You can talk, Lou. I know you got your lemon meringue there too. I'd like to say you bought it, but I'm still not sure I saw you going through the checkout to pay for it."

"Liar. I always pay for things."

"Not so sure about that. I'm beginning to think it's another one of your little problems," Carol said. "Err, strange habits."

"Snoop."

"Couldn't help being there at the same time as you, could I? Even though I hid behind the potatoes when you were rummaging in the pies."

"Disreputable, all the same."

"Reputable. Saving your reputation, my dearest one, is the height of reputable. Wouldn't want kleptomania to become another one of your questionable dysfunctions, but I see it has, despite everything I do to help. It'll be drugs and alcohol next."

"Habits!!?? Rot. What habits? What are you talking about?"

"Aha," Carol said, gaining the upper hand. "Now you're worried about being found out. But don't worry, dearest. I'll never tell …"

"…About what?" Louisa said in a hurt voice.

"Well," Carol said demurring into coyness, "peanut butter in the middle of the night, for a start. You are always at the peanut butter."

"I like it, that's all.

"Tell her," Louisa said, appealing to me. "Tell her, Christopher Robin. Tell her it's not a crime to like peanut butter."

"Leads to harder criminal habits eventually," I had to admit. "You're on a slippery slope to total addiction."

"That's right," Carol said, gaining confidence with my support. "It'll be … well … what will come next, Christopher Robin?"

"Gambling. Glue sniffing?"

"OHO!" Carol chimed in. "Don't get me started about her gambling. And glue sniffing! Can't get enough tubes up her nose. She's always drooling."

"I don't, do I?"

"Do. You do without knowing it. Remember that time we were sticking those posters together for Rag Week? You had to leave the room. Remember?"

"I was feeling rather unwell. Was that an addiction?"

"Too right, mate," Carol informed her. "Too right! You were drooling and off with the fairies when you came back into the room," she said, turning to me, nodding agreement with herself.

"Off with the fairies.

"She smells hair shampoo as well. Likes to smell all sorts of things in tubes. It's a tubular addiction. Admit it. You are hooked on olfactory stimulants and goodness knows what else. It's all I can do to keep you out of the jail cells. There's one in Durham Prison just around the corner that's got your name on the door, if you don't watch out. And if you don't stop smelling things," Carol said removing a bottle of nail polish from Louisa's quivering clutches.

"But I have to do my nails, Carol. It's not fair," Lulu whined.

"You've had all evening to do your bits for him, and I haven't. You said go and look out for him while you tidy up.

"Give me the bottle. No. Look. Give it to me. I swear I won't smell it. Just a touch up. A little touch up," she teased, grinning and subversively lifting the little red bottle to her nose.

"A touch up today…" Carol said taking back the bottle.

"…The hashish dens of Newcastle tomorrow. I just don't know how we're going to get you a teaching job with your record. You'll be totally unemployable," Carol said, relenting and handing over the nail polish.

"You'll have to rely on attracting some rich man to support your expensive habits, instead of marrying the pauper you really love."

"I'll marry whoever I want, thank you very much," Louisa said, unscrewing the top of the bottle and settling in to feed her vanity, her favourite 'habit'.

"And it's 'whomever', not 'whoever'," Carol corrected without thinking.

"Not…" Lulu sulked, tripped up.

Seeing that she had gone too far this time, Carol relented and tactfully corrected herself, reached over to give Lulu a hug, asked for forgiveness and helped her do her nails while I made the tea.

"You bugger," Lou whimpered. "You had me going that time."

And over Carol's shoulder, she said to me, "She had me going, Christopher Robin. I'm not really a bad person," she said, brightening at the love she was now being given.

"Yes, you are," Carol cut in. "… worst in the world. Don't know what anybody sees in you. Hold still while I do your pinkie."

Louisa beamed at the affected abuse.

"There," Lou said, admiring her fingers once Carol had finished, splaying them out and blowing on them to dry.

"You can go to the ball, Cinders," Carol said, joining in the admiration.

"Are you sure you're ready for this, Christopher Robin?

"Double duty at the ball?"

"Yes. Why not," I said, relishing the prospect.

"I get first go at him," Louisa said, shooting her hand into the air as if still at school.

"All right. I'll serve behind the bar while you two are on the dance floor. Then he's all mine. Just don't wear him out, that's all. I want to try some new moves out on him when you're done."

"New moves?" Louisa asked with an intake of breath.

"Sounds suspicious," she said, metaphorically sniffing at Carol's intentions.

"I'm a bit worried."

"You should be," Carol said throwing out a hip at her.

"What kind of new moves? Shouldn't you have checked them out with me first before going public? Knowing you and remembering that last shambles you took me to, we'll be thrown out for lewd behaviour before the night is half over.

"Mary's doesn't hold with lewd behaviour," Lulu whispered confidentially to me.

"Hope so." Carol beamed as we left the room. "Otherwise, what's it all in aid of?

"A bit of unrestrained bump and grind should do nicely." She grinned, throwing out another hip and knocking me sideways this time.

"First though – drinks to get us in the right mood."

Someone was rapping on my head but from the inside. I turned over to go back to sleep and there was this nose in the way. Pretty nose. It was asleep and breathing at me, so, cuddling closer, I joined it back to sleep.

The knocking persisted, growing in intensity. My head knocked, the whole world was a throbbing, spinning throb.

"Carol! You in there?" some strange, urgent, soprano voice shouted, rising in intensity with the banging and throbbing and pain.

"Wrong room, mate," I answered my dream then slammed my eyes open with the realisation that an eye above the nose next to me was open – really wide. Pretty eye, female eye frantically searching back and forth fixed its gaze on me.

"What on earth!

"Eek! Hell!!

"Shit. Shit. Shit. Oh, shit.

"No. What are you doing here?" Carol shrieked and sat straight up in bed next to me.

"What am I doing here?" she shrieked again.

"What are you doing here?"

I sat bolt upright.

"What on earth," she whispered in disbelief.

"What did we do?" she whimpered.

"We didn't?" she said, checking that she was still fully clothed.

"Couldn't," she said relieved that her armour was still intact, mostly.

"Could we?"

"You didn't…" she startled as innocently as a doe, wide-eyed and palpitating. "…did you? Did we?"

"Probably not," I said feeling intensely groggy, dehydrated and wanting to spew. I finally swung my legs over the edge of the bed and, swaying there for a second or two, debated whether or not standing up would be a good move right then, regretting at the same time that if I hadn't done anything, I should have, and if I had, I couldn't remember anyway, so what the fuck – it didn't matter.

Suddenly another groggy, groaning voice cut in from somewhere else in the room.

"It's Louisa," Carol shrieked again and searched the room for her friend.

"Where is she?"

She finally located Louisa on the floor at the foot of the bed and looking a right dishevelled frumpy yet still gorgeous mess.

"Don't. Don't. Don't look," Lou lamented holding her hands up in front of her face to block out the light and hide against prying eyes.

"I must look awful," the little mop on the floor said.

And she was right in that. She did look a mess. Hair, make-up, clothes.

Meanwhile, the hammering on the door carried on apace, punctuated intermittently with shouting and all sorts of goings-on.

Rising to take hold of the spectacle, Carol stumbled to the door, unlocked it, and a girl I had never set eyes on before tumbled into Carol's arms.

"Adelia! What are you doing here? You aren't supposed to be back until this afternoon."

"It is this afternoon," Adelia announced in a panic.

"And what are you two still doing here? And who's that?" she shrieked, meaning me, the bloke who had just shut himself in the bog.

I wretched unceremoniously into the toilet and reached for a face cloth, listening to the carnage taking place in the bedroom.

"And what on earth is IT doing in my room?" Adelia demanded in a haughty, superior panic.

"Don't know." Louisa groaned, as confused as her inquisitor.

"We went to the ball last night but seem to have lost track of things," Louisa said trying to piece things together.

"It's not what it looks like, Adelia," Carol hoped.

"I don't care what it looks like. Daddy's outside putting the horses in the barn, and I don't want him seeing all this when he comes in. You'll have to ask your paramour in there to leave, and do please make the bed before you go. I'll go out and try to intercept him – Father, I mean. Do look sharp you two. I can't be seen having you two reprobates and whatever's in the loo being here when Daddy comes in. He'll have a fit."

"…Not reprobates, Adelia," Carol groaned, sullen and confused.

"Anyway, you said we could…"

"Not with him. In here? All night? Goodness me. All sorts come to mind. Too sordid to think of. Daddy will think I'm running a brothel in my spare time. I just can't be having you in here," she said, shrieking louder, as if the intensity of her voice was going to remove the intrusion.

"Now, go. Leave at once and take whatever's in there with you…

"…Oh, hello, Daddy. You know Carol. Louisa's the one on the floor," she said standing in front of Lulu in order to hide her shoddy condition.

"Get up, Louisa. You can look for your hairbrush later.

"Are we all ready? Good.

"Then let's go to lunch," I heard her saying as she shut all of them outside in the hallway, leaving me alone and heaving in the bog.

"Smells funny in there, darling," I heard her father saying.

"Smells like sick."

Louisa chirped up brightly at this. "That'll be Carol's quiche. We had to eat it last night. She made it for the ball. Told you so, Carol, but you wouldn't listen."

I tumbled out of the bog and onto the bed in a sweat.

Minutes later, a key turned in the door. I was miserable, light headed, gutted and still lying on the bed.

Carol crept back in.

"You all right?" she whispered.

I nodded, sat up and patted the bed beside me.

"I feel awful too," she said, sitting dolefully beside me. "Whatever do you think happened last night?"

"Don't know…suppose we had fun…"

"…Too much by the looks of things…" Carol gasped, spotting something – some flimsy undergarment on the floor next to the bed and pushing it surreptitiously under the bed with her foot.

"…But…"

"…Do you think…we…er…did…? You know."

"Can't think what you mean, but – no – sadly – didn't…er…don't, don't think, that is.

"Innocent bedlam, that's all we went through last night," I said.

"Innocent bedlam…" she agreed groggily. "…Good…no…I mean, not good…but. Better shut up, Carol," she said to herself.

"Right, then…" she said as if wanting to take some sort of decisive action.

"Right, then," I said, "I think I had too much to drink."

"I think you did. I'm not too happy right now either."

We both sat there for a moment lamenting our state, leaning on each other – for the wrong reasons, but it was nice, anyway, comfy, feeling her drowsy head on my shoulder, her hair caressing my neck, my arm around her to keep her steady.

"They want me to go to lunch with them."

"Go," I urged.

"I think I'll be sick if I try to eat. Anyway," she said snuggling closer into my neck. "This is lovely. I think I'd rather stay, if you don't mind. I mean, if you'd rather I went," she said, half asleep. "I could…go," she said reaching up around my neck to hold herself up and instead pulling us both down onto the bed.

"But this is so much nicer," she said, snuggling and entangling into me to get more comfy.

"Isn't this where we left off?" she mumbled.

"Christopher Robin?"

"Yes?" I said, finding myself so blissfully wrapped up in love with this amazing creature that I didn't dare move.

"I think your elbow is sticking into my back," she said moments later in a groggy, distant, sleepy, matter of fact way.

It wasn't my elbow, silly.

Chapter 15
Elbows and Things

Two days later, we sat opposite each other in our usual spots in the library for the longest time feeling glum, saying nothing, writing nothing, no notes, not even looking at each other, steeped in a confused doldrummy mope until finally I looked up to see her taking a peek at me.

"Go on," she wrote. "Say something."

I was doubtful, frightened of what might be the final chapter in all this, so I sat mute, pretending to read, but I read a title and then fell into a vacuous despair.

A second note slid across: "Daddy's upset."

That's all I needed.

"Coffee?" I wrote back. A chat over coffee would be better than a piecemeal exchange of notes.

An uncontrolled conversation over coffee was not what she wanted right now, though. Things might be said that shouldn't be said. Things that should be addressed. Spoilers. Better to write notes, control the emotions and not hear what was bound to be miss-said or misremembered. All the same, I was proud of myself for offering to bring it all out into the open. Not like me at all. I was always the cowardy custard – or is it cowardly? I don't know. But she was not willing to face up to the consequences – if there were any consequences. She was willing to sublimate the whole thing for the time being and not have to face anything but Daddy's wrath.

So I accepted her solution and finally wrote back: "Daddy's upset?"

"Adelia," she wrote and gave me a withering look as she pushed it across. I took it to mean that she disapproved of Adelia's role in the post-mortem of Mary's Ball.

I was taken by surprise at the mention of Adelia and looked up to see Carol looking intently back at me.

This was more bad news; Carol looking frightened. It was then that we both knew a powwow was needed to sort things out, so we simultaneously declared 'elevenses', cleared up our stuff and decamped to the little Students' Union tearoom next to the library, stumbling and bumbling as we went.

"Must be serious," I said as we sat down with our tray of tea and cakes.

Carol was still looking bleak and taking deep breaths. My heart was in my mouth, not because of the possible consequences of the powwow but simply because she looked so bloody lovely.

"Daddy's not happy," she said taking a sip of her life-giving tea.

I sipped mine and awaited the next pronouncement.

"It seems…Now don't get angry. But it seems everybody is not minding their own business in all this," she said.

I nodded. "This?" I asked.

"Adelia's father has been in touch with Daddy demanding some sort of explanation for the goings on in her room at Mary's – namely you and me, er us spending the night."

"You me and Lou," I said, trying to help but not being very helpful at all.

"You aren't being very helpful," Carol said.

"Lou hasn't been mentioned in despatches yet."

"Not part of the orgy," I said, warming a little.

"Consequences?" I asked, cutting to the chase.

"I'm to go home this weekend and explain to him in person in his study."

"Tied to the rack and whipped to within an inch of your life?"

"No," she cried out in despair. "No. Look, you're still not being very helpful, Christopher Robin" she sulked. "I'm trying to be all grown up in all this, taking my part and yours very seriously, and all you can do is take the mickey. I'm in serious trouble here. Daddy could pull the plug if he thinks the worst has happened."

"You know … Thingy … babies and things."

"Then tell him …" I offered.

"What?" she sulked.

"Tell him the worst has not happened. If that's all he needs to hear. I'll tell him myself, in person, this weekend, if you like."

"Would you?" She brightened and sighed, alarmed and at the same time impressed by my heroism.

"Would you really?" she gasped.

"It will be the saddest confession of my life, but I'll do it. For you. For your sake and Adelia's and Lulu's. I'll confess that to the best of my carnal knowledge I was a complete cretin and failed to take advantage of either you or Lulu that night, when all the world knows that I should have rogered you both rotten over and over, many times throughout the night."

"Oh!" Carol, surprised and somewhat taken aback – in the nicest possible way, I hasten to add – chimed, clearing her throat at the impropriety, her eyebrows knitting in concentrated thought. She hadn't expected rogering, and the thought now perplexed her and, I hoped, gave her pause.

"Should you? I mean, could you, I mean, didn't you – at all? Not even one little tiny bit when the others went to breakfast, you didn't? When we err went back to sleep?"

"What do you think?"

"Well," she hedged a little. "Might have. I mean there was this ruddy, great thingy, you know, that I took as a sign of your intense interest at the time.

"You were intense, weren't you, Christopher Robin?"

"Very."

"Well. There you are then!" she seemed to say in triumph.

"There I am, where?"

"Nothing. Oh. Just. Oh, nothing, really. I just thought …" She blushed a deep red.

"Thought but didn't know," I helped.

"But the thingy …"

"My elbow?"

"Yes…Yes, your, er…your elbow thingy," she said, confused.

I sat quietly thinking for some time, then turning to her and looking her directly in her wondering, innocent eyes said, "Every time I look at you…"

She sat confused for a minute, then when my meaning dawned, caught her breath and squeaked, in amazement, "You mean?"

"Every time…" I nodded.

"… You look at me?" She looked amazed; some might say chuffed.

"… Or think about you," I said.

"Oh!" She sat back in her seat, truly shocked.

"You get …"

"… An elbow thingy," I cut in. "Nothing new in that. Natural, where you are concerned."

"Oh dear!"

"Completely natural – elbows and things."

"Yes … well … I suppose so. That is … I'm not sure," she said, now not so sure.

"So," I said. "I'll pop down to see daddy this weekend. If you like, you can come too, and …"

"What will you tell him?" she whispered in a wondrous, rushed, frightened hush.

"I'll tell him that, yes, his greatest fears have been realised, I rogered you and Louisa rotten that night as well as half the female population of Mary's t'boot."

"T'boot?" she gasped.

"T'boot," I said, finishing off my tea and placing the empty cup down between us for emphasis and a refill.

"T'boot," she said, deep in thought as she poured.

"Well," she said, a wonderful smile spreading across her lovely lips, "that would put the cat among the pigeons – or elbows." she giggled.

"Would it?"

"Yes," she purred. "Yes, it jolly well would," she added, harbouring a sweet, secret conviction, reaching out across the table for my hand.

"Are you…?" she ventured.

"…I mean…" she stumbled.

"Right now. Here with me…I mean…er," she bumbled.

"Am I amorous?" I helped.

"Well…yes…er," she said, clearing her throat again, unintentionally glancing downward, then quickly bringing her eyes back on a level, regaining her composure.

"You are there. I am here," I said. What do you expect?" I asked askance.

"Oh…Oh dear!

"Conundrum."

"Conundrum?"

"Yes. Err…for you, I mean. It must be well…err…disquieting for you – uncomfortable. Should I leave to give you a chance to recover?"

"I can live with it. It's rather nice, actually."

"As long as you don't stand up," she warned with a smirk. "Could be embarrassing," she whispered, leaning across the table, glancing surreptitiously round the tearoom.

"Oh?" I said, screeching back my chair peremptory to standing.

"OH! OH, NO! Don't. I mean. Well…you can if you must. But, but, but do sit down again straight away, after. After I've had a little look," she said sweetly, anticipating the worst, her eyes involuntarily fleeing to witness the object of her greatest fears.

"Goodness!" she gasped, totally unprepared.

"Wouldn't want to start a riot," I said, sitting down again, looking about lest anyone else saw her conundrum.

"Cornucopia," she whispered in breathless confusion.

"I see what you mean. I AM sorry. Did I? Do I do that?" she asked with total disbelieving, breathless pride.

"Told you. It's nothing, really. Human nature, that's all. I can't help it."

"No. It's really quite something. Incredible," she blushed and blustered becoming more intrigued with her conundrum turned cornucopia.

"I've never. Well …What about others? Other women, I mean. Does anyone else make you do that?" she asked, lowering her voice.

"Thankfully, no. It's only specifically idiomatic, I'm afraid."

"Of what?"

"Only being with you …"

"Gosh!" she said proudly, as if she had won some sort of prize.

"I better not be there when you talk to Daddy, then. Heaven knows what he'd think," she said, clearing her throat.

"Wouldn't be a good start to the conversation."

"Didn't realise that sort of thing happened … just like that, I mean."

"Doesn't, usually. Never has before you," I assured her.

"Well, I'm glad."

"What for?"

"You only do it for me," she said, settling comfortably into her seat, her eyes riveted to mine, with that huge beaming smile.

"More tea?" she asked still beaming and reaching out for a piece of cake.

Chapter 16
Punting

Punting in Durham is an ancient tradition that goes all the way back to the early days when St Cuthbert lived on Lindisfarne. As you ought to know, Lindisfarne, or Holy Island as it later came to be known, is separated from the Northumberland mainland at high tide by a narrow, shallow stretch of water. At low tide, a causeway emerges. In order to get across it at high tide, the ancient monks used a shallow, flat-bottomed boat – a punt as we now call it – propelled by a pole which they dug into the sea bottom in order to lever themselves forward from one bank to the other. When old St Cuthbert finally popped his clogs, his henchmen laid his body to rest in a punt – it being his most favourite form of transport – put wheels on it and wheeled him in it all the way to the present site of Durham City. When his body was finally laid to rest, his punt reverted back to its original use and was located on the River Wear at the present-day site of Prebend's Bridge to ferry the monks back and forth across the river at that point.

When Prebend's Bridge got built sometime later, St Cuthbert's beloved punt was used by the descendent monks for their own transportation needs and recreation up and down the river. It was found to be a perfect conveyance, for the river is generally shallow around Durham and the punt afforded the monks a lovely view of the countryside, as they poled themselves happily along in it on picnics or daytrips out to Shincliffe upstream and Finchale Priory downstream. Anyway, they had fun with St Cuthbert's punt long after he was laid to rest. And to this day, a latter-day form of the conveyance is still in use for the leisure of not only the students but also the rest of Durham. Punting is a big-time activity in this university town.

Each college has its own punts – looked after by the mistress or master of the punts – which may be booked by the students for their own recreational use (the punts that is, not the mistress or master of the punts who only oversee their use and bookings and do not rent themselves out for general use. That would be unthinkable. You cheeky thing). The public is able to rent punts from Brown's Boathouse located just above Elvet Bridge.

Tucker was the Master of Punts for St Cuthbert's Society. He tried to book himself out on many occasions to unknowing, local girls and students alike but was usually turned down by them, for despite their naiveté, word got around. They eventually found out what he was after.

"Leo," one such naïve young thing remarked to the Master of the Punts, "are you sure you know how to drive this thing?"

With Leo poling manfully on from the rear deck, they struggled upstream beyond Durham City Rowing Club. She sat in the front of the vessel looking worriedly about herself, back and forth from port to starboard.

"Steer, dear. It's steer, not drive," Leo said, jabbing in the pole, pushing the punt forward then pulling the pole out and using it as a rudder to steer.

"There's a hell of an undertow around this bend." Leo grimaced, suddenly starting to sweat, starting to feel the strain.

"Haven't we gone far enough up the stream to see the baby ducklings?"

"River, err, dear. It's a river, not a stream," Leo said kindly, gamely edging his craft back to the bank in order to stay out of the stiff current that flowed down the centre of the river.

"Never saw such an undertow on this part of the river. Err. No, dear, the baby ducklings are just up ahead. I saw them yesterday whilst out rowing with the lads."

"Is it deep enough here to row?" she quizzed, paralysed momentarily by the rapids she saw on the other side of the river, still not sure that he knew what he was doing.

"Have another tart, Amanda, dear," he urged, grunting with the effort of propelling the craft and steering at the same time. Suddenly, a bigger than usual wave hit the bows. Leo staggered to keep his balance.

"Fuckin' hell. I think they must have had a helluva rainfall upstream last night. The river's up a good six inches from yesterday."

Amanda's back stiffened visibly at Leo's use of profanity, but she took another almond tart from the little white bag on her lap, nibbling it to assuage the indignity.

"You shouldn't use language like that, Leo," she said.

"Like what, dear?" he asked, innocent of any wrongdoing.

"'F'ing 'H'ing'," she said, nibbling.

"Oh! That. Good old Anglo-Saxon, that's all, dear. It's been in the language since Chaucer was a boy," Leo said, poling now more vigorously than ever and looking more and more perturbed about the swirling, rushing water pouring past his little frail craft.

"Chaucer who?" Amanda asked in all innocence, rattling around in the little white package for another tart.

"Oh, god," Leo, tied up with bringing the punt around against a stiffening current, exclaimed without thinking.

"Fred Chaucer, for fuck's sake. Who'd you think?" he barked out of the side of his mouth, struggling to keep the bows from flipping sideways.

"If I lose it, we're in a shit load of trouble, darlin'."

"Don't think I know any Fred Chaucer," she mused, holding her almond tart into the air between thumb and forefinger in order to think.

"I know a Fred Mulberry. He lives down the street from me mam. He's in deliveries. Delivers for Tesco's," she said, grabbing the sides of the rising and plunging punt to stop herself from falling sideways out of it.

"Is it supposed to dive and roll like this, Leo?" she asked. "I'm beginning to feel a little unwell," she said letting go of the gunwale with her right hand to hold her mouth.

"Sorry dear," Leo shouted above the rising roar of the water, trying desperately to hide the fact that he had lost control of their little vessel.

"Damn," he shouted out as a particularly strong broadside sent his passenger down into the punt's midsection where she struggled to remain upright, holding back the urge to spew.

"Sorry, my dear, but this part of the river is proving to be more difficult than I remember. We'll land soon and have our picnic with the baby ducklings," he said looking bleak, holding firmly to the belief that once he got her ashore and liquored up with the bottles he had stowed away, she would prove to be as pliable as she had been after last Saturday's pie and peas supper in the local rectory.

"I'm sure…" he said, swooping toward port, righting himself then just as violently swooning to starboard…

"Fuckin' Ada, that was a big one, Amanda. Did you see that…? I almost lost it that time. Did you see it?" he asked, shitting bricks.

"Leo! I'm getting frightened. Don't you think…" But just as she was about to mention turning the punt around and making a run for it back to the boathouse, a massive surge hit the bows sending the punt spinning in a dizzying circle and levering the helmsman overboard atop his pole. Luckily for Amanda, the swinging punt took one further turn, propelling itself into the river's edge where it lodged firmly on top of a sandbank. The helmsman was less fortunate than his passenger and found himself clinging desperately to the top of his impaled pole, only metres from the beach.

"Bloody hell," he screamed at Amanda. "Do something for fuck's sake. Call the fire department," he shrieked, feeling his grip slipping down the slippery pole and dropping him nearer and nearer the raging waters.

"Jump, Leo. You can do it. Save yourself. You don't want to end up in the water. You can do it. Jump across to the bankside."

Frigid with terror, it was all the intrepid helmsman could do to hang on, never mind jumping anywhere. As he slipped down the pole toward the river, he felt the surging waters licking at his feet.

"Me toes," he shrieked. "I'm submerging fast, Amanda. See if there's a lifejacket or something under the decks. Quick. Quick. I'm going down faster than HMS Titanic."

But as luck would have it, just as his feet began to submerge beneath the waves, the pole slowly gave way in the silt and, leaning further and further over, finally vaulted him sideways back to dry land where he dropped with a thump on his bum on the sandbank next to Amanda.

"That was a close one. Did you see that? Did you find a lifejacket, dear? Eventually? Under the deck?"

But the look on Amanda's pretty little face was one of gruesome horror. So instead of pressing his case of her complete disinterest in his wellbeing, Leo shut up to consider his good fortune in not being drowned and what to do with the rest of the picnic and this pretty woman at his elbow. Leo being Leo, he was not going to give up on the intended outcome of the afternoon, and so, once he regained his equilibrium, he rustled round in the bottom of the punt and, voila, pulled out the hamper he had stored there earlier in the day.

As he placed the hamper on the sandbank next to the punt, Amanda asked, "What was that, Leo? That clinking sound coming from our picnic."

"Just a couple of bottles of ginger beer, dear," Leo said, tying off the punt to stop it from floating away and then turning to lead his intrepid party of two inland where he knew from past experience, he would find a secluded dell appropriate for the afternoon's festivities.

"This'll do dear," he said, resting the hamper on the ground, out of the way of prying eyes.

"We're out of the way of the wind here. I've brought a little blanket you can lie down…err…sit on whilst we have some lunch.

"Egg sandwich, dear?

"Bottle of pop?" he said, meaning the 12% Belgian beer he had decanted into several ginger beer bottles earlier that morning – a trick he'd learned from Beau Franklin.

"Tastes funny, Leo," she said after swigging off half the bottle.

"'Funny', Amanda? What makes you say that, dear?"

"Just that. Tastes funny. A bit like beer."

"Ah, it is, Amanda. It's ginger beer. Franklin ginger beer. They make it in Rotherham. Monks. It was made by the Rotherham Monks way back in the twelfth century."

"Tastes old."

"None's the wonder, Amanda. Because…" he said, gulping his down to catch up with her.

And quaffing the lot with one fell swoop, fortified and ready to do battle with the forces of chastity, said, "Because it is old. Bloody old…Have another, err, dear. There's plenty where that came from."

"There you go again, Leo."

"Err, what, dear? What is it?"

"Swearing. You never let a sentence go by without putting some kind of rude word in it."

"Sorry," he said, not wanting to let deteriorate a situation, which, it must be said, was turning slowly back in his favour – or so he thought, as she downed her second pint bottle of Franklin's Best.

"The very words Chaucer used when he was a boy. But I'll refrain from quoting him if it upsets you, dear. Have another pint, there's a love.

"Here's to Geoffrey," he said, lifting his bottle into the air."

"Geoffrey who, Leo?"

"Fuckin' Ada," the aggravated swain emitted under his breath. "Here we go again…

"Just a punting friend of mine, dear, who died in a boating accident not far from this very spot," he said, rubbing his hands together with glee at the sight of Amanda digging into the hamper for her third bottle of Franklin's Best.

"Gruesome affair. But I'll spare you the gory details, dear."

Chapter 17
Montagu-Smy

Nobody ever called him by his first name, for, I believe, nobody – apart from his mum and his nanny – ever knew it. He was known simply as Montagu-Smy, or Smy for short, and I suppose it was testimony to our fear of and respect for him that a Christian name was never thought appropriate. He was one of the few members of Cuth's whom you thought belonged in another part of the world, another part of the century, another part of the university. He didn't fit in at Cuth's. He knew he was from a better part of society and never failed to laud it over the rest of us. His was a unique snobbishness – a bit like Reggie Phipps. But whilst we loved Reggie's unaffected mannerisms, we despised Montagu-Smy's. Obnoxious to the core, Smy had no redeeming qualities whatsoever. He was our very own Beau Didapper, and we loathed him for it and at the same time secretly envied him.

Women were mesmerised by him. Money played a great part in this, but whilst he was denied by nature the great physical attractiveness of, say, a Beau Franklin, he had a noble profile that thrilled the ladies all the same. He overpowered them with his physicality, his belligerent, self-confidence. Poor things. They had no self-control, knew no better.

He read anthropology, and that too played on everyone's mistrust. A big-nosed, square-jawed, bloody-minded patrician, always in everybody's face. Poor guy, he never had a chance.

His usual habitat was the JCR bar with his gang of whoop-dee-doo sycophants pushing pints at each other, pushing each other to bigger and better and more outrageous boyish, priggish pranks – never at their own expense – egging each other on to bigger and better howlers.

Harry Sturge was one of his gang. An older hanger-on, he was infatuated with Smy's style, yet Harry was married with a family. He felt his domestic life needed a kick, which Smy provided for him. He competed with the other acolytes to curry favour with the undergraduate bully and eventually rose to be his chief henchman. Lean and lanky where Smy was thickset, Sturge was a comic complement to his gewgaw captain.

The narrow, winding cobblestone lane housing Cuth's was lit up one drizzly evening with a screaming rant coming from a second story apartment window opposite. Smy had been drinking all afternoon and was serenading the passers-by in South Bailey below him with his usual drunken squalor. Just Smy on another incomprehensible rant. Swinging a pint of beer above the crowd to accent his message, he leaned further and further out of the window as he gained confidence in his attack, barking out his message, his curly blond head streaming wet, his lips spattering rain and large hooked nose dripping onto the glistening cobble lane below. The large, nineteenth century streetlamp above Number 12 opposite illuminated the drama.

Sturge stood under Cuth's lamp egging on his troubadour captain to greater and greater oratory, throwing every manner of crap at him when he lost his topic or seemed to be wilting or seemed, heaven help us, to be making some sort of common sense. Taking the flying debris from Sturge as a challenge, Smy reached out to catch it and toss it back at him, hurling his own insults down at him and giving better than he got.

Invective flew up and down the rainy evening. Debris rained back and forth forcing bemused pedestrians to duck under their umbrellas and weave and curse their way past it all. Sturge was drenched. Smy too, but neither was going to give way until, with a look of dire malevolence on his face, Sturge scuttled off and out of sight several doors away into Number 8. Blind drunk to any change of circumstance, Smy continued to rail against his absent friend, punctuating his tirade with a pair of wellies that he hurtled, first one, then the other, down near the lamp. A bra followed, drifting limply to land in a puddle, and a small desk lamp that shattered upon impact, scattering glass across the pavement.

Smy was settling into his role as college tyrant orator.

"Aha," he cried out when at last he saw Sturge returning to his place opposite and struggling with a sack full of ammunition.

"Harry, you bastard. Come back for more punishment." And with that, he too ducked away from the battle scene to reappear moments later anxious to do battle with bigger and better ammo.

By this time, Allan, the college porter, who lived on the ground floor just below Smy's rooms, had had enough. He had warned them earlier in the evening, before things got too far out of hand, that their noise and disagreeable language was too much and that if he heard any more of it, he would call University Security. Allan was another decent, local man, tall and skinny, a no-nonsense fellow. To look at him, you might think that he had spent most of his life in a boxing ring. Lean and angular, his face was severe but still had a kindly aspect to it. You respected Allan at once. If you didn't, you knew he had the means to do you great harm with little or no effort.

"You lads pack it in." he scowled out of his ground floor window with his mouth still half full of bread and kippers from his tea.

"There's people here lookin' for a bit of peace and quiet of an evenin' and don't need to hear the likes of you lot caterwauling up and down the street."

Just after he had ducked back into his doorway, a badly aimed plimsoll from Sturge rebounded off it and lay right side up in the gutter slowly filling with water.

"Fuckin' prat," came the reply from above, and with it, the battle resumed apace.

"'You lot', you bleedin' idiot. What do you mean by 'you lot'? We pay your bleedin' salary, asshole."

The would-be patrician Neanderthal was incensed and lay-to with greater energy than ever before.

"Now, I've told you two to knock it off," Allan warned again a little bit later on, this time sticking his head out of his parlour window and slamming down the sash in disgust.

Just then, Damien Pettigrew wandered out of Number 12 and stood watching. Damien was an affable, unflappable first year engineering student, wise beyond his years. He liked to find a scientific answer for every problem. There was no science in his world, however, that could solve the standoff outside Cuth's. So, he hove-to just beyond what he considered to be the safety perimeter of the engagement, encouraged that both Sturge and Smy were getting closer and closer to each other with their projectiles. He watched as they unwittingly misapplied all the laws of a ballista in their throws, coming closer and closer to a direct hit without actually achieving it.

Stepping out of the shadows at last, Damien put his hand on Sturge's shoulder just as he was about to launch an old boot.

"Better to chuck it underhand," Damien offered, demonstrating the technique and nodding his head.

"Fuck off, Pettigrew," Harry spat, disgruntled at being interrupted with his bowling just as his last one bounced off the wall a couple of feet below the ranting, bleary-eyed Smy. Staggered by Sturge's near miss, Smy ducked back into his room to reload and reconsider his tactics. He moved into his bedroom to get another beer and a better angle and scored a direct hit with his first toss. Not to be outdone and shrieking with delight, Sturge lobbed a hardcover copy of 1984, which tore itself to pieces as it flew through the air. Falling woefully short, the tattered novel broke itself up and scattered itself along the wet pavement.

"No," Pettigrew implored. "You're doing it all wrong. Lob them like this! Like this! Gives you more height with less effort – better accuracy."

But the confounded, humiliated Sturge wouldn't be told, pushed his advisor back into the shadows and swilled around in the bottom of his sack for another piece of ammo.

"Piss off Pettigrew. This'll do it," he said lowering his voice, feeling its weight.

"I'll do 'im with this one," he said bringing his mum's little old, cracked brown teapot up to the light.

"Just right."

"You'll kill him if you hit him with that," Pettigrew warned.

"Too right, mate. Too right," Sturge chortled, fondling the teapot in his right hand, fitting it into the middle of his palm, caressing it and finally bringing it onto his fingertips ready to chuck.

When word got around next morning that Smy had fallen out of his bedroom window in a drunken stupor, the part about him being hit in the head by a little brown teapot was never mentioned. Smy didn't know what had hit him. Allan didn't know. He was downstairs at the time finishing his tea when he heard a scrawly shriek followed by a thud on the pavement outside his window. Sturge did know, but Pettigrew had scuttled away before the missile launch and knew better than to make silly, unprofitable enquiries. So Smy's dilemma was thought to have been of his own making, and there were plenty of passers-by who could testify that he had been his obnoxious old drunken self that night, badmouthing all and sundry, and it had served him right.

Allan grew suspicious when he saw the lump on Smy's head but put it down to bad luck in the end. He had no sympathy whatsoever for the young turd, although he hadn't expressed himself quite in those terms to the policeman who took his statement.

At first, after Sturge had lobbed the teapot and heard the diabolical shriek, he felt chuffed that his perseverance had finally paid off. Not so happy, though, when he heard the crunching thud on the pavement, and in a panic, he turned around to leg it up the lane before the coppers arrived. Why he returned minutes later, nobody could figure out, but he did just in time to see his bedraggled mate staggering back into the house, blood streaming from his head. When Sturge caught up to him inside, Smy was mumbling something about losing his grip up there then losing his balance and ending up upside down outside Allan's window. He thanked his mate for helping him get back up the stairs to his room. Apart from a bloody coxcomb, he was none the worse for wear. Apparently, a thick cloud of alcohol had cushioned his fall and blotted out any memory of the night's misadventures.

Chapter 18
A Fate Worse than Fate

"You've told Christopher Robin to go and report to your father?" Louisa asked, aghast.

"Not report to," Carol reassured her.

"And anyway, he volunteered. I didn't tell him to do anything."

"Preposterous," Lulu said with feeling.

"Poor thing," she added, pulling her legs under her on the sofa, taking dead aim at Carol who dithered with a clump of flowers at the dining table.

"Fate worse than … well … fate," Louisa said.

"Daddy's not that fierce. And I'm sure Christopher Robin will hold his own."

"Do you think so? Your father can be quite combative at times. He's very protective of his little girl. What on earth ever possessed you to tell him to go to your father about this?"

"Didn't. As I just said, if you'd have been listening, Louisa, he volunteered out of some sort of chivalrous duty to me – and you too, I must say. He thinks a lot of you, you know. Holds you in very high esteem."

"Too much, if I have anything to say about it," Carol added.

"Not surprising though, is it? I mean I am quite a catch for someone willing to offer the right sort of bait," Louisa said.

"Bait? What about Ollie? Isn't he, er…well…I mean."

"Ollie is lovely, and I'm glad he's around, but you never know, do you?"

"No, I don't, Lou," Carol said getting more and more cross with her elusive friend.

"What do you mean? Come on; spit it out. Let's hear it. What's wrong with Ollie and more to the point: what's right about Christopher Robin for that matter?"

"Nothing really, right or wrong with any of them, but…"

"But, what?" Carol said, just about to boil over.

"Nothing," Louisa said looking more and more gloomy with things. "It's…"

"Yes?" Carol said moving in on the sofa.

"It's what?"

"It's just…well. It's just that things change, don't they?"

"What things? You mean Oliver or Christopher. You'll have to tell me, Lulu. I must know if I'm about to be stabbed in the back over Daddy."

"You won't be. Believe me.

"The way things are going, you are about to come away with all the pudding and I'm going to be left with none," Lulu said, glassy-eyed and looking back on the way things were going.

"Only, dearest," she said reaching over to take Carol's hand, "don't send him to see your father. Please. He doesn't deserve that kind of thing, and you might end up losing him altogether," she said squeezing her hand for emphasis.

"Losing him? What nonsense. Whoever said anything about losing him when I haven't got him in the first place. He's just a friend. Like…Like…Like so many people – male or female. Can't someone have a friendship with a person that isn't necessarily a…a…a…relationship."

"What on earth is he going to see your father for then? Tell me that. What on…"

"He's just going to straighten him out about, well…you know."

"About whether he rogered you rotten that night, or the next day, or me – but not the next day because I was entertaining Adelia's father at lunch whilst you and he – Christopher Robin – were back in Adelia's room sleeping it off or having it off."

"Well, you are the only one – other than him – Christopher Robin – who knows anything about that one. And Lulu, dearest Lulu, if he did something with you, you don't have to tell.

"I don't want to know.

"I don't need to know, so don't say a word.

"Keep it to yourself."

"Thanks C. You're very understanding," Lulu said turning down the alarms in her eyes.

"Well?" C asked after a quiet second or two.

"Well, what?"

"Did he? You know. Did he, or didn't he? You know. That night."

"Thought you didn't want to know."

"Oh, Loueeeeesa. He did, didn't he?"

"What?" Louisa teased.

"Ravish you silly while I was out cold with drink."

"Never heard such rot. You're just trying to justify your nefarious behaviour by putting the blame on me. Wicked. Wicked. Wicked. Carol, you ought to be ashamed."

"Oh ho. Won't answer the question. I think there is more to this than you are willing to admit to. Lulu, you are so transparent. It's all coming too, too clear now. And you can't get away with it.

"Admit it."

"Admit what? I haven't done anything. And anyway, if I had, I'm not telling. So there."

"So there? So there? What do you mean you fibber?" Carol pressed her friend.

"You and Adelia. You're a right pair. I'm afraid Adelia hasn't been much help either. She's still up in arms about our little tryst. Won't be told. Still blames you for turning her room into a brothel. And I'm with her on that one," Carol replied.

"She just needs something to take her mind off things," Louisa suggested.

"We'll take her out to dinner," Carol, inspired, said with an intake of breath.

"Wonderful. Yes. We could all go," Louisa said, squinting into an idea.

"All?"

"Six of us. Diffuse the situation. Get her daddy off our backs. All of us. Have it out once and for all," the little one said with determination.

"Before Christopher Robin goes to talk to anyone's daddy, we should hash it all out over dinner. All of us," Louisa said.

"All of us?" Carol said with deep foreboding.

"Yes. Why not? You, me, her, Errol, Oliver and Christopher Robin.

At this last suggestion, Carol told her friend that she was simply mad.

Chapter 19
How Adelia Still Wasn't Much Help

"I can't see how that cad talking to your father can do me any good at all," Adelia said petulantly.

"He needs to talk to Daddy. He's the one who holds the purse strings. I'm faced with penury if something isn't done about that scoundrel."

"Christopher Robin is not a scoundrel or…or…or a cad for that matter, Dee. Surely. As much a victim in all this misunderstanding as you or I or Louisa. And if you've painted him 'scoundrel' with your father, he has little chance of convincing him otherwise. We're all…well…we're all doomed."

"Should have thought of this before Mary's Ball," Adelia said, finishing her pot of strawberry yoghurt – a treat she allowed herself once a day at lunch.

"You aren't being very helpful, Dee."

Adelia sat quietly mulling things over.

Finally, she spoke up. "I cannot talk to Daddy about this. He's obdurate. Won't listen to anything I have to say about it. Says if I'm bent on running a brothel on top of the allowance he gives me, I can run it with the proceeds of my brothel and no allowance. Told me I should put a sign up outside Mary's front door advertising my new business, put adds in the local newspapers, put a red light in my window. Honestly. I ask you. A red light?"

"Charge you and Louisa some sort of rent."

"Goodness," Carol exclaimed. "A red light? What on earth for?"

"Advertising her wares," Louisa helped from the other side of the table.

"What wares?" Carol asked in all innocence. "You're not operating a hardware store, are you?"

Adelia spent a long time over this one, took a deep breath then squared up to both of her friends and said, "Just what did go on in there that night?"

Louisa looked shocked. Carol looked afraid. Neither could say anything for some time, so Adelia continued, "It's really none of my business, and you two have every right to tell me to get stuffed, but nobody has really had the courtesy to confide in me over this business."

There was a collegiate intake of breath at this point with both defendants looking more and more earnest.

Louisa looked to Carol, and Carol looked equally glum back at Lulu.

Louisa took the lead by saying meekly, "Nothing happened, Dee. Nothing. We partied. We got totally drunk and passed out in your rooms. Honest. You and your daddy showed up, and we went to lunch. At least …" she edged nervously in her chair.

"At least some of us did. Right, C? Isn't it?" Louisa asked Carol.

But C was too gobsmacked by the apparent implications to speak. She opened her mouth to say something and a squeak came out.

"What do you think happened, Adelia?" Carol finally asked, incredulous.

"That's what I'm asking you to tell me, darlings," she said, reaching out a hand to each of them.

"Right now, I'm on the outside looking in, and the repercussions for me are disastrous. My father has threatened to cut me off completely. Somebody has to tell him," she said, a little tear forming in the corner of her eye.

"Christopher Robin will do it," Carol said decisively.

Louisa wasn't so sure. She grimaced at the thought and said, "Poor bloke. We really are putting him on the spot, you know. Next thing, you'll be telling him he'll have to appear before the United Nations to defend your celibacy in front of the whole world."

"Not celibacy, Lou. I don't think you meant celibacy. We aren't monks in the Himalayas."

"I know. I know," Louisa said in a flap, searching for the right word. "Something like celibacy. Not virginity either. Oh, help me out, you beasts. What is it I mean? Thesaurus. Thesaurus," she said scrambling around in her bag and coming up with her dog-eared thesaurus.

"Voila. Now, let's see. Virginity: 'Chasteness'. No, I don't think so. 'Chastity'…"

"Certainly not," Carol spoke as if imbued with second sight.

"What do you mean, 'certainly not'?" Louisa said.

"The implications are obvious and far too damning to broadcast to the United Nations," Carol said.

"Well then, what about 'maidenhead'?"

"Same thing, I think, Dee. Don't you?"

"Busybody-ish," said Adelia with her own grimace at the thought.

"'Purity', then?" Louisa hoped. "Not bad—"

"But …" Carol interjected. "Not bad enough. Whoever wants to be too pure in this day and age, or at least have the reputation of one who is?"

"… see what you mean," Louisa said after a bit. It often took a moment or two for the penny to drop with dear Lulu, but she usually got there in the end.

"Aha!" Louisa said with victory in her voice. "'Virtue'. That's it. I think the UN would go for that one. Don't you, Dee?"

"I wouldn't mind having my virtue paraded before the world," Carol said, mulling it over. "Happy to. As long as I was actually seen to be virtuous and not the opposite…without any."

"You mean, 'whorish'? Well," Lulu said teasing. "I would say that the former was out of the question where you are concerned and the latter more applicable," she said with a great big grin on her face and leaning over to parade it right in front of Carol.

"Surely not whorish," Carol said with mock indignation, to which Louisa nodded so emphatically that Carol took a playful swipe at her arm.

"Are!" said Lou jumping back just in time.

"Not!" Carol said, demurely pulling back behind a virtuous little smile.

"That settles it then," Louisa said. "I'll get U Thant on the phone and tell him Christopher Robin wants a quiet word with him about your virtue – or lack of it."

"Fat load of good that would do to secure my finances," Adelia said, still out of sorts.

"You can tell anybody you like, but I don't think Daddy even knows who U Thant is, let alone the United Nations. Couldn't we not just ask Christopher Robin to send Daddy a letter – no – but that wouldn't be good enough either. It needs to be somebody in authority whom Daddy could trust. One of his own ilk. Preferably somebody who was there that night?" Louisa said. "With us? Who could vouch for the veracity of our evidence? Or someone above reproach who could vouch for the good word of the accused and didn't have to be there at the time, at all."

A light went on somewhere, and as one, Carol and Louisa blurted out, "Rev Kev."

"That's who could intervene with impunity," Carol said. "The Reverend Kevin, moral tutor."

"Exactly," Louisa said. "He knows everything about everything that goes on around here."

"Above reproach."

"Stellar vicar," said Louisa.

"Should have thought of him in the first place," Carol said, intervening in Lou's intervention.

But Adelia still was not sure and mumbled something about, "How easily the incorruptible are corrupted."

Chapter 20
Rev Kev

The university's moral tutor, Reverend Kevin Bartholomew – Rev Kev – was a kindly old soul. He lived in a small house tucked away in a corner of Cuth's gardens. Once a term, he held his famous piss-up in the back room of The Rose Tree in Shincliffe to shore up his students' flagging morals by flooding the place with free beer to open up their souls and also to minister to their crumbling spirits. It was his job to see to the pastoral wellbeing of all university students, and he used this gathering to do them all at one go, in one job lot. This left him free the rest of the term to help Timmy Bickerstaff with his gardens around Cuth's, which, without Rev Kev's spectacular attention, would quickly sink into total anarchy – especially the roses, his personal favourites. The vicar loved roses. He saw each one of his students as a new species of rose that required its own special pastoral care, the same care he lavished on his flowers.

He could often be seen in his Harris Tweed jacket and big, elbow length, leathern gauntlets with pruning shears in hand, tending to the banks of roses that adorned the gardens around Cuth's and especially round the front of his little walled house. Talking to each plant in turn like a latter-day Friar Lawrence, the reverend lauded affection on each, apologising profusely to every one of his children he found necessary to improve with his secateurs.

"You see, Father…"

"Er…reverend, my dear. I'm not really a father. Wrong church…"

"Sorry, er, Reverend. You see, Reverend," Carol went on, prising out the most proper, least offensive phrase, "there is a rather delicate problem I would like your help with…"

"Mind Dolly there behind you," he warned, seeing Carol backing into one of his charges. "She's particularly sickly right now and wouldn't take being trod on."

"Er, sorry, Reverend…Dolly. Didn't mean to…" the confused young thing said.

"Quite all right, dear. Quite all right. Just needs a bit of air and sunshine, and she'll be right as rain again in no time. Isn't it odd how much like people some roses are? Dolly here and Ethelred over there. Ethelred cowers in the shade all day and thrives in it, while poor old Dolly becomes quite unwell if she doesn't get her daily dose of vitamin D. Same species, different constitutions. Quite like people. Very much like people – flowers.

"Now then, my dear, what is it you need help with. Delicate, you say?"

"Yes."

And she told him the whole story about that night at Mary's Ball and felt very much better for having done so.

Rev Kev listened attentively to her tale, not once removing his eyes from his roses. When she had finished, he lowered his little snippers to consider her predicament.

"So, what you need is some sort of message from a reputable source such as myself to your father or the father of your friend that nothing untoward took place in your friend's rooms the night of St Mary's Ball."

"Yes, Father…err, Reverend."

"A telephone call? Or p'raps a letter," he said turning fully to his postulant and gazing at her over his spectacles. Turning away from her, he put his snippers down on a window ledge and thought some more, his little, be whiskered, pointy nose sniffing out alternatives.

"You see," he said, decisively without wanting to unsettle the delicate creature at his elbow.

"You see, my dear, I would need certain assurances from not only you but also the other parties involved that no, err…indelicacies had occurred before I could issue such a warrant. Err, I would have to have a word with them myself and ascertain certain facts from them before I could do this."

Seeing his young guest's gloom at this prospect, the Rev Kev back-tracked into his previous statement a bit and said, "Oh, not that I don't believe you, my dear. I do. I most certainly do, but everyone must be consulted over the matter. Everyone. No stone left unturned, eh? That's the ticket. Should help me assuage the fears of said fathers, if, in fact, everything is above board and Bristol fashion. Now, if you don't mind," he added in his kindly way, "there's trouble around the other side of the house that needs tending to. Not unlike the little tale you have told me about your Christopher Robin and Louisa."

Oh dear, Carol thought as she closed the gate behind her.

"He's not mine. I wish people would stop saying that. And what does he mean about Christopher Robin and Lulu?"

Heartened yet somewhat confused, relieved yet full of trepidation at the same time, Carol wandered up South Bailey toward Palace Green for what she hoped would be a meeting with yours truly and Miss Adelia Pape.

Adelia, once again, hadn't shown.

I poured us both a cup and reached for a chocolate biscuit.

"Looks like Rev Kev's on the case," I said after my first bite, washed down with a scalding sip of tea.

"What did you tell him?" I asked in all innocence.

"The truth, of course," Carol said looking at me funny.

"You? What will you tell him?"

"Same," I said.

"Which is?"

"The truth," I repeated after another scalding sip.

"Do we both have the same version of the truth?" she asked with doubt widening her eyes.

"Hope so. Otherwise," I said taking another nibble. "Otherwise, we're in trouble. Why, what's your truth?"

"Nothing," she answered indignantly. "As I have already told you, nothing happened that night, or next day, or ever for that matter. It's all been a great misunderstanding. A tempest in a teapot," she sighed, dismissing it all with another sip of her tea.

"Some tempest," I said.

"Some teapot."

"Why? Whatever do you mean? What are you going to tell Rev Kev?"

I was mute at this point, feeling that my answer had already been dictated to me. I could lie to him about it all, and it would be no skin off my nose, but somehow, lying to him and to Carol's daddy would be like denying a great truth that I secretly wanted to share with the entire world.

My silence prompted an 'Oh dear' from Carol. I was dreading the next bit.

"What are we going to do?" she said, hanging her head in despair, her hands fidgeting aimlessly in her lap. She didn't slump though. Her shoulders still had that athletic squareness that I always loved about her. She sat up tall and smiled through her dilemma.

"I thought we had an agreement that we weren't going to—"

"To what? To tell the truth? Face reality?" Make things any worse than they are," she helped, still smiling.

Then a tear formed in the corner of her eye, and she drew a breath that was so lamentable it broke my already frightened, quivering heart. Seeing my distress, she reached across the table, took my hand and whispered, "Don't worry, Christopher Robin. It'll be all right. Promise."

At this point, I thought it should be me shoring her up, but this unbelievable woman was helping me, as she always managed to do. Surely, there was something in this as well, instead of all the inevitable referrals that might eventually mean an end to it all. But I had to face the fact that nothing was set in stone. We were probably not meant to be. She wasn't sure, although I was feeling kinda nice about it all. She was all tied up in pre-arranged expectations, any one of which could very easily bring it to an end. Now, I was feeling all miserable, and it was Carol who shored me up, not the other way around. All the more reason for loving her all to bits.

I grinned at her through a teary haze, and she smiled back.

"More tea," she said, lifting the pot over to my cup.

At this point, I was almost willing to put her firmly on the spot, to declare either for me or against me. But not forcing her meant no decision, and no decision right now was better than a possible outright rejection. No decision meant status quo, and I could live with status quo. What I could not begin to contemplate was outright rejection. That would be impossible to take. So, another cup of tea and hold on to what I had in the presence of one whom I trusted completely and who had my heart.

"Yes," I said. "Another cuppa."

"And?" she asked, levering the cloud from around my head.

I took a deep breath in, exhaled, feeling entirely safe in her cup of tea.

"You are a gloomy, old Hector," she said with feigning concern.

"If it will help," she said, finishing the pouring.

"If it will help, I could offer never to cross your path again."

I know she meant this in a kindly way, but the thought filled me with apocalyptic dread.

"Couldn't face that," I said.

She brightened.

"What would help then, Christopher Robin?" she asked in a hoping kind of way. "What could you face?"

"Hobnob," I said reaching for another chocolate covered biscuit.

"Can't dunk it," she said playfully. "Got chocolate on it."

"Didn't want to," I said brandishing in front of her the last Hobnob.

"Miserable sod. I wanted that one," she said, reaching out to grab it.

"Mine!" I countered, popping the last bit into my mouth. "There's one digestive left. You have it," I squabbled.

"Don't want it," she said with mock petulance, sitting back in her seat, folding her arms and glowering playfully at me across the table.

"I'll have it then…"

"No-no-no-no…Give it to me. I'll have it."

"You'll have to make up your mind then," I said handing it across to her.

"You know I'm no good at that," she glowered again.

"I know," I said, the row quelling as she quietly munched her digestive.

"You'll have to learn how to," I said.

"I know," she squeaked. "I know. But it's not going to be easy. I've always been a waffler. Can't help it. No sense of discrimination."

"No sense at all, as far as I can see. There's always a better choice and a worse choice."

"Yes, I know," she said in a hopeless kind of way.

Then she added as an afterthought, "All I know is not wanting to hurt peoples' feelings."

She sat back in her chair thinking for a while. "I just want to get along. Shouldn't need to discriminate all the time. I just want all of us to be happy."

"Status quo?" I asked.

She nodded in glum silence. I think she had been deliberating about things too.

Chapter 21
Rev Kev's Piss-Up

The Rose Tree, as its name implies, is a beautiful little pub at the edge of the cute little village of Shincliffe, fifteen minutes' walk along the riverbank from the centre of Durham. Rev Kev's Piss-Up offered free beer for as long as you wanted. In fealty to our host, though, nobody really over indulged and anyone who might be getting close to the edge was turfed out early by the landlord. There was this unwritten rule that even though there was an endless supply of the stuff, conviviality was the key. I know. I know. Sounds really strange in that setting and among a crowd of undergraduates but that was the respect everyone paid Rev Kev.

This particular evening, the weather being so mild, the garden at the riverside of the pub was in play. When the bar filled up, some of us spilled out onto the lawn to occupy various wrought iron tables scattered about it. Some wandered through the back gate and out onto the riverbank. Some occupied the saloon bar.

Idyllic. So you might think.

And I would have to agree.

However, this particular evening things got a little bit different, a little bit sideways.

Who would ever imagine corrupting an idyll?

Ten o'clock came and went. Most of Rev Kev's charges had paid their respects, downed their pints and left. Most, that is, except our group and two oafs who felt that no party was truly over until they had put their stamp on things, until they had drunk their fill and broken the place up to their peculiar requirements. We were wondering what Smy and Sturge were hatching when they arrived around nine having already done the Gilesgate Pub Crawl that afternoon. They were already six sheets to the wind.

The two raggy lads had made their way from Gilesgate down to the river through Pelaw Woods, had stumbled along the riverbank to Shincliffe and tumbled into the dwindling crowd on the lawn of The Rose Tree. They arrived along the riverbank, announcing their arrival at the back of the Free House in a squalling mood, ready to do battle with everybody still left in the place – as well as each other.

They were, of course, determined to be the life of the party, or whatever was left of it and felt it necessary to corral everybody else into their drunkenness. Smy hovered at the bar, glowering at anyone who ignored his attempts to rouse the house. Sturge just appeared unwell and was content to remain that way until unconsciousness rescued him. He teetered on top of his barstool not knowing which way to fall. A blank, drunken pallor covered his face.

Smy got in two more pints for himself and his friend, knocked his drink back with a look of superiority and hovered over Sturge who wasn't aware that another drink stood waiting at his elbow.

"Get it down you, lad," Smy ordered and slapped him on the back.

Harry looked bleak, helpless, just couldn't cope with another mouthful. He opened his mouth to tell his mate this and barf came out.

"Why doesn't somebody do something?" a little voice across the table from me asked. Lulu was astonished. She shifted uneasily in her seat.

"He looks so ill. And the other one isn't helping a bit. Well," she decided, "I'm going to do something."

I looked at Carol, and Carol looked back at me as Lulu pushed back her chair and marched over to Sturge.

"LOU!" Carol shrieked. Louisa ignored the warning.

"Are you all right?" she asked the drunkard in all innocence, not really knowing who she was about to tangle with. Harry lowered his head painfully toward the tiny Samaritan irritant at his side then blearily turned back to face the bar again. Nothing was registering just now with him.

"It's just that—" Louisa went on.

"He's all right, Ducky," Smy interrupted, leaning away from the bar and across Lulu's line of sight.

"And anyway, he's got a wife. It's me you want to be chatting up if you want a good time tonight, dahlin'," he added, leering down into her cleavage.

"I'm not your Ducky or your dahlin'," Louisa replied, irritated at the interference. "I wasn't attempting to chat him up, if you must know, nor am I interested in having a good time with you. I just thought your friend looked unwell, and if you had had any feelings for him at all, you would take him home and try to sober him up. He's had enough to drink for one night."

"Oh, you did, did you?" the drunken oaf said standing down from his bar stool and measuring himself up against this tiny, irate female.

"Are you insinuating that…?"

"Not insinuating anything." Lulu's indignation ignited. "I'm telling you he'll pass out if he has anything more to drink. Look! He's teetering now!
Quick! Catch him," she shouted, rushing to shore up the bar fly before he hit the floor. Too late. She was too little anyway. He hit the floor with a thud.

The room went silent, apart from Smy who applauded and cheered, having made no attempt to save his drinking mate.

"On yer feet, ye drunken bastard," Smy howled as he poured the rest of Sturge's beer over his head.

"Knew he couldn't hold his liquor," he said in disgust to the landlord who appeared from behind the bar. An anxious crowd huddled over Sturge, who, refreshed by Smy's liquid attentions, opened his eyes, rolled over onto his side and attempted to get onto his knees.

"Leave him. He'll be all right in a minute," his friend assured us.

"Just needs another drink is all," he said, motioning to the bartender to pour them both another pint.

"Shouldn't somebody call an ambulance or something?" Carol demanded, standing up in support of her friend despite my best efforts to hold her back.

"He'll be all right, Ducky," Smy said. "He's always doing that. Another pint and he'll be as right as rain. It's just his way of drawing attention to himself. Leave him alone long enough, and—"

"You brute," Louisa shouted. "He's your friend. Do something for him."

"Not my friend, Ducky. Nooo. Never seen him before in my life. Wouldn't admit to it if I had," he wrangled, as Louisa and Carol took Sturge's arms and helped him back onto a stool. The landlord was on the phone by now behind the bar. When he put the phone down, he re-entered the melee with a cloth to tidy up Sturge's face and jacket.

"Can't be having this," the landlord fretted. "Not in my house. They'll be here in a minute, mate," he said to Smy. "You'd better scarper before they get here."

"Nothing to do with me," Smy said in all innocence. "Somebody I met on the way to the pub. Don't look at me. She's the one set him off," he said, leering at Louisa.

"Dressed like that. No wonder the poor bugger fainted. I told her he was married, but she wouldn't have it."

"What do you mean, the way I'm dressed?"

"Tits hanging out all over the place. Red miniskirt up to your arse."

"Now look here!" Oliver shrieked coming at last to the aid of his woman.

"Bugger off, you shit-face gorilla. I eat the likes of you for breakfast."

"Well. Well. You'd better retract that last statement is all. Or. Or. Or I'll."

"You'll what, Sally?"

"This," Louisa screamed kicking the offensive lout in the nuts.

"There," she said, cleaning her hands over the doubled-up Smy.

"Somebody had to do it," she said just as the two coppers walked in through the door.

"I'd have done him one too…" Carol said later that night, sitting in the police station. "…Given the chance."

"Would you?" I said.

"Well…hit him with my umbrella."

"In the balls?"

"Well…No…P'raps not there. But I felt like hitting him; he was so obnoxious."

Lulu was bound over on her own recognisance to appear before the Beak a week hence. In the meantime, she was not to go anywhere near the plaintiff or his boozy friend or The Rose Tree. Carol was ordered to surrender her umbrella.

"Surrender my umbrella?" she asked on the way out. "Whatever for?"

Things were looking glum the following afternoon as we walked in dead silence through the centre of town.

"What will Daddy say?" Carol said as we turned up Saddler Street.

"Rev Kev!" we said in unison.

"In for a penny…"

Chapter 22
Owengate Realignment

Owengate, a right hand turn halfway up Saddler Street, led to an alleyway that led to a flight of rickety old Dickensian stairs at the top of which a door opened into Errol's scruffy digs. He had agreed to meet us there before taking us all to Castle for dinner that evening. Once again, I didn't know what to expect, either of the dinner or of Errol who by now must have been pissed off with seeing Carol and me together so often. He wouldn't go with us to Rev Kev's Piss Up, said it would be a frightful bore getting the vicar to sign off on our nefarious night in Mary's and wouldn't we rather come to dinner the day after the Piss Up in Castle Great Hall. We decided on both. A meal at Castle would have to be one up on the usual sallow offering at Dunelm House, so leaving Louisa at the bottom of the stairs, Carol and I trumped up three flights to Errol's landing at the top and pushed in through the half open door shouting our hallows.

"Not today! Lunatics," came a strangled shout from his bedroom. Errol flew out, half-naked, hopping on one foot, pulling on jeans and socks and T shirt and shutting the bedroom door behind him with a bang.

"I said tomorrow night, imbeciles."

He fretted a tattered old sweater around his shoulders and ushered us into his dismal little kitchenette, frantically filling a kettle for hot water for coffee.

"What do you mean by breaking in on a fellow halfway through his afternoon kip?" he demanded, annoyed by the apparently unannounced intrusion.

"We thought we were going to dinner tonight," Carol said, turning pink, equally puzzled, sure it had been tonight. She was breathing very heavily and obviously on edge by his weird behaviour.

"Not at all what we expected in the middle of the day, Errol."

"What did you expect then? You know I don't do any work until midnight," he said, aiming this sharpened barb at me as he stirred the boiling water into his instant coffee.

"Dinner, I suppose," Carol shot back, hurt by his repellent attitude.

"Well. You aren't getting any. Come back tomorrow. You're signed in tomorrow."

"Who is signed in tonight, then?" Carol extended her hurt, looking back and forth from me to him and me again.

Strangely, to this question, Errol fell silent.

"Anybody want coffee? Tea?" he said at last, still irritated.

"I think I'd better go then," I said, sensing an unpleasantness and not wanting to end up in the middle of it.

"Me too," Carol said without any hesitation.

What was going on between these two? Something had happened that I was not aware of. Carol simmered while Errol raked through his filthy cupboards for biscuits. Broken bits of crusts and buns came spilling out onto the counter until he spied half a roll of Hobnobs in the back and brought them out.

"Hobnob anyone?"

We left him hopping around the kitchenette, pulling on his second ratty sock and clutching the last of the Hobnobs between his lips.

"Wouldn't want to get in the way of his dinner arrangements," I grumbled on our way down the stairs.

"Could have sworn it was tonight," Carol said, still puzzled over the mix-up.

"Dinner in Castle, I mean," she added.

"He's got other plans…" I said, not wanting to re-open the can of worms, but I couldn't resist adding, "…with whoever he had in his bedroom."

This stopped Carol in her tracks. She was below me on the stairs, and I almost piled into her.

"Hadn't thought of that," came her stunned reply.

"Oh, well," she added. To each his own," she said, recovering somewhat and starting down again, then said with a wicked little giggle, "should we go back and find out?"

But we didn't.

"His business," she said as we gathered up Louisa again at the bottom of the stairs and re-entered the congestion of Saddler Street.

"What do you mean 'his business'?" Lulu asked, struggling to keep up.

129

"How about Mary's for dinner instead?" Carol said, as we marched through the crowds and little cars slowly twisting their way up and down North Bailey.

"What business, Carol? What are you two talking about?"

Not completely sure herself at this point, Carol ignored Louisa's question and pushed on through the crowds.

"If we hurry, we can just about make it before they start serving out the gruel. Mary's gruel is second to none. I have a standing guest pass in halls, and I think they will even let you in, if you promise to behave yourself." Her eyes lit up as she looked back over her shoulder at me to measure the extent of her dig.

"Promise to keep my elbows to myself," I said hopefully. She nodded with a laugh and strode on.

Marching out over Kingsgate Bridge with her long, elegant stride, she called back to me again, "Do you think that, that is what it's all about?"

"What, what is all about?" Louisa persisted, out of breath and beginning to drop back.

"Carol, answer me. What happened up there? What are you two talking about?"

When we got to Mary's dining hall, Carol was told her guest pass would not be needed for me. Adelia had signed out earlier, and her place was made available to me sitting between Carol and the jailbird.

"What do you think was going on back there?" I asked Carol as I settled comfortably onto the bench between the two squabbling beauties.

"Yes," Lulu said, jumping into the fray. "That's what I want to know," she demanded, finally cornering her friend who was not about to say, not now at least, not until she'd had a chance to think things through and fully wind up the jailbird into the bargain.

"Sixpence for the littlest sausage," Carol said, diverting Louisa's attention from Owengate and the consequences that lay there.

"Come on, you two. Ante up."

We each threw our sixpences into a saucer in the centre of the table and waited for the meals to be served.

"What's what about?" Louisa challenged again, leaning around and across me to confront Carol.

"Carol" – she thumped – "tell me."

"Dear, dear," Carol tut-tutted, staring down at her plate.

"Chops again. I so wanted a sausage tonight. Still, the wager stands, and I win because I have the littlest one. See?" she announced triumphantly, stabbing her chop with her fork and holding it up for all to see.

"What's what about?" Louisa persisted.

"HP anyone? Did anyone hear that moan from the jail cells?" Carol asked, digging into her chop.

"It was me," Louisa insisted. "I just want to know what happened."

"Nothing happened," I tried to reassure her.

"Leastways nothing that a convicted felon needs to hear about," Carol said, finishing off her chop.

"Don't believe you. You're always hiding things on me."

"Tell me. Tell me what's happening, you two," she demanded, thumping the table with her fist.

"It's nothing," I said then added, "just Errol having it off with some unknown person in his digs this afternoon. Tried to hide it behind a shower of Hobnob crumbs. But we weren't taken in by it."

Lulu looked scandalised from me to Carol and back again. Shocked to the core, she was speechless and in a bit of a panic.

"I don't understand," she finally blurted out. "You mean right there in front of you?"

"No. No," Carol assured her. "Not in front of us, silly. Before we got there. We caught them at it, as it were. Oh dear. Now we're making it all sound so sordid."

"Oh. Well…Is that all?" Louisa asked, coming to terms with the crisis. "Is that all you're worried about? Thought it must be something important – dead bodies and things."

"What do you mean, 'Is that all'? It's enormous," Carol said.

"Not really. Fair enough, I'd say – after you and Christopher Robin…in Adelia's…A week ago. Y'know."

"Oh, but Lou," Carol whinged.

"No use denying it," Lulu said.

"Turnabout is fair play."

"Fair play?" Carol said crossing her arms and leaning back to have a good old, exasperated sulk.

"But you know as well as anybody what happened in Adelia's," Carol tried to explain.

"I thought you at least would be able to see the foul play today at Owengate, not 'fair'.

"We are innocent; he is guilty. That's all there is to it."

"Innocent of what?" Louisa stuck to her prey like a terrier, sensing that she had Carol now good and proper.

"I mean, you two all afternoon in Adelia's room is innocent, and poor old Errol being found in possession of a hot body this afternoon is guilty? Come along, dearest," Louisa said, "you're just miffed that he's getting his own back…"

"But Louisa, nothing happened here that night. Nothing at all," Carol whispered her ire, not to attract the attention of the entire refectory, never mind the whole college.

"You just don't have a clue, do you? Christopher Robin, tell her," Carol directed.

I hunched my shoulders and nodded in grim support.

"Liars – both of you," Lulu said, finishing her chop.

"No matter what you told Rev Kev, you are a couple of fibbers. Now, eat your dinner before it gets cold. And I don't want to hear another word. I don't know whether you know it or not, but lying to a vicar is a mortal sin."

"Priest, Lou, priest. It's a mortal sin if you lie to a priest," Carol corrected.

"That too. Now eat up or you'll never grow up to be big and strong and get sent to hell for committing a mortal sin by lying to a vicar."

"Now I've heard it all," the doubly exasperated Carol cried out.

"Are you sure you're not just a little bit jealous because Ollie and you are…have never…I mean…er."

"What?" Louisa spun around like a tornado.

"What do you mean by…? Are you insinuating that…?"

"Not insinuating anything. Your own words. His words too, as a matter of fact. Coitus Interruptus, I think he called it."

"Terrible blight," I said. "Coitus … er … thingy."

"Coitus thingy?" Louisa squabbled louder and louder.

"Coitus thingy? Never heard such nonsense." She was now on a mission.

"Oliver and I are …"

"Yes?" Carol waited with bated breath for the reciprocal fib that was about to pop out of Louisa's otherwise chaste lips.

"Well…Oliver and I don't have to be coitus anything as far as you and your precious Rev Kev are concerned. It's our business and none of his … er, yours … his.

"Anybody's for that matter," she explained. Then a little more chastened, she explained, "we get on just fine."

"Good," Carol said sensing victory and not wanting to press it any further, not wanting to hurt.

"Now that we've established that, I must go," Carol said scraping her bench back and standing up.

"Work to do. Essays to write. Holes to fill in."

"What holes, Carol?" Lulu demanded.

"Oh, do stay a bit," she continued. "This is all too upsetting at the moment for it to be left up in the air like this. It's … not like us," she squeaked.

Carol sat down again. "What are you doing this Saturday?" she asked Louisa.

"Don't know. What did you have in mind?"

"Christopher Robin and I are going punting up the river. We thought you might like to join us," she said beaming at me.

"Don't know. We won't have to face the Spanish Inquisition when we're done, will we? Not another Rev Kev moment? What is punting, anyway?"

"Aha," said Carol spying her chance. And she told her the whole story about St Cuthbert and his punts, after which Lulu relented her concerns and agreed to bring a picnic.

"Can Oliver come too?"

"Of course – as long as you promise not to try out your coitus thingy in the middle of the river." Carol laughed.

"Might tip us all in."

But poor old Lulu was confused again and now unsure about the outing until Carol reassured her it was just a joke and not to worry. She wouldn't press her any more on her 'thingy'. But Louisa looked at her doubtfully as if the outing were bound to be full of tormenting innuendo totally out of Oliver's reach.

Chapter 23
Punting Up Thingy Creek

When the day came, there was nothing to worry about, anyway. Neither of them showed up, so Carol and I were left by ourselves at Brown's Boathouse landing stage eying our nautical journey with tremendous anticipation. At least I was. Carol was less sure and entered the wobbly punt with a small degree of dread. I held the vessel firmly to the landing stage and led her gently to her seat on a big cushion amidships.

"I've never done anything like this before," she pleaded, hanging on to both sides of the punt for dear life.

"Don't worry. Neither have I," to which she visibly gulped and held tighter.

"Is it safe? Do I need a lifejacket?"

"Probably not. The river is never more than four feet deep anywhere. If we tip, we can easily walk to shore."

"Oh," she said, still not sure and not really happy about it all until I pushed off aft, jumped into the stern, and started poling us steadily upriver.

"Oh," she said, impressed.

"That's better. Didn't know you were such an expert, you fibber," after which she relaxed and got fully into the adventure watching the world go gently by and relaxing more and more by the minute.

Fifteen minutes into the cruise, just as she was gently lulling, I announced,

"On you left – Fornication Creek."

"Oh!" she said, startled.

"We'll have to give it a miss today, though, if we're going to get our picnic in."

"Oh?" she said.

To this day, I am not sure whether her comment was born of disappointment or relief. Still, I poled on manfully past the creek with Carol gazing into the mouth of that fateful tributary, stretching her neck, I thought, to spy out fornicators on their way in or out.

"Is it really called Fornication Creek? Or are you just once again making things up?" she said hopefully, innocently.

Carol's innocence was a wonder. She was so naive about most things it acted as a barrier you felt you could never dare breach. A perfect foil for would-be assailants who never stood a chance against it. She was so innocent; she was inviolable. I'm not sure she would say this about herself. As a matter of fact, I think she would be pissed off at me for describing her so, but it was the case. Wherever she went, she had this protective dome of innocence that guarded her from churls who might want to have a go. Another reason I loved her so.

"Can't see any?" she said as we navigated past the gnarled old yew tree that marked the entrance to the creek.

"Any what?"

"Fornicators. Must be further in, around the bends. Bother. Maybe ..."

And although she didn't finish her thought out loud, we all know, or think we know, what she was secretly, innocently thinking to herself.

"...having never seen one up close," she said more in disappointment to herself than to the river populace at large.

"After all," she continued her soliloquy, "it isn't every day that you get to see one up close."

I nodded and poled on, now unsure.

"Don't really know what a fornicator looks like," she mused to herself.

"Wouldn't really know one if I saw one at large. Would you, Christopher Robin?"

"What?"

"Know a fornicator if you saw one."

I merely smiled and nodded.

"Oh? Then what do they look like, Mister Smarty Pants?"

"Like anybody, I guess."

"Oh." She smiled away from me and said to the river populace in general, "Like you or I," as matter-of-factly as you want.

"Or any of those people out there," she added.

"Anyone at all," she said, confirming her discovery.

Carol sat in silence for minutes, digesting the enormity of her discovery, then asked, "How far 'til we get to the picnic spot?"

But before I could answer she added, "Can I have a go with the poling thingy?"

"Not bad," I said, moments into her first lesson. "But once you've jabbed the pole into the riverbed, you have to pull it out again."

Carol had left the pole stuck in the mud and let go of it in a panic. We floated aimlessly on for several yards, pole-less and rudderless.

"Bother!" she said, annoyed at me but not saying anything.

"Now what? I could walk back to get it," she offered. "You said it isn't very deep."

I could see she was beginning to panic, so I produced a paddle from under the stern deck and brought us about.

"You might have said." She stamped. "…Didn't know what might happen. Could've sailed over the weir, for all I knew."

"You were getting in a panic," I said.

"No need," I said, reaching out for the stranded pole.

"You had it all under control all the time," she said, finishing my sentence.

"My hero," she said, taking the mickey, regaining the pole and jumping back onto the rear deck. She jabbed her pole in for another go, then heaved us forward, but this time tugged it out just before it stuck.

"There. Got the hang of it now."

"Good. You can take over the helm. I'll just go below decks for a kip. Let me know when you sight land."

"Aye, aye, skipper. I rather like this poling lark. Gives one a sense of accomplishment. Now" – her knees jittered at the end of a push – "all I have to do is steer us away from the bank, and we'll be fine."

We were fine after that. The little smarty pants poled and steered all the way to those shallow rapids just beyond Maiden Castle footbridge.

"Not far from The Rose Tree here," she heaved out of breath but gamely forced the punt onward to the foot of the rippling waters.

"How do we get across that lumpy bit?"

"Portage," I said. "Tie up the punt and travel overland to our picnic spot."

Carol was dubious about the overland bit, but when I pointed to the dell metres away from shore, she brightened and hove-to. She got her plimsolls wet and muddy disembarking but didn't mind a bit. We moved inland to the shade of willows blowing in the breeze and laid out a splendid lunch on a blanket.

"Don't stand in the kitchen," she warned, removing her plimsolls and socks and rolling up the bottoms of her trousers to just below her knees.

"There," she said with glee. "Nice to let the air get to them," she said, lying back and offering her feet to the sun and dozing off.

I busied myself setting out the picnic: boiled eggs, salad, ham baps and some of Franklin's special beer that Leo had recommended.

"Christopher Robin," Carol mumbled some moments later coming out of her doze.

"Why didn't you take me up Fornication Creek? If it's all that special, I mean, I should have had a go in it. Don't you think?"

"Maybe. On the way back, if you like," I said doubtfully, handing her a ham bap.

"What's really up there?"

"People in punts."

"What are they doing up there? Fishing?"

"Something like that."

"Like what? Like fishing?" she said becoming concerned. "What on earth could be like fishing if it's not fishing," she said, peeling a boiled egg.

"I mean," she said in a claggy way with her mouth full of boiled egg, "you are either fishing or you are not – fishing that is."

At this point, I was not going to be drawn. She was either having me on, or she was really the unbelievably innocent creature I had always suspected her of being. And I couldn't burst her bubble. Could I?

What would you have done?

Exactly!

Me too.

"Fornicating, I suppose," she suddenly said, her eyes lighting up with the revelation.

I held my breath.

"Whatever that is," she said, more to herself than the trees.

I breathed again.

"Unless … Unless …" she mused, "… it's some kind of term farmers gave to the creek, an old Durham or Northumbrian name for something agricultural or other. Fishing maybe."

"Yes," I quickly agreed. "That's what I'd heard. Monks named it Fornication Creek after they moved here from Lindisfarne carrying the remains of St Cuthbert."

"I suspected as much," she said triumphantly, nodding her head in agreement with her great discovery. "Probably caught great masses of fish up there using their punts," she said, starting to wobble a bit from the effects of her first pint.

"I'm feeling," she said laying back on the blanket, "decidedly wobbly. Aren't you, Christopher Robin?"

I couldn't really believe it, but I had an angel right there with me on a picnic in the countryside eating boiled eggs and coincidentally supping on Franklin's hyperbolic brew. The responsibility was enormous. What was I going to do?

What would you have done?

Thought so, you dirty beast. But it wasn't that easy, was it? I mean, trust and honour and all that.

I couldn't, could I? Couldn't live with myself if I had. Couldn't if I hadn't. Conundrum.

And so there I was in a dell with the loveliest creature in the world, full of the joys of spring, she writhing asleep on our blanket after knocking back Beau's love potion and me twisting myself inside out in refrain.

Asleep on the blanket, she breathed deeply, angelically, her cherub lips puffing out, her alabaster eyelids closed and body relaxed, asleep and vulnerable to the environs of Fornication Creek.

What else could I do? I pulled the rest of the blanket across her shoulders to keep her warm and awaited events. She was asleep in my charge, and I felt the enormity of the moment, the responsibility, the trust she had placed in me to keep her precious self safe and warm. I brushed a spider away from her hair and touched her cheek, sat beside her, guarding her, waiting for the effects of Franklin's liquor to wear off.

As it happened, I didn't have long to wait, but it wasn't nature that awoke her.

There was a movement on the river. I saw out of the corner of my eye, the image of a punt drifting slowly downstream and around the bend below us with nobody aboard. The bloody fools, I thought. For a second, I was amazed that anybody could be that stupid not to secure their craft to the bankside, but amazement was quickly overtaken by horror when I realised that it was our punt, adrift and slowly heading away from us, gently bumping into bits of branches along the edge of the river but determined to float free.

My eye followed a disturbance in the distance. Two little lads ducked out of sight among the brambles, hissing their heads off.

"Quick, Carol. They've let the bloody punt loose." And I dove in after it up to my waist to haul it back to the bank.

"Bastards," she shrieked after them. "Little buggers. Can't leave us alone a moment to indulge in Mother Nature.

"Hero again," she heckled, as I brought the punt in and tied it back up. "But get out of that water this instant," she mothered. "You'll catch your death. Pity there isn't something you could change into," she said.

"I could turn into a giant eagle and carry you out of this mess."

"Yes," she fussed all serious and grown up.

"That would be nice, but for the moment, we'll have to make do with wringing those jeans out. So, come on. Get them off and hand them over. You can cover up in the blanket until they're dry.

"No, don't worry about your knickers. Get them off as well. We'll have to build a little fire to dry your things – and stop being so coy about it. I have seen men in the buff before, you know.

"No. Stopp it. I insist. Get 'em off and here, wrap this blanket around you if you must," she blushed, handing me the blanket, as I did exactly what I was told.

"Socks as well. Come on. Might as well do the job properly," she ordered, beaming at my ridiculous attempt to hide my naked butt from her secret glances.

"Always wanted to know what a rower's bottom looked like," she said to herself, turning to the business of the fire.

"Now I know," she said in a satisfied kind of way.

"Sinewy," she said later.

"Muscles and sinews," she decided, tending to the laundry.

"You could do with fattening up a bit, in some respects, my lad," she said catching my eye with her ravenous grin.

"But in other ways … you'll do just fine," she said, folding my jeans over a branch above the fire.

"Other ways?" I asked.

"Never you mind. Just cover up before you give me some sort of seizure," she laughed, glancing involuntarily down at my nakedness.

"Every time you look at me ..." she started to remember but stopped herself from looking and instead busied herself with her duty to the drying clothes.

An hour onward, with everything once again intact – including my knickers – we set off downriver again, this time taking advantage of the current. Carol was determined to hone her punting skills, so she was doing the poling.

"See? Nothing to it," she teased. "Much faster with me at the helm."

"That's coz we're going downstream now," I said.

"Rubbish. Admit it. I'm much better at it than you. The bankside is whizzing by now. Look at it," she huffed in acclamation of some kind of superiority. I gave her a desultory, unimpressed nod.

"Soon we'll be at thingy creek. Then we can have a look in. See who else is in there and if they've caught anything or not, or what they're really up to in there, if it's not fishing."

"Believe me, it's not fishing."

"Well, I need to know, so we're going in."

And that was that.

Carol wasn't often demanding, usually quite deferential, accommodating and sweet, but I had learned over time that when she was determined, it was better to give in. Disagreement with her got you nowhere. So, we were going in. In two more bends, we were going in, and God knows what we were about to witness. I steeled myself for the inevitable, but what about Carol's sense of innocent propriety? What would she make of the scenes of depravity that we were going to witness up that iniquitous brook?

I lay back amidships and awaited events.

The sun was out. The afternoon was warming up. Listless, bored undergraduates were afloat, looking for amusement up thingy creek, and that could mean only one thing. But far from being clogged with bored, listless undergraduates looking for amusements, Fornication Creek was at first very disappointing. There was nothing going on at all in the first bit, but rounding the next bend, a punt passed us on its way out. Carol was immediately struck by the condition of the crewmembers. A young, haggard swain was at the helm punting away, and two young ladies lolled in the middle, blouses open, taking the sun, looking thoroughly exhausted.

"Poor bloke," Carol said when we were around the next corner out of earshot, "having to hump all that great female baggage up and down the river. I hope they offer to give him a spell every now and then. Shouldn't leave all the work up to one fella. He looked totally flagged. Did you see him, Christopher Robin? The poor bloke looked absolutely done in."

"Not surprising," I said, "probably comes from doing your duty of a Sunday afternoon."

"Oh, and what exactly does that mean – duty of a Saturday afternoon?"

"Oh, nothing. I agree," I said, quickly backtracking. "Those two must be a ton weight, and it is hot."

"Yes. You should consider yourself lucky that you have such an able-bodied sailor aboard to lump your ruddy great carcase up and down the river. Wonder what's going on up ahead," she said, peering off.

"It's getting very noisy. Must be the rugby fields or something. Surely, it can't be rugby, though, not all the way out here. Maiden Castle is the other way, isn't it?"

Maiden Castle Rugby pitch was in the other direction, and it wasn't rugby Carol heard going on nearby, I could tell you that without even looking.

"All that huffing, and puffing and groaning. Do they do co-ed rugby? Sounds like it's co-educational, whatever it is. Boys and girls together. Mainly women making all the noise, though. Funny …

"We're getting closer, Christopher Robin. Keep a lookout for a good landing spot. I'd like to see this co-educational rugby or fishing or whatever it is that's going on in here. There. Look there. There is another punt up there in that cove. I can see its bow sticking out. Bet they've landed to go and see the rugby. This is getting exciting. A new adventure around every corner."

She strained to urge our craft onward.

"I was right…" she shouted down to me as we neared the stationary vessel, "… there's nobody in it. But it's not tied up. Just floating akimbo. Those little boys again. I'll bet the little buggers have untied it too. Maybe we should come alongside…That's how you say it, isn't it, alongside? Maybe we should come alongside and rescue it for the owners.

I offered to push on past it, but the Good Samaritan at the helm wouldn't hear of it.

"It'll be our good deed for the day. And besides, if that punt gets into the main river who knows where it might end up.

"Getting a bit deeper here. I'm almost losing the pole. Might need the paddle out in a minute."

Dreading the moment we would actually come alongside that punt, I casually let the paddle redirect us on a bypassing manoeuvre, staying just far enough off to maintain its occupants' privacy. But Carol was determined and being the main driver of our punt counteracted against my attempted abortive movement, laughed as in turn we each vied to direct our punt first toward then away from her target.

"Pathetic," she sneered. "You'll never win with that feeble paddle."

"Might be someone in there," I warned. "Don't want to go disturbing somebody else's picnic.

"Don't be silly," she laughed, going up on tiptoes to see. "They won't mind a visit."

"Depends on what they're up to."

"Nonsense. What could anyone possibly be up to way out here in thingy creek that they wouldn't want anybody else seeing? Contraband? Smuggling?"

"There's a lot of it about," I said surreptitiously swinging the bow away from her intended course again.

"Stop doing that, Christopher Robin. You're making it very hard to…Oh. Oh dear," she said and stopped poling.

"There is someone in that punt," she said, shocked at what she thought she'd seen, swinging our punt on a wider track to bypass it, working harder now to leave it in our wake.

"Were they doing…? Were they doing what I thought…" she said, once we were clear of the scene. "…what I thought they were doing?"

"What did you think they were doing? We really didn't get close enough to see anything or anybody; you took us out of there at such a speed. I thought you were going to lend them a hand." I laughed.

"Surely not," she whispered to herself, disbelieving her own eyes.

"I've seen that bloke somewhere before."

She twisted her head sideways trying to bring a recollection forward, trying to remember some someone she had seen before.

"Where have I seen him before?" she said, squinting into the past.

Suddenly, an inkling came through.

"Now I remember. The Rose Tree. Yes, he was at Rev Kev's. It was your friend, the one with the wavy hair – and some girl. I couldn't quite see her face. You know, your friend at the Rose Tree that night?

"Beau? Beau Franklin? I don't…Not Beau, surely?"

"The very same and the girl your Leo was with."

"Not Amanda? Leo will have a fit. What were they up to?"

"It wasn't just snogging, I can assure you of that," she said, affronted by the scene in her mind and sweetly saving me from having to explain.

"Not snogging?" I asked. "If it wasn't snogging…?"

"All I can tell you is that she was…and he was…and…and, well, I'll be blowed," she said in all innocence, breathless at the thought.

"D'you think," she asked, squinting into the sun as we approached a veritable flotilla of punts anchored along both shorelines in the distance with nary a soul to be seen in 'em, seemingly.

"D'you think that's what it means, I mean – thingy creek?"

"Could be," I said gently digging in the paddle and redirecting our punt to turn around to head back out toward the main river. From that day, 'thingy' took on a whole new meaning for me.

But Carol wasn't finished yet.

"What are you doing? No, don't. We must go on. I want to confirm my theory. I want to know," she said.

"Might be best if we gave them a wide birth. You never know who you are likely to see and what they might be up to," I warned.

But Carol wouldn't be put off. As we approached and silently drifted by the first of six other punts gently rocking on that quiet tributary, she was at first mesmerised then amused and finally devastated by what we saw.

Her first comment was a breathless, "Out here in the open like this?"

Further along, "Better not go any farther."

"Goodness, I know her – and him – Rob. It's Rob and Clarissa. Both bare bottomed."

From the last observation of the very last punt came her most dramatic revelation, one that almost knocked her off the rear deck altogether. Her eyes were wide open in horror as she stepped down amidships, totally stunned. I gingerly took the pole from her limp hands and sat her down, lest she fell overboard in her trancelike state. I took over the poling and from that point took us back along the creek with Carol still reeling from what she had last seen back in the flotilla. She sat quietly going over and over the images in her head, making sure. When finally she caught her breath again, I was poling us out into the river, bringing the bows around to take full advantage of the stream.

Carol was still gasping for breath and almost in tears but didn't share her news until we were well downstream and almost parallel to Cuth's landing stage again. Managing to control her breathing with deep even breaths, she cast her saddened gaze back several days.

"Adelia," she simply squeaked.

I nodded in sympathy. She sniffed back a few tears.

"And Errol."

"It must have been Adelia in his room with him all the time. That's why she hadn't come to Mary's dinner with us. She was dining on Errol at Castle that night."

She struggled in silence with her emotions, then blew her nose, cleared her head, but then her eyes brightened again and looked clearly ahead.

"I'm glad we saw it," she said decisively.

"Yes. I am glad. Better that than going on in total ignorance, expecting one thing and knowing another. I guess I've been aware of something going on ever since Michaelmas last year, but I've never really been able to accept it."

"Do you think they saw us?"

"They were pretty well occupied," I said, and she took that as the truth, turning to look ahead down the river, shivering now in the light breeze that had come up.

I was really pissed at myself and blamed myself for her heartache, but on the way back downstream, she absolved me of any guilt, telling me that it was best we had both seen it.

Great, you might think. Get stuck in while the time is ripe. But not so fast. Hold on a minute. Winning by default was not going to be the same as winning by fair play, and I still had some way to go before being assured of any winning at all. So, I wasn't really any happier for myself to see Errol and Adelia bums up in that punt. I felt really bad that Carol had to witness it at all.

Complicated.

Hellish.

Carol was in a state, despite her rationalisation of things. So was I. It's always hard to end a relationship – even if your partner is acting like a real jerk. When I took her back to her digs, she was still shivering a bit. Not from the cold – because it was still a lovely afternoon – but from the shock, I guess.

Chapter 24
Mrs Manners' Sausage

Beau Franklin leaned in through the office door. "Er, Mrs Manners, might I have a word?"

"Of course, young man. What seems to be the trouble?"

"There's someone in my room who won't leave."

"Deary me. Is he ill?"

Beau was in a sweat.

"Still asleep. Won't move."

"Dead perhaps," Mrs Manners offered in jest, but Beau wasn't jesting.

"Is he breathing at all, dear?"

"Can't really say. Is there any way you could get the porter to come up and shift her? She's a ton weight. Might need a crane. Can't shift her at all by myself. Big boned lass. Don't want to leave her there all day. Never know what she might get up to. She has a bit of a reputation."

Mrs Manners looked the feverish student up and down and said, "She? That's different. The porter won't touch a female student with a barge pole. No. We'll have to think of something else, dear. Allan could lose his job. What on earth were you thinking inviting her up in the first place?"

"Didn't. She was there when I woke up. Could've sworn I left her at the Shakespeare last night. Came back with the lads and went to bed by me sel'."

"That must have been a hardship for you, dear," Mrs Manners noted with raised eyebrows.

"Ooh, that Beau," Elizabeth salivated after he had left the office, pouring herself another sherry. "Lovely lad, don't you think, Olive? I mean … well … he is, isn't he?"

"Trollop," was Mrs Manners' jaundiced reply.

"Surely, no, Olive."

"Can't see any good in a boy who wears his trousers that tight."

"Ooooh, I can," Lizzie enthused, rubbing her hands together. "You've changed your tune on him since, Olive. What's up wi' you?"

"Nothing's the matter with me, pet. He is pretty, I'll give you that, Lizzie, but judging by the company he keeps, not very bright."

This confused Lizzie, who said, "He keeps the company of just about every female undergraduate in the university. There must be some good 'uns in all that lot. They can't all be wrong 'uns."

"Oh, they're right about that, Lizzie. He does have a nice bottom," Mrs Manners mused, casting her mind back to his visit. "But the poor lad has no self-control, no sense of discrimination. He's anybody's. You can have him for the price of a pint of Exhibition in The Vic."

"Oh, I see. Have you … er … ever … er … had him, Olive?"

"Course not, Lizzie, dear. Course not. I'm much too old for the youth. Besides which, I can see right through him. Wouldn't be much of a catch if I did, or you, for that matter, Lizzie. So you can stop dribbling like that.

"And you can take that childish smirk off your face right now, my girl," she said, casting her eyes out through the window onto the back lawn.

"This younger generation," she sighed. "All they see in life is fun, fun, fun. They don't know they're born."

When Mrs Manners left the college later that morning, she stepped out into a picture postcard world. She inhaled it all deeply.

"Beautiful," she said, stretching up her arms as she stepped into the sunny, cobbled lane outside Number 12.

The air was still tranquil and fresh after an early morning shower.

Cathedral bells were just finishing ringing quarter to eleven.

The narrow lane wound up and away from her to her right. Edwardian and Victorian splendour merged at the top of a slight bend with majestic walls along the left side that led into town past the cathedral. St Chad's and St John's colleges ran away from her on the right, and the magnificent cathedral towers rose high over the entire town. She hurried on this morning, though, absorbing the quiet beauty of the town, dodging students who were trickling off to lectures, full of busy, full of talk. She was oblivious of their cares and woes, bent on one task this morning: getting into the marketplace on time then meeting her friend for coffee.

We've been in the marketplace before. Remember? It's where the Town Hall disco was held back chapter eight. This morning it was just as busy, busy with tables full of local merchandise. Out of its centre reared the grand statue of the Marquess of Londonderry aboard his magnificent, dirty-green, bird-shit-spattered stallion.

Olive Manners picked her way carefully from stall to stall, pouring over much the same merchandise she had seen there over most of the years of her life, but the chance of coming across something new was an exciting prospect to her, and so she walked slowly among the stalls. Campbell's had a new line in wrist watches which she took considerable time over, nodding hello to the girl behind the table, moving on casually from watches to Baxter's Pies and Cakes. She lingered over the tingling, warm pastry aroma of freshly cooked crisp meat pies.

"I think I'll have a pork pie for tea," she said to the lady behind the table.

Mrs Baxter dropped a pie into a small white packet and asked if there would be anything else.

"Two almond slices, please," Olive said, feeling particularly naughty this morning. She took one straight out of the packet to nibble on while walking around the rest of the market.

"Lovely day, Mr Thompson," she offered the portly fruiterer who beamed and tipped his cap.

"Fresh apples in today, Mrs Manners. Fresh in this morning. Juicy and crisp."

"I think Mrs Blenkinsop is coming down later this morning, Mr Thompson, to give you the college's order for the week. She's looking for gooseberries for a crumble she's got planned for tomorrow's tea."

"Right you are, Olive. There's her box in the back all ready for her, tell her. I'll add the gooseberries to save time. Nothing like gooseberry crumble," he said, tipping his cap again. Olive returned the smile, feeling a strange thrill charge through her body at Mr Thompson's use of her first name. Looking back at him as she moved on, she caught his admiring gaze resting on her rump and secretly raised her eyebrows at the thought. Although, what you would call oversized, Mr Thompson, recently a widower, had a kindly manner, a jolly smile and a nice new Rover parked around the back of the Town Hall.

Worth a chance, she admitted to herself on her way to the butcher's. A lass could do a lot worse in this day and age.

"Lovely day, Mr Gamble," she said to the moustachioed butcher whose back was momentarily turned to her, fixing a cut of pork on the back table.

"If you could slice the fat off that lovely chop, please, I'll have it for my tea tomorrow."

"Right you are, Mrs Manners," he said offering up the finished product for her inspection.

"Lovely," she said fishing in her purse for the exact change.

"Oh, and I was wondering, could you do me a nice piece of beef for the weekend. There'll be four of us?"

"Do you? DO you? Of course, I'd love to DO you, madam." The butcher smirked with his usual sly, cheeky grin. And then quickly added, "Oh you mean a roast, Mrs Manners. Sorry. Thought you might be referring to something else, err…some other service I could offer," he chuckled at his joke.

"No, thank you, Mr Gamble," she said blushing at his brazenness. "Not today, thank you very much."

"Comes at no extra cost, mind, Mrs Manners," he pressed, his moustaches bristling up at the corners in licentious invitation.

"I'm sure it's lovely, Mr Gamble, but some other time, thank you very much," she said, all a-flutter. She took his brown paper bag and on her way over to the trinket stall peeped inside and laughed. There in the bag poking its head rudely out of the top was one of Mr Gamble's huge pork sausages, unsolicited, unpaid for, yet gratefully received.

Hearing her reaction to his gift, Mr Gamble roared with laughter and blew her a kiss across the way. Startled pigeons flew up from the statue of the Marquess of Londonderry and shat some more on its head. Olive grinned back at Mr Gamble, wagged her finger and mouthed, 'Cheeky boy' at him.

"You're miles away today, Olive," the grey-haired lady behind the trinket stall said, as Mrs Manners handled several toys without really seeing them, put them down and moved on absent-mindedly to other amusements.

"Err what?" she eventually said, but even then didn't actually say it to Mrs Bedford.

"Sorry, Constance. Miles away."

"Yes," Constance said sympathetically.

"I saw that look in your eye."

"What look, Constance? What did you see?" Olive said gingerly putting down a large candle lest Mr Gamble saw her holding it. She moved along again, still dazed and breathless from the butcher's lewd attentions.

"Don't be offended by him, Olive. It's just his way," Constance said, nodding over at the butcher's stall. "He'll try it on one day and be nice as pie the next…"

"Oh," Olive said quickly, covering her embarrassment.

"No! Doesn't bother me in the least. Not at all. No! Sorry for wandering off, Constance," she said in a rush.

"Did you think…? Just wondering how Bunny's getting on with her new fella. Can't be too careful these days, can you?"

Constance nodded, then turning her head quizzically, said, "Then again, Olive, you can be too careful sometimes, as well, pet. Can't you?"

Mrs Manners didn't really follow what Constance meant; her mind was still on the inspirational gift the butcher had added to her shopping. She peeked into the bag again, and her heart rate soared.

"Fancy!" she said to herself. "Mr Gamble!"

"That's better," Constance said noticing an old lightness returning to Mrs Manners' step and her improved posture as she wandered off. Next stop, the indoor marketplace that filled the gloomy catacombs below the Town Hall. Smiling and nodding good morning to one and all, Olive Manners floated into that crowded, musty, darkened interior.

Caged parakeets, stalls full of old records, more pies and cakes, all manner of antiquity filled every recess, too interesting to resist. But today, Mrs Manners saw none of it. Her blood was up and she was strangely aware of people staring. As she approached them and as she walked away from them, they watched her. Their eyes were on her as never before, on her radiant face, her squared up shoulders, her mischievous breasts, never before so perky, pointing the way, and on her tight, beckoning rump.

"Silly old woman," she mouthed to herself as she re-emerged from the darkness some moments later, further along the marketplace. She had bought nothing more in there, choosing rather to cuddle the thoughts of Mr Gamble's compliments to her racing heart.

"Silly, silly old woman," she said as the light of day hit her in the face once again. Suddenly remembering why she had come to town in the first place, she quickly tripped across the top of the market square and then down Silver Street to a little teashop at the foot of that steep hill. As she arrived outside Hall's, the teashop at the bottom, the bells of the cathedral were just striking 11:45.

Not late. Not yet. Time to compose herself and order her coffee before Bunny got there in fifteen minutes. She found her usual table in the back corner with a view out over the river and Framwellgate Bridge reaching out across it, settled her handbag in the chair next to her, removed her scarf and jacket and sat in her usual seat next to the windows along the back wall. As she casually watched the towpath that ran along this side of the river, two young women came into view then skipped out of view up the steps that would bring them onto Framwellgate Bridge at Silver Street. Seconds later, the teashop doorbell rang admitting those two same impeccably dressed young women. They spied an empty table at the back of the shop and edged their way toward it, wrangling with each other as they slid between chairs and tables.

With due deference to the lady who would have to move her chair back to let her in, the taller of the two young women smiled graciously and nodded her thanks. Olive pulled over a little to let her pass. The other, littler student, a pretty, bouncy brunette, smiled as well.

"Lovely day," the brunette smiled and nodded enthusiastically to Olive who smiled back.

"Pull your knees in, Carol, you great oaf, so I can get by too."

The taller girl, a glorious red head, feigned exasperation, blew a swath of hair away from in front of her face and said in mock irritation, "There. Is that enough room, or should I sit out on the veranda? That might make enough room for your enormous hips."

Mrs Manners secretly hoped not, for she liked these two, their friendly abuse, their nicely tailored clothes, their cheery faces and beautiful smiles. The smaller girl, whom Mrs Manners didn't think bulky in the least, apologised for her friend by rolling her eyes heavenward. She settled herself gracefully into her chair then busied herself with the tea menu. Her face in concentration was remarkable.

A friendly squabble ensued between them over what to get, what was healthy and what was not.

The tall one finally said decisively, "Tea cake – toasted – for me and a pot of tea.

"You?"

"Buttered scone. And I'll share your pot, if you don't mind. Don't feel particularly thirsty this morning."

"Well, I am. Thirsty. So you'll have to get your own pot, I'm afraid," her friend said returning to the menu.

The bell on the teashop door rang again, a cheerful note. Mrs Manners' head turned expectantly and her smile broadened. She sat up straight.

"I thought you'd never get here," she teased as her friend approached their usual place at the back of the room.

"Almost didn't," her friend said, squeezing onto her usual chair.

"Bus was late," she puffed out of breath.

"Had to run along North Street. And then, the police at yon end of the bridge wouldn't let us cross for the longest time. Awful to-do. There was an ambulance and all sorts. Police cars."

The students at the next table pricked up their ears at the drama, as Mrs Manners' friend slid into her chair.

"Can't stay long, Ollie. Doctor's appointment. Not far. Just back over the bridge. But still. You'll have to fill me in on the run."

The two old friends chatted excitedly while the waitress hovered over orders, disappeared then reappeared with their traditional coffees and biscuits. By this time, they were on to the nuts and bolts of life. Olive was telling Bunny about her adventures in the market square this morning.

Unable to miss the story, and yet not wanting to appear nosey, the two students smiled politely at each other at first, poured their teas and chomped their snacks. The taller girl looked up when Olive reached the part about Mr Gamble's massive sausage and reached over to press the other's arm when she showed signs of splurting out loud.

"Lou, stoppit. You mustn't," Carol hissed under her breath, putting her other hand to her own lips in order to stifle herself.

"You mustn't...We mustn't...You can't." But finally catching Louisa's eye and the look of impish glee there, she burst out herself in an uncontrolled roar. They looked at each other.

Another squalid outburst.

A second of silence then they both fell about each in a pile of pure joy, each covering the other's mouth and shshshshshshing the other – but to no avail.

When they finally regained control of themselves and looked across at the other ladies in order to apologise for their rudeness, they found Olive and Bunny convulsed in a similar pile of laughter, each trying to stifle the other just like Carol and Lulu.

"Stop...no...stoppit, Bunny. You'll do yourself an injury.

"Please...don't...you'll have me splitting my hernia open if you go on like that."

"Serves you right, you awful trollop. Imagine behaving like that in the middle of the marketplace."

"I...

"I wasn't, Bunny. I wasn't misbehaving at all. It's...just...that..." she tried to say looking like she was trying to stifle a sneeze. But it wasn't a sneeze. She held it for a second, but then they both convulsed again in side-splitting laughter.

"Poor Mr Gamble. Can you imagine, Ollie?"

"No, I can't and so shouldn't you, and," Ollie said, with a twinkle in her eye, throwing her laughter at the audience of two in the corner. "...And you two young ladies should be ashamed of yourselves for the thoughts going around in your young heads."

"The very idea," Bunny said, needing to find someone to castigate. "...and put that thing out of sight, under the table or somewhere. Disgusting."

"No," Olive insisted, standing up for herself. "It warrants a prominent place," she said, sticking it right in the middle of the table for all to admire. "It's a reminder of an amorous moment I'll probably never have again, ever. I'm going to have it stuffed and mounted above my fireplace as a kind of ..."

"... kind of ..."

"... trophy," Louisa blurted out, pleased to have found just the right word, then hiding again behind her friend, lest everyone thought her a trollop too.

"Thank you," Mrs Manners demurred as the two young ladies stood up to leave.

"I think I'm going to go up to that butcher's right now," Louisa said to Carol on their way out, "and see if he'll give me one of those trophies too."

"Not likely, Shorty," Carol said looking back and downward. "Anyway, he probably saves the best ones for his taller girlfriends. Yours will be a chipolata. Mark my words. And be grateful that it's nothing more."

"Wonderful talking point though, C. Interesting centrepiece. Just think of the admiring looks you'd get around the dinner table."

"I could think of more noble talking points," Carol replied as the doorbell rang again to let them out.

"Like what?" Louisa asked hot on her heels.

But Bunny and Olive couldn't hear the reply, for just at that moment, the door to the teashop banged shut again, and they were out of range, legging it up Silver Street toward the marketplace.

Chapter 25
Bumps

"Look. There he is," Louisa said with an intake of breath. She exhaled slowly, focussing on her be-whiskered prey in the middle of the marketplace.

"Doesn't he make you feel all tingly inside?" she said scrunching her shoulders up.

Carol appeared doubtful. She was looking at a middle-aged, portly butcher with a bristly moustache and stripy apron going about his daily work, serving customers in an efficient and friendly manner.

"He's like one of those stags you see in the newsreels. You know. High on a Scottish Glenside, lord of all he purveys, dangerous-looking. You know," Lulu urged.

"Ready for the rutting season. All his concubines hovering expectantly around him."

"'Surveys', Louisa, dear. It's 'surveys' not 'purveys', although he is a purveyor of meat, if that's what you mean.

"You are getting a bit out of hand with all this talk of rutting and male dominance. I do hope you are in full control of your hormones before we go any closer.

"This isn't going to mean another visit to the police station, is it? Because if it is, you can get somebody else to bail you out this time."

"Course not. I'm in full control this time, but he does make you feel all tingly inside, doesn't he? Don't know why. He just does."

"I know why, Lou. And I think you and I should have a little talk, if you can manage to drag yourself away from your new, aged Lothario long enough," Carol said, taking her friend by the hand and tugging.

"No! No! Not yet," Lou protested.

153

"Look. He's putting something into a little packet, and look, Carol, he's giving it to that woman."

"It's his livelihood, Lulu. That's what he does for a living."

"Yes, but…Don't you think it's fascinating? Don't you want to know what he's putting into their packets? He might be doing the same thing to them that he did to that nice lady in the teashop. Look. There goes another one…

"I'm going over there…"

"No. Look. Louisa. You cannot go around searching through everyone's shopping that gets served by that butcher. You just cannot…Very unwise."

But Lulu was adamant and instead of directing her friend away from a most embarrassing scene, Carol found herself yanked bodily in the other direction toward the woman who had just been served by Mr Gamble and who was now browsing in front of the trinket stall.

Suddenly, Mrs Turnbull, for that was the name of the butcher's latest conquest, found herself standing beside a small, pretty young woman dressed in a nicely tailored mini skirt suit looking up at her earnestly like a little girl who might want some spending money.

"You don't know me…"

Just as suddenly, there came an uproar from the young woman's friend who had been standing in the background.

"Lou, no you cannot. Stop it. Come here," and yanked her back and away from Mrs Turnbull with, "I'm sorry, madam. You'll have to excuse Louisa. She hasn't been feeling at all well today." And shshshshed and tugged and bullied her squalling friend away from Mrs Turnbull's shopping bag.

"No…but…Carol…I just wanted to see if she had an enormous sausage or a chipolata in her bag. It's not too much to ask. Is it?" she complained, then turning for help to Mrs Turnbull asked, "Is it?"

"It's neither," said the shopper subduing her shock at the interruption and opening the butcher's packet to show the disturbed young lady.

"Brisket for today's tea," she said opening the packet she had received from the butcher. "See? Oh, dear," Mrs Turnbull emitted.

"There must be some mistake. I didn't order that. "Dear, oh dear," she said turning back to retrace her steps to the butcher's stall.

"I didn't order that at all. Mr Gamble," she called over to the butcher before actually reaching him.

"There must be some mistake. I didn't ask for a whole salami, and I certainly can't pay for it."

"Did you see the look on her face?" Louisa asked in a hush from behind the safety of the statue in the middle of the market square. Upon the discovery, they had edged out of the way lest the police become involved again. Lulu's record couldn't stand another conviction for disorderly conduct so soon after the last one.

"Seems to me she should have been grateful for a little extra in her shopping. Like an unexpected Christmas present," Louisa said.

"She looked utterly gruesome. No gratitude at all for his little surprise," she added.

"More like a land mine, than a present," Carol said, leading the way down across Elvet Bridge where they stopped for a minute to admire the river traffic racing by beneath them.

The water was placid, and being Wednesday afternoon, full of college rowing boats, plying their way bravely downstream directly underneath the two admiring young women.

Louisa dropped a small pebble into the river and watched as the rings spread outwards. Suddenly, a fierce looking boat appeared from under the bridge directly below them, ruining Louisa's ripples and surging onward to the grunts and roars of the rowers in the boat.

"Look," Louisa cried out. "They've ruined my artwork."

"Can't expect them to stop and go around just because you threw a pebble into the river. Here," Carol said, handing her another pebble.

"Wait 'til it's calm again and have another go."

But just as the first boat was clearing out of the way, another came roaring through from under the bridge, yards behind the first and gaining on it fast.

"They're going to crash," Carol, whose arms were dangling over the bridge wall, cried out. The warning was unheeded by both boats.

"Somebody do something," Louisa shouted.

"I just did," Carol replied.

"Oh, get out of the way and let them past," she shrieked over the side of the bridge at the pending collision.

But neither boat altered its course. Neither seemed to want to. The lead boat held tight to the bank and the second looked determined to crash into its rudder.

It could have easily pulled out and gone around but seemed bent on the destruction of both boats.

"They're going to crash," Carol yelled out in a panic, leading Louisa down the stone steps at the side of the bridge to the towpath at the bottom and along the river toward the emergency.

"Do you think they'll sink?" Louisa gasped several steps behind her faster, longer-legged friend.

"Someone might need mouth to mouth," Louisa panted, picking up speed at the thought of all those hearty, young, half-naked men depending on her life-giving skills and sped on past Carol at a gallop. Expecting to see the river littered with floating bodies and shattered boats, they both quickly pulled to a stop at Hatfield landing stage where, sadly, both boats were neatly parked and the steaming survivors stepping out of them, very much alive, back onto dry land.

"Oh," Lou emitted, disappointed that everyone was in good health and standing or sitting about the place with nary a broken limb. Some were happy and congratulating each other. Others were out of sorts with each other.

"Anybody hurt?" Carol asked, confused by the general good health among the rowers.

"Doesn't anybody need any mouth to mouth?" she asked, grinning at Louisa.

"My friend is more than ready to try out her Red Cross First Aid course on anybody who needs it," she offered.

Surpassing the surprise of the would-be rescuers were the looks on the faces of the closest group of the athletes who squinted their disbelief at Carol's offer and shook their heads at the damage that had just been done to their egos and also at the appalling ignorance of the two young ladies.

"Oh, fuck off," one dejected soul was heard to say. He had red hair.

"You fucking bastard, Franklin," he continued his rowers' lament.

"Of all the pissing times to catch a crab, you had to go and catch the mother of all fucking crabs just before we got to bloody Elvet Bridge. We were well around that bend with lengths on Castle. Why couldn't you wait until we got through the fuckin' bridge?"

"He thought we'd be better off going through Hard Arch instead of Easy, that's why. Didn't you Beau?" The stunned cox of the crew stormed in.

"Well, aye, lads," a nonplussed Beau Franklin replied. "Seemed to me the race was grossly unfair up until that point. We were miles ahead. Anyroads, I looked up and saw a couple of bonnie lasses cheerin' at us from the top of the bridge up there, and it wasn't so much a crab as a wave at me fans. Seemed like a good idea at the time, Tucker. And look. It was. There they are," the delighted, unintentional saboteur said, eying up the young ladies on the towpath.

"Well, that's a nice thing to say," Lulu said to the remark from the crewmember furthest away from them, the one with the red hair.

"After all, we were very anxious about you crashing into each other and sinking. You have no idea…"

The same dejected, red-haired young man who was furthest away from them sitting on the towpath wall, head hanging between his knees, said, "Crashing? Fucking Hell. We weren't crashing," he said, lifting his head.

It was Leo Tucker – you may already have guessed.

"We were well in the lead. Ready to bump that Castle crew until this daft pillock here saw you two and decided to throw in the towel for the chance of a bit of easy skirt."

"A bit of easy skirt?" Carol gasped.

"A bit of skirt? You ought to be damn well pleased somebody was willing to run down here and fling herself into the river to save your ungrateful, worthless carcase. Never mind a bit of easy skirt," she stormed, totally outraged by Leo's rude observations.

"Daft bint," Leo was heard to utter under his breath.

"What?" the outranged Carol continued.

"What was that you just said? What did he just say about me?" she railed, grilling her friend who, it must be said, was getting rather close to Big Beau Franklin and gazing up at his muscly bits in wonder.

"Never mind that one, Louisa. What did this one just say about me?" Carol demanded, closing in on the accused. "I remember him. He was at the Rose Tree that night, wasn't he? Leo, I think his name is. Yes, I remember now, it is Leo."

"He just said he was very grateful to you, Miss, for offering to risk all to drag his unworthy carcase out of the river," Archie, the fourth member of the crew, the boat club captain and the only really sensible one in the boat, said smiling and hoping Leo would shut up.

"Let's get back to the boathouse, lads. Nothing more for us here," Archie said pulling first at Leo then Beau and Carl and herding them back towards their boat.

"The novices should be through here any minute. We wouldn't want them to witness this debacle now, would we?"

"Err yes," said Leo, remembering the novices. "We'll tell 'em we bumped Castle and that we're just on our way back to the boathouse to celebrate.

"Excuse us, ladies," he said, dodging past the two women on the landing stage.

After pulling Louisa away from the clutches of beautiful Beau, Carol was heard to ask her friend further on down the towpath what a 'daft bint' was. Louisa could only feign ignorance at first, but when pressed again halfway up Kingsgate Bridge steps, revealed, "Bint? Oh. Bint. Some sort of umpire in a rowing race, or something. Doesn't matter, really. He wasn't your type at all. Too thin. Now my one, The Honey One, the one with the muscles and wavy hair and—"

"Gooey eyes?"

"Yes, the one with the ever so romantic eyes. The Honey One. Nicer boy altogether."

"Nicer? You say nicer? I would have said he is definitely one to steer clear of if history is anything to go by," Carol said.

"You know this boy?" Louisa asked.

"You mean The Honey One? Saw him the other day in a punt up Thingy Creek with the thin one's girlfriend doing the most friendly things to him. Right there. Right out in the middle of the creek where everyone could see."

At this news, Louisa linked arms with her friend. As they crossed Kingsgate Bridge on their way to Dunelm House, her ear was cocked for a full report.

"You didn't tell me you and Christopher Robin were out punting. Why wasn't I invited?"

Carol didn't have the heart to remind Louisa that she had been invited, but the date had been changed – for personal reasons, reasons Carol would have found difficulty in explaining. Nevertheless, Carol relayed all the gory details of the punting afternoon and revelled in a kind of wicked notoriety for her part in it.

"Yes. Well," Louisa hesitated.

"Well, what?"

"Well, what were you and Christopher Robin doing up Fornication Creek in the first place? I've a mind to tell Rev Kev. Or better still, your father. The very idea! Carol! You up there with anybody is a total scandal."

"Was it? It was an innocent diversion, surely. Totally innocent. Not his fault. He would have punted right past the place, but I said I wanted to see.

"Well," she tried to explain. "Well. Err. Just to see what it was like in there."

"And was it?" Lulu interjected.

"Was it what?"

"You know…All hedonism and bras and knickers flung into the trees and…and everything. You said you saw The Honey One with a girl doing indecent things to each other in there."

"Not really to each other. He looked like he was rather enjoying being done to by her. He was on the receiving end. Totally."

"And she?"

"She looked like she was working jolly hard on his behalf."

"His behalf? What do you mean she was working on his behalf?"

"His…You know…"

The beleaguered Lulu strained hard to understand her friend's deliberately obtuse references.

"No, Lou, that's not what I meant…" Carol said, doing her best to explain.

"His anatomical behalf?" Lulu said trying to clarify things.

"Well. If you want to look at it that way, I suppose you could call it that. Yes, metaphorically his anatomical behalf. If that's what you want to call it. I would've called it something entirely different, but, yes, you might want to call it that. If you like. Figuratively, that is.

"Very clever, Lou," Carol went on. "You made a pun or something. Have to ask Christopher Robin about it. He does English. He's good at words and double entendres and the meaning of things."

"I do English too, you know, Carol," Louisa said, a bit disgruntled at being passed over in this matter of semantics in her specialised field.

"Do you? Oh, I'd never have known it, Lulu," Carol teased.

"Well," the beleaguered, flustered girl said, "at least I would have known what Fornication Creek meant and never gone up it in a punt with a bloke in the first place."

"Oh?"

"Yes. You were very lucky, my girl."

"Oh?" Carol asked in a superior, knowing sort of way that made Louisa think for a second or two then blurt out:

"Carol!"

"Not as green as I'm cabbage looking?" Carol laughed with that twinkle in her eye.

"You evil thing. I can definitely see another visit to the Reverend Kevin in your future."

Chapter 26
The Weir

Without direct access down to the river, the ambulance had to stop at the end of Framwellgate Bridge on the other side of the river across from Hall's Tea Shop. Beneath the bridge, an empty rowing boat, a sculling boat, had been spotted well off, circling aimlessly in a whirlpool. The river eventually released it, and it drifted to shore where a couple of hearty young men waded out knee deep and dragged it to the bankside, its oars still in place and seemingly unaffected by its terrifying ordeal.

The traffic across the bridge had been stopped by police in both directions while the medics on a lifesaving mission hustled back and forth along the path between the weir upstream and the bridge. A few rubbernecking spectators followed them upstream along the towpath to the original scene of an accident – a man halfway along the weir, clinging to a snagged tree on the top of it and screaming for help.

His cries could barely be heard above the roar of the water crashing some ten feet below him on the downriver side of the weir. Interest gathered at both ends of the weir as students shouted encouragement and instructions to a man stranded out in the middle of the weir hanging on desperately to it and to life itself. The ambulance men stood around aimlessly at the Durham School end of the weir waiting for their scuba diving colleagues to arrive with a rubber inflatable dingy. On the cathedral side opposite, two impeccably dressed young women in miniskirts made their way along the tow path towards the teashop, oblivious to the drama taking place in the middle of the river. No one seemed worried that the victim clinging to the top of the weir might at any minute be swept over it to his death.

Above the far side of the river, the same side that the two young women walked along, the towers of Durham Cathedral rose imperiously into the clouds.

"Come on, Reggie, ya plonka," one bespectacled spectator shouted impatiently from the cathedral side.

"Get a move on. Don't take all day. Bloody well swim for it."

But it was all Reggie could do to hang onto the lifesaving tree that was balanced precariously atop the weir. Swimming in any direction would have swept him over and to his death. The current surging over the centre of the weir was a foot deep, enough to lift him up and push him bodily over the edge, should he let go of his tree.

"Rather not, Specky, old pal," Reggie shouted back apologetically to shore. His toffee-nosed tone was cordial with just a tinge of shiver to it.

"Don't think I'd make it against this stream," he yelled back. His head just barely above water, he was holding onto his tree with one hand and treading water with the other.

"Bloody good thing this tree's here," he burbled.

"Yes, you can," Specky, his mate, whinged. "Course you can. Only a few bloody feet."

"Rather not," Reggie shouted back politely. "Sorry. Better to wait for help."

"Well," Specky said dolefully looking about the place at the ambulance men standing about on the far side of the river, chatting and having well deserved fags after their helter-skelter rush along the towpath, "there's not much help around here," he said, peering up and down the river. "Not unless the fire department show up with their ladders. Think you'll have to swim for it. That lot don't seem to be much use. Not very interested. Wouldn't want to be on that bloody tree when it goes over the top."

"Not much chance of that. It seems pretty stuck," Reggie said trying to emit confidence.

He gave a sudden yelp as the tree moved several feet further across the top of the weir.

"Thought I was done for there," he said in a more forlorn, lonely voice.

"You still there, Specky?"

"Yeh, but not for long. Got things to do, Reg. Can't wait around here much longer waiting for you to make your bloody mind up.

"Reg.

"Reg!"

"Sorry. Sorry. Just getting a better hold on this branch. It moved just then, Specky. Did you see it?

162

"Specky.

"Specky!"

"Yeh, yeh. Keep your shirt on. I'm still here. Many wouldn't be, though."

"Specky." The pitch of Reggie's voice rose higher and higher as he felt the tree moving again across the top of the weir.

"Don't think I can last much longer here, Specky. Can't you get a rope or something. I noticed a life ring in a box back up the river by Prebend's."

"That ring was stolen ages ago. Wouldn't work anyway. Rope's too short," Specky shouted louder, for the wind had suddenly picked up and was now driving down the river buffering against the top branches of Reggie's tree.

"The life ring is on a wall in Del Fuego's room," Specky continued to explain. "Looks good. I'm pissed off I didn't think of it first. He's got two of them in there. Fancies himself a bit of a collector of Durham memorabilia."

A moment passed while Reg worked up the temerity to ask, "Specky. Think you could go and ask Carlos for the use of one of his life rings? Timmy Bickerstaff could put a longer rope on it."

"Naw. Not much point now. Your tree will be over the top and you with it long before I got back."

The tree shifted ominously again just to lend truth to Specky's point.

Then, suddenly, something wonderful happened. A rowing boat appeared out of the corner of Specky's eye. A four with a cox in it was backing down to the weir and Reg. The novice crew in the boat struggled with the backing down, some catching their blades, others missing strokes altogether in their panic to get to their friend. Colin in the bows manfully attempted to keep the boat straight. They all knew that if their boat turned sideways to the current, it would become unmanageable and would eventually be forced sideways onto the weir and over it.

"What the fuck!" was all Specky could emit.

The novice four had entered the 'pool' below Prebend's Bridge from upriver and was now attempting to rescue the trapped sculler without, of course, going over itself. Tricky manoeuvring turned the boat around and brought it slowly, slowly, ever so slowly backwards, drifting on the stream to within several lengths of Reggie's tree. As fate would have it, occupying the stroke seat of the four was that very student whose wall now proudly displayed the life ring that had once occupied a place below the bridge.

Mike, the cox of the four, carefully managed his crew who pulled carefully on their oars to reduce the boat's backwards drift, bringing it gently closer and closer to the wretched Reginald. Two lengths became one and then a half until only several yards of clear water remained between Reggie and rescue.

"Careful lads," the cox shouted. "Keep us off that tree. If it tangles our rudder…"

Carlos Del Fuego in the stroke seat of the four was, ironically, the closest rower to Reg.

"Reg," he shouted trying to hide the terror in his voice, paddling to keep the boat straight and away from the tree, "you'll have to swim for it."

"Aye, Reggie," the cox said. "We can't chance coming any closer. You'll have to swim for us. Only a couple of feet. Grab hold of the stern. We'll pull you back to shore."

"Sorry, lads" – Reggie burbled, his head just out of the water – "can't swim," he apologised.

"Never learned how. Sorry."

"Try, Reg. Try. It's your only chance," the cox screamed with terror in his voice, his eyes darting all around him. "It's your only…

"…Shit."

The boat was now drifting badly off true and in danger of coming sideways onto the weir.

"Carl," Mike screamed at his number two rower. "Pull it around. Pull it around for fuck's sake!" And as Carl drove his blade in to straighten the boat, it pulled them away from the weir and out of Reggie's reach again.

"Sorry, lads," Reggie, grinning and out of breath, shouted.

"Don't risk it anymore. You could all go over with me…" His head disappeared beneath the surface again then bubbled back up.

"Felt the tree moving again that time. Doesn't have much hold left. One little branch, I think," he burbled between blue lips, shivering with the cold and visibly tiring.

Then, "Shi-it," he shouted out of the blue, suddenly feeling himself lifted bodily across the weir as his tree detached and vaulted with him over the top. The crew in the boat couldn't believe their eyes as they saw their friend being swept atop the weir and over the other side with a wailing, falling last, 'Sh-iiiiit!' hanging in the air behind him.

In an instant, Reggie was gone, and they couldn't believe it. No time to mourn though. Panic struck the various members of the crew as they pulled and wrenched wildly at their oars picking madly at the water to avoid their own deaths. No coordinated effort. Mike screamed orders that weren't heard. Luckily, stroke by stroke, the boat gained speed, bow side's blades coming within inches of the weir but finally digging hard enough to swing the bows safely upstream and away from total disaster. Its wake described a puddled 'C' in the water.

Once they had reached a safe enough distance away from danger, they stopped, hunched over in their various despair. Total silence. Disbelief. Wonder.

Mike was the first to regain some degree of choked control.

"Right, lads. Better move further away before the river gets us too."

His first thoughts were to bring the boat safely ashore at St John's landing stage upstream of Prebend's Bridge. After that? Who knows? None of them had ever had to deal with…

Who would they tell?

How would they tell it?

They had merely been rowing downstream together with Reggie, he in his single, they in their coxed-four coached from the bankside by Specky. Reggie had gone on ahead through Prebend's Bridge, the first time any of them had been that far down the river. Mike was the first to hear Specky screaming. Then he saw Specky jumping off his bike on the towpath, tumbling in his haste to get to the river, then, strangely just standing there, casually throwing pebbles into the river waiting for Reggie to deliver himself from that tree. It didn't seem to bother Specky that the sculling boat was gone, and now that Reggie had followed the boat, all he could do was stand there and fling the rest of his pebbles into the water before returning to his bike and wheeling it off downstream, shouting derision after the hapless sculler.

"Bastard, Reggie. Fuckin' bastard."

The two hearty souls who had rescued Reggie's empty sculling boat from under Framwellgate Bridge were now struggling along the towpath with it perched atop their shoulders. When they reached Durham School's landing stage, they stopped, amused by the sight of Specky across the river jumping up and down at the water's edge. They saw a coxed four circling aimlessly in the middle of the river but couldn't see what Specky's fuss was all about, for by now, there was nobody left on the weir. The tree had gone, carrying its cargo into the rapids on the other side.

Nothing really made any sense until they saw, a hundred yards below the weir, some foolish student in Cuth's rowing kit plodging around in the shallows making his way towards the bankside, shakily choosing a rout that kept him away from the deeper pools.

"What's that daft bugger doin' down there?"

They gently put their load down beside the path and made their way down to help its sculler out of the water.

"Thanks, lads." Reggie perked up brightly at their assistance.

"Yours?" they asked, pointing to the sculling boat.

Reggie stood there shivering, numb and blue with the cold and the trauma he'd just been through. Water ran down his forehead over his eyes and off his chin.

"Couldn't help me off at the landing stage with it, could you, lads?" Reggie asked politely.

They could and did, welcoming not having to carry the damn thing any further.

"Stay away from that bloody weir," one of them shouted as Reg paddled limply out to meet his amazed rower friends who were sitting motionless in their boat in the centre of the river.

"Too right," Reggie replied. "Bugger of a drop on the other side. Don't recommend it myself," he laughed.

As he paddled his sheepish way out to the coxed-four in the middle of the pool, a barely audible, 'Daft Pillock' echoed gently off the arches of Prebend's Bridge in the background.

Chapter 27
Possession

"You still like the one with all the muscles and soft, wavy hair? Even after what he's been up to?" Carol sniffed suspiciously at Louisa's comment.

"Not 'like'. Well. Yes. 'Like'. He looks nice. A bit like your Christopher Robin."

"My Christopher Robin? What do you mean, 'My Christopher Robin'? Who said anything about possession?"

"Don't need to say anything about possession. It's all very clear to me. Has been for some time, if you only knew. In the way you look when you talk about him. You speed up and things. And change colour. Your whole being changes. I've seen it happen. Ever since that first time in the Town Hall. Try to deny it, C. There's a lot going on there that you aren't willing to face up to, or maybe you don't even know about – biological things."

Carol went quiet and whispered to herself, "Ever since the library that first time …"

"What? What did you say?"

"Oh, nothing," Carol said trying to dismiss Louisa's rot. "You do talk a load of rot, Lou."

"True. But I know you, and you'd better start facing up to the truth. There are things happening there. Physical things …" she started to say but stopped, noticing a tiny tear dropping onto her friend's cheek.

"Oh dear … Didn't mean … Oh, Carol, I'm sorry … I didn't …" Louisa said, reaching across the table and gently taking her hand.

"… All right, Lou." Carol gulped. "It's all right. Really. Oh." she sniffed, wrangling with her emotions.

"… don't know what to do, Lou," she squeaked. "Didn't mean it. Honest. I thought I was just being friendly, putting things in place. And now look what's happened," Carol said.

"Yes," Louisa said.

"Just what has happened, C?"

"I don't know," Carol said, confused.

"All my fault. Shouldn't have in the first place …"

"Should!" Louisa asserted decisively. "You had to, Carol! Had to!"

"Errol…"

"… hasn't exactly been honest in all of this."

"I know," C dithered. "I know he hasn't. But—"

"No buts, my girl. You're too good for all of his … his … his philandering.

"Better off without him."

"I know. But—"

"There you go again, giving him more chances than he deserves."

"I know. But," she said taking a deep breath and squaring up to her inquisitor, "he came around last night …"

"… And?"

"Didn't have the heart to chuck him out. Should've. Couldn't."

"And you decided to forgive him? That's what all this is about, isn't it?"

"Not entirely."

"Well, what is it, C?" Louisa demanded, losing her patience. "Spit it out. Get to the point."

"We sort of patched it up … and … and … Oh, I just don't know what to do about …"

"About what, Carol? What are you so worried about?"

"Christopher Robin, of course. Now I don't know what to do. It's all got so…impossible."

"You'll just have to tell him. It wouldn't be fair not to."

"You aren't being very helpful, Lou. You're supposed to tell me I'm a fool and not to be so silly, to stick with Errol."

"You're right, of course. You are being entirely foolish, but I still love you and wouldn't dream of trying to tell you what to do. You'll have to work it out for yourself. Dump Christopher Robin and be done with him. After all, he's been a total cad in all this and doesn't deserve any consideration at all."

This last piece of advice sounded so emphatic, so grave, so wrong that having said it, Lou challenged herself immediately.

"What's wrong with Christopher Robin, anyway?" Louisa suddenly demanded, changing course.

"Nothing, really. Well…that's just it. Nothing."

"You mean he's perfect?" Louisa said.

"Yes, I suppose, in a friendly sort of way. But that's just it."

"What's it."

"Just a friend. He doesn't seem to want any more than friendship. He's…He's…"

"Spit it out."

"I never know how to read him. I don't think he really is interested in me at all. We go out, and that's just it. We go out, and it never gets any further than that."

"You want him to go further? But he has, hasn't he? That time in Adelia's?" Louisa ventured.

"Not really. Only, I don't really know. We were all really drunk. And…aaand, well, I don't really know what happened.

"A girl needs more. A girl needs a boy to make some sort of sign. You know? Let her know he's interested,"

"I know. Without being too pushy. I know. Poor thing. It's almost impossible for him to know what to do, isn't it? He probably feels the same. Wants to but doesn't really want to go too far. You know. Doesn't want to look like a cad in the face of the incumbent."

"You mean he's behaving like a proper gentleman?"

"Looks like it. You could always ask him what his intentions were. But you're supposed to leave that part to your dad – God forbid. Poor thing. Love by vicarious intent. You could also take the lead."

"How do you mean?"

"You could have a go at him."

"And look like a total strumpet."

"Well … You are one, aren't you? I mean, maybe not that bad, but you are a tart, aren't you, really, dearest?"

Carol took a deep breath at this last tease, smiling.

"Tart!" Lou said again, grinning, trying to get more of a rise out of Carol.

"Wouldn't know how to, even if I wanted. What's the metier of a tart, Lou?" Carol asked in a confused sort of way.

"You could tell me how. After all, everybody knows how you behave. It's all over Mary's." Carol returned the tease.

"Better see Adelia for that one. She's a right strumpet," Louisa said, eying their friend who had just entered the college canteen.

"Aren't you, Adelia?" Louisa challenged, as she sat beside them.

"What?" Adelia said, not really paying attention.

"She's lost in her latest essay again," Louisa said, now trying to bait Adelia.

"Yes," Adelia chose to say.

"What? Lost in a philosophical argument or in being a great big tart?" Carol said.

"Both," Adelia said, still not paying any attention to either of them.

"Of course. Yes," Louisa discovered, "Yes. That's it. And there's always been Errol at your side. Christopher Robin can't make a move while he thinks you're interested in Errol without acting like a total caveman."

Adelia looked uncomfortable at this and chose to remain silent for the moment.

"Wish he would, sometime," Carol said wistfully. "Then I'd know."

"Then you would probably dump him for being too brutal."

"At least I would know, Lou. I'd know and be able to…"

"To what?"

"Make plans…"

"What for?" Adelia asked, all of a sudden coming out of her reverie.

"I know," Louisa said, interrupting both of them.

"You know what?" Carol asked.

"How to solve everybody's problems," Louisa replied.

"I don't have any problems," Adelia objected.

"Yes, you do, and this will solve them. Adelia, you can have Archie. You remember, Carol, the little one at the front of the boat. Carol gets Christopher Robin. And I…I get that lovely, curly haired hunky rower, The Honey One. I could do with some curly hair just about now," she said, lavishing the memory of him upon herself.

"Don't the men get any say in all this?" Carol asked.

"Do they ever? Keep them confused and wanting more," Louisa said nodding her head at her wonderful resolution. "Confused desire keeps us in control and them available for whatever we want, whenever we want it."

Carol began to smile at Lulu's innocent decision. "If life were only that simple…"

"It is," Lou exploded, "if only you knew it. Now. Time for tea," she said reaching for the pot.

"I'll be, mother. Who wants a scone and who wants a toasted tea cake?"

Carol eyed her friend suspiciously. "I'm not entirely certain I go along with all of this, especially you getting the curly blond with all the muscles…"

"Who is this splendid specimen?" Adelia asked, buttering a scone.

"Oh, nobody," Louisa said, withholding evidence.

"Just somebody we saw today with practically no clothes on and very tight shorts and who seemed very interested in one of us. And it wasn't Carol. Was it, C?"

"I could barely get a word in edgewise."

"You had already turned your nose up at him. You had already made your mind up based on a suspicion you had about him in a punt, while I…I know a delicious male crumpet when I see one and this one was one…delicious, I mean."

"All I can say in my own defence, Lou, is that you'd better watch out. Get him in a punt or feed him a pint of beer and he's anybody's, while Adelia's one is more discerning."

"My one?" Adelia asked. "What do you mean my one? You surely don't think…"

"No, not him. Perish the thought," Carol decided.

"Well, who then?"

"That sweet little boy in the front end of the boat. Archie, they called him. Sweet and sensible and won't lead one a merry dance and leave one at the altar to go off and chase after the legions of other females he'd been bedding all the while."

"Archie," Louisa agreed. "Seems nice. He was a bossy one though and sort of sweet, but thinking again, Carol, he had practically no beef on him at all. A stick insect."

"I have a feeling, Lou; Archie has more to him than meets the eye. And The Honey One a good deal less."

171

"Exactly the way I want 'em. All balls and no forehead, I think the rowers say. All balls and no forehead – that would do me just fine," Adelia said with conviction.

"And millions of other misguided women."

"Well," Louisa chirped, "we seemed to have brought the meeting to order. Time to actually put decisions into actions. Time to activate resolutions. Time to get busy. Or something like that."

"Just exactly what do you mean by that? More tea, anyone?"

Chapter 28
The Honey One

"I tell you, mate, she was all over me."

"What do you mean, all over you?"

Later that afternoon a desultory, losing crew sat nuzzling their beers in the back room of the Dunn Cow Inn.

"The leggy bint with the miniskirt up to her arse. Gorgeous. Looks like a supermodel," Franklin carried on, impressed with himself.

"I think I'm in there, lads."

Tucker was still undecided.

"Saw none o' that, Franklin. Neither of them showed any interest in any of us, least of all Carol, least of all you."

"Carol? How'd you know her name?" Beau was incredulous that Leo should or could know anything about her.

"Carol. Flynn knows her," Leo explained.

"Flynn knows that? Tell you what, if he knows that, I'm a monkey's—"

"Get him a banana with his pint, Archie. Flynn's in love with the lass. She's the one that spotted you in that punt with my Amanda up Fornication Creek. Thieving bastard."

"Eh? The one that started laughing when she saw us?"

"The very one, mate. The very one. They were out having a picnic when they happened to come across you two perverts twisted up like conjugal snakes. Serves you bloody well right for going off with my lass."

"Not bloody likely. Not bloody likely. Him? With her? Don't believe it. Don't believe it," Franklin said pulling his lips away from his pint and shaking his head in dismayed disbelief.

"If you'd spent more time with your eyes in the boat instead of watching the totty on the bridge, you mightn't have caught that ginormous crab under Elvet

Bridge. We would've caught that Castle crew and maybe the next one on from them, mate. Instead, it was us who got bumped. Still, you're such a shite rower, you were bound to cock up sooner or later," Leo said, hanging his head in dismay.

"He er … He had his end away yet? Flynn – and that bint – I mean."

"Ask him yourself, why don'tcha. I don't bloody well know, do I?"

"I might well be doing that before the night is out. The other one, the little 'un. Could have shagged her on the spot."

"I'm afraid," Leo said, "she is also spoken for."

"Spoken for? What do you bloody well mean 'spoken for'? What's that supposed to mean? What kind of Victorian language is that?"

"Hands off. That's all."

"Who says?"

"A bloody big Hatfield rugby player by the name of Oliver says so. That's who. Huge bloke. Eats the likes of you for breakfast."

"Bollocks," Franklin said, totally unconvinced.

"All right. All right. I warned you."

"I'll have that little filly bedded by ten o'clock Saturday night," he declared. "Oliver or no Oliver. Did you see the way she was looking at me back there? She'll be easy, mate; don't you worry," Beau said, nibbling at the edge of his beer.

"Go on then, Franklin. A pint says you won't," Leo sneered.

"You're on, Tucker. It'll be a pleasure supping your beer. The easy part is that wench. Hard part is separating you from your cash."

"Pleasure will be all mine to see your miserable crippled carcase twisted up inside that beat up old dustbin outside Hatfield's gate," Leo said, seriously cheered up and rubbing his hands together with the prospect.

"Err, by the way, she's in Mary's but lodges with that Carol up Western Hill. There's a bloody big dustbin at the bottom of Western Hill too, in case you need somewhere to hide from Ollie. Just thought I'd mention it, Franklin, just in case you feel you've bitten off more than you can chew, which I know you have."

"Tucker, you are such a gobshite. No wonder you can't hold your beer or your women. They're easy pickings for the likes of me, or anybody else for that matter."

"Yes, Beau. Of course, Beau. They'll both be at Van Mildert tonight for the disco. Shall I come along and hold your coat, Beau? You'll need excessive amounts of bog roll when you start to shit yourself."

Leo knew he had him hook, line and sinker. If there was anything Beau could not resist, it was a challenge to his mojo. His very being depended on regular conquests, and he knew it was only a matter of time before she would be begging him to bed her. He knew this as a matter of right, his right to any woman he pleased.

Leo, on the other hand, had seen big Ollie, and he chortled inwardly at the thought of the confrontation.

The Van Mildert disco later that night was unusually quiet. It sounded raucous from a distance as we walked up to the college gates, but once inside…Deadness. A few isolated couples gyrated on the dance floor.

Errol worked a disco from behind a table loaded with musical gear – records, turntables and speakers. A few bored hangers on stood around, idly looking guilty, furtively rustling through album covers, waiting for the chance to duck out and get back to Cuth's where the real action was that night.

"It's a bloody morgue," Leo said as we all stood around cradling our beers to our chests, waiting for the punters to arrive.

"Thought you said she'd be here, Leo," Beau grumbled, out of sorts.

"Don't worry, bonnie lad. It's early. It'll pick up. You will have plenty of chances to ply your trade once the totty starts to arrive. Just give it time, mate. They're all off in their rooms doing their homework like good boys and girls…"

"Hello, you." Suddenly, Carol was at my shoulder, a pint in each hand, smiling, engaging.

"Just let me put these down. Back in a sec."

She tottered over to the disco table, relieved herself of her burden then scuttled back.

"Didn't know you were going to be here tonight. You could've said something! Who are these reprobates? Ah, yes, I recognise this one from that boat that crashed today. You were all very grumpy about it. Little wonder. But I was ready to jump in and save you, should needs be."

"Beau," I said, identifying the mad stalker.

"Ah, yes. The Honey One. Maniacal puntsman," she grinned and blushed.

"And?"

"You know Leo."

She nodded.

"Archie."

"The cute, sensible one. I remember. Bossy too," she said, measuring him against Louisa's earlier appraisal of his parts.

"My job, m'lady," Archie said bowing courteously.

This pleased Carol, so she went further.

"How so? Your job?"

"Somebody has to keep this lot in line," he said.

"Ahhh. Quite right too. Disorganised rabble," she laughed.

"Wait a minute, Archie. I wouldn't say we were a rabble," Beau cut in.

"Well, I would," Leo chirped in. "Especially that crab you caught that lost us the race."

"And where were you, Christopher Robin, while all this crashing was going on," Carol asked.

"Way downstream. Chasing Reggie over the weir in his scull," I said.

"Oh my god. Did he capsize?" Carol gasped, clasping hold of my arm.

"Spent most of the morning camped out on top of the weir. Then decided to dive over it. He survived it though. Many wouldn't have. He has an irritating tendency to bob to the top of most life-threatening situations. Got right back into his boat. We escorted him back up the river just to make sure he didn't get into any more trouble."

"Good. Is he all right? Whatever was he doing to end up on the weir?"

"Says he didn't see it until it was too late, the pillock. The story of Reggie's life. He's gone back to cricket until he sorts out common sense."

"Shouldn't he be in a bigger boat?" she asked. "Surely that would be much safer."

"Not if he was in it," Beau said, looking about the room that was starting to fill up.

"He brings mayhem to anything he tries," he said. "Err, is your mate here, the petite one?" he said suddenly.

"My mate? My mate?" Carol asked taken off guard.

"Don't know what you mean. I've got lots of, ah, mates."

"The one that was with you on the towpath today. Couldn't take her eyes off me. Brunette. Smallish. Nice tits."

Shocked by Beau's mouth, Carol turned to me with a look of incredulity, flustered a second, then erupted.

"Could be any female in Durham," she replied, "by the sounds of it. Let me ask around of my 'mates' with 'nice tits'. I'll see if any of them remembers you. But then, how might they ever forget?" she added.

"Aye," Beau said. "Go on then. There's a good lass. I'm sure she'd appreciate seeing me."

"I will," Carol said, shocked and totally pissed off with him and looking daggers at me.

"Shall we have a look around?" she said, dragging me off to the other side of the room.

"Don't mind Beau," I said, getting her to myself.

"He's too full of himself to know when he's being offensive or merely being full of himself."

"He means Lulu, doesn't he?" she sparked and sputtered.

"Well! I wouldn't introduce her to him if you paid me. The nerve…But then he is rather beautiful, isn't he?" she had to admit.

"He thinks so," I said.

"Lulu's crumpet. The Honey One," she said.

"So she is interested in him."

"Appears so."

"Interested in who?" A little person had suddenly appeared from a hole in the wall, all ears and eyes and gorgeous.

"In 'whom' dearest English scholar," Carol corrected.

"All right, if you must – 'whom'," Louisa said, hands on hips, eyebrows inclined.

"Your crumpet," Carol explained. "The one with the wavy hair; the one you idolised at first sight down by Elvet Bridge. The Honey One."

At this, Louisa's eyes lit up. She became very interested, ducking around us to see who else was in the room beyond.

"But you wouldn't like him up close. Not at all handsome. Rather ugly, I would say. To be avoided at all costs."

"You mean that wonderful man we met on the towpath with hardly any clothes on…?"

"You wouldn't be interested in him clothed. Unprepossessing. Not at all good looking with clothes on. Has no taste whatsoever, apart from Yorkshire fop."

177

"There he is," Lou squealed with delight, seeing him from afar, despite our attempts to shield her from his masculine glow.

"Get out of the way, you two. I do believe I've just spotted the future father of my beautiful, tall, blond, blue-eyed children," she said, waving generally about the room but mainly at the future father.

"… likes doing that," Carol said. "Waving helps to show off her figure, which needs no introduction at this point.

"Is that man actually licking his lips? Lou, Lou, do be careful. You might want to consider his reputation."

"Believe me," I said following in their wake, "it's not his reputation she's after at the minute."

"You might be more circumspect, Louisa," Carol said reeling her in, taking her by an elbow and steering her out of trouble toward the bar.

"Oh dear, Carol." Lou struggled. "One can't be an old maid all one's life."

"Just be more careful with this one. He has a reputation…"

"I know. I know," Louisa squealed in delight.

"Perfect for me: muscles, wavy hair and a shadowy past. What more could a girl ask for?" she sighed.

"Your moral tutor, that's what. Calm down. At least let him make the first move."

"Why? I'm in love and ready to have his blue-eyed babies. Get thee behind me, Carol, I'm going in with both barrels blazing, and devil take the hindmost."

She took a deep breath, hitched up her famous breasts and marched toward the gathering at the other side of the room.

"How'd you do?" she said holding out her hand to Beau.

"I'm Louisa. What is your name, wonderful man?"

And as we all stood around gobsmacked, expecting Beau to strip her on the spot and have his evil way with her the way he usually did, in front of the assembled populace, he just stood there looking gormless, gazing down at this adorable creature and holding out his hand to make her acquaintance. No groping, no grabbing, no slobbering tongues. Not a bit of it.

He just stood there, mesmerised. Totally out of sorts, unable or unwilling to make his usual play. Tongue-tied. Was it us standing near that put him off?

Lulu smiled her best, most glorious smile, holding out her hand, awaiting some sign of life from her newly made acquaintance.

"Lulu," she offered again.

"Beau," Leo prompted, nodding to him to at least shake her hand.

"Well then, that's settled," Leo blurted out, in a hurry to move on to the bar. "He's out of circulation at last, and the rest of us are free to work on getting our ends away without fear of being stabbed in the back by the biggest backstabber of them all.

"Congratulations, Beau. Here's to a wonderful married life … hope you both will be very happy together. Now. Back to more important business. Best bitter," he announced to the general assembly, as he moved off toward the bar.

"Only hope he doesn't change his bleedin' mind before the night's out. There's a certain little someone over there I've suddenly become very fond of," he said, pointing the way with his empty glass and following it the way a cat follows a wiggly piece of string.

Lulu moved in very close to Beau, smiling fondly up at him – a mistake, we all sensed but not yet a fatal mistake. Beau was just as moved as she and stared down at her fondly with a big, stupid grin on his face. Beau never did 'stupid' very well.

"Looks like you've scored there, Beau," I said elbowing him in the ribs.

He just stood there with that gormless look on his face, returning Lulu's dumb show.

Carol thought somebody should say something.

"Lou? Lou? Are you feeling all right, Louisa?" she asked, rushing at her, taking her aside.

"Honestly. Get hold of yourself, woman. It's not as bad as all that. Is it?"

Louisa could only nod and grin in Beau's direction unable to take her eyes off the lad.

She opened her mouth to say something, but no sound came out. She squeaked instead. She blushed crimson and suddenly moved away from her new paramour to clutch Carol's arm, as a child clings to her mother.

"This is ridiculous," Carol scolded, annoyed at Lulu's behaviour.

"You are behaving like a five-year-old. I'm going to do something odd in a minute unless you come to your senses."

Errol appeared from behind the disco table looking curiously at the two women.

"Errol," Carol said. "Thank goodness, you've arrived. Do something. I think Lulu's having a fit. Look at her all gooey and lost."

179

Taking the hint, Errol snapped his fingers in front of Lulu's face, the way magicians do to de-hypnotise their victims.

"Lou. Louisa," he commanded, "snap out of it, woman."

Startled, he turned to the rest of us. "She's in some sort of a trance. How much has she had tonight? May need medical attention if she doesn't come around. "Lulu, it's me, Errol."

Disappointed at his feeble effort and diagnosis, Carol stepped in again.

"Oh, never mind, Errol. Of course, she's in some kind of a trance. It's Beau here and his blue eyes. It's called infatuation, and it could be fatal if we don't do something about it before he gets her clothes off."

Louisa sighed and, still in a trance, began to unbutton her blouse.

"But soft, what light through yonder window breaks…" she began to recite.

"Now that's enough of that, my girl," Errol snapped, stepping in again. "Quoting Shakespeare at a time like this is going to do no one any good at all. Neither will disrobing in front of all these men," he said doing up her buttons almost as fast as she undid them.

"Carol," he shouted in a fluster. "Do something, can't you! She'll be bloody well naked if you don't step in here and stop her."

He turned back to look at Louisa, but by this time, her blouse was almost completely off.

"No you don't, my girl," he shouted, pulling the flimsy garment back around her shoulders and chest before she could get her bra off. "You aren't going to impress anybody by going around topless."

To which, Leo remarked from over at the bar, "There might be some of us who wouldn't mind, Errol, old friend. Give her a few moments, there's a love, to impress me at least. Haven't had a good impression in years."

"Carol!" Errol cried out for help.

"Don't look at me. She's a grown woman. Far be it from me to interfere with her rites of passage." Then turning to her mate said, "Better cover up Lou. Errol's getting more than his fair share of bountiful bosoms. I don't think it suits him. And Leo looks like he's ready to faint."

"Leo," I said moments later to a dejected figure returning from the bar with a pint in each fist and a scowl on his face. "You'll have to do something about your friend, Beau. He's about to jump all over little Louisa. She's disrobing, quoting Shakespeare, and I'm afraid they will both be regretting their next move if somebody doesn't do something."

Leo thrust one of his pints at me and looked quizzically across at both Lulu and Beau.

"I don't give a monkey's about Beau or his new conquest. I've just had my heart broken by him for the tenth time this term, and it's about time somebody took him completely out of the running."

"Ah," Errol said to the newly bereaved, "Leo, is it? Yes. I've heard about you. Now let me see. You say Beau here has done you irreparable damage already this year a number of times. Yes? And you wish him to be put in his place.

"Well," Errol said.

"I've got just the fella," he said stepping to one side.

"Oliver here would like a word with your Beau."

Fully expecting Big Oliver to be right behind him, Errol turned around to find a large area to his back occupied by no one at all. Oliver had slipped out for a wiz, leaving Errol flapping in the wind.

Beau wasn't listening anyway. He was busy being escorted out of the building by a besotted, semi naked young lady who had nothing more to say to anyone else. Apparently, it was time for some sort of action, and she was taking the bull by the horns and accepting nothing less from him. Floating high on a cloud of pheromones, the happy couple drifted hand in hand through the disco rabble and out the front door of Van Mildert College.

Sometime later, they were discovered fully clothed on a park bench down by the river gazing deeply into each other's eyes. Across the river, the illuminated towers of the cathedral rose majestically out of the trees. We thought that the two lovers would at least be naked and asses deep in the bushes by now, exercising the various rites of spring they were both being subjected to, but no, they were sitting hand in hand gazing off across the river.

"Great," Leo said, leading us back across Prebend's towards Cuth's.

"Out of commission at last, poor thing. Never thought I'd ever see the day, but it hasn't come too soon for me and the multitudes of young women who have been duped by his dubious charms.

"You're well in there with your totty, though, Flynn. She's nothing to look at, mind you, but it is said she plays a mighty game of scrabble of an evening."

I said nothing. I knew I had a long way to go. But I knew when I started it would be a dodgy road filled with potholes. Potholes had loomed large earlier that evening as she settled herself down behind the disco turntable with Errol, leafing intently through stacks of record albums with him and no longer interested in my presence on the dance floor.

Just resting?

Or sending out a signal loud and clear that nothing had yet been settled between those two. Even more disturbing was the sight of Adelia in the background flitting through the shadows, seemingly no longer part of Errol's attentions either.

Chapter 29
Osborne's Bash

Prof Osborne sat behind the desk in his office on the second floor of St Cuthbert's Society, his elbows on his desktop and fingers forming a pensive 'A' under his chin. The grand windows at his back overlooked the lawn below. Glorious sunshine poured in through the windows illuminating the hat stand near the door on which hung his dusty old gown and umbrella. The professor rarely ventured out without his umbrella, which acted as a walking stick. Lifting its tip to just the right height between strides then placing it briskly onto the ground at the step, he measured his pace with a lively 'one-two-three' cadence. In this way, he walked the distance to and from his home above the banks of Pelaw Wood each day, smiling at everyone he met, pointing a friendly umbrella at those in the distance who might not be able to hear his cheery greeting.

This morning, though, the principal of St Cuthbert's Society was glum. He was searching for words to tell a student that his academic torture had come to a merciful end at last. Not an enviable job. Osborne wanted everyone in the place to be comfortable and usually stayed in the background. He oversaw the entry of every new student in September, sat at high table during meals and took his place in the middle of the college photo every June. But other than this, he was rarely seen around the place. He enjoyed his anonymity and felt it a sign of success that he was not involved directly in the running of the college. Henry Havelock, his subordinate, did most of the running, but even he left the undergraduates to their own devices.

Prof Osborne was not happy this morning. And even though the sun shone brightly through the windows at his back, he did not look forward to the visit of the student concerned.

He fidgeted with his fingers and with the pens on his desk, looked longingly behind him at the sun on the lawn, got up, sat down, sighed deeply and spying his dusty old gown on the hat stand, lifted it off, brushed it off, slipped it over his shoulders and sat down again.

"That's better," he said to himself, but thinking better of it, of the occasion at hand, and the effect the wearing of a gown might have on the condemned student, he stood up and quickly placed it back on the hat stand.

Knock, knock, knock.

Henry Havelock poked his head in around the door.

"He's here, William."

"Goodness."

"What do you want me to do with him?" Havelock asked.

"How does he look?"

"As well as anyone on death row might."

Havelock withdrew his head but was immediately called back in.

"Would you. Err. Do you think you might be able to take this one on for me, Henry? Upset tummy. Not feeling up to this particular execution."

Havelock grimaced and declined the invitation.

"Previous engagement, I'm afraid," Henry said, meaning his unfinished pint down at the JCR bar.

"What about Mrs Manners? She doesn't mind doing things like this. Good at executions. A glass or two of sherry always puts her in a favourable state of mind. I could chat her up if you like, William."

Osborne waved him off and reluctantly told him to send the condemned up.

"Righto, Principal," Havelock said and slid out of sight, closing the door behind him.

Because he was focussed on events to hand and not on the flowerbeds surrounding the lawn or the wood pigeons cooing in the trees outside his window, Prof Osborne could hear the steady, heavy trudge of someone's size thirteens on the stairs approaching his office. He looked again at his gown on the hat stand, thought better of it, reached across his desk, drew the cup filled with pens and pencils toward him, thought better of that, pushed them away again, sat casually back in his chair, then sat up again and placed his folded hands on his desk, attentive, ready, compassionate – so he thought – and awaited events.

The person outside on the landing had reached those hallowed doors with the imposing, some would say deathly, sign beside them: 'Professor W. G. Osborne: Principal' screwed to the wall next to them.

Knock. Knock. Knock.

Prof Osborne cleared his throat.

"Come in," he pronounced.

Now, William had rehearsed this part of the interview many times on the towpath this morning during his walk in to work. He didn't want to predict his fell pronouncement by sounding too severe and yet didn't want to sound as though the condemned had been invited up for tea and scones.

Something dignified, yet friendly.

As he approached Prebend's Bridge on his walk-in this morning, he thought he had it just right and was happy with it. But now that he had finally made that introductory remark to the morning's proceedings, he wasn't sure he had hit quite the right tone and immediately felt ill at ease that he might have frightened the poor sod outside from taking the door handle at all.

Osborne waited.

The door handle turned and the door opened a crack.

Ah. At least the victim hadn't been scared off. Bravely, he entered the room, or at least the cast on his arm entered.

"Dear boy. What have you done to yourself?" Osborne said with the utmost concern and, wanting to disarm the situation, looked desperately around the room for a chair to assuage the casualty that now faced him.

"Do come in. Please. Please. Have a seat," he said to the peremptory head inclining into his office. Rushing to drag a chair from the window to a spot beside his desk, he led the victim to it by his good arm.

"Dear boy. What have you done to yourself?" the concerned, misbegotten, would-be executioner said.

It wasn't enough that we have set out to send him down, but we've tried to kill him in the process, the beleaguered Prof thought to himself.

"It's nothing really," Lucien Fenwood-Gross said and winced a little as he said it.

"Rugby. Cuth's v Hatfield. Couldn't dodge their hooker, I'm afraid."

And he winced again, seeing the effect that the first wince had had on Osborne. What Lucien had neglected to say was that he had only been a spectator at the match, had turned around to comment to a friend just before the play crashed in on them from the field. The result was a sprained wrist.

"Stout fellow," Osborne effused in admiration of his service to the college.

"Didn't leave the field until after the game. X-rays. Got this put on yesterday," Lucien said, almost holding back another wince.

"Well," Osborne said, picking up his phone and getting through to Mrs Blenkinsop in the kitchen.

"Yes," he enthused to her.

"Got an injured warrior up here, Mrs Blenkinsop. Tea for both, please, and," he said smiling at Lucien, "toasted tea cakes and scones.

"And could you butter the scones, please, Mrs Blenkinsop? Don't think Mr Fenwood-Gross can manage a knife at the minute."

Lucien returned the smile and settled back in his chair to await elevenses.

"Err, did we win the match?" Osborne enquired of his warrior, nodding his approval of the young man's heroism.

"21–18," Lucien said with aplomb, neither wanting nor seeking admiration for his role in the victory, for there had been none.

"And what position do you play, dear boy?"

Without hesitation, Lucien replied, "Lock forward, Professor. Err, lock forward," rather demurely, for he neither wanted nor sought approbation for his role in the victory. If the truth be known, Lucien had played lock forward in one game once for St Mary's middle school against St Joseph's and had been so frightened by the experience refused to play it ever again. He sat now with his head bowed lest the good professor enquired further.

"Give as good as you get, I'll be bound. You're a healthy size for a forward. Not many would get past you, I'll be bound."

Lucien just grinned self-consciously at this. He had never made a tackle in his life, ran away to the other side of the pitch rather than come to blows with anyone on it. He did rather like the cuddling that went on in the scrum though, but once that bit was over with, he just stood about dodging the mad tugging and frugging that took place, waiting for the next cuddle to form.

"Ah, the tea has arrived," Osborne said rubbing his hands together, relieved that his prime duty this morning had been usurped by pity and an admiration for a true sportsman who had given his all for the college rugby team. True heroism was rarely recognised these days, in favour of the fanaticism that most young people displayed for pop groups and the like, Carnaby Street fashions and the like. Nobody was ever carried home on his shield anymore. Pity. The world could do with a few more martyrs and a few less namby-pambies.

The ceremonial of disbursing tea over with, the two fellows sat back to enjoy a buttered scone. Osborne manhandled a little table up next to Lucien's chair to make him more comfortable. Sports talk ensued during which the guest fumbled his way through references to sports he had no knowledge of at all. Cricket was a complete mystery to him, and he finally had to admit it to his principal.

"Never went in much for cricket," he said dismally, launching himself at another toasted teacake. "Couldn't see why they had to bounce the damn ball, instead of just tossing it straight at you. Makes it very difficult to hit."

Osborne looked cross-eyed at this and said nothing, for he revered the game and saw little in it to quibble about.

"Seems to me trying to chase a little ball bouncing all over a field until it stops bouncing is impractical and a waste of everybody's time," Lucien added.

Now, this very action of chasing a little ball all over a field until it stopped bouncing described all of those activities which Osborne held dearest, so he tactfully withheld his opinion on it, preferring to answer with only a measured 'Yes' and asked his visitor if he would like anymore tea.

"Had a roaring good time with him," Osborne told Henry Havelock after the visit.

"And you didn't need Mrs Manners' help with him after all? Henry asked.

"What for?"

"Chucking the blighter out."

"Oh. Never thought of that. Didn't come up. Was that what he'd come for?"
Havelock raised his eyebrows.

"Well. We were getting on so famously; I couldn't really send him down, now, could I? Him with his war wound and all. Stout chap, Fenwood-Whatsit."

"His what?"

"War wound, Henry. War wound. Broken arm. Didn't you see? Had it in a cast. Broke it in the match against Hatfield rugger buggers on the weekend saving a try, poor old soul. Self-sacrifice is the fellow's middle name. Don't come any finer.

"Send him down?

"After all he's done for the reputation of the college?

"Couldn't hear of such a thing.

"I'm sure he'll bear up next semester and come through with flying colours. Send his department head a note, will you please, Henry: 'Talked to the fellow; splendid chap; past misdemeanours a mere blip in an otherwise brilliant career; rethinking sacking him; do come to tea with Edna next Thursday.'"

"Will do, Principal. And err Fenwood-Gross?"

"What? Yes! Why not? Capital idea, Henry. Invite him to tea as well. Couldn't do any harm letting his department head see what a decent sort he really is, and what a mistake it would have been had I followed his advice. Don't think the English department really knows the man. Otherwise…"

And so it was settled. Tea next Thursday with Fenwood-Gross, the head of the English Department and a few others to fill out the table. When I met Lucien next day in The Three Tuns, his spirits had picked up several degrees.

"Well?" I asked, fully expecting to be told the grisly details of a dressing down by Prof Osborne.

Henry just lifted his pint to his lips and drew off half the liquid in the glass before looking up with a dumbfound expression on his face. He put the glass down on the table, thought some more and finally announced, "Resurrected," and sat there savouring his new lease on life.

"What do you mean, 'Resurrected'?"

"Just that. Amazing recovery.

"Thought I was a goner when I went into his office. By the time we had finished elevenses, he'd told me his whole history about how he'd come to be in Durham in the first place, and his wife and kids and grandkids. Nothing at all about my failing grades and an unbelievably bad reference from Lynwood. None of that. We got on famously. What a bloke! Unbelievable. Best mates by the end of it, him and me.

"And now this," he said, handing me the note Henry Havelock had put in his pigeon hole.

"Me, invited to tea next Thursday at his place, and I'm to bring a friend, if I like."

"Bloody Hell," I said.

"Bloody Hell indeed. Not only unexpelled but invited to rub elbows with the great and the good. And a free meal thrown in which can't be bad in these austere times."

"Calamity avoided," I said, lifting my glass to his good fortune. "Avoided and doubled," I said and finishing off my drink, enthused.

"One more for the road?"

"At least," he replied with a roar. "At least, dear boy. Can't wait to tell Father the good news. Apparently, he and Osborne went to Kings, Cambridge in the same years. Osborne can't place Father but seems to remember the name."

And that was how Henry and I happened to be at Prof Osborne's little shindig. By the time we got there, the guest list had multiplied, and we found ourselves in the presence of a number of Durham's rich and famous.

His house was in a lovely, quiet terrace of Edwardian stonework atop Pelaw Woods bank. Two steps out his front door and Osborne was on the towpath that took him through the middle of town following the river to Cuth's. The man had definitely fallen into the best of all worlds. He lived in an idyllic countryside setting and was only minutes' walk from the shops downtown.

"Do come in chaps," Prof Osborne said shoving a glass of sherry into our hands and ushering us into a spacious parlour laden with fancy grub and booze.

"Don't know if you've met Harry at all," he said showing us to the fireplace in front of which stood, or rather lounged, a fellow I'd noticed upon entering and didn't relish having any part of that night. Harry Sturge leered back at us with his cocky, snooty grin. Grinding his teeth with the pleasure he was obviously giving us in seeing him, he held out a limp hand to me. I remembered him from that auspicious Rev Kev piss-up at the Rose Tree, but he hadn't remembered me. He wouldn't have acknowledged it if he had. He considered himself part of a completely different set to which the rest of us could never belong.

Timidly beside him stood his wife. Thin and waif-like, barely coming up to her husband's shoulder, Alice looked for all the world as if she didn't want to be there, at least there and standing next to him. From the look of dread in her eyes, she was clearly well aware of Sturge's miscreant behaviour around the town and didn't think him suitable anymore as a dinner partner. She was a pretty lady in her thirties, mother of two young children and fed up with all of Harry's antics and all of his tiresome, bull-shitty boozy ways – his misguided attempts to regain lost youth. Her face lit up with the chance to talk to someone else, and she stepped forward to meet us ahead of her husband.

Lucien's plate was immediately filled with piles of sandwiches and cheese from the various tables which he navigated in and around with brutish dexterity. Alice followed, and I followed her chatting about the weather, Osborne, Cuth's and beer, all 'too bloody boring' for Harry who slinked over to join another group in the room, a group sporting a cute little brunette in a becoming yellow print frock whose back was to me at the moment and whose raucous conversation seemed to be leading the storytelling and whose smart little rump could be mistaken for no other than Carol's Louisa. My emotions soared to see her there, in her element, joyous, animated, filling the room with her own brand of humour.

Her arms and elbows and hips flailed out in all directions, holding her audience transfixed with her stories. But where was Carol? Or Ollie? Or The Honey One, for that matter. She was there by herself, holding court and doing a damn good job of it.

I was really keen to dive into Lulu's group but decided to stay with Alice and Lucien for the time being, watching Harry sidle up beside Lulu and slide his arm around her waist. Not skipping a beat, she pulled his arm away without looking up to see who it was and carried on her monologue. Sturge persisted with his groping by stepping close again, reaching around and planting his hand firmly on her butt. Her high heel crunched firmly onto his foot, and he jumped back, limping, chastened, dismayed but undefeated. By this time, Lulu recognised Harry as the guy she was sent to the local clink over that night at Rev Kev's piss up and wasn't standing for anymore of his crude behaviour, yet she didn't want to wreck the evening by belting him across the chops. Lynwood and Osborne wouldn't have approved.

"Serves him bloody well right," Alice said, her eyes caustic with the sight of her husband limping in circles and finally finding the edge of a table to hold on to.

"Never learns, that boy. Thinks he's God's gift to women. All women. There are some who take it, but that one obviously agrees with me," she said just loud enough for everyone to hear.

I nodded and held my breath.

"Stone in your shoe?" Alice asked him with venom.

"Come over here and I'll cripple the other foot for you," she hissed, incensed by his attempt to ruin her only night out this month.

I sensed that this warning was one not to be ignored. Harry's lopsided grin said it was all in fun. His bloodshot eyes belied the excruciating pain in the foot he dearly wanted to rub but wouldn't give in to. Lulu just carried on entertaining her audience without missing a beat.

I could have hugged her for that. There she was, little and defenceless against this lout, yet fending him off like a diminutive Superwoman.

As the evening wove its way through hors d'oeuvres and the buffet main course and endless conversations about the machinations of the English department, I finally managed to catch the little minx's eye and nodded behind me in the direction of the French doors that led out onto the patio. She and I convened there with wine glasses and wobbly plates full of goodies.

The night was mild and calm, the evening air full of sweet scents from Mrs Osborne's flowerbeds wafting in from all directions. Lulu was in fine spirits, and although hidden by the night, her eyes glowed up out of the darkness with the festivity that she had ignited inside her.

"There's a river down there, somewhere," she said, leaning out across the stone wall at the back of the terrace.

"Great response to that jerk," I said.

She just giggled.

"Isn't he the one…?"

"Yes. One of the louts at The Rose Tree," I said.

"What on earth is he doing here?" she asked.

"Osborne invited him. God knows why. The guy's a buffoon. You certainly put him in his place. Good on ya."

"Hope I didn't do him any permanent damage," She giggled in the darkness again. That his missus in there?"

"You're a dangerous woman to get on the wrong side of."

"Not really," she cooed, retreating from the wall and moving back closer to me. "It's getting a little chilly out here, isn't it?" She gave this as the reason for her snuggling close.

It wasn't really colder. As a matter of fact, the breeze had warmed, but I didn't mind her using it as her excuse to snuggle and didn't mind the warm softness of her body next to mine on such a moonlit night.

Her tone softened and deepened.

"Didn't know you'd been invited tonight either. Could've come together if…"

"I'm Lucien's guest," I said in a whisper, not wanting to break the spell.

"Lucien? Lucien F-G? Wasn't he being sent down for doing nothing at all for two years?"

"Apparently not sent down at all. That's what I thought. Looks like he smooth-talked his way around Osborne, and Lynwood has let him have another go."

"Good. There's hope for the rest of us then."

"You don't need to worry, Lou. You're in line for a first. At least that's what I hear."

She looked around and back up at me pulling my arms down around her for warmth.

"Rubbish," she said in a dreamy way. "Who told you that?"

"Two people."

"And which two might they be?"

"Carol, for one and Adelia for another."

"Oh! Dearest is too optimistic, I'm afraid. Be glad to get a third, the way things are going."

"A good solid third is nothing to be ashamed of," I said, tightening my arms, swaying her gently from side to side and leaning my chin on the top of her head.

"But I'll put money on you coming out with a first or…or…"

"You'll eat your head." She giggled, and thought about releasing me but thought better of it and leant her head back into my chest.

"Better not let Beau or Dearest hear about us tangled up like this, or…" I whispered into her ear.

"Like what? We're merely conserving body heat against a cold, buffering nor'easter. Otherwise, we'd freeze to death."

She giggled, looked back at me and twirled deftly out of my arms, away from some brink.

"Why'd you do that?" I asked, sleepily.

"You know what 'otherwise' did?"

"No. What?" I asked, somewhat foolishly, clawing at thin air.

She stopped in mid-twirl and fell back easily into my arms again.

"There. See?"

"See what?" she said in an absent-minded snuggle, this time facing me. The difference was amazing. Her hair. I rested my face there in that fabulous swirl, intoxicated by her scent, her succulent curves moulding into me.

"Christopher Robin…?

"Christopher Robin…?"

"Umm?"

"Christopher Robin…um…err…did you really go up Fornication Creek with Carol?"

I hesitated several seconds before answering. "Ummm. Maybe."

"What's that supposed to mean? Maybe!"

We swayed a little. She moved her head to look sideways up at me.

I could sense her eyes piercing through the night, glaring at me.

"Well?" she asked in a husky, more mature voice.

"Why?"

"Wondering."

"Wondering about what?"

"Just…It's just that…" she said, drawing out her answer, making me wait either because she liked the closeness, or she was just prevaricating.

"Ye-ess?" I asked.

"Well. I was just wondering what it was like."

"Like? What do you mean 'like'?"

"Well. Um. You know," she said dreamily.

"Oh, I don't know…What if one was to go in there?"

"Fornication Creek?"

"Yes. That's what I mean. What happens in Fornication Creek?"

"Didn't you ask Carol?"

"Not really. Couldn't," she snuggled.

"Wouldn't do to ask her."

"So you ask me."

"Yes."

"Lou, should we be doing this?"

"Doing what? Now you're just trying to change the subject."

"This," I said, squeezing her into me.

"Oh, this," she said, squeezing back. "I don't know. It is rather nice, though, isn't it?" she asked dreamily.

"Where were we?"

"Fornication Creek."

"Ah yes. Well …" She hesitated. "Beau has asked me, and I said I would get back to him after I'd made some enquiries on the subject."

"With me?"

"Yes. With you. Of course with you. Couldn't really ask Dearest in the state she's in these days, could I?"

"State?" Things were beginning to open up or close down, depending on how you chose to see them.

"Well, for a start…" I began.

"Yes. Go on," she urged.

"Well…"

"You just said that. Do come to a point…"

"Going anywhere with him is not advised," I said.

"Advised…What do you mean, advised?"

193

"Just that. Ask anybody…"

"Which 'anybody' in particular? You? But that's why I'm asking you. Dearest says you and she went in there and lived to tell the tale."

"Going anywhere with Beau is not a good idea. I can vouch for that. And Fornication Creek is the worst place I can think of – with him."

"What about with you?"

"Me?"

"Yes, you…What about going up Fornication Creek with you? After all, you are the world's expert."

"Wouldn't recommend it."

"Not you either?"

"I mean, it wouldn't be like I – or Beau – was being your tourist guide."

"Goodness …" The night went silent. I could feel her heart racing. I felt like I needed to swallow hard but didn't dare.

"What would you be doing then …?"

I could feel her eyes looking up at me again, expectantly, innocently.

"This?" She manoeuvred her hips and asked in a dusky, gypsy, deep-throated, erotically charged whisper.

"Certainly not," I said weakly.

"This?" she manoeuvred again.

"Possibly," I said.

"Possibly this," she repeated, "but not this. What can it mean? I am baffled," she said easing her pressure on me. "You aren't any help at all, Christopher Robin. Not any …" she said getting up on her tiptoes to give me a peck on my cheek. "… Help …"

Another peck.

"… at …"

And another.

"… all."

A fourth peck on the cheek before releasing her grip and twirling out across the night away from me.

"I suppose I'll just have to go and see for myself," she said, ending her twirl at the stone wall with her back to me.

"And since Beau is the only one gallant enough to offer me passage, I'll have to accept his offer," she said, gazing at the moon off through the trees. For some reason, just then, just as the moon was on the rise, she turned to look across at me. The moonlight caught her face. Hippolyta, proud but never ill met. Fascinating, savagely beautiful and proud. She took my breath away. She was a goddess on a mission, and nobody was going to stop her.

Was I her mission?

I didn't even entertain the thought at this point. Beau was on her mind, and I knew I was merely a stepping-stone, or so I thought.

Leaving Lucien in the middle of a drunken scrum in Osborne's parlour, I offered to walk Lulu back to her digs hoping that Carol might be in, worried that not only would she be in but in with Errol. But she wasn't and they weren't. So that was OK.

"Not a split infinitive all night, or dangling participle all evening," Louisa remarked as we walked arm in arm up Western Hill.

"Not a preposition out of place," I said.

"It's what you might expect in such elevated company," she said.

"I longed to hear a misplaced modifier, but nary a one…"

"Nary a one," I agreed.

"You still haven't delivered that book, Christopher Robin," Louisa said as we walked up to her door.

"*The Romantic Poets* one, remember? You promised. Need it for a paper I'm working on."

"I know I'll never get it back, if I do."

"Yes, you will. Yes, you will, you beast! With interest," she insisted.

"Aha. What kind of interest could you possibly offer on such a loan? My expectations are exploding."

"Just you wait and see. I've been planning it for ages, but you will have to deliver it to my bedroom window in the middle of the night. It's Carol's idea, really and a good one. Can't wait to try it out," she said in all innocence.

"Middle of the night?"

"Yes, well, early evening. Couldn't have you waking up the entire house."

"Your bedroom window?"

"Yes. No balcony on it, I'm afraid. You'll have to tap on the window to get me up, although I'll have been feigning sleep, waiting all along with great anticipation."

"In your nightie, I expect."

"You'll have to wait to find that one out," she answered coyly.

"Negligée?" I hoped.

"Not telling, silly. It has to be a surprise."

"Pleasant, I hope."

"I think you'll be…"

"Shocked?"

She didn't answer.

"Aroused, then?"

"You'll have to wait and see, Christopher Robin," she insisted with great glee in her voice.

"Stop trying to winkle it out of me."

"Carol's idea?"

"Yes."

"Will she be in it?"

"Hope not. Well, maybe, but she'll be asleep. So you'll have to whisper. And throw little pebbles at the window. Don't shout: 'I'm here with your damn book. Come and get it.'"

"Not to shout," I confirmed.

"No. Be very quiet. And you'll have to whisper."

"How will we be able to understand each other from such a distance if we whisper."

"That will be made abundantly clear, my lad. Understanding is the easy part."

"Your lad?"

"Yes," she said, squeezing my arm.

"And it's not that far. I am on the ground floor, you know. There. That window there at the side of the house."

"Ah, not far at all. No climbing trees and things."

"Right," she said, proud of herself. "Well within leaning out and reaching distance."

"I'll go and get it right now," I said, pulling away from her.

"No. Not tonight, surely. Some other, unexpected time," she said in a rush. "It has to be a surprise for me. But come to tea at Mary's tomorrow, if you like. It's pork chops again."

"My favourite," I said.

"Bring a sixpence," she called after me, as I headed back down the hill. "It might be your lucky day. And don't forget that book but come some other, unexpected night with it," she said with a wicked, self-deprecating smile.

"How will I know which day?" I shouted back up the street.

196

"Friday," she shouted back. "That's as unexpected as I can offer."

"My lucky day?" I whispered, but by this time, her door had shut, and I was once again left dangling in the middle of a split infinitive.

Chapter 30
The Harlot's Third Option

Halfway through the term, I moved into a three-bedroom terraced house in Kepier Terrace, just off Claypath and around the corner from The General Gordon. Better than the digs I had been in on the outskirts of Durham, the new place was shared with three other students and within five minutes' walk of the city centre. No grumpy old landlady to skate around in the mornings and explain to, whenever I returned home late at night. The new place was perfect, three smallish bedrooms and a squashed-in bathroom upstairs, and the living room on the ground floor turned into a fourth bedroom. Two female students occupied the top floor. I was the third tenant up there and lived in the little front bedroom that looked out onto the street through a little window. Damien Pettigrew was in the big downstairs room. The kitchen had just enough room in it for a chair or two, a record player balanced precariously on a stool, a sink and a cooker. Damien kept the kitchen spic and span, washing and dusting up a storm whenever our backs were turned. Nothing was off limits to Damien's fastidious washcloth. This irked the two girls no end. They were slobs at heart and didn't like to be reminded of it by this know-it-all, pinnied male.

I didn't mind. I liked Damien. Brought up in Richmond, he couldn't help his toffee-nosed, upper-class ways. He was always cheery and always saw things with the practical mind of the engineer. Damien gently helped us understand how the world of numbers worked. Anything that didn't have a number didn't fit into his world. Anything out of place, he found a place and a number for. Anything untidy, he took as his responsibility in life to rescue. I suspect that in later life Damien would turn out to be the last of the really true English gentlemen. He was never perturbed. He handled life's challenges with the aplomb of a maharishi, an English, upper-class maharishi.

I can't remember much about the two girls upstairs. They lived in their own world of boyfriends and daily academic routines that I didn't attempt to enter or participate in. One of them went out with a mate of mine. The other was rarely there.

Just as I was getting into the swing of my new digs, I was reminded by a little note in my pigeonhole in Cuth's about the book I still hadn't got to Lulu and where had I been for the last few days.

"I've been waiting in the library."

The note was signed 'C'.

I made my way dutifully along to the library at the appointed time, found my way through to our usual table, parked my stuff, opened my books and awaited events. Nothing happened for a long, lonely five minutes, then in the middle of *Joseph Andrews*, the chair opposite scrunched backwards. I held my breath and looked up to see Carol piling her things all over the table. My heart beat faster.

She said nothing as she organised her rubble into appropriate piles. Texts on the right, notebook in the middle, pens and pencils at its head and bag on the left.

"You forgot the cat," I said at which I was roundly shshshshed while she settled herself comfortably onto her chair and began her work.

After ten minutes of silence, a voice appeared as if from out of nowhere.

"Well?"

I looked up to see her looking, troubled, back at me.

"Well?" she said again in a whisper.

Remembering how I had left her that night at Van Mildert disco, hooked once again on Errol, I held my confused breath then heard myself whispering back to her, "Moved into my new digs last week," I said lamely as a kind of apology.

"You might have told me instead of leaving me…leaving me…leaving me pending."

I took a deep breath. Didn't know what to say, so I said, "You're never pending."

Someone shshshshed us again from a different table.

She looked up brightly from under her hair band at this but remembering she was supposed to be cross with me, feigned attitude and returned to her books in a cute little huff. I was being given the silent treatment.

She was in charge of the silent treatment, so according to silent treatment protocol, I deferred until, quite out of character, I ventured a, 'Well?' of my own.

She looked up with a scowl on her face. It appeared I was really in deep shit this time. For what, I had no idea.

"Sorry," I wrote and pushed the note across. A limp attempt at reconciliation I know, but it was all I had.

Not a nibble. She continued working up a storm, hair askew, falling over her headband, across her forehead. Totally against study hour protocol, we disengaged for the rest of the hour leaving me wretched and confused.

"You might have said," she finally pushed a note back across the table then stood up and started loading up her bag, ready to leave.

"Said what?" I bravely uttered.

"You and Louisa," she hissed in a sulky funk and sat down again.

"Me and Louisa, what?"

"Your romantic evening under the stars, is what.

"She told me all," she said very loudly and was immediately roundly hushed from all quarters. We decided to decant to the Union Teashop to answer questions and set things right. I needed to explain, so I followed her like a little puppy. She was still out of sorts and totally in charge.

"It's not as if it matters. Not as if..." She looked across at me over the brewing pot of tea.

"But. You might at least have said something to me about it all, leaving me to pick up scraps of evidence here and there from Lou and wondering...and wondering...and won...oh, it's just no good..."

"Just that," I said.

"What? Just what?"

"Nothing. An evening under the stars. We found ourselves together at Prof Osborne's party and went out to chat on the patio."

"... not what she says." She feigned sulking and stirred the pot. "... not that at all ..."

"I walked her back to your place, and ..."

"... And then you arranged your erotic assignation. She told me all about it. Deny it if you like, but ..."

"You arranged it all," I said in my own limp defence.

"It was your idea. I was merely going along with things in the hopes ..."

"Yes?"

"Well. In the hopes that I might see you there at your digs, that's all."

"You can see me anytime. When you're interested, that is. No problem there, if you're interested, that is," she said, playfully trying to corner me again.

"Seeing Lou half naked in her slinky negligee hanging out of her bedroom window is another thing. You might want to think of that," she said.

"But it was your idea. She said it was. Look, I'll give you the book. You can deliver it to her. No need for an assignation, or a negligee, or her pale, white, ample bosoms bobbing under a midnight moon."

"Thrust out." I was corrected.

"All right then, thrust out under a midnight moon."

"Wantonly.," she giggled.

"Wantonly? Never Lou!"

"Yes Lou! As wanton as they come. You mustn't have noticed," she added as a kind of sop and giggled again. I was consumed and distracted by what I can only describe as total, abject, breathless adoration of Carol at this. I was dizzy with it. She must have recognised the dumb look on my face and cleared her throat. It was all getting a little too carried away for a teashop and quietly satisfied that she had me squirming; she calmed the blood by pouring the tea and offering me a toasted teacake.

"Harlot. There's no other word for it, unless it's tart."

"Butter?" she asked.

"Poor thing just has no control of her libidinous, thrusting bits-and-pieces when there's a full moon on the go. Like a werewolf. The moon does that to her. And a balcony – which we don't have, by the way. So you would have been stymied on that one."

"I was happy with the negligee and ample, naked, thrusting bosoms bit. Don't need a balcony. Would have meant a climb. I don't climb balconies very well."

"That's a shame. My window has a tree," she said brightly, looking wonderingly across at me as if having discovered The North West Passage.

"I'll deliver it to you then – If she's not in, that is."

"If she's not in?"

"Yes."

"But it's Louisa's assignation. You're not going to disappoint her, are you? Ample bosoms and all."

"I thought you didn't want it."

"Didn't want it if I hadn't been told. Want it now that I can vet the affair and keep you two in line. I'll be secretly there behind a curtain, just in case."

"What? In case of what?"

"You – silly. Getting too amorous. I know what happens to you, especially when there are ample bosoms on display. And I don't have to tell you Lou's are wondrous, if not monstrous."

"You don't have to tell me," I said, rather unwisely.

"You've noticed then?" she asked, raising her eyebrow and blushing.

"Sort of. Kind of," I squirmed, realising I'd just screwed up again and desperately trying to come up with a way out of this new unwise incrimination, but wise old Carol jumped on it immediately, and I knew I had to tell her in order to preserve some sort of verisimilitude.

"Sort of, kind of? What do you mean, sort of kind of? Have you and she…?"

"Not really, but she did wander a little close to me under the moon that night on Osborne's veranda.

"You snogged her, didn't you?" She laughed out loud with great glee and satisfaction that she had me trapped. "Come on, you blaggard. Own up. Tell all. And remember Lulu's already confessed to it, so if you don't. If you don't tell all…"

"Yes? What?"

"I'll know," she said, nodding her head and grinning. "The stories must coincide, or I'll know."

"Know what?"

"That you're a blaggard, silly and not to be trusted around impressionable young women. That's what. Now. Fess up and take your medicine like a good boy."

So I fessed up about the body contact and waited while my delicious inquisitor mulled it all over.

"Wow," she exploded with her discovery. Her eyes popped, those glorious orbs popped, almost sending me backwards off my chair.

"Lulu didn't tell me that part. You say she pressed her ample bosoms wantonly into your manly chest while you and she were on the patio? Wow. It gets better and better, but I'll have to visit her for confirmation, so you had better be telling the truth, my lad."

"Your lad?"

"My lad." she nodded again; her whole face contorted in glee as she reached out for my hand across the table.

"But," she relented, "poor you at having to go through the Spanish Inquisition just to get a book to her. Have another cup of tea. I shall have to talk to Louisa right away. She missed the body contact on the patio bit and needs a chance to get her story right, accurate…more accurate.

"Were her nipples erect and piercing your shirt?" she persisted, grinning.

"When?"

"You know, silly, back on the patio."

"I couldn't remember any piercing, but she smelt amazing."

"Lou always does well with her smell," Carol admitted, dispossessing my hand and reaching across for a scone. With a mouthful, she went on to explain,

"It's the harlot's third option. If she doesn't get you with the face or bosoms, the smell is next. From what you've told me, she had everything going that night. Are you sure she didn't know you were going to be there at that party? Sounds like she knew you were going to be there, and she was lying in wait, ready to pounce. She doesn't usually go out like that with all guns blazing unless there's big game in the hunt."

"Me? Big game?"

"Who else? She'll be taking you home to Daddy next. Then watch out."

This confused me, and I don't mind saying, pissed me off. Was Carol ditching me yet again in her kindly, matter-of-fact way? Passing me off to Lulu? Errol must be back in the picture. If I had had any gumption, I'd have had it out with her and put an end to it, one way or another. The possibility of a negative answer, though, was still too cataclysmic for me to contemplate, so I didn't. I preferred to follow the old standby: if you don't know it has happened, it hasn't happened.

Don't ask.

Chapter 31
Décolletage

"In the dead of night?"

"Dead of night," Carol assured me.

We were scrunched up on the tiny sofa in her digs.

"Must be. Has to be. She's been getting ready for this for days. You cannot disappoint her."

"What if I wrapped it up nicely in a parcel and sent it through the post instead?"

"Won't do. Not in the least," she said aghast at the thought.

"Has to be delivered in person," she said.

"I could just give it to you, and you could pass it on."

Carol sat up, looked daggers at me. That wasn't going to 'do' either. She sat back down again.

"Pass it on? Simply passing it on won't work, I'm afraid," she said, getting more perturbed with every one of my daft suggestions.

"I know. I know," I said cowering away from her ire.

"She needs to know you care. It's...it's...it's...well, it's symbolic and romantic and things. A bit like...well...a bit like this," she said, snuggling again.

"And you don't mind?" I asked.

"Course not, you ninny. She's my best mate. She's about to swoon under your dark, foreboding, manly gaze."

"What about her...?"

"Her what?"

"You know."

"No, I don't."

"Her ... delecottage?" I asked in all innocence.

"Her what?"

"You know. Her …" I motioned about my person and finally pushed up imaginary bosoms."

"Ah … Her décolletage. You mean her ample, thrusting bosoms, her pale, ample, thrusting bosoms. Well …" She snuggled closer in order not to reveal the intimate content of the next bit to the whole world.

"Yes. Well. Lulu and I have been working on that too. A lot," she said, inclining her head in emphasis. And I'm afraid you will have to wait to find out. It's her secret weapon, or weapons. It's really the focal point of the assignation. I've been helping her with it. And I think we've finally got them right."

"Right?"

"Yes. You'll see. I'm rather proud of that bit."

"Oh, you mean she's going to hang them out over the window sill like some harlot in Amsterdam."

"No, silly. It's all really quite dignified. Intimate."

"Dignified. That's what I'm afraid of," I said.

"Understated," she whispered.

"That too," I said with some dismay in my voice.

"Well. Look. What would you have her do? The girl cannot be expected to perform a pole dance for you right there in the middle of Western Hill."

"Wasn't expecting a pole dance."

"She's not doing one. And that's that."

"Understood," I said bowing my head to her higher principles.

"It's meant to be intimate…and understated…" she said.

"But I could have a word, if you—" she said.

"No. Don't. I don't mean…" I fumbled, now out of my depth.

"She's not shy … well, I mean … she is really quite shy. Really. But for the sake of verisimilitude … we had been – at first – planning on a loose-top-button-display rather than a full cleavage one – if you know what I mean. But now I'm giving the plot away, so don't do any more prying. No more prying," she repeated.

"No more prying," I assured her.

"Good. Anyway, it's not all set yet. There are a few loose ends to tie up."

"Sounds like quite a production."

"Oh, it is. You'll see.

"She's really quite excited."

"I guess spur of the moment has gone out the door?" I asked.

205

"Spur of the moment? Oh, you mean improvisation."

"There's a lot to be said for it, improv, I mean. Then again, if you leave it up to it – spur of the moment – a lot can get missed, a girl can get confused, and who knows what might happen. Best to have a script."

"Nightie or jammies?" I asked.

"Negligee of course. Don't be silly. Couldn't see having a real balcony scene with jammies, could you? Dear me. Unheard of."

"Just wondering what my motivation should be," I said.

"Motivation? Lust, I suppose. Just every day, common or garden lust. Why? What did you expect it should be?"

"A cuppa tea after? Hobnobs. Chocolate ones."

"Chocolate hobnobs? What next? I ask you." She sat up in mock horror, looking to the heavens with that delightful grin.

"Chocolate Bourbons would be nice," I ventured.

"Ingrate. You'll be wanting jam on it next. Just think. You will have the express reward of attending a young nubile woman at her window in her negligee, if you're lucky – maybe pyjamas, if you're not – in the dead of night with all the rewards such an assignation might reap. What more could you possibly ask for?

"Chocolate hobnobs?" she playfully derided. "Out of the question. Only for really grand, state occasions. I do think you are playing it up a bit, Christopher Robin. Chocolate hobnobs? What can you be thinking? Totally out of the question."

All the while, throughout the conversation, our voices became lower and lower while our heads got closer and closer until, by the end of it all, her head was on my shoulder with her smiling lips bare millimetres away from mine.

"Christopher Robin?" she whispered, quiet moments later.

"Yes?"

"I think pyjamas would be best, the best option, I mean. Don't you?"

"Negligee," I said without hesitation.

"I mean," I added. "No chocolate hobnobs … a fella should have some kind of reward for services rendered."

"What do you mean, 'services rendered'?" she said, sitting up and turning to me earnestly, looking directly into my eyes.

"The book, of course. Book delivery to her boudoir in the dead of night. Delivery services."

"Oh," she said with some gratitude in her voice.

"I thought you meant something else," she said.

"What else could I possibly mean?" I teased.

"You know," she said, punching my shoulder.

"Don't know what you mean."

"Yes, you do. And you're not to do any of that sort of thing. Hear me?"

"I hear, but a bloke should have some perks, especially after missing so much sleep and door-to-door delivery."

"Door-to-door delivery does not include that kind of reward, I'm afraid."

"Doesn't it? I was hoping…"

"You can just stop hoping. She's my mate, and you're not to lead her on, not like you are doing to me."

"Not? And what do you mean, me leading you on?" I asked.

"The topic of another conversation…" she said, prevaricating.

"The topic of a now conversation," I insisted heroically.

"Explain, please. Why do you think I'm leading you on and that I'm not entirely serious when I …" I added quickly.

"Yes. Go on. When you…"

"When I say that you are the most beautiful woman on earth."

"That's better," she said, snuggling closer again. "That's much better. As long as you're not leading me on or demanding negligees as payment, or hobnobs, for that matter – chocolate-covered ones indeed."

"If you only knew."

There must have been abject terror in my voice when I said this, for she sat up with, "Oh! Oh. I see. Dear me," she said, looking troubled. "Dear me," she said again, either for emphasis or because she didn't know what she had started and didn't want to go any further, or just that she couldn't think of anything else to say. Anyway, her exclamation was genuine. She was shocked.

"Then it is true. You do like me."

"Kind of, sorta."

"I see," she said, truly shocked.

"Why?" I asked.

"Well. It's. I'm. It's…"

"Yes?"

"What do you mean, 'kind of, sorta'?"

"Nothing special. It's the way your eyes smile," I said.

"My eyes?"

"And generally just the way you look."

"Oh?"

"Yes."

"And just how is that? The way I look," she asked, genuinely interested, as if she didn't know how she looked or the effect the way she looked had on everyone-me-everyone.

"Simply?" I asked.

"Yes," she said in a rush to find out. "Keep it simple. Succinct and to the point.

"Succinct?"

"Yes," she said, demurring. "And …"

"To the point?"

"Yes. Go on, Christopher Robin. Out with it. I can take it."

"Well." And here I had to stop and look her up and down to drag the point out. "Simply the most wonderful woman I have ever met. In my whole life, that is."

"In your whole life?" she said enthusiastically, cherishing the idea and going pink at the same time.

"Well …" she beamed, treasuring the thought. "That is high recommendation coming from you."

"And the way you speak."

"Oh my goodness. How do I speak?" she asked with genuine surprise.

"Just like that. Just like that. Innocent and sweet. And…"

"And? Yes? What? I'm all ears. Compliments only, please. And don't lead me on. You can go on now," she said looking altogether pleased with herself.

"The way you are."

"Am I? Goodness. How's that? I mean the way I am."

"Like…"

"Yes? Go on. Like what? Flighty, like a kite."

"Not in the least. Well. Yes. Now that you mention it, you are flighty like a kite. Yes."

"Well, that's nothing new. I knew that already. You have to tell me something new or else it doesn't count."

"Bloody lovely," I said.

This stopped her in her tracks. She was hoping for a more grown up, sophisticated image, one that she had been trying to cultivate, like an aloof, sophisticated super model but hadn't quite pulled off yet, mainly because she was still too young. But I would guess that she would always be too young and would always be more like bloody lovely than a super model.

"Are you disappointed?"

She thought for a bit then shook her head.

"Innocent, sweet and vulnerable," I said, drawing out the image.

She drew a deep breath. "I suppose we are all vulnerable in one way or another.

"You are vulnerable…" she said, all of a sudden, turning the tables on me.

"Am I? How so?"

"You aren't going to like this, Christopher Robin. But…One of your most endearing qualities is your vulnerability."

I squirmed. This was not going to be pleasant. But the look on her face said the opposite, so I sat still to take my medicine.

"You think you are a big tough grown up man, but to me, you are an innocent little boy."

"Oh? Like when?" I said, challenging her to destroy me.

"Well," she thought, pressing her tongue to her upper lip.

"Are you firing from the hip?" I asked.

"What does that mean?"

"Shooting with both barrels."

"Now that's you being vulnerable again. See what I mean? There's no need. See? You always take the worst possible view of yourself. Stoppit. I'll be nice. Don't worry. Promise," she added.

"Good. Fire away."

She took some time to consider her words before she fired.

"For a while now, you've had the chance to claim your winnings, but out of some perverse sense of your own vulnerability or sense of fair play or a lack of confidence, call it what you like, I don't know – you hold back, do nothing, let others take the lead until I'm at a loss to know what to do. Lulu sees it too. She can't understand it. You are vulnerable to your own sense of fair play."

"I wouldn't see it that way," I said.

"Anyway, what's wrong with having a sense of fair play? Having a sense of honour or decency."

"Is that what you call it? All's fair in love and war, you know.

"Well then…Do it. Be a caveman for once in your life and don't give a damn for the other man. Claim your spoils. Do it. You've won me – many times over – but you are reluctant to collect your winnings.

"It's very irritating, you know," she said lowering her voice.

"A girl must know where she stands, be collected from time to time. And must also know if she has a chance. I'm never really sure with you. Do you have somebody else in the wings? Do you, Christopher Robin? It's so infuriating. It's your impossible vulnerability again. I can see that. And it's sweet and lovely. But …

"But … I've said too much. You are upset. I should go. I should go before…" she said in a rush.

"Before what?"

"Before. Before. Don't you see? Do I have to spell it out in any more detail? You know, ever since you went on that clandestine assignation with Louisa," she said with a tear forming in the corner of her eye.

"Which assignation?"

"The one where you and she stood breathless in the moonlight…"

"Prof Osborne's Party?"

"Yes," she said in a blaming kind of way.

"Well. Ever since that, I've wondered just what is going on with you, with you two. That's why I've been pushing this balcony scene."

"You didn't need to, you know," I said.

"I did. I did."

"Why, especially when you didn't need to?"

"Well. Well. I had to know if you two …"

"If we two? If we, what?"

"If you two were, well, you know. I had to disregard my own chances, my own feelings in favour of a friend. Rather like your fair play."

"Your sense of honour and decency?" I asked wiping away the tear that now hung on the tip of her nose.

"Dishonourable honour," she burbled.

"I had motives," she said.

I considered this for some time before saying, "You thought you were doing the right thing. You do it and it's OK. I do it, and I'm a vulnerable fool. Well, I guess I am a fool. I was always a fool for ever thinking you and I …"

"What?"

"You know. Could ever be on the same page together. You have always seemed to be unobtainable to me, beyond any woman I could ever dream of …"

"Yes?" she urged, feeling that we were finally getting somewhere.

"All those times," I said, trying to explain. "All those times we were together and nothing happened. I really wanted … hoped something would. But could never be quite sure."

"About what?" she asked, exasperated.

"About you. About me. About you really feeling anything about me. About you just being polite," I said.

"Polite? Polite? When have I ever been polite? Rude perhaps but never polite. What do you mean, polite?"

I thought for a while trying to frame the right words to suit the occasion.

"Humouring me. That's it. I could never be sure that you weren't just humouring me out of some weird obligation to friendship."

"Now that's just rot. You dolt. You didn't know? All this time," she went on. "All this time I've been looking for a way to get through to you. Giving you appropriate hints. A clue here, a nudge there. Come and get me, I'm yours. That sort of thing."

This took my breath away. Well, wouldn't it yours?

"I've always been," she went on. "Ever since that lovely proposal in the library that time. You took my heart. Swept me off my feet. Ask Lou."

"Is that what Osborne's evening was about?" I asked.

"Yes," she said with all the assurance she could muster.

"A test."

"Yes.

"We both needed to know. And you bugger, you passed it. But I knew you would anyway. I didn't realise at the time, though, that it wasn't your intentions that were being tested but your sense of fair play. Another time, another place and you would have jumped all over her. But being the gentleman you are" – she blushed and lowered her eyes – "you wouldn't be drawn. Couldn't be. Plan failed. Gentleman through and through.

"Sorry," she admitted.

"What for?" I said.

"Clandestine motives …"

"Oh."

"There. I've told you all."

"And do you feel better now?"

"Feel somewhat … exposed …" she said.

"… But I'm sure it's good for me to tell all. Now there's nothing left to tell."

"Oh, yes there is," I said, playfully rounding on her.

"What?"

"Errol."

"Oh … bother. I knew this was coming …" she said.

"And?" I asked.

"Only that. I knew you would bring him into it…"

"And?"

"Don't want to talk about him."

I raised my eyebrows but said nothing, was ready to not talk about him, when Carol suddenly did.

"He's a dear friend, a dear old friend," she said in a rush as if wanting to get it over with in a hurry.

"I can't just …"

"Can't just, what?"

"Can't just stop, just like that. Don't want to hurt him, you see."

"And so, we are here," I surmised.

"Yes. Er. No. What do you mean?"

"US. Me and you. Here as on a darkling plain."

"There you go again, quoting people that I don't know – Tennyson or somebody. Distracting the whole conversation."

"Matthew Arnold," I said.

"Yes, well … I suppose we are here, and so is Errol – here. And all I can say is I wish he weren't. Here, that is. And he's dear to me and I can't treat him badly, even if you want me to."

"I didn't say that. But he is here. It's as if he's there standing right beside you."

"I know," she said sadly, looking beside her at some gloomy ghostly figure there.

"It's nothing," she said as delicately as possible, placing her gentle hand on my arm as an assurance.

"Promise," she said as further reinforcement.

"Now. More tea?" she asked, brightening, pouring me another cup and looking for all the world like nothing was amiss, at least nothing that couldn't be fixed was amiss. And whatever was to happen to us over the next few weeks, I trusted her to do the right thing by me, always.

There was nothing else I needed to say or feel about us but trust. This had been laid out already. Trust. A comfortable assurance. She was there for me in trust, and I trusted her totally.

Chapter 32
Crackerjack

"A right little crackerjack, she is."

Franklin was in front of his mirror adjusting his hair, getting ready to go out.

"I wouldn't call her a crackerjack," I said, knowing that at least some kind of courtesy should be used in the description of the lady in question.

"You tellin' me what to call my lass?" He huffed over the last tuck of his cravat, not even bothering to look at me.

"Not crackerjack. That's a box of caramel popcorn."

"Just what she is," he said with total confidence in his assessment of the girl he'd only known a couple of days.

"And…The proof's in the pudding, mate. You'll see."

"I'll see what?"

"Just what a little popper she is. Now. Pass me that bottle o' smelly, mate. Special Cologne," he said, lavishing the stuff about his person.

"One sniff o' this and she's anybody's. Especially mine." He grinned, dimples flashing all over the place.

I winced at the suggestion that tonight sweet little Louisa might be subjected to Beau's brutish view of romance, feeling totally guilty for putting these two together in the first place. Was this going to be another test? I felt like the father who was about to let his daughter go out on her first date with the village churl.

"Where are you taking her?" I tried to make the question less loaded with indignation and loathing than I was filled with.

"Gilesgate. Her, me and the lad here," he said making a sweeping gesture past his crotch.

"A couple of glasses of wine and Bob's your uncle. Just you wait, mate, but don't wait too long. Coz when I get her back to hers, I expect the premises to be completely vacated for her and me and him," he said indicating his celebrated 'lad' with another grandiose low sweep of his left hand.

"You really think she'll fall for that?"

"Never missed yet. World famous, he is."

"On a pub crawl down Gilesgate?" I was incredulous.

"She'll love it. Feet won't touch the ground. Can't miss," he said, giving his hair a last smooth-over and adjusting his crotch ready for the off.

"How many drinks do you plan on plying her with?"

"Doesn't matter, really. One or two should do it. Get her in the mood. Women usually don't need anything to get them in the mood wi' me, anyroads. The lad's reputation precedes us. She'll be salivating as we speak," he said, sweeping his golden locks back then letting them drop – just so.

"And I'm feelin' – good," he crooned to his reflection in the mirror.

"There's one thing you can do for us, though, mate, that would be a great help."

"Oh? And what's that, Lochinvar?"

"Get that Carol out of their digs before we get back. We can't come back here. Leo says he'll be working and can't have the bumpin' an' rollin' goin' on next door.

"So…

"I'll be takin' her back to Western Hill for a bit o' rumpy-pumpy after. Need a clear landin' strip, if you know what I mean. You could bring her mate, what'sername, back here, if you like. I know you'll be the epitome of discretion with her. You being you, and her being her. Take her out to the Dun Cow first – on me, if you like – as long as she's out of her place by the time we get back. I could stretch to a couple of glasses for her and a pint shandy for you. Anymore and you'll have to pay for it yourself. And keep your filthy eyes off the dolly new maid in there behind the bar. I haven't broken her in yet. Looks a tasty lass. Think I'll have time for her tomorrow, once little Louisa is hooked."

I had to tell him that I had no interest in aiding and abetting his scheme for tonight, that I had other plans, and he would have to find some other landing strip to take his catch to for rumpy-pumpy. Not bothered at all with this blockage to his festivities, he addressed his reflection in the mirror one last time.

"It's a hard life being the only Romeo in town for all these gaggin' women. It's a hard life, but somebody's got to do it. Gotta go. Already late, but she'll forgive us when she sees the bounty in store for her." He beamed as he fled the scene in a rackety rush dodging past Mrs Manners who had stopped at the top of the stairs to catch her breath.

"Err, Mr Franklin." she withered and dithered, holding on to the banister for support.

The Honey One stopped several steps down from her.

"I'm glad I caught you before you left," she said, her breathing even more elevated now.

Beau's hair flopped down over his forehead with his arrested descent.

"There's something I need to talk to you about," she said, inhaling his special cologne and feeling a little giddy, hanging on tighter to the banister. Her chest heaved with the strain put upon her heart, and her face reddened with what might have been her effort in climbing the stairs. Or was it that little blond wave of hair falling down across his forehead that made her heart pump so erratically? Was it the dimpled cheeks that she had flirted with all those times in the college office? Or was it his smiling, succulent lips claiming her lips in a dream?

"Yes, Mrs Manners?"

His delphinium blues dilated wide in anticipation.

"I…you…err…I wanted to talk to you, Mr Franklin…"

"Yes, Mrs Manners?" he said climbing back up one step, one step closer to her.

"What is it?" he said in all innocence.

"Nothing…err nothing. Only…"

"Yes? Only what, Mrs Manners?"

At this point, the dear lady began to feel quite unwell or depending how you see it – well – young again – thinking his smiling eyes were for her and her alone, not knowing that they were looking several hours ahead to the tryst that he had planned for a certain young lady from St Mary's.

Mrs Manners took courage from the young man's bright, happy smile, and without thinking, launched herself directly at those rosy lips that seemed to beckon. Before he knew it, the young lad had been accosted from a great height. Not only had she hit her target, but once the target had been achieved, she hung on to the lad as if her very life depended on it.

Poor Mrs Manners.

When she realised what had just taken place and that she had Mr Franklin in an unrequited headlock, she recoiled in horror and began to shriek at the top of her lungs that she had been accosted and that her attacker had very nearly carried her off to his bedroom to have his wicked way with her.

A full register of students flooded out onto the landings as well as the bottom and first floor of Number 8 to see what in the world was going on. What was the woman going on about? Why was she so hysterical, and why on earth should Franklin pick on her when he had almost every female in the university willing to throw herself out of a window to gain only a little part of his very special attention? Beau was just as mystified as the rest of us and far from seeming to want to carry her off to his lair was actively peeling her fingers from around his head, and ears and nose.

Poor Mrs Manners.

Poor Beau.

What a pickle.

Once free, Beau dashed downstairs without looking back and fled the scene before his admirer could gain another hold. The door downstairs slammed shut, and he was gone.

Mrs Manners looked across at me and then at Tucker who had popped his head round his door to see what the fuck was going on.

"Only wanted to talk to him about his battels sheet," she said, straightening her blouse and smoothing down her skirt, her chest heaving and eyes dilated with excitement.

"Do you think he'll be back soon?" she asked him.

Leo's head ducked back out of sight.

"Not bloody likely, missus," Leo offered from behind his closed door.

"Poor bloke's had a fright," his weak, distant voice was heard to say.

"Won't be back here before the night's out. You'll have to get in the queue, missus," he said, gazing off across the gardens out the back window of his room.

"Should be right royally shagged before he comes back here in the morning, though. Better to take a number and come back tomorrow evening, dear. He'll be feeling more like it by then," he mused.

"Bastard!

"Not that I would be interested in … that ... but … bastard!" he uttered again in despair.

Feeling desperate myself and in need of some kind of support against the coming evening, I asked Tucker out for a fortifying pint. He refused on the grounds that he had done bugger all this term and needed to spend some time in his books. It was important, he said. But he might get up to the General Gordon for a game of darts later, if I was interested.

What could be more important than the wellbeing of little Louisa who was on the verge of making the worst mistake of her life?

"Not my worry, mate," he said still gazing off over the gardens through his window. And that was that. So, I set out by myself to see what I could do to intervene in Louisa's fall. As I marched along North Bailey, I was greeted by the unmistakeable voice of Lucien Fenwood-Gross who had spent the afternoon in the Union in the company of doleful Specky Neville whom Lucien had just abandoned in the hopes of finding brighter fellowship for the night.

"Halloo," came Lucien's greeting from somewhere behind me, as I was walking past the cathedral.

"I am in need of sustenance and happy conversation. Specky is in a funk back in the Union with his head at the bottom of a pint of Guinness. He mumbles something from time to time about honouring one's debts, payments or something or other, shows me little packets from his pockets as proof of his debts, has another drink then falls back into his funk again. I'm afraid he's sinking fast. His dealers, he says, are closing in on him. I've escaped or rather run away before he pulls me in with him. Drag me off somewhere, Flynn, anywhere, please."

On our way through the marketplace, I updated him on the dire fate of my friend and my mission to save her from the clutches of The Supreme Fornicator.

"Can't be as bad as all that." Lucien puffed, out of breath, as we struggled up Claypath, heading for Gilesgate, the scene of Franklin's intended debauchery.

"After all, she's seeing him of her own free will and old enough to know what she's doing, whether you approve or not. I think what you really need is a bracing pint and healthy reassurance that despite your worst misgivings, everything will be all right.

"It couldn't be that you're a tiny bit jealous of Franklin's prospects for the evening. She's that lass you hooked up with at Osborne's shindig, is she not? A comely wench, if memory serves. Pretty eyes. Although her eyes are the least of his intentions tonight."

I had to agree that she had very attractive eyes, and although I didn't mention it, I must also agree that I was feeling pissed off with her attentions toward Franklin. Anybody else's interests in her would have brought no ill will. Franklin was different. It took Lucien's view of the situation, though, to bring my emotions into perspective.

Lucien wheezed on up Claypath, and as we approached the Travellers' Rest, he stopped a minute to catch his breath.

"Just what are your intentions if we happen to bump into them? Fisticuffs? A good telling off? Drag her back home to face the ire of her papa? Believe me, there is nothing you can do tonight that might help her make the right decision about him, other than letting him run his course and letting her make her own mind up; letting her make her own mistakes and face them afterwards. Fathers have tried for millennia to protect their daughters against The Cad and generally all to no avail. Best we stop in here at The Travellers' and think things through. Wouldn't want you to regret forever your actions tonight. Wouldn't want you pushing her in his direction by unpropitious action. They also serve who stand and wait, dear chap. They also serve a nice pint of exhibition in here. Let's go in.

"Mmmmm, smells lovely," he said absorbing the beery, hoppy, brewery aroma that wafted out the door as we entered.

Considering Lucien to be useless at most things, yet very astute when it came to beer, common sense and human nature, I gave in for the moment to his need for fortifying drink and brought the first of many pints over to our table near the front window. The place wasn't busy yet, and so we were able to hear each other without having to raise our voices. Many problems were solved over the course of the evening. Customers came and went, but we were still there exchanging life's tragedies when Lucien decided it was time to move on to other climes. We stumbled out onto the street and made our beery way up to the General Gordon and found the cool, dark Saloon Bar there ravaged by a company of friends who welcomed us with open arms into their game of darts.

To Leo's question about whether or not I had located Beau and Louisa, I had to lie that we had scoured the town and had come up empty handed. He fired his dart into a double one to end the game.

Colin said that Beau had probably taken her to his lair in the boathouse, to which Agnes, Leo's friend for the evening, replied, "Don't be so daft, Colin. They're probably having a very nice evening somewhere quiet and romantic, walking under the moonlight along by the river. If he's got any sense, he'll keep well out of the way of that dirty, old boathouse. Spiders and things running about the floor. Turns me ill just to think about it."

"That's just it," Leo said toeing the line for their next game of darts, "Franklin and sense don't mix."

"He'll have shagged her rotten by now, if I know our Beau; taken her to some sleazy dive to get her soused up for another go at her starting right about now," Tucker said, checking his watch.

He hit a lucky double ten to start his next game.

"Jammy bastard," Colin muttered out the side of his mouth, stood up to the mark and missed with all three of his darts.

Agnes missed.

None of Specky's darts stuck. He sat down again in a sulk, emptied his pint and skulked off to the bar for a refill.

"Mine's a pint, Herbert, while you're there, my dear," Lucien shouted wistfully, to which Specky mumbled some inaudible insult and returned with his Guinness in one first and nothing in the other.

"Good god, Herbert. I didn't say I wanted a Guinness."

"Fuck off, Lucien," Specky spat. "Get your own fucking drink."

"Temper, temper. What's up, Specky, my lad? Out of sorts…or funds…or just out of charity?" Lucien asked with polite arsenic in his voice.

"Or just the stingy old bugger you've always been. You still owe me one from the Union. And, by the way, have you paid that special bill yet? The one you were talking about back there?"

"Piss off," Specky scowled, set his drink down and picked up the darts to take his turn at the line.

Lucien turned to the rest of us, raising his eyebrows. Something was on Specky's mind.

"Right," Specky said suddenly, as if an alarm had gone off somewhere, "I need a piss," and shuffled outside to the bogs in the back of the pub.

The mission that brought me out that night was soon forgotten, though, with a rumbling squawking banging and crashing that came from the back yard of the pub.

"Sounds like a fight out there," Leo said, nodding towards the disturbance.

"Do you think somebody has finally done him in?" Lucien asked with almost complete disinterest in Specky's fate.

"Sounds to me like he's been throttled and stuffed upside down in a dustbin," he added, casually rising to his feet and lumbering off to the bar.

"Drinks anyone?"

We gave him our orders.

"Oh … oh, aye," Leo mumbled, toeing the darts line again, aiming, teetering on his right big toe the way he does and delivering the point of his dart to nearly where he wanted.

"Damn …

"Oh … yes, Lucien. And a pie, if you please. I'm feeling famished at the minute," Leo said, looking sternly embarrassed at Agnes who laughed at the accusatory nature of his comment and fired back:

"Don't look at me, Leo. I'm not responsible."

"I am feeling weak, dear," he apologised. "A pie would prop me up for the rest of the evening. Give me the energy," took up aim again at the dartboard, teetered …

"… to …"

…delivered the dart, missed and lost his train of thought.

"Damn and blast. Whose arrows are these, anyway?"

"Yours, Leo, dear," Agnes answered caustically with a flippant, burbling laugh at his feeble attempt.

"Yes, well, they're damp. Can't throw a damp arrow…A pork one, please, Henry – with HP on. Pork pie with HP sauce, if you don't mind."

"Can't stretch to HP, Leo. OR a pie for that matter. Exchequer will only stretch to a pint for you," Henry said, poking at a dismal pile of coins in the centre of his hand.

"You'll have to give me the money for the pie."

Missing this last bit from Lucien whilst pulling his darts out, Leo cocked an ear to the continuous dustbin rumblings coming from the back yard of the pub.

"I think Specky's being attacked out there. I'll just go out and see if he's all right. Protect my investment. Owes me a pint," Tucker said looking self-servingly over his shoulder.

"Owes me several, when it comes to it."

"You'll be lucky," Colin called after him.

"Join the queue. Specky's never repaid a loan in his life. He's probably out there right now fighting off his dealers," somebody else said, don't know who, doesn't matter, really.

Suddenly, there came a god almighty bang, then all went quiet out in the yard.

Leo recoiled into the snug without ever reaching the back door, a grim look on his face.

"They've done for him this time," he said staggering toward his seat.

"Nonsense," Agnes said. "It's just a cat out there rummaging in the dustbins for scraps. Or Specky with his bad eyesight falling about drunk."

All baited eyes were turned toward the back door.

No one appeared. Then…

"See?" Agnes said.

"Cats," as one huge, self-satisfied ginger Tom poked his head around the door before stepping confidently across to Leo and past him, stroking its tail lovingly across his leg. The cat, whose name was Boris, sprung easily onto a stool in front of the bar before jumping nimbly onto the bar top and over to his little round cat bed on the other side between the row of single malts and cigars.

"Specky's turned into a cat," was Leo's first thought.

"Couldn't be Specky," Colin said. "Wrong hair colour."

"Doesn't seem to want to fight, either."

"A benign Specky. Just doesn't fit. Can't be Specky," Colin decided. "He'd've had your face off by now."

The cat smiled out across the bar at us, purring at the attention he was getting.

Specky staggered back in after another round of darts had finished with Colin winning.

"That was a near thing," Specky said, chastened by events in the back alley.

Nobody looked up.

"Robbers," he said with hurt in his voice, reaching out for sympathy.

Nobody gave a fuck.

Then, out of nowhere, in through the backdoor strutted first Montagu-Smy, scowling at, daring Specky, and then his mate Harry Sturge threatening death. They passed through the pub with nary a word, slamming the front door on their way out as a kind of warning.

The air in the General Gordon was taut.

After a suitable pause during which he trawled the hearts of the assembly for some kind of sympathy, any kind of love, Specky said, "None of you give a fuck, do you?"

"None the worse for wear, Herbert?" Lucien said from the middle pages of a week-old Daily Mirror.

"I could have been killed out there," Specky said, looking around desperately for a reaction.

"Appears you weren't," Leo said in the middle of the next game with Colin and me. "More's the pity," he whispered out of the corner of his mouth.

"Nothing to rob," Colin added.

"No harm done," I said.

"Could've been though, but…"

"Who were they, Herbert?" Agnes asked.

"Your dealers?" she added quickly, cynically, unkindly.

Agnes was a no-nonsense kind of Cockney lass and usually came to the point and was often right.

For a millisecond, the bar went quiet then just as quickly carried on with its business. Darts flew and talk resumed as if to stifle any hurt or to give Specky a chance to find a response. But Specky didn't. He was in no state to. Countless pints and god know what else in his system left him bereft, and he just slumped over in his corner, breathing hard and looking deeply, furtively, into the nature of things.

"Will they be coming back in here after you, Herbert?" Agnes asked.

"Coz if they are, I'm away home before the fight breaks out.

"Did you pay them?

"Specky, did you pay them?" she hissed.

Herbert lifted his head and stared at her malevolently, said nothing, just stared and stared.

"Goodness," she said. "That's an awful look. Hope it doesn't mean what I think it means, coz I'm not at all frightened of you, Specky Neville."

"Let him alone, Agnes," Leo said kindly.

"I'll let him alone when I know I'm not going to be in the middle of some gangland take down."

"Hardly gangland, is it, Specky? Just your mates paying a call. That's all. Isn't it, Specky?

"Specky – isn't it?" Leo said looking closely at the slumped over figure.

"Fuckin' Ada," he cried out. "He's passed out, Agnes. Agnes," Leo implored, "he's passed out!"

"He's all right, Leo. Just give him a nudge. Get him up and walk him about. He just needs his juices flowing again.

"Specky," she said, giving him a prod. "Get up, Specky. You're not fooling anybody."

When I nudged him, he just fell to the floor.

"Out cold," I discovered.

"He's either unconscious or dead," Leo said, sniffing at him suspiciously.

"Never could hold his beer. Come on Specky, old fella," he said reaching down and urging him to his feet.

"My god, I think he's…"

"Put him back, Leo. You're choking him to death grabbing him by the neck like that. Put him back. Somebody call an ambulance."

And somebody, I don't know who, got on the blower and dialled 999.

He had been beaten up in the alley so severely that a rib was bruised. That, plus his high alcohol content finished his dart-playing evening.

"It's all your fault, Leo," Agnes scowled after the body had been removed to the infirmary.

Leo was aghast at her accusation.

"You shouldn't have grabbed him by the neck like that. Damn near choked the life out of the poor daft little sod."

"I was just administering first aid, Agnes. More than you were likely to do for him."

"Me? Wouldn't touch him with a punt pole. Never know where he's been," she shuddered.

"At least I didn't try to choke him to death in some misbegotten act of first aid," she added as an afterthought.

Continuing his turn at the dartboard, Leo didn't miss a beat.

"I may…" he said firing his first arrow into a seven…

"Have…" shooting a three…

"Saved his…" double top…

"Life, Agnes. There, I've done it – double top.

"I win…

"Colin – double top," he triumphed. "I've won!"

"Mine's a pint, mate," Leo said with glee.

"Saved the life of a dear, misunderstood mate while shooting a double top at the same time.

"See that, Agnes, dear?"

"Yes, Leo. Heroic, I'm sure," she said ignoring his moment of glory, holding out her glass to him for a refill.

"Do something really useful and get me another Cherry B."

"I shall, dear. I shall. Right after I've phoned the BBC's Sports desk. I'm sure they'll be very interested in my little double. David Coleman, no less. Yes," he prattled on. "I'm sure old Dave will be very interested," he mumbled, shuffling off to the bar and returning, still prattling, handing her refilled glass across to her but spilling a bit on the way.

She jumped on him immediately.

"Sorry, dear. Sorry. Must've got carried away. Must be the elation of the moment," he said feeling very smug.

"Not often you win at darts, Leo," I said.

"Or save the life of a poor, daft, little sod of a mate," he said looking directly into the caustic grimace of his true love.

"Hardly saved his life though," she said.

"Hanging on by a thread, Chris, my lad," he said, turning to me. "Hanging on by a thread. I could see his little hourglass emptying with every breath. All I could do to struggle back from it and into a double top.

"Whose shout is it by the way?"

"By the way," Agnes replied in her dour way, "it's still yours. A glass of half-spilled Cherry B does not constitute a round."

Chapter 33
Poor Specky, Poor Lou, Poor Beau

Some pints later, a droll, rag-tag, band of pilgrims spilled out of the General Gordon onto Claypath heading downhill toward Sweaty Betty's Chip Shop. Louisa and her perils with Beau were now a bygone memory. Upon reaching The Travellers' Rest, however, the memory of Louisa's calamity was jolted back into stark reality, for there up on the mezzanine floor at the back of the pub was that very maiden, alone and looking wistfully out toward the street, just as I happened to glance in the door.

Her date for the evening was nowhere to be seen. Lulu, alone and looking miserable, was reason enough for intervention and rescue, and I was going to be the lad to do it. Swiftly making my apologies to the others and threatening to join them later at Betty's chip shop, I broke off from them, entered the closely packed pub and shouldered my way through the din to the bar for a pint and a wine and then to the stairway at the back that led to the damsel on the upper deck.

Louisa grinned sheepishly as I approached. I plonked myself down opposite. "Oh, dear," she said. "You."

I said nothing for a minute or two, allowing the dust to settle before getting the gory details from her. She was unusually quiet, choosing to sip her wine and gaze longingly out over the balcony at what I thought to be a memory of the absent cad who had obviously dumped her.

I could see that she needed some time before talk and so sipped quietly at my pint.

Finally, I offered, "Noisy in here."

She nodded, took a deep breath and sighed, returned her gaze to the lower floor.

I nodded. After several more minutes of unprofitable silence, hers and mine, we both stood up to leave.

She wanted to talk but at the same time didn't, so I respected her fragile state and gave her support as we made our way back to her digs. Halfway across Framwellgate Bridge, she stopped to look back and up at the whispering, gloriously illuminated cathedral towers along from the castle.

"You don't have to be my escort, you know."

"Just in case," I answered.

"In case of what?"

"Bad'uns on the way home," I replied.

"Bad'uns? Here? Don't be silly."

But I was silly and insisted on being her escort for the rest of the walk home. She remained quiet and within herself for a while. Taciturn. Cut off. I took this to mean that her evening had not gone well, and that the romance with Beau had faded. Must have. Couldn't think of any other reason for her to be alone.

We walked past the bus station with salt and vinegar smells coming from Frampton's' fish and chips shop pulling me sideways up the alleyway.

"If we could just stop a mo'," I said.

"What for?"

I pulled a hungry face, and she laughed. Frampton's queue was short, so our business in there was concluded quickly, and we were again on our way with Lou rustling into my newspaper intermittently, coming up with a juicy fat chip, snorffling it off and returning to the trough for more.

"You said you didn't want any," I complained as my hoard of battered haddock was quickly cut in half.

"Didn't think I was hungry, but – appears I am," she said fisting a particularly large piece of fish down her throat.

"Magwitch," I said, reminded of *Great Expectations*.

"Not," she said with feigned hurt, reaching for another treat.

I steered away from her, protecting my treasure.

She laughed and swooped again. I lifted the newspaper high, out of her reach.

"Sod." she giggled. "Let me have some."

But I held her off until desperate measures took over, and she pulled my arm down. I had to give in when she threatened to disable me amidships. We walked up Western Hill plundering the rest of the meal in fistfuls, each determined to eat our fill and fighting over the vinegar-drenched crumbs of salty batter left in the bottom of the trough.

"There's that man," Louisa suddenly said of a couple she spied scuttling quicker than us up the other side of the street.

"Who? What man?"

"You know. In the marketplace. Mr Gamble, the lewd butcher. Gives out rude bits of meat to unsuspecting housewives. And that woman too. I know her from somewhere," she said, staring across at them.

"Where have I seen her before?" she quizzed herself.

"Probably the butcher's missus," I said, not really clueing in to the mystery woman yet. But then I too had a fright.

"That's Mrs Manners," I said, stunned and stopping to get a better look to make sure.

"No. SSSSHHHHH. Quiet. She's the one we saw in the teashop. Carol and I. The one he gave the sausage to. No…Don't look. Very rude," Lulu said stopping and hiding behind me in order to get a better look without being caught, peeking around me then pulling back in again.

"Looks like his little gift worked," she mused, thrilled at her discovery.

"He tempts unsuspecting women with pieces of sausage that he leaves in their bags as a kind of subtle invitation."

I couldn't understand what she meant and must have looked really stupid. She punched my shoulder. "You know," she giggled.

"Invitation to dinner?" I said, still not understanding.

"No, silly," she giggled again. "You know," but she wouldn't say more until it suddenly dawned on me:

"Oh! You mean …"

"Yes, silly. I mean …" she guffawed, this time out loud, drawing the attention of the two across the street. They glanced quickly over at us then put their heads down forcing the pace up the hill.

"Didn't know Mrs Manners was married," I said still clueless.

"You know her?"

"We share an acquaintance," I said, hedging around the Franklin incident that afternoon.

"What do you mean an acquaintance?" she asked, torturing me with a dig to the ribs.

"What do you mean? Tell me. Tell me. Tell me, or I'll dig you again."

So I told her all about Mrs Manners and her mad infatuation with Beau, the unpleasantness earlier that night. It stopped Lou in her tracks.

"Oh," she said. "Poor thing. Then I wasn't the only one," she said deep in the memory of her failed evening.

We walked on, Lou thinking deeply, quietly about things. When she finally got it all straightened out, she said, "He is rather pretty." Her eyes were glowing with the memory.

"Never really dawned on me," I said, not wanting to become involved in the sordid lottery of Beau's beauty.

"I can see why older women might dote – in an old maidenly, motherly kind of way," she said, still disentangling herself from her own emotions.

"If you'd rather not talk about him," I said.

"No. No, no. I'm a big girl and up for a bit of self-chastisement."

"Did he …?" I asked, suddenly, out of the blue.

"I mean, you know. Did he? Did you?"

"Did he take me down to his lair, you mean?"

"Yes. I guess that's what I mean."

"We happened to wander past the boathouse," she said wistfully, looking around and up at me for some kind of reaction.

I held my breath.

"He … err … we … err. Funny, he had a key to the doors."

"I nodded cynically."

"Big doors. Hard to open. Even big strong he had trouble with them."

She stopped talking for a minute, considering what to say and what not.

She watched her feet reaching out ahead of her miniskirt, missing the cracks in the pavement, finally skipping over the last two and doing a twirl at the end like in hopscotch.

"There," she announced triumphantly, "did it." She looked up at me for some sort of praise.

I smiled.

We stopped.

She took a deep breath.

"Hopeless," she sighed, coming back to the topic at hand.

"And no," she declared adamantly, "we didn't. He wanted to. I didn't. He left me there, unfulfilled, you might say – him, not me, you'll be interested to hear. Wasn't very happy. Stormed out of the boathouse, leaving me to close up those big doors by myself."

"Bastard," I said feeling sorry for little Louisa having to fight against those huge boathouse doors.

"I managed," she crowed.

"Should have left them open," I offered.

"Couldn't, could I? It's your boathouse too. Couldn't leave it all undone like that with robbers all over the place. Your boats. Your oars and things – whatever you call them.

"So I pushed and pushed one side to the other and left. The lock is still undone, hanging there loose. I don't possess a key. But it looks as though it's closed from a distance," she said proudly, lifting her head again for approval.

I approved.

"I'll go down later and lock it all up. I have a key," I said as we parted outside her digs.

"What on earth do you need a key for?" she asked, full of suspicion.

But just then, before I could fumble an answer, Carol pulled up in Errol's Daimler, jumped out looking from me to Louisa and back to me again and without saying a word to me gathered Louisa in her arms.

"We've been all over the place looking for you," she explained. "Thought we were meant to meet at the Traveller's Rest for dinner.

"He wasn't interested in dinner," Louisa had to say.

"We've been very worried," Carol said, cross and yet relieved at the same time.

Louisa looked at me and nodded.

"Did Christopher Robin rescue you from him?" wise old Carol said, beaming at last at me. "Wasn't a very good idea in the first place, was it, Dearest?" Carol said, cuddling her friend.

Strangely, non-committal at this, Louisa chose to close the evening without closing the incident or even the relationship. She and Carol turned and made their way towards their digs. Just before they got to the door, Carol turned back to me, waved and called out, "Don't forget tomorrow morning. Ten o'clock."

Errol poked his head out of the car window. "Lift anywhere, old fellow?" he asked kindly. I declined. He started the car with a choking cough, ground it into first and pulled away, off down the hill and disappeared, spluttering, into the grey night.

The riverbank was deserted when I got to the boathouse. A shove on either end of the doors brought them completely together. Glad that Louisa had the presence of mind to secure the boathouse in the first place, I fitted my key into the oversized, ancient lock, clicked it shut and turned to go.

Suddenly, from out of the mists, a familiar voice drifted across the river, "Just came back to do that me'sel."

"You been doin' a bit o' late night sculling?" Beau shouted from the middle of Bath's Bridge."

"Tidying up for you."

He hurried the rest of the way across to the boathouse to check.

"You forgot to lock up," I said.

"Owt nicked?" he asked apologetically, genuinely concerned that he had left the place undefended. "Thought I'd go for a midnight paddle," he said, examining, then opening the lock.

"Clear me head.

"Give us a hand wi' a sculling boat, and I'll let you get away to bed."

"It's dangerous going out on the river at this time of night," I said, as I pushed his sculling boat away from the landing stage. He said it was the safest time to go out. With no one else on the river, he would have it all to himself.

"Apart from wrapping me'sel' around Elvet Bridge, it should be as safe as houses out there," he said, yanking on this bowside blade to turn the boat downstream. I wasn't so sure of this and seconds later decided to get a bicycle from the boathouse to follow along behind him, just far enough back to keep him in sight.

The upper part of the river went okay down past Brown's Boathouse at the Elvet Bridge bend. Beyond this, things got a bit tricky, for me, not for Beau who seemed to have some kind of internal navigation system that kept him safely in midstream. Beyond the lights at Brown's Boathouse, the path was plunged into pitch black, leading up to Hatfield landing stage. Not at all the same as cycling it in daylight. I couldn't see a thing.

Beau paddled smoothly along as I crashed into trees, bumped through potholes and smashed into shadowy, furtive beings coming at me out of the darkness with no time to stop or turn before ramming. It was getting desperate on the towpath, but I managed the wibbly-wobbly bits above Hatfield boathouse steps, you know, the steep, twisty uphill bit, the darkest bit where no light from streetlamps or street windows penetrates.

Takes a lot of hard peddling to get up to the top of that craggy hill, but I made it, slipping and sliding and spinning the back wheel. Stopping at the top to catch my breath, I squinted off along the trail for pedestrians. Below me in the centre of the river, the puddles from Beau's oars revolved with a swish on either side of his wake in the flat, calm water. It was idyllic. He was in a sublime state out there. By now, he was well ahead of me downriver out of sight, paddling doggedly on, coming to terms in his own way, with Louisa's refusal.

Or so I thought.

I caught my breath, got back on the bike, dodged around several couples out for a stroll, wheeled confidently downhill and under Kingsgate Bridge.

Suddenly, the wake and puddles from Beau's boat disappeared. He was no longer visible on the river. I panicked, braked hard and came to a skidding stop, flailing about in the darkness for any signs of the scull, upturned or not, or a body. There was nothing out there. No wake. No puddles. No boat. No Beau. Shit!

Calamity.

Back I went in a panic to check under Kingsgate Bridge, straining my eyes for any signs of an upturned boat or its sculler.

Nothing.

Back again downstream to where the puddles had stopped and the last vestiges of them were now only white circular ripples in the moonlight.

Beau was gone.

He couldn't be any further downstream. There would have been puddles.

Panic?

I was beyond panic at this point. I was delirious with the possibilities and what to do, so I gave it another three or four journeys up and down that part of the riverbank, checked out the three college landing stages, all within a couple of hundred yards of each other. Still nothing.

Finally, before calling 999, or on my way to finding a phone, I decided to peddle down to Prebend's Bridge and rummage about downstream for any sign of a boat. When I got there, Lucien and Reggie were ambling across Prebend's with their snouts joyously deep in their orders of fish and chips.

"Probably balls deep in some lassie back along the bankside," Lucien said, unhelpfully, fishing in the bottom of his newspaper for the last dregs of batter, not really interested in the fate of one of our school chums, his death, his drowning, his body dragged out of the river somewhere below downstream by a local fisherman perhaps, some days hence.

I went berserk, declined the offer of Lucien's fistful of batter and stood gazing morosely out over the bridge at the expanse of water below it, spreading out into eternity.

"Has to be some bloody where," Reggie said, gazing too to keep me company, chomping deliciously, disinterestedly on his vinegary dregs.

"Might be in those deep weeds over there. Looks as good a place as any for a cadaver to lodge." Munch, munch, munch, chomp. He trotted down the bankside to have a disaffected, closer look.

"Not here," he shouted back up to us.

This really got me spooked. I just couldn't fathom that we were really contemplating all this stuff; that the body of our friend might actually be out there somewhere, floating alone and uncared for.

"Gotta go, lads," I said at last.

"Where? Anyway, what can you possibly do tonight? Too dark," Lucien said, seeing my distress.

"Better to wait for the morning, old boy."

"999," I said. "They have to be informed."

"Coastguard's your best bet," Reg called up from below, practising his googlie delivery off into the darkness, using the towers of the cathedral above us as an imaginary set of wickets.

"Draglines and such."

This made me freak out totally, even more than before, and I hared off in a sweat up the lane to Cuth's, to use the phone in Number 8. It had to be done. I didn't want to call the authorities, for this very act brought a macabre ending to things. The last act in my responsibility to Beau would be handing that very responsibility over to the police.

When I staggered up the steps into Number 8, the phone was in use.

Tucker was on it, arguing with someone, adamant that he hadn't left her purse in the General Gordon. It was Agnes.

"Leo, I need the phone."

"It's her bloody money," he stormed back at me, oblivious of my mission. "Says I lost it."

"Can't she just pop out and check?" I urged in a rush to get hold of the phone.

"Right," he agreed.

"Right. Agnes," he hollered down the phone.

233

"Just pop round the pub and check. You aren't far. It's…" after which came a torrent of abuse from her that must have been heard the other side of Newcastle. He held the phone to his chest to stifle her rant.

Then he turned to me with that withering, hopeless look on his face. You know, the one he uses when he thinks you're an absolute turd for butting in on his romance, the one that says, 'Why don't you just fuck off and mind your own fuckin' business?'

"Good one, Chris. You've really set her off this time. Remarkable how you always manage to do that. It'll take days to calm her down from that. Good one."

"Leo! I need the bloody phone. Call her back in a minute or two."

"Oh, aye! Aye. You know where my bollocks'll be in a minute or two? Hangin' from the flagpole at the top of the cathedral, that's where."

And he pointed dangerously upward with his middle finger, meaning that there was another phone two floors up.

So I took his advice, not wanting to start World War III at that very minute and leapt two storeys at a single bound. Might have known. It too was occupied.

"Downstairs," Ian whispered over the back of the phone and gesticulated.

"I need the phone, Ian," I insisted right in his face.

"There's been an accident.

"It's Franklin."

"Oh?" Ian backed off hanging up with a look of dread on his face.

"Is he all right?"

"Gotta phone the police," I said, not willing to publish Beau's real fate, preferring denial for a little longer.

"Oh," he blurted, his eyes bugging out of his head, shoving the receiver at me.

I had to restart dialling several times, missing numbers in my trembling haste.

"Is this the police?"

"Hee hee heeee," came a disturbance from somewhere along the hall.

"I want to report an accident," I said barely able to hold the phone steady.

"Hee hee hee," the girl continued her enjoyment in one of the nearby rooms.

"There's been an accident on the river," I forced myself to say.

"Accident you say, Sir. Just what kind of accident, Sir?" the formal, female voice at the other end of the line demanded.

"Uuum. Gerroff, cheeky. That's off limits," I heard the same gurgling female voice coming from a room down the hall and gesticulated to Ian to go down there and pull the door closed.

"Tucker at it again," Ian surmised and marched off to stifle the intrusion whilst I explained things to the constable at the other end of the line.

"I'll bet he's in there shagging the ass off some lass," Ian grumbled. Setting off on his mission.

"It's not Leo," I called after him. "He's downstairs on the other phone with Agnes trying to explain things. Probably Colin and Vicky. Try Colin's room and get them to knock it off for a bleeding minute," I hissed after him, my hand over the mouthpiece.

"Eh? What?" came the startled response from the police lady at the other end of my phone line.

"Uh, sorry ma'am," I said not wanting to seem to be overly familiar, yet at the same time not really sure how to address female constables. "Just somebody down the hall making a racket."

Then getting on with the subject at hand, I decided to face up to the brutal truth of the evening. I blurted out, almost choking in the process, "I want to report a drowning…" and with that, staggered back against the wall, nearly fainting with the magnitude of that statement. It sounded a ridiculous thing to say, but what else could I say, and so I repeated it word for quivering word and waited for a gasp or something from the other end of the line.

Nothing.

Then, "Yes?" as if this wasn't enough to mobilise the entire Durham Constabulary onto the banks of the river.

But still…nothing from the other end.

"Yes, what?" she returned.

"What do you mean, 'what?'" I demanded, imitating a demented, indignant Tony Hancock preparing to explode. "Somebody's drowned. What the bloody hell else do you want me to say? Get help, can't you…?"

"Well, Sir, you can begin by calming down and giving me your name and address and location, then…"

Just then, Ian ambled nonchalantly back to me from down the hall, informing me "… not Colin," and he waited a second or two to let that information sink in, then declared as casually as possible, "Franklin. In there in his room with some lass."

My jaw dropped. The phone dropped from my hand and bounced, bounced, bounced idly against the wall, slowly rotating as it unwound its cord. I heard a highly disgruntled voice squawking from it, as I silently addressed Ian.

"'sright," he said as casually as anything. "They're at it right now.

"In his room."

Ian always had this calmness about him. Never ruffled. Never interested. Never held a grudge. Never bothered. He took life in his stride, as we all should do, and was a great example to those of us who fly off the handle at things.

"She threw a book at me when I barged in. They're in there screwing as we speak …" he confirmed by nodding his head. "…the bastard," he concluded with envy. "I thought you said he'd had an accident or something," he said, picking up the phone and casually replacing it on the hook.

Yes. Like you, I wondered who his female companion for the night might be and how he had come to be there with her in the first place. And yes again, you might be right to assume that it was the lovely Louisa in there, who had somehow met him on his way home and settled comfortably into his arms, but far from me to let it out. If I knew who it was in there with him, it would be crass of me to identify her, wouldn't it? After all, it was no business of mine and no great item in anyone's CV to be seen in the Supreme Cad's room. Revealing her name would damage her reputation immeasurably and start people talking.

So, I can't tell you. Or, I won't. Sorry. You'll have to figure that one out for yourself.

I left Cuth's that night feeling seven storeys high. I couldn't care less who was in his room. My only thought was that he was very much alive and doing the sorts of things that he thrived on, that we all loved him for and, at the same time, abhorred him for.

Rain had started to fall when I left the building. The cobbles were slippery and reflected light from the streetlamps and one or two small windows on the way. Puddles were forming on the pavement, fed by downspouts as much as the falling rain. I rode the bike back to Kepier Terrace in minutes and was about to turn in when I saw *The Romantic Poets* lying there on my bedside table, beckoning to me.

Chapter 34
Rowing Lesson

"About time, what? You said 10. It's ..." Carol said listening to the cathedral bells tolling quarter past way off in the distance. "... 10:15. That's not late. It takes time to walk all this way. Half an hour. Really, I'm on time," she said, threatening me with her whole beautiful being against any further argument. I was defenceless against this. I knew when I was beaten.

"Yes," I said, melting. "Or ahead of it."

"That's better. You are learning," she said with that fiendishly wicked grin, squinting sideways into the morning sun that was shining directly into her eyes.

"You may have a sausage roll," she said, holding out a white paper bag to me.

"Got it from the market on my way through."

"Not Gamble's?"

"The very one, disreputable though he may be, he makes jolly nice sausage rolls," she said with her mouth wrapped firmly around hers. "Not as big as the bribery ones though," she said, disappointed.

"Bribery ones?"

"He tries to bribe unsuspecting housewives by sneaking great big sausages into their shopping when they aren't looking. Very unscrupulous."

"Sounds like the decent, friendly thing to do," I said, not letting on that I knew from Lulu what it was all about. Was I not letting on, or just afraid that any mention of Louisa at this point might unbalance a very pleasant morning?

"You might," she said finishing hers with a last delicious mouthful and a smirk. "But if you understood what his real motives were, you would think again, my lad.

"Coffee?" she asked, producing two steaming cups from another bag.

"Breakfast," she declared contentedly, leading the way over to the park bench that sat beside Cuth's landing stage for just such occasions. "Breakfast picnic," she said, settling down as if she didn't have a care in the world.

I had invited her to 'Go on the water' this morning, but at this moment, I somehow had the feeling we weren't going to get that far, judging by the comfort she was taking in the breakfast picnic.

A sculler drifted past us on the far side of the river.

"Is that what you expect me to do?" she asked with fear in her voice.

"Not at first."

"Why not?"

"Takes time."

"For what?"

'Balance for one."

"Looks simple to me. He doesn't seem to be having any trouble. Doesn't look like balance comes into it at all," she said, gaining in confidence as another sculler swished past, this time going the other way on this side of the river.

"Nor does she," she said stowing our rubbish back into her paper bag. "Let's go," she said, standing up, eager to try it herself.

"Louisa not able to drag herself out of bed this morning?" I asked. Carol had intended bringing her along.

"It appears," she said, puffing, helping me to push the gargantuan boathouse doors apart, "she has other things on her mind."

I hesitated bringing up events that might be still raw to her and let it go at that.

"This'll be fun," Carol said looking at the equipment littering the interior of the boathouse.

She hadn't brought anything to change into, or a towel just in case…

Both would have come in real handy, as it turned out.

"You just said," she sputtered some moments later, water streaming down over her face as she waded back from the middle of the river to the edge of the landing stage, "you just said don't let go of the handles…"

"Blades," I said, correcting her.

"Blades then," she obliged, sputtering up at me and standing chest deep near the edge of the river.

"And I didn't … and I still fell in …" she said out of breath and looking for a dignified way to get out of the river.

I wasn't sure whether it was me she was angry with for her dunking or herself – or both.

I hauled her up and out of the river onto the landing stage. At the time, gripping her from behind didn't seem to be an issue. It was simply a way of getting her out, dignified or not. But looking back on it later, I was amazed at the matter-of-fact way I reached down and round from behind her, and without thinking, cupped her breasts in order to pull her out backwards onto the landing stage. She allowed it without any protest, in fact seemed to accept it, as the normal form of rescue; and as a matter of another fact, she leaned back into me, encouraging it. I didn't really think about it at the time, wanting to get her out of the water in the safest, quickest way possible. Either way, she was undeterred and despite being sopping wet, wanted to climb right back into the boat and have another go.

Can you believe it?

"I'll get the hang of it this time," she spurtled, with water still streaming down over her chin, and her clothes clinging like glue to her curves. I felt so responsible for the dunking, but I have to tell you, I didn't mind the effect the water had outlining her glorious body through her thin, translucent tracksuit. She either didn't mind or didn't notice it. All she wanted was to get straight back into that boat and make it work, even in the state she was in. What a star!

She looked really disappointed when I declared that she had learned enough for one day.

"Tomorrow?" she insisted as I ushered her back through the boathouse, up the rickety wooden stairs and into the changing room. She was shivering and blue with cold by the time we got up there. The changing room was never the warmest place at the best of times. Thing was, she had no clothes to change into and no towel to dry herself off with, so I stayed and took charge of rooting out the necessities from the musty, old lockers around about.

As she started peeling off her wet things, I averted my gaze by hunting through the lockers for anything to put on her. Luckily, I found just enough gear for her cover herself up in.

She pulled off her sodden top without even a nod to impropriety, passed it to me and I dumped it onto a seat beside her.

"Help me with this, would you?" she offered, delighting and surprising me at the same time, turning her back to show me her bra clasp, confident that what she was exposing to me was totally acceptable.

"And don't look," she commanded with a cheerful grin as her bra popped off in my hands. She fluffed out her hair with a towel that I dug out, then patted it across her shoulders and breasts – which I wasn't supposed to look at but did and at the same time noticed the glee in her eyes noticing me taking full notice of her pink-tipped nipples. Her voluptuous breasts swung out and back and around as she laboured to dry herself off. Marvels of nature, they settled as she casually dropped a tatty, old, green rowing top over her head. The breath-taking view quickly disappeared under humungous folds of clothing, which dropped down over her butt. Next, without a though she stepped out of her wet knickers, wringing them out before handing me them too, to add to my haul, then rubbed the towel up and down her legs, inside and out before bending to press a foot into the right leg of an oversized, discarded tracksuit bottoms. Left leg.

I couldn't help looking.

"You looked!" she kidded and stopped to admonish me.

"Didn't," I lied, looking all the time. Her pert, steaming bottom, covered in a light down, flared out, majestically, confidently, unashamed of being on display and out in the open.

She stood there on one leg, balancing, holding onto my shoulder before attempting to pull up the other leg of the tracksuit.

Beaming at my attention, she blushed scalding red, slowly pulling the bottoms up, wiggling her bum before enclosing her glorious cheeks in that sloppy, mouldy old bit of kit. I dug out two odd, woolly, socks from another locker, and she was ready to slip her sodden plimsolls back on.

"There. How's that?" she said, posing, looking like a beautiful ragdoll.

"I liked the other outfit better," I said.

"You mean the one where I had nothing on," she giggled, going at her hair with the towel again.

"Doesn't count. Too easy. This top is very scratchy," she complained after finishing her hair, looking down at her nipples spiking out through the rough material like tent poles.

"Don't jiggle them so much," I offered.

"Can't help it," she chided. "Nothing to hold them down with. Oh, they are very itchy and being very bad to point like that" – she moaned – "and you are being very bad to stare," she said, proudly displaying them to me, making no effort at all to stop them or hide them. Then her arms were on my shoulders drawing her luscious eyes close to mine.

"Thank you for saving my life, my knight in shining armour," she whispered closing her soft lips on mine.

"You do nothing but save us – me and Lou – these days." Her eyes glowed.

"'Twas nothing, My Lady."

"Remind me to reward you in kind." She breathed in deeply, which issued a tickle in her nose and drew her away to sneeze.

She sneezed.

"In kind?" I said.

"Yes," she said, returning her arms to my shoulders after the sneeze.

"Something nice," she said, her eyes suddenly dilating with an idea.

"Dinner. That's it. I'll cook you dinner."

"Didn't know you cooked."

"Don't. Gotta start somewhere, and you can be my first victim. Next week?"

"Next week," I agreed.

"No Errol?"

"No Errol," she confirmed.

"Just us?"

"Just us," she confirmed again, then thought again.

"Oh, and maybe Lou. She needs feeding from time to time. If you are OK with her being there."

"Could be tricky," I said.

"How so?"

"Don't know how I'll be able to properly ravish you after dinner with her being there," I said with the tip of my nose gently rubbing hers.

"Oh!" she squeaked and pulled away an inch or two, her eyes crossing in concentration. "Hadn't thought of after-dinner ravishing," she said, comfortably settling back in close.

"Have to think about that. Ravish, you say?

"After dinner …

"Well…

"Then…

"Lulu will have to forage."

"Poor Lulu," I said.

"Poor Lulu," she said, her forehead touching mine.

"Must go. French lecture in twenty minutes," she said taking her damp bra and knickers from the seat and stuffing them into her bag.

"You realise you'll have to explain all this to daddy this weekend," she said on our way out. "Just kidding. He is coming though, and there is still the matter of Mary's and Rev Kev's letter he wants to talk about. Don't tell him about today. It was lovely," she said planting a great big snog on my lips.

"Enjoyed every minute, my hero."

"Parting is such sweet sorrow," I said.

With a wave back, and her oversized rags flapping loosely about her in the wind, she bolted off to her Baudelaire in Elvet Riverside.

Chapter 35
But Soft, Wot Light...

"Book!" That's all the note said.

"What's that, Chris?" Leo asked leaning over my shoulder whilst rummaging around for mail in his pigeonhole.

"Overdue notice from the library? Funny way to get books back."

"Not the library," I replied.

"Oh?"

"Invitation to a balcony scene," I said, casually turning the note over to see that the other side didn't contain more instructions. It did.

"Oh, yes," he said sardonically, crumpling up a load of post and throwing it into the wastepaper basket.

"Come alone." The back of my note said. And the 'alone' was underlined several times with a funny little mask next to it. Around the mask curled the imperative: "Eight o'clock. Tonight!!!" With three more exclamation marks.

"Bugger!" Barrie growled. No longer interested in my imperative, he held his own in his trembling hand and said, "Must be some bloody mistake. I paid that bill weeks ago. Have to go and see Mrs Manners and get it straightened out." he fussed.

"Bloody hell. I paid it last month," he suddenly remembered and with that disappeared into the college office where Mrs Manners and her cronies were just starting on their second round of afternoon sherry.

"But soft, wot light through yonder window breaks..." I called out to the startled maiden peeping out between her curtains.

It was very late. Events had prevented me from getting to Louisa's window at the appointed time, so when I eventually did get there hours late, I fully expected no one to be up. I called up to her anyway and, as directed earlier in the week by Carol, and threw pebbles at her window. Finally, the curtains stirred, and a sleepy face appeared between them.

"Oh, *The Romantic Poets*. At last." she yawned, opening up her window as far as it would go and leaning out.

"Did you bring it? You did get my note? You are very late, Christopher Robin. Whatever possessed you to come at this time of night? I've just got off to sleep. Thought you weren't coming. Gave up and went to bed. Carol is fast asleep. We waited for ages. I thought you were some sort of burglar or something, rustling around in the bushes like that at this time of night.

"Was it you throwing stones at my window?" she said.

"PJ's. I might have known," I said in mock dismay as she opened her curtains fully, displaying herself to the indiscreet moonlight.

"You 'might have known' what, Christopher Robin?" Louisa demanded leaning and twisting out of her window stretching down to reach the book.

"Might have known you'd be in PJ's and not your negligee."

"Was earlier. Carol made me wear it. She went to bed, so I got into these. Much more comfortable," she said, straining down to get the book.

"It's no good. You'll have to reach higher. Jump or something. Throw it," she umphed, reaching as far down as her arms would allow her.

"Throw it. No, wait. Don't throw it. Might get damaged. I'll go and enlist the help of someone with longer arms to fetch it up for me. I'm sure she won't mind being dug out of bed at this time of night. And what on earth are you dressed in? What's in that cap? A feather! Very good. An Elizabethan feather. Just wait here a mo. I'm sure Carol would love to see your lovely feather.

"Oh, and by the way, she's in her PJ's too, but I'll have to get into costume, now that you are wearing that feather."

She went away to bang on Carol's door.

Suddenly, a light came on in the next window over. A sleepy-headed Carol, also dressed in pyjamas, rushed her curtains back, opened up her window, yawned and stretched into the moonlight. She resembled a fawn awakening.

"What are you two doing? It's very late. Can't a girl get any sleep around here without you two caterwauling outside her window?" she said still yawning.

"Not caterwauling," Louisa said reappearing, defending our questionable late-night activity.

"See if you can reach Christopher Robin's book down there for me, C, will you please."

"Oh," Carol said, finally coming to life.

"The book. Now I see. But surely you don't want me leaning out of the window to retrieve his book, in the moonlight, Lou. Not me. Not at this point in the script. The stage directions at this point say that it must be you in a state of accidental, unintentional undress who lends her ample, half-naked bosoms to the plot – hideous though they may be – by reaching wantonly down to him in the moonlight. And where is your negligee, my girl? You are seriously out of costume."

"Was going to do a quick costume change, but it's too late now. And what do you mean, 'hideous'?"

"Why else would you bind them up like that, unless you're ashamed of them?"

"Not ashamed, Carol, just…just shy."

"Wrapped up in the most unbecoming Winnie-the-Pooh pyjamas. I ask you! So we'll have to improvise a bit," Carol said.

"Improvise? What do you mean, improvise? First of all, I'm improperly dressed for it (according to you) and second, my arms won't reach," Lou said flailing and stretching and twisting downward at me again just to prove the point. "See?"

And just as she did this, the force placed upon her dear little Winnie-the-Pooh PJ top exerted by her impressive proportions, popped loose a button – the second one down – the one whose job it was to guard her modesty at all possible costs.

"Ooops. Sorry, Christopher Robin. Didn't mean that." Louisa gulped levering herself back into her room to hide her embarrassment and cover up.

"There. You see." Carol laughed.

"No, Christopher Robin. No. I didn't mean 'see' as in 'look'. I meant it as in 'understand'. Stoppit! Stop looking." she laughed.

"You must avert your manly gaze at this point in the plot," she said, continuing to direct things, "while the harlot gets her bits right.

"Louisa, you strumpet," she said, laughing uproariously at Louisa's embarrassment.

"You might have at least spread events out a little, instead of declaring your intentions in one go like that right at the start. You have to create an air of romantic tension in the scene if you want his passions to rise, not throw yourself out after him right at the start like that."

"Not doing anything of the sort, Carol," Louisa said, out of sorts and out of sight back in the shadows of her room, fixing the problem with a safety pin and reappearing when she was once again decent.

"There," she said, certain that now her bits were safe.

"Better," Carol approved, leaning out and around to check Louisa's repair job.

"But will it hold? Better had, eh, Christopher Robin? What do you think, meeting your paramour under the moonlight with only a safety pin guarding against your feverish attentions?"

"Never mind that, C," Louisa said eager to get on with getting the book.

"Reach down with your orangutan arms and retrieve his book for me, there's a pet.

"You'll not have to mind her hairy arms, though, Christopher Robin. She hasn't had a chance to shave them in the last hour, and you know how fast it grows on ungulates. Oh, how it grows and grows. The poor thing is beset with arm hair."

"Don't listen to a thing she says, Christopher Robin." Carol giggled, squeezing her shoulders together in delight.

"Here. Look. See any fur or fuzz or anything growing out of my skin? Beautiful and pristine as a baby's," Carol said reaching down and across but just coming up short of the book, even though I edged it out towards her fingertips.

"No, don't, Carol. I can do it," Louisa said suddenly reaching out below her friend. I'm all pinned up and decent now. I can get it. Your services are no longer required. Shoo."

"Get away you scamp. You're in no condition to …" Carol hissed back.

"It's all right," Lulu insisted between clenched teeth, as her fingertips touched the book.

"You don't need to…"

But suddenly, as fate would have it, or luck or chance, Lulu's safety pin, which as it turned out wasn't so safe, gave up the ghost and with it, the top button of her pjs went pop as well, leaving her seriously unsustained, unpinned and in a quandary about whether to complete the book transfer or grapple with her gaping shirt, so to speak. She chose the shirt and in doing so let go of her hold on her window sill and tumbled out of her window and into the arms of the unsuspecting yet delighted me who waited there below her, hoping against hope.

In one easy movement, I caught her up and held her out to Carol who looked down on the scene, brimming over with laughter.

"There. Now you've done it, Louisa. I knew there was a subtext going on here besides book lending. You do have ulterior motives. We have found you out, you harlot," she scolded, wagging a finger down at us.

"You've been planning it all along, haven't you? Look. Here. Christopher Robin, put her back," she commanded with glee.

"And you can take that great big smirk off your face, my lad. And you as well, my girl. Look. Stoppit both of you. Even though she is completely at your disposal and … and … and very … my goodness. Louisa! All wobbly and – look at them. Just look! They are on the loose. Behave, you two!"

At this point, I wasn't sure whether the 'you two' referred to Louisa's two rogue breasts diving and winking in and out of her loosened shirt or to her and me. Didn't matter, I held her close, afraid that she might fall to the ground, and she helped by linking her hands around my neck and kicking her heels in delight.

"Louisa, cover up, you baggage. Have you no shame?" Carol laughed and fussed.

"No, Christopher Robin, don't look. Louisa! Cover them up. You're not helping one bit. Just look at them stabbing out like that."

"Put her down, Christopher. Put her down. And do stop looking. She's too exposed like that."

"No, don't put me down, Christopher Robin," Louisa answered. "I've no shoes on. I'll hurt my feet on the gravel. You hang on to me while I pull my shirt together," she said taking her arms from around my neck and seeing to her pyjamas.

"Hand her back in up here then. No. Wait. Better still, I'll go around and open the front door, if that's all right with you, Louisa. I know it's not in keeping with the script or subtext of your scabby little rendezvous, but needs must, and I do think you are looking too comfortable there in the arms of our young swain with a feather in his cap.

"And…

"He's not too unhappy either by the looks of things. Do feel free to put her down when you are able to, sometime this side of Christmas. Lou, take that gormless look off your face," she shouted after us, as I carried the delicate maiden around to the front door where Carol stood waiting to let us in.

"And Christopher Robin, do remember your sore elbow," Carol said helping her friend back down to the floor again, covering her up and looking intently at me, flushed with the moment.

"Too much pressure on that precious instrument, and we will all be in trouble again," she said, effervescent with joy.

"Wouldn't want that, now, would we?"

"What on earth do you mean, Carol? Elbow?" Louisa asked, setting about her decency again.

"Never you mind, Louisa. Never you mind. It's just an old war wound he has to be careful of. Flairs up every now and then," she said, grinning at me whilst helping her friend's décolletage.

Chapter 36
Daddy

Daddy arrived by train several days later.

I had no idea what to expect. Hearty shake of the hand? Thorough dressing down? Upper class twit of the year? Two knobbly, hairy, Neanderthal hands gripped tightly around my neck, squeezing the life out of me?

Bearing in mind just what was about to take place, I should have at least been terrified. Should have.

Wasn't.

Ignorance was my defence, I guess. I preferred it that way, suspecting that if Carol were anything to go by, the dad couldn't be too bad, and anyway, I had nothing to answer to. Nothing to lose and everything to gain. And so, I looked more and more forward to it as the moment approached.

The day before his arrival, a hastily scribbled note lay in the bottom of my otherwise bare pigeonhole:

"Can you meet The Aged for me, please?

I have a seminar in the morning.

IT arrives on the 11:45 from Warwick.

Can't miss the old fuddy-duddy.

Brilliant blue eyes. Lovely, kind smile.

Grey hair, of course. Sorry, not much help there.

A bit doolally. Not yet totally senile. Oh, and he will have left his bag on the train. Can you retrieve it for him?

A copy of this morning's Mirror clasped firmly in his right hand opened at the half-finished crossword. Umbrella in the other. Pencil behind his left ear. Pipe in the upper pocket of his jacket. Not in his mouth, though.

If you miss him, or if there are hordes of other look-a-like daddies getting off the train, I have told him to look out for you.

Don't forget to jump on the train to get his bag for him.

Ta,

C

PS: Meet you at the Dun Cow for lunch.

PPS: You can bring him too, if he behaves. If he doesn't, put him on the first train back home."

Wondering what exactly she had described me as, as a target for Daddy to look for, I set off for the station with enough time to stop on the way to collect my breakfast at Driscoll's Bakery in North Street. A bag full of sausage rolls did me all the way up to the train station.

There were only two platforms, one on this side going north and the other side going south.

With no way of knowing which train was from Warwick or Clapham or the moon for that matter, I sat on a bench at the end of platform 1 eating my snack, examining each carriage that arrived.

As expected, a number of possible trains came in and left with none of them giving up Daddy. A fourth possibility 'whoo-whooed' down the line as it was passing the cathedral. This had to be him, so I stood up, trying to look as respectable as possible and watched, as each carriage went by. The train eventually pulled to a hissing, steaming chunka-chunka-chunka stop.

Doors flew open emitting all sorts of travellers onto the platform, commuters mainly from York and Darlington but no doddery, white-haired old bloke carrying an umbrella. Disappointed, I made my way to the exit to stand there and wait, just in case he was one of the last ones off. The crowd dissolved past me, and the platform bloke was just about to signal 'the off' to the train driver when I happened to see a white head nodding asleep on a window halfway down the middle carriage.

I shouted, "Wait!" to the conductor who was just about to put his whistle to his lips and blow us all off the face of the earth.

"I think that old guy should be getting off here," I explained, gesticulating frantically at the sleeping passenger, but I was too late. The whistle blew. The train started up and nothing could stop Daddy from going all the way up to Newcastle before he found out.

Then, suddenly, out of the blue, "Christopher Robin?" someone at my elbow asked brightly.

I turned to look and...

"Daddy," the gentleman behind me said kindly, introducing himself, extending a hand and smiling as beautifully as I could have imagined, no, more beautifully than anyone could have imagined.

He smiled and nodded and smiled.

"How do you do?" he said, flourishing an umbrella.

"Carol has told me many things about you, all the way down to your sausage rolls," he said, eyeing the little white bag. "Don't mind if I do," he said reaching into the bag and wrestling around inside it for one. "Haven't had a thing to eat since brecky ... Famished."

Suddenly, I remembered his bag left on the train.

"Your bag," I said. "You left your bag..."

"Didn't bring one," he said nibbling away at elevenses as we walked along the platform.

"No need. Going back this afternoon. Can't stay. Got to get back by tonight. Meeting the vicar. Something about Publishing the Banns," he said smiling benevolently over me.

"Carol said I should start the prelims right away for you two. You are C of E, aren't you?"

This was a blow that fair took my breath away.

Banns?

"Seems you have to get on top of things like this or it could take forever," he said gazing out across the town skyline. Suddenly, I noticed a twinkle in his eye as he took a sly sideways look at me.

"You are joking?" I said in a sweat. "I mean, the Banns?"

His twinkle turned steely. "Course not, old chap. Can't start too early with the preliminaries. Get ahead of the game.

"I don't mind though. Better to get rid of her as soon as possible. That's what I say. Takes a load of pressure off the exchequer. Fees and things. Food. Make-up. Clothes. Costs me a ruddy fortune, she does. Not to mention the constant aggravation. She is a nuisance. But you will have seen that.

"No," he continued. "Hand her over to you as soon as possible. That's what I say. Let somebody else take it all over," he said, strolling amiably downhill, twirling his brolley.

All at once, he stopped, thought deeply with his chin on his chest and said finally, "You won't mind, will you, old chap?"

I stopped to take in his fell pronouncement, confused and not knowing what to expect next.

"Can't pay a penny toward the ceremony, I'm afraid," he said emphatically, pinning me with a warning, blood-shot eyeball.

"You'll have to fund the lot, I'm afraid. Just coming out of a very bad quarter myself, and things aren't likely to improve in the next…so…" he said with deep regret.

"Still. Must be getting on. Point me in the direction of the nearest pub. I feel the need of much fortification before seeing her. You will join me, of course, dear boy. The first round's on me. Could do with a spot of lunch as well before the crap hits the fan. I'm afraid she isn't going to like what I have to tell her," he said just to put me at my ease.

"By the way, dear boy. How are you going to be able to keep her at the level to which she's become accustomed? Must confess, I've spoiled her all her life. She and her brother still get away with murder.

"You are going into a reputable profession when you leave here? Something with a bit of money behind it. Carol will take a lot of keeping. Sorry to heap all this on you at once, but it is the nuts and bolts of life, y'know."

Shock upon shock. The nuts and bolts of life were flying about my head like shrapnel. I was fairly reeling by now and wondering what I had got myself into. Maintaining a steady outlook, although my heart was tumbling out of my chest, I led the way down toward town, acutely aware that no matter how I tried to feign a semblance of self-control, I must have had the look of a scared rabbit.

The nearest pub was easy. We had agreed to take The Aged to lunch in the Dun Cow, so he and I settled in the back room to chat and wait for Carol's lecture in Elvet Riverside to finish. After our second pint and several pies and salads, the door opened and she appeared in all her splendour, beaming, crept up behind Daddy, folded her arms lovingly around his neck from behind and gave him an unrelenting hug.

"Isn't he lovely?" she said, squeezing the life out of him. "Hope he hasn't been too much of a nuisance," and squeezing again.

Then with mock gravity, she squared around in front of him.

"Now, what have you two been talking about? What have you been telling him, Daddy?" she asked looking from him to me and back again, stopped, registered the mood in the room, saw the look of doom on my face and gasped.

"You haven't…Not the Banns again. You old bugger. Not the nuts and bolts of life?

"Honestly, Daddy! Oh, no, not with Christopher Robin."

"I told you not to this time, you imp. You've used that one for years now with just about everyone I've ever met.

"You're incorrigible.

"He didn't, did he?" she asked, turning to me.

"Not the level to which I've become accustomed?"

Like an elderly Dennis the Menace, Daddy beamed at his evil little joke and pulled out a chair for his daughter to sit on then got up to totter over to the bar.

"Sorry," she said. "Thought he'd got over that. Really! The very idea. What must you think. The very idea. Hope you don't mind," she said, plonking her bag full of books on the table and swinging her knees under it.

"He will have his little joke. I should have warned you. Sorry. Don't be too cross. It's his way of dealing with stress, I think."

"By heaping it on me, I guess."

"Were you? Stressed, I mean. Well, you shouldn't have been. He means well. Sorry.

"Did you mention Mary's Ball?"

"I thought the nuts and bolts of life were enough to be going on with," I said briskly as Daddy returned with a tray of drinks.

"I've ordered lunch," he said. "Hope you don't mind, Polly," he said using his daughter's favourite nickname.

"As long as it's not pork pie," she said looking earnestly aggrieved up at her father.

"Nothing wrong with a nice pork pie, darling."

"Can't get my mouth around it, and when you finally do break in, it's full of goo."

"Jelly's the best part, darling. Nourishing. You didn't use to turn your nose up at my pies. Seems to me this university lark's had a bad effect on you," he said looking toward me for support and grinning.

I bit into my pie to show him solidarity.

"Traitor! Whose side are you on? You're just doing that for his sake," Carol said with a smirk. "I've never ever seen you eat one of those."

"Good for the figure," I lied, having bonded firmly with The Aged P.

"Pork pie and a pint. Nothing like it," I said, lustily swigging off half my drink before settling the glass back onto the table.

Daddy followed suit and, planting his glass firmly onto the table too, said, "I can see we are going to get along famously. Now, my dears, what did you drag me all the way up into the frozen north for? Something about Adelia. Her father says she's very upset. Something about you and Louisa turning her room into a brothel."

Carol turned glum then lightened in the same second.

"Hardly a brothel, Daddy. Overnight bivouac, perhaps."

Daddy looked on suspiciously, nodding, listening to her now with deep sincerity while she explained things as best she could. He nodded cautiously as she went over the good bits, glancing at me from time to time to gather my reaction to things. I stayed out of it for the time being though, lending support and only joined the fray when it was time to produce the letter from Rev Kev.

Daddy measured the full import of the weighty document.

"And so you see," Carol implored, "Adelia's father has been badly misinformed. It's shocking the way things have been twisted out of shape," she said looking from me to him and back again.

"It's funny, you know," he said at last after giving the issue enough breathing room, "your mother and I went through similar scrutiny all those years ago in Cambridge, and all I could say then, and all I can say now is it's no one else's business but yours and yours," he declared looking from Carol to me.

"I'm only sorry Adelia and her father felt the need to get anyone else involved in it in the first place and even more sorry you two have been bothered by it at all. Now, get on with your lives and let's have another pint. I'll need several more to face racing back up that hill to the railway station for the four o'clock back home."

Just then, the door broke open and Lucien Fenwood-Gross popped his head in to survey the atmosphere inside.

"Ah! Flynn, my boy!" he said, helping himself to a seat at our table and lowering his weight onto it. "I thought I might find you in," he said, looking brightly from one to the other and holding out his hand for introductions, which once concluded, he added, "It seems I've fallen behind."

"Here," Carol said pushing her father's next drink across toward Lucien. "You can have this one. It's extra to Daddy's requirements," she said, looking daggers at Daddy.

"No, no, Father. I insist. You and I have to be going. I promised Louisa a turn with you before you go to see Rev Kev, and if we hurry, we'll just be able to catch her coming out of her Milton. You two stay and catch up," Carol said, rising out of her chair and taking up her books and bags off the table.

Daddy followed suit in an apologetic tumble, stumbling across to the door after his daughter.

"See you off at the station," I shouted after his retreating form.

He tipped an imaginary hat and was gone.

"Daddy!" I said to Lucien.

"Daddy!" he confirmed, nodding his head and grinning like Oliver Hardy.

Suddenly, Carol's head popped back into the room. "See you at four?" she asked and mock grimaced toward her father waiting outside.

"See you later," I agreed and was left to spend a delightful hour helping Henry reorganise his life and catch up with his beers.

"Quite the dolly bird," he observed, amazed, halfway through a sombre, quiet patch.

"Nice lady," I said, never having thought of her as a 'dolly bird'. Still, I nodded at his peculiar description.

"So far Daddy has proven to be a brick."

"Fairly serious stuff, though," Lucien went on, "if Daddy's been summonsed."

"Needed his opinion on something," I hedged.

"Could have asked me, old fellow. After all, I am your academic superior, a kind of moral tutor…after Rev Kev. Of course."

"You?"

"Me," he affirmed.

"A kind of councillor. I'm dismayed you haven't used my superior intellectual acuity to help solve your dolly bird problem."

"The only powers you have that might be helpful to me, at this very moment, my friend, is to order the next round on time, which is, about, now," I said handing him my empty glass.

"Next time I need advice I will certainly seek you out."

He wandered off to the bar leaving me to contemplate Daddy's visit.

Chapter 37
Dinner

"I like Lucien," Carol said later that evening.

"Oh," Lulu chimed in. "Lucien Fenwood-Gross? Me too. He's a lovey. Like a cuddly dumpling."

"Didn't know you knew him, Lou," Carol said.

"That time at Prof Osborne's soiree. Met him there."

"Says you're a dolly bird," I had to say just to keep things in perspective.

"Me?" Carol was amazed and confused at the same time.

"Why on earth a dolly bird?"

"You are, Carol," Louisa chimed in. You are a dolly bird, besides being a strumpet…at least that's what your father says you are."

"No, he did not, Louisa," Carol said, lifting her shopping bags onto the kitchen counter top.

"He most certainly did."

"I believe the word he used was courtesan – and he used it in the nicest possible French way, meaning the kind of beautiful woman one might find at court in France in the eighteenth century."

"I'm not quite certain that was his meaning, Carol. I think he meant strumpet, or to be more exact, tart. What do you think, Christopher Robin?" Louisa asked.

"He meant strumpet, didn't he? Just like the kind of woman one might find walking the streets at night in twentieth century London," Louisa said with that twinkle in her eye.

"What are you doing, Carol, with all those bags and stuff?" Louisa asked.

"Dinner," Carol said with mock confidence, carefully unpacking her shopping.

"Ah. Then you won't be needing me here," Louisa said, beginning to pick her things up with the intention of leaving.

"Certainly do," Carol replied, strangely and unaccountably eager to get Lou to stay, taking Louisa's things from her hands and putting them back down again.

"I thought..." I began to whisper my objections but was cut short immediately by something Carol had going on in her fiendish little brain.

"You'll be my chief guinea pig," she said in a rush to Louisa.

"You are commissioned to try all the dishes before I release them on the general public."

"And the dishes being…?" Louisa said doubtfully, confused by the fuss Carol was suddenly lavishing on her.

"Pizza. I'm cooking pizza tonight."

"Ugh. Why on earth that? I recall your last one with suspicion if not dread. Think I'd better be off then," Lou said, pulling a face and picking up her things again, on her way out. Carol fled after her, turned her around at the door and insisted she put her things back down again and sit down at the table while she finished unloading her shopping.

"That was a Tesco's own. Not mine. My one is going to be fabulous," she said, doing a twirl ending up facing the fridge with a wooden spoon in her hand.

"I've engaged Christopher Robin, who," she said flashing a smile at me, "I am told is an expert on pizzas, to help with every step of the cooking. Although it can't be very hard to produce a pancake and cover it with icky goo. Just needs the right spices – that's all – and sufficient wine to dull the taste buds."

"Does he know that your experience with cooking is absolutely nil?" Louisa said, turning to me for confirmation.

"As a matter of fact," she went on, "her so-called attempts at the culinary art have been given a government health warning and come wrapped up in one of those pretty yellow plastic police banners used to keep the public well back from a crime scene."

"Far from criminal, Lulu, my pizza is going to be spectacularly successful. All I need to know now is how to get this packet of flour open."

"Here, let me help," Louisa intervened, pulling at the packet and exploding the contents all over her and the kitchen.

Carol came to her aid, fussing and dusting the flour off her face, out of her hair and off her jumper.

"Trust you to draw attention to your ample bosoms yet again by pouring flour all over them," Carol said patting the white stuff from Lulu's lightly floured breasts, "and getting me innocently to bash them about in the company of an adult male. Honestly. You are incorrigible. Look at you. Look at them.

"No! No! Christopher Robin. Don't look! You are still too eager. Avert your manly gaze. These floured paps are not for public consumption, lightly floured or not lightly floured."

"Perish the thought," I said watching Carol doing her motherly dusting of Louisa.

"You missed a bit," I said, surveying the undulating topography and pointing to the offending lump clinging imperiously to Louisa's left one.

"Let me get it," I offered.

"Hands off," Carol warned but too late.

"Needed a deft flick," I said, leaning well back out of Carol's reach. "There, you didn't feel a thing, Lou, did you?"

But Lulu was keeping quiet, basking in her preening, like a kitten under its mother's tongue.

"It's no good," Carol said unable to get the deep-down powder out of the wool. "You'll have to go and change – and no, Christopher Robin, you won't be needed to help her with it. You can stay with me and roll out the dough for the pizza as soon as I can gather enough flour off the floor to fill this bowl.

"Scat, Lou. Put on your big swampy navy-blue jumper," she called after her through to her bedroom.

"The old, shapeless one that will hide those…things completely from Christopher Robin's view. Your powdery one is giving him palpitations at the moment, and we wouldn't want him expiring on us tonight, not before he's had the chance to taste my wonderful cooking," she said, fully absorbed in finding the pizza page in her cookbook.

"Let me see, now. Do we want a Margarita pizza or some other long Italian name I cannot pronounce?"

We opted for the unpronounceable one and waited festively for the oven to transform it from a doubtful, glutinous Salvador Dali mess on the countertop to a glorious, fully cooked and crisp Monet.

"Perhaps it needs a little more wine," I ventured as it lay at rest, steaming and fully exposed in its cooking tray on the countertop.

"More wine," Louisa agreed not wanting to hurt Carol's feelings and itching, at the same time, to open a second bottle.

"It should be fine after one or two more glasses. I always find wine improves the flavour of most things, given time…"

"And enough wine," Carol added.

"A necessary ingredient," Lou reminded everyone.

"Absolutely," I said. "We almost forgot it."

Suddenly, there came a knock at the front door.

"Ah! I wonder who that can be," Carol said in her furtively conspiratorial voice, smiling knowingly at me.

"Go and answer the door, dearest Lulu, whilst I pour you – and whoever's out there – another glass of vino."

"Why me?"

"Because, dearest one, it's your turn, and besides you are closest to the door, and because you are dying to know who it is, and also because if you don't, you will be sorry for it for the rest of your life. That's why."

"Goodness. Didn't know who answered the door to be so…"

In the meantime, I had gone out and pulled the door open. There was nobody there. Just a dark, empty, front step. I turned to report my discovery to the others and was just about to close it again when a familiar Yorkshire accent assailed me from the darkness.

"Flynn. Flynn, you fuckin' bastard," it hissed from somewhere the other side of the rhododendrons. Two eyes appeared within the leaves, and when I shook its branches, a sweaty face popped through.

"Is she in there?" it asked sheepishly.

"Who?" I teased.

"You bloody well know who," he threatened again.

"Who is it?" Louisa's head nudged out beside me.

"Oh!" Truly shocked, she recoiled at once to use me as a barrier between her and Beau.

"Who invited you up here?" Louisa demanded, which I thought, coming from her, to be rude.

"Statuesque, red-headed bint," Beau said, still in the rhododendrons. The branches shivered as he talked.

"Told us to come to tea. Said you were pissed off at us, so I thought—"

"You thought you'd come up here and unpiss-me-off," Louisa helped but still not quite hitting the right kind of conciliatory tone.

"Look you two; come in out of the rain. Stop airing your lovers' spat to the whole neighbourhood," Carol tut-tutted from the kitchen. And with that, she swept outside and practically dragged both of them by the ears into the kitchen.

"This has got to stop," she said, putting her foot down, and halfway through her next glass of wine.

"You are both miserable, and, well, it's time to stoppit."

Lulu lifted her nose up at the thought, cuddling her glass and not in the least bit interested in discussing it.

"Carol," she whined, "you have absolutely no right to—"

"Yes, I do, Lou. Now shut up, drink up and let's have some pizza and some fun."

"And you," she said turning to the latecomer, "who do you think you are calling me a 'bint'? 'Statuesque', perhaps, but I'm no 'bint'." She mused, admiring his admiration.

Beau shat himself and giggled. "Sorry, missus." He pulled his forelock and, looking suitably contrite, downed his glass of wine in one guilt-laden gulp.

The evening went downhill after this. Beau got rat-arsed pissed and ended up making a right balls up of Carol's attempt to reunite him with his true yet unattainable lust.

Louisa declared total war on Beau, saying she never wanted to see him again after which he puked up all over the rhododendrons in a rage on his way out. I really couldn't blame her. She too had had too much to drink, though. Anything to drink would have been too much for her, owing to her body weight and her lack of experience with alcohol. Carol felt very ill. She said it was the pizza, but I know it was her inexperience with booze. She went off to bed early leaving me to look after Louisa at which I was a total failure once again. All of my efforts at mediation got totally nowhere, but not wanting to incur a second visit from Carol's daddy or Louisa's daddy or even Beau's daddy for that matter, I staggered off home leaving the two girls snoozing comfortably, knowing tomorrow for them was going to be a living hell.

"Don't look at me like that."

I scribbled the note next morning and pushed it across the library tabletop to Carol who didn't look at all happy.

"Not looking at you like anything," she returned, then added: "Feel ill still. My head hurts. What can I do? What do you do when you have alcoholic poisoning? Shouldn't have had that last glass of wine."

"You shouldn't have had the third, fourth, or fifth," I tried to help.

The notes slid back and forth at regular intervals.

"I feel great," I wrote trying to deflect blame and at the same time raise her spirits by giving her a good example to follow.

"Did I do anything foolish last night?" she asked.

She looked up morosely, took a deep breath and tried to smile, encouraging me to deny she had acted like a jerk.

"You ate the goldfish and sang some bizarre but memorable Icelandic rugby anthem out the front door at the top of your lungs whilst swinging your bra in circles at the policewoman just as Beau was spewing up in the rhododendrons. Otherwise, nothing too bad, really. Nothing the policewoman said would amount to a real crime. Just intensely embarrassing for you and Lou for the next month or so."

"I suggest you two move," I said, trying my best to be helpful. But for some reason, even this didn't help.

Since neither of us was going to get any work done in the library this morning, we decamped next door to the Union tearoom where a brewing teapot placed halfway between us on a nice tablecloth seemed to loosen up our brain cells a little.

"You could move in with me," I said, buttering a scone. "There's space for a spare bed in the broom closet down the hall. I could throw out the brooms and the ironing board to give you a bit more room."

"Daddy would have some objections," she noted, her head lolling closer and closer to the tabletop, despite the healing properties of the steaming pot of tea.

I couldn't think what he could possibly object to, and I told her so, especially since I had offered to move the brooms and ironing board and especially since he had told us that we are not his business.

"Yes, but" – Carol struggled to form her words through the dulling fog of post-traumatic alcohol syndrome – "but that's not to say he doesn't care. Correct?"

"Cares very much. Don't know anyone who cares more about you if it isn't me."

"Correct," she said.

"Correct," she repeated but then lost the thread and waited for it to trickle slowly back to her.

"No. Wait a bit. It's not that he doesn't care. It's that. Let me see…It's that he trusts us to make our own decisions in life, just like his parents – my grandparents – let him do all those years ago.

"There. I'm glad I was able to think that bit through, b'cuz I thought my brain had fallen out of my head for some reason," she said, shaking her head as if something loose inside it that wasn't working properly might fall out and leave her at last clearheaded.

"He has always trusted me. Can't say that he has any reason to trust you though. You have been a bit of a cad in all of this," she teased.

"Cad?" I said, lifting the lid and stirring the tea.

"Yes. Cad. With Lulu. She's still not willing to elaborate, but…"

"Is it about the book – which I shall never get back, by the way."

"She's not saying. Anyway, it isn't the balcony scene in which – I must tell you – you behaved magnificently."

"How on earth have I ever been a cad to her then? I couldn't have been. Not in my wildest dreams. You have made a miss-a-priori cognition there."

"No such thing," she said, giving me a withering look.

"What?"

"First of all, there is no such thing as a miss-a-priori cognition. There is such a thing as an a-priori cognition but not the other way around," she insisted, still looking a bit green around the gills.

"Anyway, miss or not, you have made a mistake based on the facts of things. I have never been unfaithful to Lulu or anyone else for that matter. Always held her in the highest esteem. Did for her as I have done for you and would do for anyone else. And I didn't look, when I had every right to, err, under the circumstances."

"I seem to remember you taking a little peek," Carol said, then swung the discussion back on track. "For her as you have done for me? Just what on earth do you mean by that?"

"You know exactly what. Nothing I wouldn't do for her," I hedged, feeling backed into a corner, feeling a little bit guilty of pending accusations whatever they might be, not wanting to defend myself for fear of hurting her.

"Nothing," I explained, hoping that would answer her squinting inquisition.

"Well. I should hope that you would do for me at least some of the things you wouldn't do for her."

Trying to catch her at her own little game, I asked earnestly, "Like what?"

"Can't think at the moment, really. My brain is a tepid jelly right now, but I will think. I will remember loads of things that you have done to her that she disapproves of and holds you in deep misesteem of. Or something like that," she said in a muddle, shaking her head again.

"No such word," I said.

"Misesteem – no such animal."

"It's not an animal, silly. It's the way Lulu feels about you for all the contemptuous things you have done to her. But she forgives you. She jolly well does forgive you because she is such a lovely, err…forgiving person…

"…But I am feeling extremely unwell at the moment," she said as a look of deep foreboding dropped down from her lovely eyelashes.

"…And if you'll forgive me, I think…" she declared, getting up and making a dash for the loo, which was just around the corner behind her.

Poor thing.

Still, it serves a purpose, that hazy spinning of the room, that clammy feeling down the back of the neck, that shunting of the gut that can only mean one thing, and poor, sweet Carol was in the throes of it at that very moment.

Poor, poor thing.

"Thank god, I've never had your drinking problem," I offered when she finally got back to her seat, giddily, carefully lowering herself onto it, eyes wide with her new experience.

"Will it go away?" she moaned in all innocence. "I don't think I'll ever touch another glass of wine, ever again in my life," she said very slowly, deliberately in order not to slur.

"Lots of water, that's the way to deal with it. Lots of water and bed rest. Sleep it off. You'll be better in the morning. You'll see."

"Morning! But what will I do about today?" she squeaked.

"Never you mind, I'll look after today for you. First, we'll have to get you home and tuck you in," I said, fussing. "You should never have come out today in the first place, let alone drunk so much last night. We live and learn. Live and learn."

"Yes," she said quietly. "Oh, I don't feel at all well."

Chapter 38
Cad

After taking Carol back home and putting her to bed, I strolled with Louisa back through town, wrangling on our way toward separate lectures. Hers was Blake and mine Milton. The centre of town bristled with all manner of townish activity. Shoppers, sellers, students with their college scarves wrapped around their necks pushing on stoically up Silver Street, clinging desperately to an excuse; a mother with a toddler in tow idly drifting past shop windows, clinging to the belief that it could all happen again, and we two literary scholars wandering together and apart, dodging around and between the crowds, attempting conversation but knowing it was all no good. Me because I didn't understand what on earth Lou was on about, and she because I was so dense and 'male' into the bargain.

"Carol says I've been a cad. Don't understand it."

"You have," Louisa offered. "You were a cad. The next day."

"The next day, what? Day after what?"

"The day after the balcony scene. You probably don't even know what we are talking about. You probably aren't even aware that what you did was entirely out of order, the way you men see things."

"But how? What do you mean?" I asked feeling accosted, very male and caddish, trying to remember what happened the day after the balcony scene.

Finally, exasperated by my lamentable blockheadedness, Louisa threw up her hands and turned to face me full on. Cornered by this fiercely beautiful female with larceny in her eyes, I reeled backwards out of range, or so I thought.

"Why did you do that?" I asked, feeling the full impact of her bag on the side of my head.

"What did I do?" she asked, walking on ahead, now speeding up to get separation between us.

"You deliberately thwacked my head," I said feigning hurt and staggering after her.

"You deserve it. Two timing, cad."

At this news, I had to stop and gather my thoughts. We were at the edge of the marketplace at the top of Silver Street. I couldn't, for the life of me, figure out what the hell she was on about but was willing to listen and ready to turn on the slightest evidence.

"I saw you."

"Saw me what? What are you talking about?"

"You and that girl," she said incensed now. Indignant. Literally vibrating with acrimony.

"Up there. Up Claypath. The whole world must have seen it. You cannot deny it, Christopher Robin. Dragging that girl into that alleyway just past the cinema…And…And…And doing goodness knows what in there to her.

"And…and…and…That's not all," she stammered with passion. "You didn't come back out. Not that I saw, at least."

"Bloody hell," I shouted.

"Bloody hell what?" Louisa said, shaking with anger.

"You took some unknown female off the street and into an alley and did goodness knows what to her. And there I was, rushing up to say hello.

"What a naïve fool I must have looked. And you disappeared with her before I could get there. But it's none of my business, is it? You don't have to explain a thing. It's your private affair.

"Just … just … just don't say anything. I really do not want to hear the sordid details. However, if you don't explain yourself," she said wresting her arm from my grip, tears streaming down her cheeks. "Just don't expect anything else from me except thin cordiality and deep, deep loathing.

"Just what were you doing in that alley all that time?" she sobbed.

"Putting her to bed," I said which must have been a shock to Louisa, the way I said it.

"Oh!" Louisa was stunned and, in her confusion, walked in blind circles around the market stalls trying to gather her thoughts.

"I thought at least you'd be more circumspect than that … after all …"

"Nothing to hide at all," I said, cherishing the drama I was generating with my obtuse, bone-headed explanation.

"I bedded the wench. And that was that. Is that what you wanted to hear?" I said, more out of indignation than truth.

Gobsmacked, Lulu went silent, not expecting such a forthright confession.

"And that's all you have to say?"

I could see she wanted a better explanation; one she could handle and take back to Carol who obviously knew nothing of the incident.

"You could at least say she was your cousin or something, an aunty come to visit you for the day."

"She wasn't. Just some random girl," – which was a bit of a lie too but not that far from the truth.

"Random? In what way random, may I ask?"

"Looks like you have asked, and so all I can tell you is that she was random. I didn't even know her name."

"Some blond, random floosy you bedded and you didn't even know her name. I find that hard to believe."

"Did you get a good look at her," I said, feeling hurt by Louisa's abandonment.

"You seemed to have seen that she was blond. Did you get a good look at her hair, her face or her clothes, for that matter?"

"Tracksuit. She was wearing a purple tracksuit. Probably some rower floosy of yours you dragged up off the river for a quick…bedding, I suppose," she said between impassioned gulps of air, wandering off in a daze towards Elvet Bridge.

I just looked on and nodded.

"Couldn't agree more," I shouted after her. "You have hit the nail on the head," I shouted, enjoying the melodrama, dragging it out as much as I could. I knew it would be too cruel to let it go on too much longer, but for now, I played the injured party, following closely on her heals.

Poor Lulu.

Feeling like the cad I was being accused of, I chased off after her towards Elvet Bridge, now wanting to explain the whole thing properly, but by the time I got there, she had been swallowed up by the crowds of shoppers and students teeming both ways, and I completely lost sight of her until seeing her cute little rump in the distance hurrying up the steps into Elvet Riverside Lecture Halls. I called out, but she chose not to hear and disappeared inside, swallowed up by the crowds of undergraduates filing in to lectures.

By now, I was desperate to set the story straight and reclaim her good opinion, put things right, explain properly. Her lecture hadn't started yet, so I stood at the back of the lecture theatre scanning the packed hall for any evidence of her presence.

I had gone too far.

Desperate to make amends and cheer her up, I searched back and forth for her with no results. I was about to turn back out of the lecture theatre when I noticed something familiar in a distant corner.

She was sitting by herself, alert and ready for the pearls that were about to be cast by Prof Lynwood on the stage, resplendent in his robes behind his lectern. Louisa ignored me when I settled in beside her, said nothing, affected disdain, quietly awaiting the main event, still heaving with anger.

A sniff.

A tissue.

Doing her best to shut me out, she fished in her little pencil case for a pen and began to write the date and the lecture topic at the top of her yellow notepad, her luxuriant hair dropping between us, a barrier to any further communication. This was now reaching catastrophic proportions.

Lynwood continued to fuss behind the lectern.

Louisa squiggled on her notepad next to the date, doodled a triangle that grew branches and eyes and ears. I reached across with my pencil and drew a noughts and crosses grid at the top of her page and even started it off with an X at the top right-hand corner. She responded quickly by rubbing out the intrusion, giving me a withering scowl and turning her back to me, shutting me out of her life for good.

This terrorised me. I had no answer to it. This was the open-minded, happy-go-lucky, delicate, sweet Louisa deciding that I wasn't worth the effort any more, that I was the lowest thing that crawled on the earth, banished forever from her thoughts.

Powerful stuff.

Feeling totally alone and insignificant, I sat back in my seat, folded my arms across my chest and breathed in deeply to calm my racing pulse. This was news indeed. Enmity that I didn't deserve. Certainly more sinned against than sinning, I felt at that moment that this place held no more wonder for me. I understood too that having her good opinion meant more to me than I had ever realised.

Lynwood looked out across the waves of expectant, eager young faces, gripped his gown lapels, cleared his throat and began. The droning voice and heat of the building conspired to send me off within a matter of minutes. When I woke up some time later, the hall was emptying, the professor was gone from the front, and Louisa's seat was empty.

Can't tell you how I felt at that point. Abandoned too, I guess. Frustrated. All the emotions of rejection and isolation swam around my brain as I lifted my frame from my seat and hauled my miserable carcase up the steps toward the back of the lecture theatre. Hoping to see a lonely little person waiting for me in the foyer, I was even more desolate to see the place empty.

"I hope my ranting in there didn't disturb your nap, Mr Flynn." It was Prof Lynwood behind me, coming out of the lecture theatre, arms overflowing with books.

"I feel that if I have no other effect, I have at least served that particular purpose. And thank you for not snoring. Snoring can be so off-putting."

"Sorry, Professor," I fumbled.

"That's quite all right, old man. Tried to think of ways to make Milton less tiresome, but for the life of me, he always seems to end up sending people off."

"Milton?" I blurted without thinking. Suddenly, it occurred to me that it had been Milton and not Blake. Why was Lulu in the wrong lecture, my lecture?

"Yes," Lynwood said, gently spilling books as we walked. "You have every right to think it was Porky Pig, considering the attention you were giving it, but I can attest to the fact that we were deep in the workings of *The First Book of Paradise Lost*," he said, stooping, as did I, to retrieve his dropped texts.

"And not Disney's top ten. Mind you, I wouldn't mind giving a talk on Elmer Fudd and Co. sometime. I think I could count on total audience attention."

"You could sell tickets," I said.

"And hot dogs during the interval, my boy. Yes," he said, standing up again with his books in some sort of manageable order, "we could do with some new material around here. Milton's fine for the stuffy old crowd that likes that sort of thing but give me Sylvester the Cat and Tweety Pie. There's drama for you! A few feathers fluttering in the breeze then, voila, Tweety is back up and at Sylvester with a baseball bat again without a thought of ornicide," he said as we stepped outside into the sunlight.

"I'm going to table a motion with the committee. We need a balance," he said, wandering off ahead of me.

"No wonder attendance is dropping. Less *Hell, Fire and Damnation* nonsense and more contemporary arts. Less Milton and more Porky Pig. That's the answer.

"You've been a tonic, my boy, a revelation. Come to tea this afternoon."

He darted off, his robes billowing out behind him.

Just then, from the other direction, the green camouflage jacket and red hair of friendship hove into view dodging through the crowds heading for Dunelm House. The Pinball Wizard looked concerned about something and didn't see me at first.

"Lunch, Leo?" I suggested. He brightened up at this, and we pressed on into the canteen for a bite to eat.

"Trouble?" I asked as we set our pots of yoghurt down and settled into seats next to the windows overlooking the river.

"Agnes," he sighed with that grim, crest-fallen look on his face.

I nodded, not really ready for more woe but willing to listen to his tale.

"You'd think there was some easy way of getting on with women, wouldn't you? Just when you think you've got them sorted out, it starts all over again, only in a different way. What is the answer?" Leo asked.

"Lynwood has the answer," I said.

"Loopy Lynwood?"

"Yes. Lynwood." I nodded. "Didn't you hear him just now? You couldn't have been paying attention."

"What is it then? What's his solution to the world's eternal problem?"

I took a deep breath before answering then exhaled slowly.

"Porky Pig."

"Porky Pig," he said brightening.

"Ah, yes. Porky Pig. Should have known. I can see it now. The panacea to the illness that afflicts half the world's population. Porky Pig. What else? That man's a fuckin' genius. And there I was having a lovely kip in the middle of his lecture just now, blissfully ignorant of all this. Should have stayed awake."

Then he suddenly turned to me with that look on his face.

"Do you know what she's gone and done yet again?" he asked totally out of the blue, twisting his face into a credible imitation of the Grinch. "Agnes, I mean."

"Not again?"

"Yes, again. And it's the second bloody time this week. Two firsts in a week," he withered answering his own question, totally out of sorts. "Could have spaced them out a bit to, say, one a year. Once in a lifetime would do me. Makes me look like a total cretin in front of all my friends."

"Which you are, by the way. In front of all of us," I helped.

"Which I am, thank you very much.

"Very embarrassing, as you can imagine. People are starting to look at me. People are starting to ask questions. What in bloody hell am I doing going out with a bloody Einstein, they ask. What are you going to do about it, they ask.

"What can I do about it?" he exclaimed, finishing off his yoghurt by sticking his tongue inside the pot and ringing it around.

"Grow a brain cell?" I offered.

"Can't do it. I tried. Even tried doing some work to pull my lamentably poor fail up to at least a third. Almost crippled me. Didn't bloody help.

"You saw me…" he said in desperation.

"I did! Last week in the library. You were trying very hard to finish your essay on time and get it in. Almost worked," I recalled. "The colouring-in bit was good; the best bit, I thought. Although I don't think colouring-in counts."

"Almost worked," he remembered with optimism in his voice. "Took my little worn down pencil stub and paper into the library and did some research for once."

"You asked the librarian where the coffee machine was …"

"That's research, isn't it? You have to know where the coffee machine is."

"Wouldn't actually call it research though," I said.

"Got me out of the library, though."

"After only five minutes in. You really didn't give yourself a chance."

"Had to get out, hadn't I. Couldn't stick around like a spare part after that dolly bird of yours settled in opposite us."

"Carol? She was OK, I thought. Didn't say a word. She didn't interrupt your earth-shattering discoveries, did she? Worked away quietly on her French like a good 'un, as I recall."

"She didn't have to outwardly interrupt. She was there. That's all that was needed from her. Don't know how you stand it, mate."

"Stand what?"

"Her. Being there – in all her splendour. Her being anywhere near does my head in. Why couldn't you find a homely looking lass?"

Taken aback by this, I quietly turned the theory of homeliness over in my head leaving Leo room to think about his denunciation.

"Near is what I like about her," I said. "The best part of her, as a matter of fact. Near is heaven. Far is hell."

"Other way around for me," he declared with self-satisfaction.

"Torments me to buggery," he declared with a withered grimace.

"I gotcha," I said. "Next time she shows up, I'll tell her to pull an empty coal sack over her head, just so she doesn't set you off."

"Good," he said with withered relief in his voice. "Another one taken care of. Now all you have to do is sort out Agnes for me.

"Dearie me," he lamented. "The things we have to do to keep the world right. Is it opening time yet?"

Chapter 39
An Unpropitious Day
in the Sun: Philandering

It didn't get any better over the next few days. Lulu just wasn't interested. As far as she was concerned, I had committed a mortal sin and that was that. I would see her off in the distance in crowds around the town, but before I could close in to explain, she would disappear. Looked like we had just missed each other, but I knew better. She was deliberately avoiding contact, ducking around corners and darting behind buildings and people. Silly, I know, and I knew too that it would just take minutes to clear the air with her, tell her what really happened that day in the alley but pinning her down to do this was looking like impossible.

Carol wasn't much help. She just said Lou was out of sorts over The Honey One and didn't want to talk about him. Nothing about me. When I pressed her, she said Lou hadn't mentioned the Claypath alleyway incident to her, or if she had, it wasn't having any effect; although, Carol wasn't around as much either and made the excuse that she needed to get work done before she could come out to play. Both of them in their own way were drawing away from me. I needed time with them together to sort this whole alleyway thing out. They – especially Lou – were growing distant. I was devastated. Miserable. Felt abandoned.

"Such is life," Leo explained to me.

"Part of life's rich tapestry," he said. "Give it time," he said. "An' if they don't come back – sod 'em. Plenty more fish in the sea."

"Cuth's Day next weekend, mate. Bring 'em to Cuth's Day. Get 'em sorted.

"One or two Britvics on the lawn. Packet o' crisps and you'll be well away.

"Spend some money on 'em. They'll love you for it."

"Me and Agnes'll be pressing daisies all afternoon on the lawn listening to the bands. Beau is taking his latest conquest. Don't know who yet. Could be anybody's.

"You'll be the odd man out if you show up single."

"Drinking my way to oblivion on the lawn, eh?" I said.

"Something like that. Not such a bad idea," he said, reconsidering oblivious drinking. The more he turned over the idea of being a singularity at Cuth's day, the more he warmed towards it.

"Agnes might get in the way of things, if you know what I mean. Oblivion and such. You and me all afternoon on the lawn with nobody to get in the way, to interrupt the flow of beer and intellectual conversation." He thought some more about the possibilities this might offer, weighing up the pros and cons.

"Might be able to get Beau to dump whoever he's picked up for the day. Three of us. Sounding better all the time. Boat Club piss up perhaps. On the lawn…"

And by the time he'd finished, Leo had outlined a plan that began to sound much like many other afternoons: lunch, beer and lolling about on the lawn in the sun waiting for dinner and blind sobriety.

Colin arrived late but wasn't impressed.

"Doesn't sound much different from the usual. As a matter of fact, it is just like any other afternoon at Cuth's, as far as you're concerned," he said.

"That's it," Leo enthused. "You have it in one, me old son. That's the genius of it. Cuth's Day without being slave to propriety…"

"You mean without the women around to curb your drinking," Colin said.

"Sheer genius," Leo enthused. "Couldn't have put it any better me self. Took Flynn to come up with it," he said, decanting the blame.

"Always knew he was good for something. Never knew what, really, but now…this…stroke of genius.

"Cuth's Day. All the trappings. Lolling in the sun on the lawn all afternoon without anybody to get in the way of a pint or two, without being the slave to propriety," he said, mulling the phrase over in his fevered little brain.

"Have a pint. Go off and have a game or two – croquet, swat the rat," he said waving in the direction of Del Fuego who had just joined the table.

"Settle back in the sun. Undo me shirt. Take me socks off."

"Steady on, Leo," Colin said getting more and more worried about Leo's plans.

"Les singing *Cushy Butterfield* and *The Blaydon Races*. Les doesn't usually blossom until he's had four or five. *The Lampton Worm* perhaps. His *Lampton Worm* is a gem.

273

"Punt fight down on the river later. When we are all suitably imbibed."

"Stagger back up here for another tipple. Mine will be yet another pint of Best Scotch. Your round by then, Crabtree. First of the year for you, you tight git, but you always come good by Cuth's Day.

"Don't you worry, me old son, we won't leave you out."

"I think Vicky would have something to say about that," Colin said bravely.

"Keeps an eye on me drinking, does Vicky. Doesn't like seeing me paralytic."

"They don't like seeing any of us having a good time," Tucker reminded him, defending his stratagem.

"She doesn't mind me having a few pints with me mates. Doesn't like the day after much, though," Colin said, defending his snivelling.

"If you get to feeling unwell, you could help Del Fuego with Swat the Rat."

"Specky might have something to say about that," Del Fuego said.

"Might be peeved if somebody took his place," he said, pulling that face to illustrate something delicate.

"Specky's job is to drop the rat into the top of the tube. Takes a steady hand. He's good at revving up the punters. Passionate is our Herbert."

Leo considered this option before saying, "Bloody well revs me up with his ranting and goings on. He's a maniac. Needs a different job. Something to quieten him down, not rev him up. How about the tea and cakes stall? Couldn't get too passionate over tea and cakes, could he?"

"There then. That's settled. Tea and cakes for Specky, so Colin can do the Swat the Rat when he feels – when Vicky feels – he's getting too close to his limit. I for one am now looking more forward than ever to our unpropitious day in the sun."

Leo read English. He did little with his professors to promote his degree, rarely attending lectures and sleeping through most that he did drag himself to. It was testament to his genius that he made it through at all. This man's main interest in life was his next pint as well as getting his leg over whenever the opportunity presented itself – which, it must be said – was not often enough. Hence, his abiding Beau-envy. Hence, Leo's peevishness at the minute brought on by his largely celibate state.

The Great Day was approaching, and I was in a quandary about what to do with Carol and Louisa. I wanted to invite them both, would love to see them both, but it looked like this wasn't going to happen. Louisa was still convinced that I was some kind of two-timing cad who couldn't be trusted, and so I finally decided to take the bull by the horns and explain what had really happened that day in that alleyway.

"Can't see you before Cuth's Day," Louisa's note said in response to my invitation.

"Too busy at the moment, dearest. Let's talk about it on Cuth's Day," Carol returned with only two days to go and me in a tizzy about everything. What else could I do but acquiesce? – a skill I had learned to employ greatly ever since meeting those two. At least there was a 'dearest' thrown in which gave me some hope. And leaning very heavily on that, I deposited into their pigeonholes their invitations to Cuth's Day lunch, kind of like lighting the blue touch paper and standing back to await results.

Lunch arrived on that glorious day. The lawn behind Cuth's was resplendent in white tablecloths gently ruffling in a warm breeze. You know the kind of day it was; no need to describe further. The tables were packed high with all sorts of grub, and everybody seemed to be having a great time, trying their hands at the various games, feeding their faces and lolling about on the lawn drinking their beers or Britvics or whatever else they chose. The bands would arrive later in the afternoon and play 'til the wee small hours. I was the only morose person there, for you see, no Carol or Lulu had arrived. Hoping that they might eventually turn up, I joined the lads and lasses who had circled the wagons on the lawn outside the bar.

Several hours passed imbibing but still no special guests, and the afternoon was slipping by without any sign of them. I wandered off in a desultory funk, ending up on Prebend's Bridge gazing out across the river, fully aware that I had royally screwed up somehow and that my Elysium had come crashing down all about me.

A seagull flew past.

And then another lonely seagull.

Two seagulls wheeling in the breeze over the river.

Two.

Ironic.

Pairs of resplendent students wandered up and down the towpath or behind a morose and lonely singleton gazing out over the bridge parapet. I was reminded of the magical moment when I had bumped into Carol that morning as she was stepping down the other side of the bridge, all smiles, out of breath, pink with the exertion, so I thought, but now when I remember that morning, she was blushing pink not with exertion but with delight. And I had missed my chance.

"Don't do it," suddenly came a cheery warning from behind me. It was Tucker, his pint in one hand and one for me in the other.

"Courtesy of Crabtree, skinflint extraordinaire," he said, handing mine across.

"Didn't think we were such a boring bunch that you would be forced to top yourself."

We stood side by side on that parapet, sipping our pints, gazing off at the miraculous view of the cathedral towers and the weir.

"Err, well, yes," he began, as he often did, hoping that some kind of sane conversation might follow.

"Didn't think that you were that far gone."

I smiled, but he must have sensed the emptiness.

"Punt fight starts in a bit over by the Count's House. Sup up and we'll wander down. Have a look."

I nodded agreement and drank off half my pint. I could see Leo had something to tell me that he was waiting the right time for. Must have been bad. He kept waiting and gazing off over the water.

"Well," I said, "what's happened?"

"Beau has arrived…"

"And?"

"Got this new lass in tow…"

"New lass? Not Louisa?"

"That little firecracker your—"

"…splendid…" I said, intervening.

"Your splendid lass hangs around with…No. Not her. Haven't seen either of those two at all today," he fished, looking sideways at me to gauge my reaction. I must have looked squalid, because he shut up for a while before finally venturing:

"Didn't you say you invited them around to lunch?" he said as gently as ever he could.

When I didn't reply, Leo carried on with his monologue trying to drag me out of my funk and back into the festivities of the afternoon.

"Anyway, Beau's arrived, plastered. His new lass, plastered. They are both plastered."

I nodded, a kind of disinterested, non-committal nod and returned to the rest of my pint whilst gazing out across the river like some daft lovelorn jerk out of one of those cheap romance novels. Must have looked a right pillock. But Leo wasn't having lovelorn at the moment. He was still on about Beau and his new dolly bird.

"They were doing some serious cuddling when I left. You'd think they'd at least find a convenient bush to do it behind or a rock to do it under, not right there in the middle of the croquet lawn. Him in his coif and cravat and her wearing god only knows what.

"She's not a small lass, quite large, really. Fills out most of the lawn all by herself and wearing…

"… wearing nothing at all …" he said with considerable amazement in his quivering voice. He took another drink, examining her image in his head.

"… A pink blancmange, it looks to me. Diaphanous veils. Leaves nothing to the imagination. I for one would rather be given the right to imagine what was under the veils, instead of it being flaunted like that for all to see."

"Poor Beau," I offered, still not very taken with Leo's news.

"Don't think he cares. He's totally paralytic. His senses have been addled. He'll wake up with a horrible headache in the morning and no memory at all of her and what he is doing to her right there in front of High Table: Prof Osborne, Henry Havelock, Rev Kev, their tidy wives, the lot, whilst the rest of us poor, daft sober sods will have the grotesque memory of it stuck in our heads for the rest of our lives.

"…It's horrible!

"At least Specky tried to cover her up with the table cloth off his cake stall which, it must be said, wasn't big enough.

"Your Louisa would not be best pleased if she saw Beau right now. Not pleased at all. Better that she and her glorious mate, whatshername, haven't seen any of it.

"Offensive," he said, ending his rant with the kindest word he could think of.

"Frightening," he added as an afterthought.

"What is whatshername's name, by the way…?"

"Carol," I said quickly.

"Carol," he confirmed just as quickly and not wanting to linger on a heartache, dropped the subject.

Meanwhile two hundred yards or so behind us, upstream at the Count's House, the punt fight had begun in earnest with much male and female shrieking, screaming and splashing echoing through the bankside willows. Before this year's particularly ignoble event, Cuth's had two punts which were set against each other for the traditional battle. Rival gangs of students in various degrees of sobriety aboard the two vessels manoeuvred clumsily around each other. Once within throwing distance, they pelted each other with bags of liquid food colouring and bags of flour. When the bags ran out, the battle was deemed to be over, but this punt fight turned out to be different from all others held before it. It was the bloody Battle of Neville's Cross all over again.

With private scores to be settled, two of the combatants opted for a duel to the death.

Sturge and Smy in opposing punts dragged the event down to their crudest of crude level, and anything within reach was hurled at the opponent until nothing loose was left on board either punt. Their only resort now was a desperate ramming tactic. Eventually, everyone on both sinking punts abandoned ship whether they needed to or not, splashing, jeering and throwing invectives, at last attempting to overturn each other. Finally, these noble vessels, brave servants to Cuthbert for many decades, were flipped over and left derelict just off The Count's House, sad, sunken hulks, monuments to Cuth's Day.

Two dozen drunken, dazed, exhausted combatants crawled out of the river and lay about the bankside gazing in wonder at what they had done.

"Things got out of hand," one of them was heard to say.

"Didn't mean that," another said.

"Yes, you did, you twat," Specky levelled at Del Fuego.

"Wasn't me who started it," Del Fuego said looking all woebegone and miserable. "Somebody chucked a paddle. Just missed my head. They were trying to murder us after that bastard Smy rammed into us."

"Which pillock jabbed that punt pole through our bows?" Ian said, sitting bewildered on the bankside holding a hanky to his bleeding nose. "We sank like a rock.

"Don't know how I came to be under the damn punt. Bloody murderers. Nobody heard me under there. Could have done for me. Who pulled me out, by the way?"

Colin raised his hand. "I was trying to shove you back under, Ian, only I got it wrong."

Just then, Big Al casually remarked, "There's somebody floating head down in the water out there. Is there a life ring about, somebody?"

But the life ring wasn't there, was it? It was one of a pair Del Fuego had proudly displayed on his wall in Cuth's. So Al waded in up to his waist and dragged the body out onto the towpath.

"It's Sturge," Al mentioned in a disinterested way.

"Do us all a favour and throw it back in," Les said.

"Is it dead?" a disinterested bystander was heard to enquire.

"Partly," Al returned, about to administer a life restoring thump to his back.

"What the funken hell is that supposed to mean?" Leo asked casually.

"He's either dead or he's not dead, Alan. Can't be somewhere in between."

"Well, you come and look after him, then, Leo," Alan said, getting out of the way to let the supreme diagnostician in.

Rocking back and forth on his heels and cuddling his pint firmly to his chest, Leo leant over Sturge to take a look, nodded sagely to the soggy gathering and announced, "Looks partly dead to me. Why don't you pat him on the back again, Alan, to get the phlegm out."

"Get the bloody phlegm out, Leo? He's got half the contents of the River Wear in there, bedsteads an' all. It'll take more than a pat to bring that lot up."

"Nonsense. I've got every confidence in his innards."

Meanwhile, Alan jumped up and down on his chest several times to make him spew.

"There now, Harry, feeling better…?" But before the enquiry was finished, Sturge was on his groggy feet, fists clenched and taking dead aim at his absent mate, Smy.

"Where is he? I'll kill the bastard," he threatened, thrusting out at no one in particular.

"Last time I saw him, Harry," Leo said trying as best he could to be helpful, "he was wandering away up the towpath arm in arm with your wife."

"Did someone mention unpropitious?" Leo asked on our way back up the path to the party.

"Both of our punts have been sunk; a near drowning; Beau and his new missus misbehaving on the lawn in front of our revered principal and his wife and his party of university toffs; Flynn is as miserable as sin, with or without the attendant diversions, because his women folk have refused to entertain his call of the wild.

"It has been a right cock-up from the start, a right cock-up. And I fear there is more to come before lunch is served. Has anyone heard from the likes of young Herbert or Reginald? God knows what those two have in store for us before the day is out."

"Hardly my women folk, Leo," I said.

"Hardly here, Flynn. Not here at all, from what I see. You, mate, are scuppered, cast adrift, a singularity. Your harem has deserted you in droves and gone back to their original habitat. What were those two called, Errol and Oliver?

"Face it, my friend; you need to spend the rest of this day making the acquaintance of other ladies, many of whom will be suitably enough plastered later in the afternoon for your evening revels.

"Look," he said as we entered the lawn. "There's one diaphanously displayed lady out in the middle of the lawn looking suitably adrift – and glum. Shall we go and cheer her up. She appears to be all by herself."

"Beau's tart?" Colin said, never one to mince words.

"Britvic?" Leo asked the abandoned lady whose name we found out was Helen.

"Err, drink, Helen?" he repeated, teetering backwards and forwards on his heels.

Helen, who was a healthy-looking, big-boned lass 'covered' in a gossamer see-through frock that left little to the imagination, said that she preferred beer, a pint. And so, Leo scuttled off to bring her a pint, encouraged by one who shared his taste in drink, a no-nonsense kind of gal who looked the equal of him and Beau and the rest of the lawn put together, for that matter.

Leo scuttled back with her beer and stood rocking on his heels awaiting a result. When none came, he offered.

"Couldn't help noticing, dear, that you were escorted here by our friend, Beau," he said, bowing obsequiously and continuing his concern for the welfare of this destitute young lady.

"Buggered off, did he?" Leo said in his well-meaning way, holding his pint close to his chest whilst he prised as much as he could out of her.

She looked back up at Leo bowing there above her. Once on the grass, he was certain that he might not be able to easily get up again. She looked back up at him, squinting around him with the sun pouring around his head into her eyes, put her pint to her lips, took a swig and, after the style of Mae West, "By mutual consent, Honey. Why? You thinking of taking his place?" she said, ironically patting the grass beside her. By the twang in her voice and her confident manner, this girl was from the States.

Definitely American.

Leo was at once smitten.

"Very well then," he said thoughtfully, "in that case, dear, I think I shall give up using compound sentences for the time being," he said, easing in beside her and looking back up at the rest of us with that sly, predatory grin on his face.

"Did somebody say something about unpropitious?" Colin said moments later back at the bar. We had decided to leave Leo to his own devices out there in the middle of the arena with the American lady who looked like she could and very well might eat him alive well before lunch was finished.

"Knowing Leo," Colin said, "he'll want to serve her on the lawn in front of the great and the good just to go one better than Beau.

As it was now well within the lunching hour, Fairport Convention was setting up, ready for the off. Twangling and testing their instruments, the group made good their sound and began, drowning out any attempts at conversation for the next little while. We all leaned in to each other to be heard.

"Didn't I see Smy over there at the back of the queue with Sturge's woman?" Ian said, not daring to single himself out to the illustrious thug by pointing but rather nudging toward Smy with the point of his elbow.

"Came in with her," Big Al said, "but she seems to have made good her escape from him. Yes, there she is further back in the queue talking to that smallish woman in red and that bloke in a Castle scarf."

My heart sank.

I made good my escape into the bogs at the back of the JCR bar to gather my thoughts and hide my confused little mojo. If Louisa and Errol were here, Carol could not be far away. And who was with whom, I asked myself as I buttoned up my flies, chased after my fleeing nerves, took a deep breath and checked the mirror on the way back out to the coliseum.

Nothing had changed in the meantime. The food queue hadn't moved and Louisa was still there at the back of it chatting to Alice. Errol had disappeared. This made it slightly easier for me, so I retrieved my pint from Al, took a deep breath and bravely made my way toward the back of the queue. Standing directly behind the small person who meant so much to my life, I trembled on the precipice of a nerve ending, inhaling her scent and looking directly over her head at Alice.

"You got my invitation then?" I squeaked nervously toward Louisa whose back was still to me and who was not in the least bit interested in anything I had to say at the moment. Alice caught my remark, looked first at Lulu to see what she would reply and, getting nothing from her, stifled her own response to my question. For what seemed like an eternity, we stood becalmed there in the middle of the crowd.

Suddenly somewhere from the depths of the moment, a voice rose. Without turning around to address me directly, Louisa spoke to me or to Alice or to the bloke directly to her left, I couldn't say which, but she spoke.

Good. This was progress. This was…

I tipped forward onto my toes listening intently to hear what was being said, desperate to beg her pardon, to ask her to repeat it, anything to establish contact. And then suddenly, she turned to face me. She didn't have to say another word, for there written all over her face was the misery she still felt after seeing me pulling that girl into the alleyway off Claypath. I felt crushed. How could I do that to her and leave it all unrepaired.

I took a breath, steadied the ship and tried to begin to explain.

"Did you also notice how wet she was?" I stammered out of the blue.

"How wet I was…we were. Did you?"

Lulu looked back into that specific reference, concentrating hard on a memory. Her head began to shake from side to side. Her face was full of doubt, anguish and disbelief. Her beautiful vermillion lips pursed. I waited several lifetimes for her to examine that event again. All at once, she concluded, "No."

That's all.

I collected this as evidence and nodding my head in the affirmative, uttered, "We were. Absolutely sodden. Both of us."

"Oh," she said quietly, a penny slowly dropping somewhere.

"From the river. Yes, you were," she affirmed, finally 'getting' some of it, turning her head sideways in order to better understand.

"Yes. Her from falling out of her sculling boat…" I stammered.

"And…" I wanted to add.

"You from jumping in after her, and…" she said with a sudden intake of breath, examining these new facts in miniscule.

"…and dragging her out," she said quietly, turning the new evidence over.

"…and that's why…" she said putting two and two together.

"…I had to get her back to her place up Claypath and dried out," I explained.

"…Simply that," I added, quietly.

"You rescued that girl!" she decided, a breathless smile crossing those fabulous lips.

"You saved her life!" she concluded.

"Wouldn't say that. Wouldn't go that far. She needed help. Isn't very tall. And it wasn't looking very good for her for a while…her being so…short. So I jumped. Not strictly protocol in the circumstances, but I guess I panicked. A bit. That's all.

"She shouted out she couldn't swim," I added.

"That's all," Louisa said to herself, now beaming with delight.

"Dragged her sopping wet back to her place up Claypath where her roommate saw to a change of clothes for her and a cocoa for the three of us," I explained in a rush. "It being a chilly walk back."

"That's why you didn't…

"…come back out for a bit," she said in wonder, finishing her own sentence this time. "You had cocoa, and didn't…"

"Sorry," I apologised, "for not having ravaged her rotten during her moment of need."

"I thought…" Lou stumbled.

"Yes. I know," I said.

"But. I thought you we in there such a long time because…" she said, not finishing her accusation out of respect.

"Yes. I know."

"You…You…You pillock. Why didn't you say something?"

"Tried to. Loads of times. Nobody would let me," I said plaintively.

"And you weren't philandering?"

"Wasn't," I said.

"Didn't," I added and added even further, "Wouldn't even if I knew what it meant – 'philandering'."

"By the way," I said as, beaming, she tugged me forward to stand beside her.

"…having it off," she offered in a conspiratorial whisper, silencing my further enquiry. "With many women whilst betrothed to another. English scholar," she accused, flashing those dark, harem eyes.

"Oh," I said stupidly.

"That."

"Yes, quite."

"Betrothed?" I ventured.

"Yes," she said beaming in an irritated kind of way.

"Who, may I ask, or whom?" I dithered.

"You may. And it is 'who'."

"Oh…"

"Not me, you pillock."

"Ah. Yes. Well…"

She said nothing after this and re-engaged Alice who turned out to be much more articulate and level-headed than me at this particular moment.

"Not there, Christopher Robin…" Louisa cautioned me later on in the day as I stupidly moved with my paper plate filled with sandwiches and drink towards Leo and his newly acquired lady friend who were lolling next to the rhododendrons.

"They're having far too much fun for my liking," Louisa bossed. "Let's go over there under that nice tree. Perfect place for a picnic."

Chapter 40
Egg Salad Sandwich

"We've tried this picnic thing before," I said later, eating an egg salad sandwich opposite Louisa and Carol who had arrived late.

"Yes, we have," Carol said. "And you were dreadful at it."

"Did my best. Had it all planned out. Those boys…"

"Don't go blaming 'those boys' for your ineptitude," she said, sitting opposite me on the lawn with her legs tucked up under her bottom.

"I ask you, Lou. There we were…" Carol tried to explain to Louisa my ineptitude at picnicking.

"No, Polly, don't. Don't include me in your sordid, little tryst," Louisa said.

"I don't want to know how good he is at picnicking or punting or anything else for that matter."

"Those two over there seem to be very good at it," Carol said observing Leo and his new friend across the way.

"Very good, I would say," Louisa said, nibbling. "They look like they want to win first prize. Your friend is excellent, if you count carnal intercourse in public as part of the picnic rubric."

"Do you think they know they can be seen by the whole world?" Carol asked.

"Don't think they care, Polly," Lulu replied, casually looking towards the rhododendrons.

"Perhaps somebody should pop across and tell them," Carol said, looking over at me, "prise them apart or something. Throw a bucket of water at it."

"Ah, there's motion in the undergrowth. Someone's coming through," Louisa said as Sturge hove into view through the bushes. He lingered above the young loving couple, gesticulating all over the place with his pint and finally guffawed at a joke he made.

"He's kneeling down next to them. Your friend Leo doesn't look too thrilled. Look at the sour look on his face. Don't think he admired the joke."

"Or the jokester," Carol said sitting up herself and turning a little to get a better view.

"Who else is that with the lout?

"Another lout…"

"That great oaf, Smy?" Carol asked, peering off through the leaves.

"No," Louisa said, squinting herself to get a better look.

"No, not him. Too pretty for Smy. Oh my god, it's The Honey One, it's Beau, come to reclaim his woman I expect," Louisa said turning cloudy.

Later that evening as we walked back up Saddler Street, stiff from sitting for hours on a hard wooden bench, once again waiting for Louisa in the police station, Carol wondered if the band would still be playing back at Cuth's Day.

Louisa was dizzy from her second arraignment in as many weeks.

"I didn't really mean to hit him, you know," Louisa said.

"But you did. Hit him, I mean," Carol reminded her.

"More like a smack. A tiny tap that wouldn't hurt a fly. A swat."

"That's what started the whole thing off," I said, stumbling on and off the curb to avoid the slow-moving cars that squeezed their way to and from Palace Green.

"And it wasn't the swat that caught everybody's imagination. Pouring your pint over his head is what did it, really."

"He had it coming to him," Louisa said.

Carol nodded stoically, and then asked, "In what way, Lou? I mean, how did Beau have it coming to him just for sitting down beside that woman?"

"It wasn't that," I said.

"Wasn't it Christopher Robin?" Carol asked.

"Have I missed something?"

I raised an eyebrow at Lulu inviting her to intervene.

She struggled on up Saddler Street, stepping off the curb into the slow-moving traffic and back again, separating from us then coming back. Carol reached for her hand and pulled her close for safety and away from the cars.

"What was it then, my girl?"

Lulu looked toward me pursing her lips.

"He's a cad. That's all. He needed a pint poured over him, and I did it, and I'm not sorry. And," she said with deep conviction, "that judge agreed with me. He was a nice judge."

"I know he was a nice judge. But if he hadn't 've been, you'd've been stuck in jail all night with me having to explain the whole thing to your father to come and get you out…

…of jail, that is, in the morning."

"Oh, I don't think it was as serious as all that. It was good of Beau to admit it too, in front of the judge. Point in his favour. Don't you think, Lou? I mean, Lulu, he looked like he was sorry for that night."

"Not sorry enough to my mind," Louisa said.

"You are being a bit harsh on the poor bloke. Did you see how he looked at you while confessing his sins to that nice judge?"

Louisa looked back at that bit and seemed to relent her attack, walked on quietly.

"The judge did say you and Beau were not to come within fifty yards of each other for the next two weeks."

"Then what?" I asked. "Britvics at ten paces?"

"Believe me," Louisa assured us, "I don't ever want to see him again, ever, in my life, again, in any capacity, at anytime, anywhere," she said, throwing her arms up in exasperation.

"Oh?" Carol said throwing her glorious eyes up to heaven, the way she did, the way that no one else could, the way that shook me to the core.

"And you can just stop that right now, Christopher Robin."

"What, Polly? What did he do? What is he doing?"

"Tell you later, Lou. Not for public consumption in the middle of the Queen's Highway," she said sending a knowing smile in my direction while forging on along South Bailey to the wee small hours of Cuth's Day now heading for the next morning.

"That's better," she whispered taking me by the hand and drawing me close.

"You haven't done that in such a long time. I was beginning to wonder…"

"Wonder about what?" Louisa asked.

"What is he doing, Polly? Tell me you beast…Or…"

"Or what?" Polly challenged her friend.

"She'll pour her beer over your head," I said, staggering under the weight of Carol's blushing admiration.

Chapter 41
A Sturdy Lass

"You saw it," Leo enthused.

"I saw it, Leo, and it was wonderful, purposeful, full of purpose," I said.

"Vigorous," Colin chimed in. "Full of vigour, I thought."

"Couldn't have lasted the night at that rate," Leo said with some doubt in his voice.

"You got her back to the room, though."

"That was a feat in itself," Leo said, in a self-congratulatory way.

"Chuffed at that," he added.

"…and had your wicked way with her, I suppose, Leo," Colin persisted.

There was an awkward, searching silence at this point.

Leo ducked under a low-hanging tree limb as we ascended the crooked towpath on the other side of the river from the Count's House, you know, that steep bit on the outside of the bend.

"Couldn't, could I? I mean, she was six sheets to the wind and unconscious when she hit the bed. Mind that branch."

"Chivalrous of you, mate," Colin noted.

"Didn't think you had it in you," I added.

"Neither did I. Sorry, now I did. I had set her up all night with pint after pint, and all I got for me pennies and pains was a dull snoring, until she finally woke up at one the next afternoon. 'What's for lunch,' she said. What's for lunch? I bloody ask you."

"After everything you spent on her on Saturday…" Colin said.

"She expected me to buy her a lunch on top of it."

"Got rid of her after that, did you, Leo?" I suggested.

"No," he exclaimed. "NO, bloody hell not. She's still up there now, listening to Elvis on the wireless. I think she thinks she's moving in."

"Worrying," Colin said.

"You can't afford to feed her on top of it all. Cost you a fortune, as well as the space she'll be taking up."

"Bloody well can't get stirred in me own room," Leo affirmed.

"That's something I thought I'd never hear you say, Leo."

"Oh, aye. Aye. I don't mind the odd visitor but bloody hell…

"Besides," he decided in a most un-Leo-like way, "…got work to do. Exams next month. Idleness is not next to godliness … mind that rock … I need some sort of a plan."

"Plan for what?" I asked.

"Getting something out of the last three years," Leo said throwing his scarf around his neck against the suddenly chilly evening breeze.

"And now this …"

"This what?" Colin asked, puzzled by the obtuse, rambling conversation.

"Lodger. Her indoors. Helen."

"Thought you were all for it. I mean, having a woman all to yourself and her being American into the bargain," I said.

"There's a time and a place for these things. Now that life is bearing down on me, now that I need some space and time to salvage a degree …"

"Tell her to get out, then," Colin advised.

"Easier said than done, mate. Easier said."

"Come on, Leo. You can't have it both ways. Either you want her or you don't."

"Not as easy as all that," Leo said.

"Seems to me it is," Colin said.

"Make a decision."

"That is exactly it, in a nutshell," Leo admitted.

"Tell her it's a part-time relationship, and you'll see her every other Thursday for teacakes in the Union." Colin said.

Leo fell unusually silent after this last suggestion until we got to the top of the rise in the path, the bit that comes up behind St Oswald's church.

"Trouble is, I kind of like the company…If you know what I mean."

"Curb it. Temper these wild sexual desires, is all I can say. Put her to one side for a bit. At least until exams are over," Colin said.

Leo gave him that look. The one that asked him if he was insane, said nothing, just gave him the crazy, insane look.

"Nothing then…"

"What do you think?" Leo said sarcastically as we emptied out onto Church Street heading for the Spread Eagle further down opposite Dunelm House. Another summer's evening was drawing in. I was feeling cast adrift after the Cuth's Day debacle. We were all in need of an anti-depressant wallow in our local.

As we crossed Church Street, Leo spotted in the distance the unmistakable figures of two dear friends heading in our direction.

"Isn't that your missus down there, Flynn, and her bijoux feloness?" Leo asked, glad to change the subject from his headache to my heartache. I followed Leo and Colin into the Spread Eagle without confirming or denying his observation, led them to the bar, and since it was my round, called the bartender across.

"Could've sworn that was your Carol down the street," Leo said, chasing my heartache, his lips hovering over his drink.

I said nothing. The wound from Cuth's Day morning was still too raw; the memory of Errol leaving Cuth's lawn in the wee small hours with Carol and Louisa in tow was still so devastating that I hadn't had time to come to terms with it. But that was me all over. Jumping to conclusions. Thinking the worst.

"Leave it be, Leo, can't you?" Colin said coming to my rescue.

"Shit," was all Leo could say. "It hasn't happened to you an' all, has it? First me. Now you and her. But…thought you two were well away when Helen and I left Cuth's that morning. Just goes to show what a few hours can do. Isn't it amazing? First you think you've got it. Then…"

"Shut up, Leo," Colin said looking across at me. I must have looked a sorry mess because Leo did just that.

Looking ambulatory and contrite, the way he did, he said to himself, "Err, yes. Shut up, Leo."

"Shut up, Leo," he repeated to himself.

"And drink your beer."

Anything that was said after that was meaningless. I didn't hear it. Colin and Leo went on about how fickle women were. I descended into a funk of galactic proportions, a funk hole the size of the universe. They swore that women were a liability not to be entered into this side of sobriety. I nodded occasionally, not part of any of the conversation, and as the night wore on, I knew I really only wanted to be back in my room and unconscious in my bed, away from all the hurt and pain and sorrow that this apparition was causing me. My head bobbed closer and closer to the tabletop.

"What on earth do you think you are doing?" A little voice suddenly jabbed me out of my self-mortification.

"We thought we saw you coming in here," she jabbed again.

"Come on. Get up. Get up. We thought we saw you slinking in here earlier on with your dubious mates," the ministering angel prodded.

"Why didn't you answer when we waved at you?" It was Louisa. I had no idea where she had come from or what she was doing in my stupor.

"The least you could have done was wave back. I said you were just being rude. Now get up. Get up," she commanded.

"I'm going to take you home. Carol's still in her department party, or she would've been in to see to you. So I said I would. Now, on your feet, my lad. One sorry foot in front of the other," she commanded.

"Mind that chair. And out the door."

The door opened. I knew this by the cool fresh air that wafted past my spinning, boiling head.

"Now tell me, Christopher Robin, just what do you mean by standing us both up tonight." Struggling to keep me upright, she held my arm around her shoulders and levered me across the road.

A sturdy lass, I decided in my inebriated state. And I told her so – in my inebriated state.

"You're a sturdy lass, Lulu."

"Thank you. I'll put it in my curriculum vitae. Should create immense interest for prospective employers. Now, if you can just manage to lift a foot over this curb. Yes, it's a curb. Left foot forward. We'll not go across Kingsgate Bridge though. I think that would be tempting fate. Let's go around by Elvet Bridge, and if we come across any nice policemen, try to look at least a little bit sober for them."

"Sorry, Lulu," I heard someone saying from somewhere next to me.

"Sorry about what, you heavy great lummox?"

"Being such a drag." It was me that time who said it, but it still sounded like an out of body experience.

"You are being silly," she said stopping to shift me onto her other shoulder. "You are not a drag, even if you might be the heaviest lummox I've ever tried to carry home. Not a drag. Maybe lovely," I heard her whisper to herself. "Maybe, but never a drag." she humphed.

"And no. Come back here. We don't have time to look out over the bridge at the river just now. No time for Pooh Sticks. There's that ruddy great Claypath Hill to get you up, and it's going to take—"

Suddenly, I was swept up and lifted up higher by a mighty force of nature.

"Was that a mighty force of nature that just arrived?" I asked of the little person who was no longer supporting me by herself.

"Yes, it was," replied a voice not unlike Carol's.

"Mighty. And a force of nature... Poor Lulu. You do get yourself into some ridiculous pickles, Christopher Robin. It's a good thing she was here. It's a good thing she is a sturdy little elf."

"What do you mean elf?" Lulu demanded.

"Minimus, then." Carol humphed into my ear, struggling to keep me moving forward.

"You take that part of him, Lou, and I'll carry this, and I think … we … should." she groaned. "… be able … to … make … a go of it."

"Should be," Lulu huffed and puffed. The rest of the portage to Kepier Terrace was beyond my memory.

I do remember them getting me up to my room, though, with the help of Pettigrew who was just finishing tidying up. He was always very handy when it came to the mechanics of things, especially levering a drunken person upstairs and around the corner at the top of the stairs, past the broom closet which Carol sniffed at suspiciously and through the bedroom door and onto the bed where I was unceremoniously dumped.

"There," Carol said from the foot of the bed.

"There," Lulu repeated, very pleased they had managed.

"Do whatever it is you need to do to get him into bed, Damien. Come on, Lou. I'll be by in the morning with sausage rolls for breakfast," she said, disappearing back down the stairs, her voice diminishing in volume as they descended.

"Whatever did he mean by that remark he made outside the General Gordon, Louisa? Whatever did he mean by it?" Carol said as she opened the door onto the street.

"Something about some person in an alleyway somewhere down there he wanted us to meet."

"Oh. Just some woman he pulled out of the river who lives at the bottom of Claypath. Nothing really…"

"Nothing really? Nothing really? Louisa, what on earth are you talking about?" Carol demanded as their wrangling talk disappeared gently into the night.

The rest of their muffled remarks entered my bedroom through the little window that looked out onto the lane.

Next morning wasn't very much fun. I was glad Carol didn't fulfil her threat of breakfast sausage rolls and spent most of the morning in agony. I heard the two girls down the hall leave the house early and Damien a little bit later. The rest of the morning was an unremitting hangover that I struggled with various treatments to overcome. To no avail.

Having nothing to do in town, I hung around the kitchen playing records and drinking loads of tea and other non-alcoholic brews, dying to see either or both of my rescuers, knowing at the same time that I was in no fit state to see anybody. Damien came back around mid-afternoon full of the joys of spring and proceeded to lecture me on why the Mini was such a sound car, mechanically, that is. Why it handled so well.

"It's because," he said, "there's a wheel at each corner, instead of anywhere else. And it's got front wheel drive."

"Oh," I said, doubtful of his reasoning but willing to accept his genius in such matters. He smiled condescendingly and poured more tea.

Several tea cakes later – which he magically produced out of a white paper bag and toasted – the tea cakes, not the paper bag – he suddenly remembered who he had seen in the marketplace while buying the teacakes.

"Those two who dragged you in last night; your two women folk," he said without batting an eye.

"Carol and Louisa? Lifesavers. They were in the market?"

"Yes."

"Doing what?"

"A lot of laughing and pushing and pulling at each other whilst getting something from the butcher's. When they saw me, they collapsed in a heap. They were in an uproar. Couldn't for the life of me think what the joke was."

"Did you happen to see what was in the packet they got from the butcher?"

"Didn't dare look. Totally inappropriate for a chap to spy into women's shopping like that. No, didn't look."

"Why?" he asked from behind a nibble.

I steered the conversation back to the mechanical advantages of some cars, and he was pleased to illuminate.

"At least," he said after his review of most cars on the road today, "they got into one that does not have supreme handling."

"Oh?" I asked, not really wanting to hear.

"Daimler," he said in a disinterested way.

"Parked in the marketplace. Waiting for them whilst they finished their shopping."

"Didn't happen to see who was behind the wheel, by any chance?" I asked, my heart racing.

"By every chance, I did," he replied, full of himself.

"I make a study of such things. Snooty looking bloke in a Harris Tweed jacket, a Castle scarf and zippy up boots. He had to jump out to let one of them – the littler one – into the back. The door was stuck. Typical Daimler."

"And the taller of the two?" I asked but, fearing the worst, as usual, didn't really want an answer.

"Got in the front with the Tweed jacket."

"Were they – he and she – very friendly at the time, do you think?"

"Couldn't say, apart from the peck on the cheek he gave her before she got in."

"Peck on the cheek?" I asked, now very interested.

"Just a peck?"

"Just a peck," Damien confirmed adamantly.

"And…And…And was this peck, was it reciprocated in any way, shape or form?" I asked, now very desperate to find out.

"Not before she got in."

"Oh. Good."

"But once inside, she reached across and gave him a hug."

"But not a peck. A hug, not a peck. You have to be precise with this part, Damien. Did she give him any sort of tactile facial appreciation of his worth to her whilst they were inside the bloody car?"

"Not that I could see from where I was standing, but then again, I really couldn't see what was totally going on inside the car. They don't handle the best, Daimlers, and visibility inside them isn't good, especially when they are screaming away from one at a rate of knots."

"He drove away fast?"

"Very."

"Out of the marketplace?

"Yes. Up Saddler Street towards the cathedral, I think."

"And Castle," I said, my dismal funk growing apace.

"No wonder she didn't appear for breakfast this morning. She probably spent the night with him…in his room." I mused, desolate and confused. "What was she – they – she doing in there?"

"Couldn't say," my informant advised me.

"Had to get my shopping done," he said rattling the paper bag that, by the sound of it, still had some teacakes.

"Disaster?" he asked, nibbling delicately around the toasted edge of one.

"Another hurdle, maybe," I said.

"How does one find out?" he said.

"Ask," I supposed.

"A terror-laden question," Damien concluded.

"Life-changing," I said.

"That bad?" he said. "If it's going to change your life, the obvious solution is: don't ask it."

"Cowardly way out," I said.

"Live to fight another day," he said hopefully.

But when he saw the look in my eyes, he said, whilst popping another teacake into the toaster, "Ask it."

"Simply that?"

"Yes, I'm afraid. Be brave. Go up to her and ask her. Tactically, morally, logically, it's the right thing to do."

"Is that what you would do?"

"Not on your nelly."

"But you advise me to march right up to her digs and ask her face to face."

"Have it out once and for all," he assured me.

"The heroic option. Best thing to do," he added, "if – that is – she wants a hero. She may not, and if so, you are then in deep shit, but at least you'll know where you stand…"

"Yes," I said thoroughly at odds and confused with my options.

"Then again…"

"Second option?" I asked.

"Third option," he corrected.

"Third option, then," I said.

He said, perfunctorily, "Put the kettle on and we'll have another cup of tea."

"Oh…good," I said with considerable relief.

"No," he cautioned. "That's not the third option. A cup of tea is never an option."

"Delaying tactic?" I asked.

"Strategic intervention, a pause whilst formulating a plan."

"Well, what is your third option then?"

"Don't know yet. That's what the tea break is for – forming one."

Finally, after several cups, Damien looked very sternly at me and announced, "I think you'll just have to wait. You don't seem to be able to take the bull by the horns…"

"…Too dangerous…" I said.

"…Quite. Could get out of hand. No. You don't need to take the bull by the horns at this point. Wait and allow things to mellow a bit…"

"Great," I said, "and allow her time to run off and marry Errol. Bide my time whilst she and he patch up their differences and drive off into the sunset in that clapped-out Daimler, leaving me revolving in their wake, a revolution – I might add – that could last a lifetime."

"Yes…" he said, now in some doubt about his third option, "… there is that. There is certainly that. But …" he had an addendum.

"But, the way things are going, from what you have told me, this will not happen, and…and you must allow her time to come to her own conclusions. I feel she has already made her decision about him. You are a shoe-in, by the way. Just give her time. There is strength in this. Believe me."

"How much time?" I asked which he didn't answer.

"Hours? Days? Several eternities?"

"You see, I believe you and she are seeing this completely differently. You see it as a time-limit thing, and she sees it as a time-to-go-shopping-in thing before you next get together."

"It's done, you feel?"

"It's done. Couldn't have put it better."

"Nothing more I can do, you think?"

"Nothing. Absolutely nothing. Go about your business. Take your mind off her completely. Let things come to you."

"Good. Yes. Good. I'll take my mind off her completely, until…"

Until the library several days later.

She wasn't there. Nothing unusual in that. She often wasn't there. I was often not there too, but then I'd hear about it from her. Why was I absent? What was I doing not to be in the library? How could I be so thoughtless without letting her know? She could miss a day, and it didn't matter to her; no harm done. Nothing unusual in her deserting me. But. Let me miss once, and my head was immediately on the block.

She wasn't there in the library, but Leo was.

What a shock.

He had his head in some work he had on the go and was oblivious to the rest of the world. In sign language from the far end of the room, I asked him what the occasion was. He stuck a finger up his nose to show me that it was none of my bloody business then held up some paper or other he was working on and went back at it, dutifully carving out a thesis. I could hear the grunts and straining brain cells all the way across the room. He wasn't used to the library's cone of silence, and whenever in there, you could hear him grunting away at whatever he was doing, talking to himself in low mumbles, whispering, congratulating himself or swearing at his lamentable results. It was like a Saturday afternoon on the terraces at his beloved Crystal Palace, or was it Millwall? – with him losing badly.

This was Wednesday morning with rowing outings in the afternoon, so when we were finished in the library, we wandered along toward the boathouse picking up the others on our way. Colin and Beau met us at the foot of Kingsgate steps. Colin was unusually quiet for the rest of the walk to Bath's Bridge. Beau was ebullient, full of himself and this week's conquests. Reggie shouted down to us 'Chaps', from Elvet Bridge that he might be a minute or two late. Something inaudibly toffee-nosed about something or other, a cricketing book, I think, he had to pick up from one of the shops along Old Elvet, but not to worry, he wouldn't be long.

"Chaps," he called us, "Chaps."

And he immediately struck off again across the bridge, his bowling arm rising above his head describing the perfect arc of the perfect googlie he had been working on with us for the entire year. We stopped and watched as the arm flew up and around, followed by his hair flapping in the breeze, again and again and again, until finally disappearing out of sight into the crowds at the other end of the bridge.

"Good old Reggie," Colin said as we all stood and watched the display.

"Born in the wrong century."

"Fancies himself a coach now," Beau said with some envy in his voice.

"He's coaching the novice women's four, Beau," I said.

"Aye and making a right balls-up of it," Beau said with that faraway look in his eye.

"Wouldn't mind making a balls-up of coaching the women he's got in his little crew."

"They seem to be enjoying it," Colin said.

"Aye," Beau said wistfully. "Think I'll ask if I can be his assistant."

"Don't you think you've got enough – women that is – to be going on with?"

"Never enough. Never enough women."

"Until you meet that special one, eh?" I said then looked over at Beau who didn't seem to be listening anymore.

"Eh? What, Flynn?"

"Never enough women until you meet that special one," I repeated.

"Aye, well…" he said with a look of embarrassment.

"Seems to me I've got a ways to go until that happens, mate."

"Make hay, eh?"

"Aye, summat like that. Plenty of living to do until that fateful day," he said seeming to make heavy weather of the notion. He put his head down and forged on into some storm in his future.

I somehow knew what and who he was struggling with at that moment, and it wasn't a notion of the future but someone very much in the present.

"Can't be all that bad," I said.

"Oh?" he said, his eyes wide with some kind of stinging reality, something he wasn't coping with well. And then he said nothing at all for some time, making heavy going of things beyond his comprehension.

"Whadya mean, Flynn?" Leo weighed in.

"About what?"

"Goldilocks there having it bad. We should all have it half as bad as him."

"You're just put out because you can't even handle his cast-offs," Colin said.

"Aye, Leo," Beau said. "I set you up with Helen, and what do you go and do with it?"

Leo said nothing.

"An own goal, mate, that's what," Beau persisted.

"Bollocks."

"There you were set up with the ball on the penalty spot. No goalie in the net. And you go and shoot into your own goal. An own goal, you pillock, from the other end of the pitch."

"Bollocks. We developed a mutual understanding, is all," Leo said.

"And what was that? your mutual understanding? That you preferred to shoot into your own goal?"

"She said she wanted more out of the relationship than I was willing to give her."

"A Cherry B and a packet of crisps? She wanted more than that, and you couldn't spring for it? Tight git. Skinflint. You couldn't get the girl another packet o' crisps, and she dumped you. Bloody hell, mate. Serves you bloody well right.

"Would it help if I gave you sixpence for another packet next time you're out with a lass? We could do a whip around before you go out of an evening. Sixpence each. That's it. Sixpence each so Leo can get his leg over. We'll come up with the lass and the crisps as well, if you like.

"All you have to come up with is the balls."

"Seems to me, Beau, that at the minute you've got the money and the balls and yet you've not got the lass," Leo said, peering contemptuously back over his shoulder at Beau.

"Bollocks. Got plenty o' lasses on the go all over. Always have. You're talking bloody bollocks, mate." Beau was putting a brave face on it.

"Plenty mebbes, but not the one you want," Leo said, heating up.

"And," Leo said turning around and facing him.

"She's the one that really counts. Isn't she, mate? She's the one that really matters," he said, turning back around again to catch up with the rest of us.

"She's the one that can't be bought with a hundred boxes of crisps or that goldilocks hair of yours or even the fancy scent you put on, because unlike the rest of your conquests, she knows what you're really like."

"Oh, aye, and just what am I like then, Leo – just what?"

But Leo didn't have the heart or the balls to tell him, so he shut up for the time being.

Colin, however, being the shit-disturber that he was, broke in and offered to the general populace, "A right prat, sometimes, Beau, that's what."

"Not you an' all, Brutus?" Beau actually sounded offended at this.

"It's a common fact. And you don't need me to tell it you. The way you treated that lass – all your lasses, as a matter of fact. But her especially. And still expecting her to fall into your arms in spite of it."

"They're all fair game," Beau said, rushing to his own defence.

"Aye, I suppose. But so are you. And that's why you're feeling like shite right now. You've had a comeuppance, and you bloody well deserve it."

"Thank you, reverend Crabtree. Let me know when you're giving your next sermon, and I'll be sure to book a front row pew.

"Louisa and I parted company ages ago. I couldn't care less about her."

"Who said anything about Louisa?" Colin said.

Beau was momentarily silenced by this and bothered at the same time. You could hear the wheels grinding in his head.

"I gave her a chance. She wasn't interested. End of story."

Even for the Honey One, this was a sad turn of events, so we all shut up, walked on in silence for a bit and gave him some space. After all, he was a mate, a mate with a massive ego. But right now, you could see the hurt little boy in him, and it wasn't a pleasant sight.

Finally, Leo broke the silence. "Some chance," he said contemptuously.

"What was it, Beau? The kind of chance you give every girl that falls for those goldilocks, little boy looks of yours?"

"Why not?" Beau insisted, still not seeing the point.

"She's no different from any other lass I've ever been with."

"That's just it. You still fail to see the point. She's given you the point, but you missed it."

"Which is what, Romeo?"

"I think the word you're looking for is respect. The only thing in this world you only ever respected is you."

"You an' all? You an' Crabtree? The two of you. There's a seminary up the road you both need to go and see about joining. Me? I'm staying right here on the lookout for more totty who also happen to be on the lookout for a bit o' rumpy pumpy."

Chapter 42
Dirty Great Pile of Stones

Several afternoons later, Pettigrew met me at the door to Kepier Terrace with his pinnie on. He'd been doing the kitchen, and it sparkled. It was the last week of term.

"Your friend Carol dropped by earlier," he said, wiping his hands on a tea towel.

"Wanted to know why you weren't there last night. Didn't say exactly where 'there' was, but from the look in her eyes, you were supposed to be somewhere special and weren't, and you are in trouble."

"Shit! Thought that was tomorrow night. I'm sure it was tomorrow."

"Apparently not, old friend. How good are you at eating humble pie?"

"Did she say anything else?"

"Nothing much. Going home on the weekend. Daddy is picking her and all her things up. She's out tonight. A birthday party. She's going with her friend. Errol's party, I think she said. Is that the bloke with the Daimler? No chance to get together before she goes home, apparently.

"Didn't stay long. I offered her a cuppa until you got back, but she couldn't stay. Said she had to go out and buy a new frock for the party."

This was another dismal turn of events. Carol partying with Errol.

Unsettling.

I guess I knew the term might end like this. The evidence of the last few weeks said Carol and I were pretty solid. Errol hadn't been heard from. What had happened to turn it all upside down?

I couldn't have expected an invitation to Errol's birthday. Didn't get one, so I thought, and gate crashing tonight would be churlish. No. The best thing to do was to let events play out tonight, stay away, and maybe I would get a chance to see both ladies before their fathers arrived to take them home for the summer.

Maybe I wouldn't. Maybe tonight was going to be final. Carol would sail off into the sunset with Errol, and I was cast adrift to languish the night away, alone in my little garret at the top of the stairs before leaving for London at the end of the week and the summer job I'd picked up there.

I wasn't really good at languishing and headed into town to find some friends. By the time I got to Cuth's, the lads had left for any one of a dozen watering holes around the town. The place was as empty as my heart, and I now entertained the idea of gate-crashing the birthday party but managed to talk myself out of that.

Agnes shouted down to me from the second-floor landing that she thought they had all gone out to the Vic to drown their sorrows about having to leave at the end of the week. I asked her if she wanted to join me in my search for them, but she had too much packing to do and besides didn't want to get in the way of Leo and his new 'whore'. By the time I got to Prebend's Bridge, I heard her calling after me to wait. She had changed her mind and would like to get some fresh air. So I waited mid-bridge for her to catch up.

"You don't look so well," she said as she settled in beside me to take in the view of the cathedral downstream.

"Is something the matter?" she asked.

Despite her hard-nosed, no nonsense Cockney exterior, Agnes could be relied upon when times got rough. She sensed trouble and waited for me to excise my demons whilst we gazed out across one of the most breath-taking panoramas in all the world.

"Do you think the guys who built this place knew just what a winner they were on to all those years ago?" I said trying to dodge her question.

"You mean that bloody great monstrosity up there?" she said dismissing with a wave of her hand my idyll, the river, the weir, the wonderful old buildings at either end of the weir, the castle on a hill in the distance and the glorious towers of the cathedral halfway along atop the tree-lined bankside.

"Dirty old church should have been pulled down centuries ago…" she carped.

"And replaced with what? A canteen for the people who laboured all those years to build it?"

"Could have done a damn-sight worse," she complained, tossing pebbles into the river.

"There's enough stone in the damn place to build several council estates out past Gilesgate. I'm sure nobody thought of that when they were erecting their false idols to their pagan gods around here."

"This bridge?" I asked, including it in her diatribe.

"Oh, the bridge serves a purpose, I suppose. Gets me from here to yon side of the river without getting me feet wet," she giggled. "But that dirty great pile of stones up there? Well, I don't know."

"Looks nice," I said, defending the cathedral with all my might.

"I don't know," she said in that sour way she had.

"Lovely to some. But I just can't get over the cost to build it and keep it up when there's other things the money could be spent on."

"You're just pissed off that the Scots didn't manage to pull it all down years ago on their way to Neville's Cross. Too many English arrows to contend with. That's your only problem with it. Now admit it, Agnes."

"I'll admit to no such thing, thank you very much. There will come a time in the not-too-distant future when the working class of the North will have their way with things like that and monstrosities such as that will be demolished as an act of social conscience and necessity."

"And replaced with…?"

"…A ruddy great flyover using those ugly towers up there as supporting pillars. Or crushed underfoot to form the foundations of a new millennium pleasure dome."

"You should bring it up at the Big Meeting next week on the race course. I'm sure the lads over there would be very receptive to your brave new world. Meanwhile, we'll just have to put up with that ruddy great pile of rocks blocking our view of worthier things like Woolworth's and Tesco's and that cute little tearoom at the bottom of Silver Street."

"Turn it into a multi-storey bicycle park!" she demanded. "Imagine how many bicycles you'd be able to get into it."

"No cars?"

"Not after the revolution. Walk it or bike it."

"I guess that rules out your idea of a flyover then, unless you want to get the bikes out of the middle of the city. Make it a pedestrian-only precinct."

"Only pushbikes and prams allowed and, of course, pedestrians."

"So with the prams you are allowing for the procreation of the species. Future generations. As long as they don't walk on the grass."

"Oh, aye. They can walk on the grass all they want."

"As long as they mow it and keep it tidy?" I asked.

"They don't have to mow it," she said, concerned that her public shouldn't do anything they didn't want.

"Who mows it then? After you've torn down that beautiful edifice and grassed it all over."

She saw what was coming and with capitalism as the only logical conclusion, decided quickly. "Sheep. It will be an agrarian revolution as well. Can't have smelly old gas lawnmowers fucking up the countryside. Sheep will do the job very nicely and fertilise as they go." She giggled.

"And what will you do with the university buildings? They're all over the place blocking your revolutionary view."

"And serving no real purpose, apart from tearooms for the idle rich. I'd turn them into daycare centres for working class mums. Turf out the addled-brained profs that pose as superior intellects, and turn it over to the kids and their mums.

"It's going to happen, Flynn," she said emphatically, patting the blocks of the stone bridge that had spanned the river for centuries, at the service of the city. "It has to."

"Bollocks," I said, patting those same dear old benevolent stones.

"Besides," I said. "You'd never get it past the council."

"The council's a load of old tossers," she moaned.

We wandered off across the bridge in search of absent friends. The Vic was empty, so was the Spread, Waterloo and Three Tuns. As a last resort, I popped my head inside the Dun Cow. A table full of them in front of the window at the far end glowered back at me. Agnes made her excuses before I entered and left, worried that Leo might be entertaining his new 'whore' in there.

"Mine's a pint, Flynn," Leo shouted before I had time to sit down.

The rest of them placed their orders, including Beau whom I was surprised to see sitting there, grinning back at me. I set about getting the orders in at the bar.

"Nothing better to do of an evening, young Flynn?" he asked.

"Thought I might get around to a birthday party later," I mentioned to Beau after handing out the round.

"Build up some courage first."

"Oh, aye?" he said.

"Town Hall," I said.

"You could've been there with Louisa, if you'd played your cards right. Remember her? The one you loved and lost not so long ago."

"Me? Lost? Couldn't've been me. Never lost a bint in me life, me. Who's been spreading vicious rumours?" he asked, defensively gulping down half his pint in one go.

"It's all right if you don't want to talk about another one of your carnal failures, Goldilocks," Leo said. "We'll understand."

"Failures? Bollocks."

"This'll be the second time in as many weeks. You're losing your touch, mate. Wenches around town are wise to you. What happened this time? Try to get into her knickers, and she wasn't having any?"

"Bollocks," he glowered, shoved down the second half of his drink and got up to leave.

"Have a go at the new barmaid on your way out," Leo called after him. But Beau didn't hear and walked right past the bar without so much as a peck after her beaming, trembling smile. The door slammed. Beau was gone. The barmaid remained behind the bar sullen and lacking something.

"Something wrong with this," I said.

"It's a sad, sad time," Leo lamented, "when he walks past a woman and doesn't even look up. Not a smile."

"Probably got a dose of the clap," Colin said in his usual phlegmatic way. "Out of action for a bit. You'll see. He'll be back at it soon. Soon as he's paid a visit to the doc. Penicillin, that's the answer for Beau. You'll see."

Leo took a long sanguine slurp of his drink, sat back like the old sage he was, belched long and loud before proclaiming to the void left by Beau.

"There's more than a dose of the clap that's eating at his vitals. And we all know what. Lack of confidence in his old todger. It has suffered a blow he might never recover from. Suffered a mighty blow."

"Oh, aye, Leo. And that's where he's off to now? Looking for a lost mojo?"

"Yes," Leo proclaimed, loving every minute of it. "Hasn't had a woman in eight hours, poor thing. He might never recover," he declared with that evil little, self-satisfied smirk on his face.

"Never," he added, placing his empty glass firmly on the table.

"Who's for another?" he asked, actually putting his hand into his pocket, then removing it quickly, to announce, "Your shout, Crabtree."

I eventually shook myself free from the Dun Cow and worked up enough courage to sneak by the Town Hall to see what was going on with Errol's birthday party. The racket could be heard all the way down Old Elvet and only got louder as I approached the market place. The square outside the Town Hall was electric. A band was hacking away inside and booze-blasted punters overflowed into the marketplace, staggered about or sat dismally on the steps and central statue of the Marquess.

A townie fight broke out somewhere over there; lads were being pried apart by their lasses; lasses were cursing and wrestling other lasses. The lads stood around having a good laugh at them and their scratchy, slappy fights.

Couldn't see anybody I knew in the hordes, but as I got closer, and the crowd came into clearer focus, I discerned a mate of mine – Specky with his head between his knees sitting on the top of the steps looking like death warmed up. Del Fuego, teetered above Specky imploring him to get up. They'd better leave before things got worse, he said. Word had spread that there was going to be trouble, and it seemed that Specky was at the centre of it.

A rage suddenly blistered out from the main doors of the Town Hall with Smy and Sturge at its centre. Smy's ruddy red belligerent face blared out of the doorway in search of prey.

He was steaming mad at somebody. Sturge did his best to hold him back, but on this occasion, as on many others, once he'd had a bellyful there was no holding this maniac back. He shook loose from Sturge's grip and tore down the steps after Specky who was too pissed to know that he had become the target of Smy's frenzy.

"Daft little git," Smy spat, standing above Specky.

Del Fuego tried to get between the bully and his drunken friend but was shoved aside down the steps.

"All yours now," Sturge shouted, grabbing Del Fuego out of the way.

"I've got this one." At which point, seeing two friends in a mess, I walked up behind Sturge and in jest shoved a forefinger into the centre of his back.

"Stick 'em up, you dirty rat," I said in my best imitation of Jimmy Cagney.

Sturge wasn't impressed and turned to me with a wry grin on his face.

That was the last I knew of that particular event.

I saw the grin but not the fist and waking up on the ground in the middle of the market square some moments later saw nothing but the figure of a horseman spinning out of blurred control above me.

"Not again. Not you again," someone kind kneeling next to me said.

"Help me get him to his feet, you lot," she fussed, appealing to the general population roundabout.

"I think he's all right. You're all right, aren't you, Christopher Robin?" she said pulling my arm to at least get me to sit up, which I didn't want to do right at that whirling moment.

Louisa dabbed the corner of my mouth with a hanky and generally ministered to the wounded groggy soldier sitting on the ground. I'm sure she would have had my head wrapped many times around with bandages torn from her petticoat, if she had any.

"You've got a nasty cut on your mouth, and look, look here, a bump on the side of your head where you fell," she continued.

"Other than that, I think you'll be all right," she said, wiping the dirt off my jacket and closing in on me – which I didn't mind so much, coming out of my delirium and levelling off in a mild trauma.

"I think I'll just sit here for a mo, Lou, if you don't mind," I said, being cuddled ever so close to my ministering angel and feeling for all the world like I'd been knocked out and gone to heaven.

I was in the middle of a circle of friends standing above me, all looking grave. Lulu knelt beside me, stopping me from keeling over again. Specky and Del Fuego leant in close until Tucker pushed his way to the front, worried to death that my injury might interfere with my round.

"You've pulled some stunts to dodge it, Flynn, but this is the best one yet. Somebody help me get him up," he said looking around desperately at the assembly, "and get him over to the bar before he completely loses it again.

"Here, missus," he said to Louisa. "Give us a hand to get him up onto his hind legs, will you."

"Oh god. What's that?" I groaned seeing Harry Sturge sitting below the Marquess of Londonderry holding his head.

"Did I do that?"

"I wish," Lulu said, leading me out of the crowd and into the Market Tavern. "I clocked him one when he hit you.

"Whatever possessed you to want to get into a fight with him?" she demanded.

"Didn't. Just looking out for Specky."

"Oh? Which one is he?"

"The one bereft of all sense."

"That could describe any number of people here. Including you, I'm afraid," she said leading me to an empty table inside the pub.

"You sit here whilst I go and fetch you a cup of tea."

She brought back a pot, which we sat over, inhaling its restorative steam.

"Why weren't you at the party?" she asked, sipping at her drink.

"Wasn't invited," I said, swilling my cup.

"Rude of you not to have come."

She heaved a great sigh, lifted her gaze to stare right through me.

"It's not good enough, you know."

"What? What's not?"

"You know bloody well what's not. You.

"You avoiding us – me and Carol – all this time. And now you don't even show up for the party."

"Told you I wasn't invited."

"Were too. Carol sent you that card. Errol told her to. They both wanted you to, you great pillock."

"And where are they now?" I asked.

"Errol's in the bogs spewing his guts up, I suspect. Carol left yonks ago looking dreadfully unhappy. Took a bottle of wine with her. She's looking grim. Spent the whole night looking out for you. Gave up and said she was going home to curl up in a good book and get her head sorted out. I tried to stop her, but she was adamant. You know how she is when she gets adamant about something. Thoroughly miserable. I stayed behind to keep a watch out just in case you showed up. And here you are, brawling in front of the Town Hall. Disgraceful," she said, fed up to the teeth with me.

"Getting into fights with people. It just won't do," she said catching her breath and turning her head to the side to hide a tear welling up in the corner of her eye.

"…She waited all night for you.

"And you…

"…You couldn't care less.

"What is the matter with you?"

This unexpected denunciation staggered me. It was as though I'd been punched in the face again, but this time by one whom I adored and admired and trusted beyond belief.

"I just thought," I stammered to get hold of my thoughts.

"You just thought what, you imbecile?" The tears were visible now, trickling down the front of her cheeks.

"That…"

"That, what? That you could go around playing with people's feelings like this, and that they wouldn't be hurt?"

"Had no idea that I was hurting anyone. Let's face it, Lou," I said, summoning up the courage that I never thought I had.

"Face what, you idiot?"

"Carol and Errol…"

"Carol and Errol, what? Don't you see? Haven't you seen it all along?

"Why do you think…?

"Just what DO you think?"

Then, without waiting for what I thought, she let me have it with both barrels.

"…You thought Carol and Errol were still…?

"After all this time? After everything she's done – I've done – to keep her in your thoughts…you bloody idiot. Blind bloody fool. You couldn't see it, could you, even though she's been hitting you over the head with it for months now and agonising over you…"

"Agonising over who?"

"You, you…you…you jerk," she said using my vernacular. This really hurt.

"Both of us. Ever since that beautifully silly library thingy. She couldn't get you out of her mind."

"But Errol, the party, tonight, everything…?" I gasped.

"Mostly made up by you to avoid the truth, I suspect."

"Truth? The truth about what?"

"The truth up until just now when she stormed off home and into a good book swearing she had to pull herself together; the truth that she had to stop trusting people."

"The truth about what? Trusting who/whom/who?"

"You. Idiot. But now…

"I don't know. You have a lot of mending to do if you want to pick up the pieces, but I'm afraid, there are far too many pieces after this little incident. I'm afraid. Well. I'm afraid…"

"What? Spit it out, Lou. What are you afraid of?"

"I'm afraid…" She took a deep breath. "I'm afraid your ship has sailed, that's all."

She stammered with the passion of the moment, the enormity of her pronouncement.

"She said it's hopeless; you're hopeless. That's all. Before she left. She said that she was giving up and going to plan B, whatever that may be."

I sat there for some moments completely gobsmacked, speechless, hurting beyond hurt for this lovely creature sitting in front of me crying her eyes out, for me, the world's biggest jerk, but most of all for the one I most wanted to be with who was heading home tomorrow with thoughts about me that I couldn't take.

Chapter 43
Drizzly Night

And so I meandered up Claypath, alone, in a daze, heading to a cold, lonely room and some kind of oblivion I didn't know how I was going to deal with. Just as I opened the door to the yard in Kepier Terrace, a slow misty drizzle began. Wonderful. What next? The house was empty, dark and cold. Damien had left for his home in Richmond already. The two girls upstairs were still out on the razz.

Nobody home.

Dark, lonely, cold, drizzly night.

I left the light on in the kitchen downstairs for the girls, whenever they might return later, and went to bed in my garret upstairs next to the broom closet.

The wind outside my room knocked the washing line in the yard against a post creating a ting, ting, ting, that wouldn't stop, keeping me awake, remonstrating against my stupidity. A hardening rain blew against my little window pain. I tossed and turned for ages until finally waking sometime later, realised that I had managed to defeat my raging conscience and had actually slept for an hour or so. The rain had stopped pelting the window, but the tapping was still there, only it was louder now and intermittent as if someone was banging on a door somewhere.

As if…

Shit. Sounded like…

It sounded as though someone was trying to keep me awake, get me out of bed. It was as though…

I got up just to make sure and looking down into that little yard illuminated by the downstairs light saw a woman leaving the yard.

Without thinking, I thrust open my window and called down to her.

"Carol! I'm here. Don't go. Please. I'm sorry. Don't go."

She turned back into the yard, and the moon coming up over the house illuminated her beaming face eagerly peering up at me and her right hand brandishing a bottle of wine above her head.

"Thought we could do with a drink," she called back up, waving the wine more vigorously.

"Genius," I shouted back down.

I heard her trying the door which always stuck until you gave it a god almighty shove.

"Kick it. You have to give it a kick," I shouted down.

"Wait there," she called back up confidently, her rump half in and half out of the house.

Doing as I was told, I waited, listening to her make her ham-fisted way along the partially lit hallway and up the dark stairs, bumping into things and generally making a ballsup of the process until all at once she was breathless, rain drenched and there at the top of the stairs mock-collapsing under the success of climbing to the top in the dark.

"Thought you were bent on bringing the whole house down around us. What on earth do you want, so late at night?" I whispered to her from my doorway, my heart in my mouth.

Ignoring my ignoble greeting, she swarmed, out of breath, towards me from the top of the stairs. "Look what I've brought you," she cooed, as she lodged tightly into my encircling arms, holding up the bottle.

"It's open. Nicked it from the party tonight," she announced in a triumphant, enthusiastic whisper. "Thought we could do with a drink before bed, a night cap," she nodded, all the while her joyous face and lips entangling with mine.

"Had a chat with Lulu when she got home tonight," she finally said, stepping back and reaching down to ease off her sopping wet shoes.

"She said you were in a fight with someone in the town square. Very unwise, Christopher Robin. Said you had a bump and poorly face. Poor you. Let me see. No, don't turn away. Let me see it," she said dabbing a hanky onto my mouth.

"Nothing really. Just a scrape. You'll live," she said, ungenerously, I thought.

"Anyway…" She stopped to think what she was going to say.

"Anyway. We had a talk, Lou and I."

"Oh? What about?" I said reaching for her, in the eager semi-dark.

"Mainly you, you jerk. That's what she called you," she giggled. "And I'm inclined to agree," she said, continuing first aid with her hanky."

312

"Oh. And what did you two decide about me?"

"That you are a jerk and that couldn't be helped. That is a large bump."

"No difficulty in that," I said. "I am. Can't help it."

"Can't help what, exactly?"

"Being such a jerk and so head over heels in love with you."

"Oh. You are? Still? Even though…"

"Even though," I said.

"That's nice," she said stopping her ministering to my poorly mouth and, taking dead aim on it, placed her lips on mine very hard and for a very long time. Her lips were soft nectar, quivering soft nectar. Finally, she released them to take a breath. "We sorted it all out, Lou and I. She's finally come to her senses," she said looking me dead in the eyes.

Another sweet kiss. Then she leaned away from me again, looking more serious.

"…Abandoned any thoughts of Beau and is seeing Archie tomorrow night. He walked her…"

…she stopped and thought for a bit, thought about what she had just done, the snog, I mean, seemed to like it, measured the distance between us and launched another juicy snogging onto my hungry lips, parted a breath away and whispered, "…home from the party tonight. Nice chap. Speaks highly of you, although he says your catches need work – whatever they are." She thought some more and said, "Christopher Robin, what are catches?" I slipped my aching arms around her, pulling her towards me. This time it was me making the running. Unbridled running, you might say. Anyway, she pushed herself back away from me, coz she was finding it hard to breathe again.

"Here," she said, out of breath, brandishing the bottle she had brought.

"It's open." she struggled, as I wrapped her in another snog she tried to dodge around but couldn't.

"Me too," I said, finally out of breath too.

"You too what? You great oaf."

"Me too, I'm open too."

"That's settled then," she said, standing away and removing her dripping cagoule and dropping it onto the floor.

"Christopher Robin," she said breathlessly, feeling around in the dark again and finally realising, although I couldn't see why she hadn't noticed it in the first place.

"Christopher, umph, Robin, umph…you haven't got any clothes on. Is this the usual way you greet your guests?"

"Always," I replied taking her in hand, stroking her hair and what not.

"That's nice. I like that…and this. Then I'll be your guest for the night. If that's all right with you; if you don't mind, that is. If you haven't any other, more pressing plans."

"Quite all right. I think I can fit you in," I said snagging her wine and placing it on my little bedside table before lunging at her again. In the darkness of my room, her beautiful, joyous face was illuminated by the streetlamp shining through my window.

"You can have the broom closet," I said, drawing her towards me and crushing her lips against mine, her breasts against my chest. "I took all the brooms out earlier…and cleared out…that nest of mice…Might be a few spiders left…but…"

"Bugger that, mate. I'm having this room," she giggled and struggled to say around my hungry mouth devouring her lips, her eyes, her cheeks, chin, neck and ears.

"You can have either the broom closet…" she said pulling away and dodging around my insatiable attack.

"Or…

"This one…with me…in it," she struggled to say, giggling and umphing all the while.

"That's nice," she said, "Keep doing that."

"This room please. The one with you in it," I said.

"Drink?" I asked trying not to forget my manners in the turmoil.

But there seemed to be no time for that now.

Her eyes glowed tenderly as she calmly stepped away from the bed, pecking at her buttons, pushing me back onto the bed then slipping off her blouse and undoing her bra.

Breathing heavily, she lowered her lips to mine. Another delicious, tender snogging.

"You'll have to get this off," I umphed this time.

"Just a mo then. You are very bossy all at once," she said somewhere in the night above me.

"This?" she announced triumphantly holding her skirt in the air.

"Yes. Now these too."

"Knickers as well? I ask you. Whatever next? What will Daddy say?"

"Won't tell him, if you don't."

"Like this?" she whispered dropping her knickers onto the floor beside the skirt, pushing me down and crawling on top.

"If you like." I snuggled to get a better angle.

"I do like," she said in a deep, demanding voice.

"Like this?"

"Yes. Just like that." She trembled onto me.

"And this," I asked, knowing that all care had fled from our night.

"Bossy boots," she whispered all over my lips, then sitting back up on top she quietly, insistently rocked and lunged back and forth until totally out of breath and totally out of control. Hours later, she at last toppled forward like a floppy ragdoll onto my chest.

"You are a wonder, you know."

"Am I?"

"Yes," she gasped, her glowing eyes centimetres from my nose. "And I want all of you again and again…"

"Now again?"

"Yes. Now and…oh godddd, forever."

And we worked together to see to it that she got her trembling wish.

Somewhere in the middle of a dream later that night, I heard her sleepy sweet voice tangled up with my arms and legs, utter something. I listened for more information, wriggled a little to test the soft warmness there.

"Can't sleep," she said from under a pile of damp hair in the dreamiest of dreamy voices. "Need some help," she said, patting her hand all over me, finding me and taking control of things.

I snuggled into her neck and, wrapping my hand around her breast, pulled her closer. She adjusted her hips backwards onto me.

"You are all elbows tonight. Did you know that? All lovely elbows. There. That's better," she snoozled, reaching back behind her to adjust things.

"Not my elbow," I said feeling her delicious, hot, encircling, thrust peeling me back.

"Should…have…known," she said engulfing me, settling around me with another more urgent backward thrust of her hips.

"Oh god," she squealed, "here it is again.

"Christopher Robin? Christopher Robin…? Christoph…"

id for some time, some measureless moments or hours, that was all she
she was so busy and so out of breath.

Her sibilant breathing abated afterwards when at last face to face again she
ispered deliciously into my eyes in the dark, "Night night."

And we slept.

End